Taming Kate

Kate edged closer to Charlie. "Please just hold me tonight. But I can't give myself to you. That I can only do with the man I marry."

Charlie shut his eyes against the vision of femininity enticing him beyond all reason. "Kate . . . woman, you're askin' for too much." Mumbling a defeated curse, Charlie pulled Kate into his arms. "All right, then, Kate. You win. Just for tonight. But if you try to give me the slip tonight, I'll blister your butt."

She laughed. "You mean you're not man enough to control one headstrong seventeen-year-old girl?"

"Are you woman enough to handle me?" He reached out and slid his fingers over her shirt to touch the button between her breasts.

A gasp escaped her. "Charlie! You promised!"

His hand slipped beneath the shirt to caress the breast. "You laid out the rules, Kate, but my cooperation don't come without a price. I've just got to have another taste of you, woman."

Other **AVON ROMANCES**

Taming Kate

EUGENIA RILEY

AVON BOOKS ◆ NEW YORK

TAMING KATE is an original publication of Avon Books. This work has never before appeared in book form. This work is a novel. Any similarity to actual persons or events is purely coincidental.

AVON BOOKS
A division of
The Hearst Corporation
1350 Avenue of the Americas
New York, New York 10019

With love to my precious Aunt Sister, for taking me along on that most memorable evening of great food, scintillating conversation, accordion music and gospel singing, during which the entertainment was so lively and mesmerizing that I plotted this book—

Many thanks!

The author extends special thanks to Mrs. Norma Siviter Assadourian, Head, Special Collections, Smith Library Center, Southwestern University, Georgetown, Texas, for showing me the Edward A. Clark Texana Collection, which was most helpful to me in establishing the background for this book.

Special thanks are extended to Mr. Roy Fish of Nacogdoches, Texas. Also gratefully acknowledged as excellent background sources consulted in the writing of this book are *Comanches* by T.R. Fehrenback and *A Dictionary of the Old West* by Peter Watts.

****

It should be noted that, while the names "Tonacey," "Paha Yuca" and "Piava," used herein, are names that may be found in Comanche history, the characters created under these names herein are purely fictional.

Chapter 1

Mid-August, 1859
Nacogdoches, Texas

The sun was hot enough to raise blisters on a tin roof. In a clearing just outside the small town of Nacogdoches stood a ramshackle one and a half story frame house, surrounded by the lofty green pines of East Texas. In the yard stood six young women about to witness arson.

Dressed only in her camisole, bloomers, and a thin wrapper, seventeen-year-old Kate Maloney grimly circled Mrs. Eberhard's boarding school, sloshing kerosene from a jug. Kate's lovely face was clenched in a mask of relentless fury; she was smack in the middle of the most murderous rage she had ever known.

As Kate went about her dire task, she was followed by an entourage of five weeping schoolgirls, all of whom, like her, wore only their underclothes and wrappers. The five younger girls had been begging Kate to abandon her madness for several long, hysterical moments—all to no avail.

"Kate, please don't burn down Mrs. Eberhard's school," twelve-year-old Gretchen wailed. "She'll beat us all senseless."

Kate didn't miss a step as she rounded a corner

1

and poured kerosene onto the front porch. She drew herself up proudly and turned to face her younger classmates. "It's about time the old shrew got a dose of her own medicine," she asserted with green eyes flashing. "Just look at you, Gretchen—there are welts on your face from where that old witch hit you with a willow switch. And you, Betsy—your arms are covered with scratches, thanks to that she-wolf. I've had all her stinking abuse I can stomach."

"But Kate, burning down Mrs. Eberhard's house won't help at all! She'll only get more worked up than ever!" freckle-faced Sally interjected.

"She'll lock us all up in the root cellar and throw away the key!" Gretchen added in a terrified whisper.

"Not if I've a breath left in my body, she won't," Kate maintained as she emptied the rest of the kerosene onto the gallery.

As Kate set down her jug and pulled a box of matches from the waist of her drawers, an hysterical shriek went up. "No, Kate, please stop!" several of the others beseeched, looking on in horror.

Kate calmly turned to the sobbing group. "Anybody need to fetch somethin' out of the house before I set her up? That old biddy burned all our clothes—but if there's a rag doll or a sewing basket any of you have taken a shine to, my advice is, get it now."

The other girls exchanged lost looks. Then fourteen-year-old Betsy turned to Kate with an expression of panic. "But—what about Mrs. Eberhard's things?"

"Who gives a polecat's behind about the old biddy's things?" Kate countered angrily. "She didn't hesitate to destroy most of our belongings, and now she's going to pay!"

Thirteen-year-old Hannah, the most devoutly religious of the girls, rushed forward and grabbed Kate's arm. "Oh, no! Mrs. Eberhard's family Bible!"

"What about it?" Kate asked with strained patience.

"If you burn her Bible, we'll all spend eternity in a lake of everlasting fire!" Hannah declared.

"Oh, hell and high water," Kate said disgustedly. "Go fetch it. I'm not saying I cotton to barbecuing the Good Book myself—just so all of you understand that it's the Almighty I'm fearin', not that mad dog Eberhard."

"Yes, Kate," the others sniveled in unison.

Kate watched with thinly disguised impatience as Hannah rushed into the house to fetch their teacher's Bible. "And, mind you, don't step in the confounded kerosene!" Kate called out after her. "It's the house I'm aiming to set ablaze—not your Sunday slippers."

As the schoolgirls waited in tense silence for Hannah to return, Kate grimly thought over the events in her life that had brought her to this appalling pass. Though Kate was still quite young, hers had been a rough, turbulent existence; her mother had died at her birth, and she had been raised by a cantankerous Irishman who thought women were good for two things only—having babies and obeying their husbands. Kate had never known true love or acceptance, certainly not from her father, and she'd been labeled "difficult" all her life. Her predilection toward being a tomboy had not helped matters: "It ain't right a female should shoot like a man or ride astride a horse," Jeb Maloney had always said.

As a young child, Kate had gone through a string of governesses, all of whom had thrown up their hands at her recalcitrant behavior. Afterward, her father had shuttled her from one boarding school to another; yet, again and again, Jeb Maloney had been informed by the boarding school head mistresses that there was no controlling his obstreperous daughter.

Then, soon after Kate turned seventeen, Jeb had heard of a new boarding school out in East Texas, run by a strong-willed German woman. Sure his problem was solved, Kate's father had promptly shipped her off.

That had been two weeks ago, and from the very moment Kate Maloney and Berta Eberhard had laid eyes on each other, total and unconditional war had been declared.

Berta Eberhard ruled the girls in her charge with an iron fist, subjecting them to brutal sixteen hour days of lessons, Bible study, and chores, with no time out for rest or recreation. The slightest infraction was punished by a swift, sadistic beating, along with hair-raising threats that gave the younger girls nightmares—in which they were locked up in Berta's hotter-than-hell root cellar, or their hair was cut off, just like Samson's in the Bible. Not only that, but the cruel school mistress made all of her charges wear oppressive black wool dresses, even in the blistering August heat.

No one had ever dared to defy Berta's absolute authority—until Kate Maloney appeared.

Kate had at once been outraged at the physical and emotional abuse she witnessed at Berta Eberhard's school. Yet, in another sense, Kate's arrival in Nacogdoches had heralded the beginning of a great adventure in her life.

Kate Maloney had always been a loner. But from the moment she had arrived at Mrs. Eberhard's school, the other girls, all younger than she, had looked up to her. From the instant Kate had stared Berta straight in the eye and drawled, ''I'm not wearing that black shroud—and if you don't like it, you can go kiss a sidewinder,'' she had been proclaimed the heroine of the day. Never mind that afterward, Mrs. Eberhard had locked Kate in her room until she at last donned the scratchy, suffocating uniform. Thereafter, the other girls' days passed in an endless series of skirmishes and outright battles between Mrs. Eberhard and Kate—all of which they watched in horror and fascination. Kate had gone from loner to leader, from maverick to champion of the oppressed.

And Kate had discovered that this was a role she loved.

Then the heat wave had come—the heat wave that had raised temperatures in Nacogdoches way above the century mark, and tempers even higher. Still, Mrs. Eberhard had persisted in forcing the girls to wear the stifling black wool clothes, even after one of the younger girls had passed out from the heat and another vomited. At that point, Kate had had all she could take. Earlier today, while Mrs. Eberhard had been in town fetching supplies, Kate had gathered all of their black uniforms and sold them to a passing peddler.

Two hours ago, upon returning home and learning of Kate's perfidy, Mrs. Eberhard had gone into a frenzy, chasing Kate with a switch. When Kate had proven too difficult to corral, the German woman had lashed out indiscriminately at the other girls, viciously switching several of them. This, more than anything, Kate could not abide—seeing her friends suffer because of her own misdeed. She had come forward and accepted her punishment; her back still stung from the cutting blows the woman had inflicted.

Yet the nightmare for Kate and the other girls had just begun. As the six watched in horror, Mrs. Eberhard had gathered all of their other dresses and had burned them in the yard. Then she had headed off

for town, leaving the girls with only their underclothes and wrappers to cover them, telling them
spitefully that she was going to buy black wool for
new uniforms, and that they would stay up all night
sewing them.

That was when something had snapped in Kate,
when she knew that drastic means were called for.
Never in her life had she so longed to get her hands
on her father's Colt Dragoon. Since she had no gun
with which to give Berta a good scare, another, desperate plan had quickly formed in her mind. As soon
as Mrs. Eberhard was out of sight, Kate had fetched
the jug of kerosene from the shed—

Hannah emerged with Mrs. Eberhard's huge family
Bible, her reappearance interrupting Kate's turbulent
thoughts. "Kate, won't you please reconsider?" the
girl implored.

Kate shook her head. "That battle-ax beat us and
burned all our clothes, so now I'm going to burn
down her damned house."

"Kate, please, don't!" Laura wailed.

"Hell, I'm doing the old bat a favor," Kate
asserted as she prepared to strike a match. "This
old shack is so rickety, it's little more than a feast
for the rats and the termites as it is. Now all
of you—get back! All hell's fixin' to bust loose
here."

The other girls shrank back in horror. Once Kate
was sure her classmates were out of danger, she
smiled with fierce triumph, lit the match, and tossed
it on the porch. She watched in vindictive pleasure
as hot flames danced across the gallery, igniting the
moth-eaten curtains at the front windows. The heat
rose in hot, shimmering waves toward the roof, and
the acrid odor of burning kerosene and wood filled
the air.

In the background, the other girls shrieked lamen-
tations and clung to each other. Kate stepped back

a bit to admire her handiwork. She pulled a cheroot from behind her ear and slowly lit it, savoring the taste of the tobacco. Grinning her pleasure, she stood outlined by the snapping flames—a beautiful young woman of Irish heritage, with riotous black hair, delicate features, a peaches and cream complexion, and eyes green and wicked enough to give the devil himself pause.

The house was totally enveloped in flames by the time Berta Eberhard returned in her buggy, with three bolts of black wool on the seat beside her. The large, middle-aged German woman lumbered out of her conveyance and hurried toward the girls in the clearing, her arms waving wildly and her plump features florid.

"What happen? What happen?" she demanded furiously.

Kate held up the empty jug of kerosene and her box of matches. "Guess," she replied with a smirk.

Berta Eberhard lost control, going at Kate with both fists flying. "You witch! You harlot! You set my house on fire! I kill you for this!" she shrieked.

While the woman was at least twice Kate's weight, Kate was younger and much more agile. She easily dodged Mrs. Eberhard's savage blows and administered a swift kick to the shin which left the older woman doubling over and gurgling in agony.

"You gotta corral me first, you miserable old shrew!" Kate spat.

The German woman somehow managed to straighten herself. "I go get the sheriff," she screamed at Kate, her features livid, her hat askew. "You will hang for this!"

"And you can burn in bloody hell—just like your house!" Kate yelled back. "You think you can treat us worse than the scum in your slop jars. Well, it's high time someone taught *you* a lesson, you old harridan!''

Mrs. Eberhard shook a fist at Kate. ''You brat! I make you pay for this!''

The woman whirled and hobbled to her buggy, shouting her outrage in rapid German.

As soon as the buggy lurched off in a din of flying hooves, the other girls hurried toward Kate. ''Kate, she said you're going to hang!'' fifteen-year-old Laura wailed.

''Nonsense,'' Kate retorted. ''They may throw me in the calaboose, but they sure as Sunday ain't gonna hang me. My pa'll skin me alive when he finds out, but I reckon he'll spring me first.''

''Oh, Kate!'' Two of the younger girls burst into tears.

''Now, calm down, every one of you,'' Kate ordered. ''It's over now—Mrs. Eberhard is out of business. You're safe and all of you can go home.'' Astonished to feel tears stinging her eyes as she stared at her frightened, vulnerable companions, Kate lifted her chin and added bravely, ''That's all I ever cared about. You're my friends, you see, and I couldn't abide seeing that old hag hurting you no more.''

''Oh, Kate!'' The other girls rushed forward to embrace her, and the six friends huddled together, trembling.

The house was little more than a heap of burning cinders by the time Berta Eberhard returned with the sheriff. The middle-aged, mustached man looked decidedly ill-at-ease as he approached the girls with the irate German woman.

''Are you Miss Kate Maloney?'' he asked Kate.

''I sure am,'' Kate replied, smiling poisonously at Berta.

The sheriff coughed. "Miss Maloney, Mrs. Eberhard here claims that you—er—"

"She burn down my house!" Berta Eberhard cut in, her bosom heaving. "She's a hell-cat, a she-devil! She deserve to hang!"

The sheriff raised a hand at the seething matron. "Now, hold it a minute, Berta." He turned awkwardly to Kate. "Is what Mrs. Eberhard says true, miss? Did you burn down her house?"

"I sure did," Kate drawled. Flashing a look of contempt at Berta, she continued indignantly, "And did this old bat tell you what she did to us? Beating us and burning our dresses and making us wear black wool from head to toe when it's a hundred and twenty in the shade?"

As Kate spoke, Mrs. Eberhard puffed up like a toad. "You a lying little hussy!"

"And you're a malicious, hateful old bitch!" Kate hissed back.

As the two women lunged for each other, the sheriff dived into the fracas, forcing the two raving females apart. "Now, wait a minute, both of you!" To Kate, he said, "What you're saying may be true, miss, but it still don't justify your destroying this woman's house. I'm afraid I'm gonna have to take you in."

Mrs. Eberhard smirked at the sheriff's words, but Kate was smirking, too, as she held out her wrists. "Be my guest."

The sheriff colored as he shifted from foot to foot. "Oh, no, miss, it won't be necessary to handcuff you."

"As you wish, Sheriff," Kate replied.

The sheriff turned to Mrs. Eberhard. "Ma'am, I'll be sending my deputy along directly with a wagon to fetch the other girls. I reckon they'll have to stay at the hotel in town until their folks can be notified."

''Ain't that a cryin' shame,'' Kate added spitefully to Berta.

Mrs. Eberhard shot Kate a look of utter scorn. Kate merely winked at her friends.

As the sheriff led Kate off, she was still grinning.

Chapter 2

Ten Days Later
Round Rock, Texas

Jeb Maloney was cussing a blue streak. Sitting at his table at the Round Rock Saloon, he pounded his fist in outrage as he reread the letter he'd just received from the sheriff of Nacogdoches.

Across the room from Jeb, at the piano, a hefty woman with flaming red hair was plunking out an off-key rendition of "The Yellow Rose of Texas." The customers of the saloon—mostly ranchers or drovers from the area—observed Jeb Maloney surreptitiously and gave his table a wide berth as they came and went from the bar. The big, burly Irishman and his hair-trigger temper were legendary in the small Texas town.

Finished rereading the letter, Jeb crumpled it and ground his jaw. His daughter, Kate, had been thrown in jail for burning down Mrs. Eberhard's boarding school! Never in his life had he felt so disgusted with his offspring. This was far worse than the time Kate had put a king snake in the Mother Superior's bed at Ursuline Convent, or the time she had hung her teacher's drawers out on the flagpole at Miss Turner's Institute for Young Ladies. This—why this was downright criminal—arson, to say the

11

very least. This time, there'd be the devil to pay before he got his feisty, headstrong daughter off the hook.

Jeb shook his head in exasperation. He'd never been able to control Kate—she'd been a maverick from the minute his housekeeper Conchita had slapped on Kate's first diaper. Perhaps if his dear Margaret had lived . . . But Jeb's young wife had died bearing their daughter. Jeb had tried not to hold his wife's death against the girl, but the little spitfire had tried his patience sorely for all her seventeen years.

The trouble was, Kate had never got it through her head that she was a girl child, not a boy. From the time she'd been a little tyke, Jeb had caught her again and again hanging out with his ranch hands; she'd sweetly finagled many a drover into teaching her how to ride or shoot. Jeb had sworn on his wife's memory that he'd reform the wayward girl, to no avail. He'd ushered her through an endless parade of governesses and boarding schools, yet not one of them had been able to control her. Full of mettle and defiance, she was nothing like her sweet, gentle ma had been.

Though Jeb hated to admit it, his daughter was the spitting image of himself. But a woman had no place carrying on like a man! The girl was every bit as ornery as Spuds Gilhooley, the cantankerous Irish neighbor with whom Jeb had been feuding for almost twenty years.

Now this business in Nacogdoches. Jeb stroked his stubbled jaw and shook his head. When he had first heard about the iron-willed Mrs. Eberhard and her school out in Nacogdoches, he had assumed that his problems with his daughter were finally solved. He had foolishly concluded that the German lady would be able to whip Kate into a proper lady. Thus, he had shipped his recalcitrant daughter off to be taught some manners.

Now, it was obvious that if anyone was doing the teaching, it wasn't Mrs. Eberhard. It was clearer still that no woman could ever redeem his hellion of a daughter.

Jeb wondered dismally what he would do next. He was half-tempted to let Kate rot in jail, but it was no permanent solution. During the past year, he'd been seeing a widow lady from a neighboring ranch, and he was seriously thinking of getting hitched up again. But he knew he could never seek his own happiness until he dealt with Kate.

The girl was seventeen now, he mused, too old for school. Which meant that the only alternative left was to marry her off.

But where in blue blazes would he find a husband man enough to handle her? Or even one willing to take her on?

With ill-disguised contempt, Jeb glanced about the saloon, studying the other customers—ranchers, drovers, muleskinners, and miscellaneous drifters. What a sorry lot they were. He knew of no man in Round Rock with enough grit to stand up to his daughter. Indeed, a number of eligible men in town had already borne the brunt of Kate's notorious temper. Why, the whole countryside was still buzzing with gossip over the incident last year when Kate had shot the hat off the circuit rider's head, just because she claimed the preacher had given her a "leer." Hell, the girl was downright dangerous; she could ride and shoot as well as any man. So, even if Jeb could manage to convince one of the locals to wed her, he was sure the little spitfire would plant the hapless fool in the ground by sundown.

No, his only hope was to find an outsider—a stranger who'd never met Kate, someone with nerves of steel and a will stronger and more dauntless than his daughter's. The man would have to be an upstanding sort, too, else Jeb knew his own conscience would never give him any peace.

But where in the hell would he find such a man?

As if in answer to Jeb's question, the saloon doors swung open and a tall, dark stranger strode in. At once, all the occupants of the saloon turned to eye the man covertly, warily, for this newcomer radiated an unmistakable aura of power and danger. His frame was towering, lean and hard-muscled, his features sharply honed, his hair and eyes near-black. He wore a blue broadcloth shirt, a leather vest, and tightly fitting shot-gun chaps. His hat was black, his boots and gunbelt hand-tooled. A Colt revolver and sheathed Bowie knife were strapped to his muscular thighs.

Silence stretched tauter than a tightwire as the broad-shouldered stranger sauntered over to the bar and ordered a whiskey. As his menacing gaze roved about the room, others promptly turned away, resuming their poker games or ruminating. The stranger downed his drink and ordered another.

A moment later, Bart, the bartender, brought Jeb a fresh bottle of whiskey. "Who's the *pistolero?*" Jeb asked Bart under his breath, nodding toward the bar.

Bart followed Jeb's gaze. "Him? That there's Charlie Durango."

"Charlie Durango?" Jeb repeated in disbelief.

"In the flesh," Bart replied, striding off.

Jeb studied the man with intense interest. So this was the infamous Charlie Durango—former Texas Ranger turned bounty hunter. Durango was a legend in these parts; he had a reputation of being mean enough to send a rattlesnake slithering out of his path. Rumor held that Durango would do any job, no matter how dirty, as long as it was legal and the price was right. Durango had stalked practically every outlaw or renegade whose face or name had

ever appeared on a wanted poster; he always got
his man, but rarely turned in his quarry alive.

While Jeb had never actually met Durango before,
he had certainly heard plenty concerning his dauntless reputation and his various exploits. Indeed, one
of Jeb's best friends, Gil Buckley over in Travis
County had once hired Durango to take care of his
rustler problem. Later, Gil had told Jeb that the man
had taken to his task with tenacious dispatch, rid-
ding the ranch of maverickers within weeks. Charlie
Durango was a man of his word, Gil had said, if
utterly ruthless. "If you want a job done right, hire
Durango," Gil had advised.

Hmm. If he wanted the job done right . . . Would
Durango be able to handle Kate? Jeb's hand clenched
on his whiskey glass. As much as the thought
stunned him, he couldn't get it out of his mind.
Clearly, the bounty hunter was the type of man no
one dared to cross—A man like himself. And Jeb well
knew that only such a man could ever hope to tame
Kate.

As Bart made another pass by Jeb's table, Jeb
caught the bartender's sleeve. "Tell me what you
know about this Durango character. What's he doin'
here—where's he bound?"

Bart glanced toward the stranger. "I hear tell he's
holed up right now at Sam Stockton's hunting cabin
south of town." In a low voice, he added, "The
scuttlebutt is, Durango's plumb whipped from
bounty huntin' and Injun fightin', and he's aimin'
to retire."

"Retire?" Jeb repeated in a shocked voice.

"Hell, the man must be pushing thirty," Bart replied.

Jeb frowned thoughtfully. "Why don't you tell
Mr. Durango that if he'd like to join me at my table,
the whiskey's on me."

Bart's eyebrows shot up, followed by a swift, nervous nod. "Sure, Mr. Maloney, whatever you say."

Watching Bart stride off toward the bar, Jeb was thinking fast. So Charlie Durango was aiming to settle down. Hmm. Perhaps for the right incentive, he could be convinced to take Kate on.

But would it be right to saddle his daughter with such a hard man? Jeb's cold blue eyes gleamed with outrage. Hell, the girl deserved no less after the way she had carried on. Besides, if the Texan was interested in her, he'd make it clear that he'd tolerate no abuse of his daughter. He just needed to find a man strong enough to handle Kate and keep her in her proper place.

Jeb watched Bart say something to the Texan and point toward his table. After a moment, Charlie Durango got up with his empty glass in hand and strode toward Jeb.

"So, you're inviting me for a drink, neighbor?" Charlie asked. His soft drawl did little to mute the lethal menace radiating from his whipcord-taut body and dark, probing eyes.

"Sure, Mr. Durango—Jeb Maloney's the name," Jeb replied confidently, extending his hand.

Charlie accepted Jeb's firm handshake with an equally strong grip of his own. "Pleased to meet you, Mr. Maloney."

"Have a seat."

Charlie sat down and removed his hat. He held up his glass, which Charlie filled with whiskey.

"So what brings you to Round Rock, Mr. Durango?" Jeb asked.

Charlie shrugged. "I'm between jobs at the moment, on a bit of a furlough. I'm staying out at the Stockton hunting cabin. Sam and I rode together when I was in the Rangers."

"Oh, yeah, I know Stockton," Jeb replied. "He usually comes through to hunt deer when the weather grows cold. You—er—got any firm plans, Mr. Durango?''

Charlie took a slow sip of his drink and asked softly, ''What's on your mind, neighbor?''

''I might have a business proposition for you.''

Charlie chuckled. ''So does everyone.''

''I've heard you're hankering to settle down.'' Jeb gave Durango an assessing stare.

Setting down his drink, Charlie took a pouch of tobacco from his shirt pocket and began slowly rolling a smoke. ''I might be.''

Jeb smiled engagingly. ''Generally speaking, when a man wants to settle down, he thinks about choosing himself a mate.''

''Could be.'' Charlie lit his cigarette and took a deep draw.

Jeb leaned forward. ''What I'm trying to say, Mr. Durango, is that I've got a daughter I'm aiming to marry off. And I was wondering—well, if you might be interested.''

Charlie's dark eyes glittered suspiciously. ''What ails this girl you're trying to foist off?''

Jeb was at once indignant, fixing Durango with a magnificent glare. ''Why, nothin' ails her, mister. You'll never find a prettier little filly, or a smarter one, neither.''

Charlie harrumphed. ''And how old is this paragon of virtue? Forty-five?''

''Seventeen.''

Charlie still looked highly skeptical, his eyes narrowed on Jeb. ''And you're sayin' nothing's wrong with her?''

''Nothing, I swear,'' Jeb asserted. ''Besides which, the man who marries my daughter will inherit all my land one day, and . . .'' Drawing a deep breath, he finished, ''What I'm tryin' to say, Mr. Durango, is if you're interested, I can make it worth your while.''

Yet Charlie shook his head, a cynical gleam in his eyes. "Now, hold it right there, mister. First off, I ain't interested in your land or your money. Next, I can smell a bamboozle a mile away, and I can tell you right now that your deal stinks. You've never before met me, you know nothing about me, and now you're telling me you want me to marry your daughter?"

Jeb squirmed in his chair. "Well, it's not exactly true that I know nothing about you, Mr. Durango. You see, Gil Buckley is a good friend of mine, and he's certainly vouched for your—er—character."

"I remember Buckley," Charlie conceded. "Still, why would you want to hook your seventeen-year-old daughter up with a man like me?"

Jeb sighed, deciding his only recourse was to tell the truth. Avoiding Charlie's eyes, he muttered, "Because you're the only man I know who might be able to handle my daughter."

To Jeb's surprise, Charlie laughed. He looked highly amused and intrigued. "What do you mean, handle her?"

Wordlessly, Jeb uncrumpled the letter from Nacogdoches and handed it to Charlie. After tossing down his smoke and grinding it out beneath his boot, Charlie spread the letter out on the table and read the contents with a scowl.

When he was finished, he glanced up at Jeb, grinning. "Your daughter has been arrested for burning down a boarding school in Nacogdoches?"

"That's about the size of it," Jeb acknowledged. "She's rotting in the hoosegow at this very moment."

"Does she usually carry on in this manner?"

"Oh, mister you have no idea."

As Charlie listened in fascination, Jeb launched into a long discourse concerning Kate's recalcitrant behavior over the years. While hearing of Kate's various, outrageous exploits, Charlie uttered more than one disbelieving expletive; at one point, when Jeb told of how Kate had turned half a dozen squealing piglets loose in church, he fell back in his chair with a look of amazement.

"And you're asking me to marry this girl?" Charlie asked afterward, his expression still dumbfounded.

"Mister, I'm begging you," Jeb said. "I've reached the point of desperation with the girl. I've come to the conclusion that—well, it's gonna take a man stronger than me to handle her."

Charlie chuckled. "Now that is a compliment."

"But, mind you, I'll permit no abuse of the girl," Jeb went on. "Nor will I tolerate any philanderin', so if'n you're not quite through sowing your wild oats, son, you'd best say so now. I'm simply looking for a strong, upstanding husband for the girl—and from everything I've heard, you fill the bill."

Charlie stroked his jaw for a long moment. "Maybe I do," he conceded at last.

Jeb was most pleasantly surprised. "Then you'll marry her?"

Charlie broke into a grin. "Maybe I will."

"And you're prepared to give up your rambling ways and settle down for her?" Jeb challenged.

"I'll admit I'm aimin' to retire soon."

"Then we have a deal?"

"Maybe we do." Yet even as Jeb was extending his hand, Charlie held up his in caution. "But with one important condition. I want to see the goods first. I ain't marrying the girl if she's a bad looker."

Jeb was all smiles. "Sure, mister, you can see the goods all right. And you've got yourself a bargain," he added, shaking the Texan's hand.

"So when do I get a peek at the girl?" Charlie asked.

"Soon as I spring her from the calaboose."

Charlie's deep laughter could be heard all the way across the room. To Jeb, he said softly, "Then I reckon I'll be hanging around town until you fetch her home."

As the two men continued to discuss a few more details of their arrangement, Jeb inwardly heaved a great sigh of relief, knowing he had hooked a live one. Kate was a winsome creature. He was sure this Texan would have a hard time resisting her.

A she-devil straight from hell the girl definitely was. But a bad looker—never!

Jeb Maloney's dilemma was solved.

Moments later, as Charlie Durango mounted his palomino and headed out of town, he too was feeling self-satisfied.

Charlie cantered Corona down the shady expanse of Stagecoach Road and waded him through the low water crossing at Brushy Creek. Protruding from the creek bed was the raw monolith of rock after which the town of Round Rock had been named. He proceeded uphill, heading due south toward the Stockton cabin. It looked like he'd be staying there a bit longer than he'd originally planned.

Charlie grinned. He'd been stunned moments earlier when Jeb Maloney, a total stranger, had proposed that Charlie marry his daughter. But, damn, if that little hellcat Kate Maloney didn't sound intriguing!

Actually, though he'd told no one, Charlie was looking for a wife. At thirty, he was growing tired of the rough, dangerous existence he'd been living for so long. He'd grown bone-weary of dusty trails, gun battles, Indian fighting, and tracking down the scum of the earth. Not to mention, smoky saloons and whores who tried to knife him in the back just to steal his money. For several years now, he'd had a yearning to turn respectable and settle down. That meant getting hitched, having children, and, for once in his life, finding a home to call his own.

In fact, Charlie had been preparing for his eventual retirement for some time by investing a heavy chunk of his savings in a gold mine up near Pikes Peak. His partner had recently written, saying he was close to reaching a major vein. As soon as the strike came in, Charlie was planning to relocate to the Denver region.

He'd be needing a wife to take west with him. Indeed, in the recent letter, his partner had said, "Bring a female along when you come—there ain't none here to speak of."

Charlie Durango liked women as well as the next man. But his problem was, he'd never met a woman who would be exciting and fun enough to spend the rest of his life with, a woman with enough grit and spunk to face him down when he was wrong, yet who was loyal and courageous enough to always stand beside him. The women he'd met heretofore had come in two basic varieties—whores who only wanted to use him, and mealy-mouthed virgins who cowered at the sight of him. Neither type was marriageable material, as far as Charlie was concerned.

Yet, now, at last, he may have heard of a woman who was his equal. He shook his head and grinned. Burning down a boarding school—now *that* girl had spit!

If the Maloney girl's looks were passable, Charlie knew he would likely marry her and take her along to Denver. Her feistiness didn't bother him in the least.

Hell, Charlie Durango liked the idea of having a wildcat to subdue in bed.

* * *

While Charlie was gloating over his victory, Jeb was preparing to leave town, purchasing extra supplies at the Oatts' store. He was exiting the rock building with a hefty bundle of goods when he practically collided with his nemesis, Spuds Gilhooley.

Both men backed off and eyed each other warily. While Jeb was huge and barrel-chested, Spuds was gaunt, bowlegged and swaybacked, gray-whiskered, with the mean, intense look of a weasel. The two men lived on neighboring spreads and had been fighting their boundary dispute for almost two decades now. They often took pot-shots at each other from opposite hillsides, but always missed. Folks in town had commented that the two men enjoyed their feud too much to actually kill each other.

"Well, ain't you a fly in the ointment," Jeb drawled at last.

"Well, ain't you a pea in the shoe," Spuds jeered back.

"Get out of my way, Gilhooley," Jeb countered, shouldering his massive frame past Spuds and through the doorway.

Jeb was striding off toward his horse when Spuds called out shrilly, "Hold it a minute, Maloney. I'll be having a word with you!"

Jeb turned and scoffed, "Oh, yeah? Seems to me, you usually do your talkin' with your shootin' iron, Gilhooley. That is, when you ain't rustling my cows."

Spuds shrugged. "If them longhorns of yourn is too lame-brained to stay on your range, then it's open season."

"Open season, my butt," Jeb retorted. "It's you clipping my fence and mavericking them onto your land."

"Says you. And I say you're just a low-down coward who up and stole my crick."

Now Spuds had Jeb's undivided attention. The

rancher's face turned red with outrage as he waved a fist. "I ain't stole your crick, Gilhooley, it plain shilly-shallyed onto my land. You can ask Judge Kennedy about that. And you call me a coward again, you misbegotten little runt, and by damn I'll—"

"Bribe the judge again, like you done the last time we was in court?" Spuds asked with a sneer.

Jeb advanced on the other man like a raging bull. "That's an outright lie! Why, you lowdown, dirty—"

Both men were about to reach for their guns when the Round Rock sheriff, George Winston, strode up between them. Having spent years trying to prevent bloodshed between the two warring Irishmen, Winston quickly took charge. "All right, you two geezers, back off," he ordered gruffly. "I ain't having no gunfight on the streets of Round Rock at high noon. This here is a civilized town."

The two men glared at each other for another moment, then heeded the sheriff's warning. Spitting a wad of tobacco toward Spud's feet in an unmistakable gesture of contempt, Jeb turned on his bootheel and stalked off to his horse.

Spuds watched, his grizzled features twisted in fury, his firing hand twitching next to his holstered gun.

None of this was lost on the sheriff. "Now, Spuds," he cautioned, "you'd best let it lay. You shoot a man in the back in this town and you're gonna swing. Make no mistake about that."

Spuds glowered at the sheriff, muttered a curse, then pivoted hard and strode away. Inwardly, he was still burning with anger. Jeb Maloney was a coward and a water thief. Spuds vowed he'd get his creek back, even if it meant he had to fill Jeb Maloney's britches with buckshot first . . .

Jeb, too, was still seething as he tied his bundle to

his saddle straps, mounted his horse, and started toward home. Spuds Gilhooley had become a real burr in his saddle of late. After he dealt with Kate, he'd fix Spud's wagon for good, he vowed.

Chapter 3

J eb Maloney's expression was grim as he and two of his wranglers rode into the town of Nacogdoches on the ancient *Camino Real*. The men had endured a brutal three day ride from Round Rock in the blistering heat, and Jeb's temper had grown shorter with each mile.

At the public square, they turned north, passing the pillared court house and the two-storied Roberts Saloon, once a Spanish trading post. Finally, they arrived at the small, stone jail building just south of the old Caddoan Indian mounds. The three dismounted and tied their mounts, as well as the appaloosa pony they'd brought along for Kate, to the hitching post.

Jeb turned to the others. "Why don't you two go wet your whistles while I see about the girl?"

"Yes, Boss," they replied in unison.

The two men strode off toward the saloon, while Jeb set his jaw in a firm line and turned toward the jail. The instant he swung open the heavy door, he heard the unmistakable sound of feminine laughter. The sight that greeted him made his blood boil.

The door to the building's only cell stood wide open; inside the tiny cubicle sat his daughter Kate. The girl wore only her underclothes and a loose wrapper. She was perched on the edge of her bunk

25

with a smoking cheroot dangling from her lips and a sheaf of cards in her hand. She looked pleased as a cat licking cream. Across from her on a straight chair sat a thin, middle-aged man with a silver star on his chest and a poker hand clutched in his own fingers. He looked edgy as a greenhorn sitting on a cactus.

"Well, Sheriff, you gonna' ante up or fold?" Kate was asking.

"Please, Miss Kate," the man replied, throwing her a beseeching look, "you already won ten dollars offen me—"

That's when Jeb stormed forward and roared, "What in the blue blazes is going on here?"

The man dropped his cards and struggled to his feet; Kate took a long draw on her cheroot and eyed her father warily.

The red-faced sheriff, meanwhile, hurried through the opening to greet his guest. "May I help you, sir?" he stammered to Jeb.

"Looks like you're helping yourself to my daughter!" Jeb bellowed.

The sheriff's eyes grew huge. "Oh, no sir! I mean, I was—er—just keepin' an eye on the girl—that is, I mean—well, until you arrived, sir. I mean, you must be—"

"Jeb Maloney from Round Rock," Jeb retorted, drawing himself up to his full, menacing height as he glowered at the lawman. "And I repeat, sir, what in the Sam Hill are you doing with my daughter, and why is she in this scandalous state?"

At Jeb's words, the sheriff looked miserable, avoiding Jeb's eyes. "Well—er—I brought Miss Kate one of my wife's dresses to wear, seeing's all her other clothes was destroyed, but she flat out refused to put it on. Said she—er—wanted the judge to see the evidence of what Mrs. Eberhard done to her and the others—"

"What the hell!" Jeb stormed over to Kate, his eyes gleaming with murderous resolve. "Daughter, you will dress yourself properly at once, or I'll see that you're horsewhipped."

Kate, who had been watching the exchange with some amusement, stood to face the man confronting her, the man who had been her nemesis all her life. Jeb Maloney had greeted her in exactly the manner she had expected—with utter contempt. Now, despite his powerful, intimidating presence, she took a lazy draw off her cheroot and drawled, "Hello, Pa."

Jeb Maloney's face turned the color of blood sausage, and his nostrils flared as he heaved in short, furious breaths. "Get that goddamned cheroot out of your mouth, girl, before I make you eat it! The very idea—you, practically a grown woman, gambling and smoking and displaying your wares like a two-bit whore—"

"Whatever you say, Pa," Kate retorted, dropping her cheroot on the floor and grinding it out beneath her slipper. Her expression remained remote, hiding the deep, cutting wounds her father's harsh words inflicted.

Jeb whirled on the sheriff. "Who do I have to see to get the girl sprung?"

The sheriff chewed his mustache and shifted nervously from foot to foot. "Well—er—you might speak with Judge Hamilton over to the court house. But you'll have to know, sir, that Mrs. Eberhard is mighty riled about her house being burned—"

"Folks that gets their houses burned down around their ears generally is," Jeb snapped back. Tossing Kate a scornful look, he added to the lawman, "I suppose I'll have to pay the woman off—"

Kate sprang forward, her eyes blazing and her fist waving. "No, Pa! Don't you dare give that old she-devil a plug nickel until you hear my side of it!"

Jeb whirled on his daughter. "She-devil, my hat! You're one to talk, you foul-mouthed brat! Now shut up, miss, or I swear, I'll take you all the way back to Round Rock tied up in a gunny sack!"

At her father's words, Kate's chin came up and she seethed in silent outrage. Her father had already turned back to the sheriff and was asking for the whereabouts of Judge Hamilton's office at the court house. A moment later, Jeb Maloney stormed out of the building without giving his daughter a backward glance.

The red-faced sheriff went to his desk and picked up the brown calico dress Kate had refused to wear for days now. Walking over to the girl and extending the frock, he said gently, "Er—Miss Kate, if I were you, I'd be putting this on."

Kate took the gown and bit her lip, fighting tears. "He wouldn't even listen to me. He didn't even care."

The sheriff nodded. "I know, miss. And I allow it was a terrible thing Mrs. Eberhard done to you and the others. Truth to tell, no one in these parts can abide that old witch. But your pa is mighty worked up at the moment. Perhaps later—"

"He won't listen," Kate cut in bitterly. "He never does."

"I'm sorry, miss."

The sheriff turned away awkwardly; Kate blinked back tears and, resigned, donned the gown.

Late afternoon had crept in by the time Jeb Maloney made all the arrangements, convincing the county judge to release Kate into his custody and paying off Mrs. Eberhard. The small group was grimly silent as they rode down *La Calle del Norte* back toward the *Camino Real*—first Jeb; then Kate, in her calico dress; then the two wranglers, Pete and Miguel.

The trail out of Nacogdoches was peaceful and quiet, but the three men were ever-watchful of the piney woods surrounding them. While the fierce Comanche Indians had recently been officially removed from Texas by the U.S. Cavalry, renegade bands were still known to attack settlers.

Near dusk, the group paused to make camp in a clearing near a rushing stream. The two wranglers cared for the horses, built a fire, and heated up some tins of stew, while Jeb kept watch over Kate. Father and daughter had spoken not a word since Jeb had gotten Kate released from jail, but the scathing looks the two exchanged revealed their mutual animosity.

The stew was palatable, and the hoecake Miguel had baked near the fire was smoothly textured. The foursome washed down their repast with strong coffee. After the meal, Kate dutifully went off to the stream to wash their dishes under the watchful eye of Miguel. She was hoping her show of domesticity might soften her father. After she returned to the fire, the two wranglers went off to water the horses for the night, leaving her alone with her pa.

Sitting on a large rock, Kate dried the last of the tin cups with a dishtowel. The night surrounding her was balmy, filled with sweet scents and soothing sounds; the sky above was vast and black as a Texas sky could be, and dotted with a thousand glittering stars. Yet all the wonders of nature seemed lost on Kate tonight. She observed her father surreptitiously as he stared into the flames and smoked his cigar. It still rankled that he had refused to listen to her. Was there no getting through to the man?

Swallowing her pride, Kate decided to make one last stab at explaining things to him. ''Pa, why won't you hear my side of the story?''

Jeb tossed his cigar into the fire and looked up at her with blue eyes blazing. ''Because there's no defense for what you did, daughter. Do you have any idea how much I had to pay that German woman to get her to drop the charges? Hell, the old bat could build ten new houses for what she squeezed out of me! I'll never forget the sight of her, holding out her hand and smirking smug as a fox sucking an egg.''

"You shouldn't have given her a penny!'' Kate cried, gesturing angrily. "She was cruel to us, beating us and—''

"Then my hat's off to the woman, is what I say!'' Jeb cut in. "Though obviously, she wasn't able to beat a whit of sense into you!''

"Oh, why do I even try to talk to you!'' Kate screamed back. "You never listen!''

"That's because you've never had a respectful, decent word to say to your father.''

Kate's hand slashed the air. "Who are you to talk of respect and decency? You're just takin' it out on me cause Ma died, just like you done all my life.''

"Shut up, girl!'' Jeb bellowed, waving a fist. "Don't you ever speak of your ma in that insolent tone of voice.''

"It's the truth and you know it. You just won't admit it. You've hated me from the day I was born. Why don't you just say so?''

"Maybe I would if you'd shut your confounded mouth long enough for me to get a word in edgewise.''

"Then be my guest,'' Kate challenged, tossing her curls in a gesture of defiance. "I'm all ears, Pa.''

For a moment, the two glared at each other, with only the snapping of the fire and the distant nickering of the horses to fill the raging silence. Then Jeb said gruffly, "Get ready for bed, daughter. We've a long ride ahead of us tomorrow.''

"Then what?'' Kate cried bitterly. "Pa, why do you insist on taking me home? You know we'll go on fighting each other till we're both dead or hell freezes over. Why don't you just let me go?''

"Never!" Jeb retorted. "You think I'd set you loose to disgrace me by plying your trade in some saloon or brothel? I'll see you saved from your own willfulness if it takes my dying breath!"

"Then prepare to meet your maker, Pa, cause you ain't never gonna change me!" Kate railed back. "And furthermore, you know damn well I'm gonna' run away the first chance I get."

Jeb stared murderously at his daughter. He was getting damned tired of Kate's recalcitrant, contemptuous attitude and her utter lack of remorse for the wrongs she'd done. He decided it was high time to teach the girl a lesson; indeed, she'd been begging for a good scare all day. Throwing her a meaningful sneer, he said softly, "Oh, don't be so sure you'll be running away, daughter."

Kate lifted her chin. "So you're gonna' stop me? You and which army?"

Ignoring her flippant remark, he continued, "You see, I have plans for you."

Kate scowled suspiciously. "What plans?"

"I'm marrying you off."

"In a pig's eye, you are!"

Jeb smiled a slow, cruel smile. "Oh, I think you'll be willing to take a husband once you hear about the alternative."

"Alternative? What alternative?"

"I'll have you committed to an asylum for the insane."

Kate howled with laughter. "You must be out of your cotton picking mind!"

Jeb leaned forward and hissed, "No, it's you, daughter, whose sanity is in doubt." He shook his head and uttered a low, clucking sound. "Burning down boarding schools and refusing to wear proper clothing for a woman, not to mention, playing cards and smokin' cigars like a man—now that surely sounds like demented behavior to me. And I'm sure

I'll have no problem finding a judge to sign the order and seal your fate.''

"You're serious!" Kate gasped, her eyes huge.

"Damn right, I'm serious. In fact, I've already got an asylum picked out down to Austin—one of those places where they lock you up and throw away the key.''

"You wouldn't dare!" Kate blustered.

"Try me.''

The two glowered at each other for another charged moment. Then Kate heaved a furious breath. "Pa, it's you that's gone plumb loco. You really think I'm gonna marry this fool you've picked out?''

"There's no doubt, daughter.''

"Who is he?''

Jeb chuckled. "Oh, you've never met him.''

"How old is this saphead? Forty-five?''

Jeb glared at his daughter. "Fifty-six.''

"Fifty-six!'' Kate shrieked. "Why, that's even older than you! The geezer must have both feet in the grave by now.''

"Yeah,'' Jeb drawled sarcastically, "and he's also got gout, rheumatism, and rotting teeth. And I only wish I could find someone more deserving of you.''

Kate was too appalled to speak, staring horrified at Jeb. At last, in a deadly serious tone, she said, "Pa, I'll never marry him. I'd sooner hitch up with Satan in red longjohns.''

Jeb reached into his pocket to extract another cigar, lighting it and taking a long draw before he spoke. "Then enjoy your asylum, daughter.''

Much later, when all four had settled down on their bedrolls around the fading fire, Kate's mind was seething in the darkness. Never had she felt such helpless rage and gnawing frustration.

Her father had sprung her from jail, all right, but,

just as she'd feared, Jeb Maloney had steadfastly refused to listen to her side of the story. As always, he was absolutely unwilling to acknowledge that she might have been right. In his eyes, she was worthless, an utter trial, and perpetually wrong.

Now, her father was determined to marry her off to a man old enough to be her grandfather. It was a nightmare!

Kate knew that the only avenue left open to her was escape. She lay tensely awake for long moments, watching the embers die and listening to the three men as they shifted about on their bedrolls. Once she heard only the deep, regular sounds of their snoring, she got up quietly and crept toward her pony.

She hadn't gone more than ten feet when steely fingers gripped her arm. She whirled, furious, to face Pete, one of the drovers.

"Miss Kate, your pa told me to be on the lookout for this," he said lamely, though his grip on her did not slacken.

"Pete, please let me go," Kate implored in a tense whisper. "You know what Pa's planning to do to me—"

"I'm sorry, Miss Kate," Pete said. Over his shoulder, he bellowed, "Boss!"

Kate somehow resisted an urge to cringe as her father came forward in his longjohns. He glanced with cold dispassion at Kate, then nodded to Pete. "I been expectin' this. Tie her up."

"Why don't you just let me go?" Kate screamed at her father's retreating back. "I hate your everlasting guts!"

Later, as Kate lay with her wrists tied to a sturdy sapling, her slim young body at last shook with sobs. Her tears fell on the hard, unyielding ground.

* * *

Two days later, at high noon, Charlie Durango was standing in the door of the Round Rock Saloon, sipping a beer, when he glimpsed a fascinating sight. Jeb Maloney was riding down Stagecoach Road with two of his wranglers; in the center of the group of men rode a proud young woman Charlie knew had to be Jeb's recalcitrant daughter.

The sight of the girl took his breath away. All the sounds surrounding him receded as he stared, captivated, at her. She was haughtily beautiful, her firm chin thrust high, her long black curls tossed back. She had the prettiest skin and the most trim, enticing figure he'd ever seen on a female. Her wrists were tied to the saddlehorn, and her countenance was magnificently disdainful as she stared bravely ahead.

So this was the daughter Jeb Maloney wanted him to marry! This was the little spitfire who had burned down a boarding school and planted a nest of ants in her governess's snuffbox. The girl was clearly a breath of heaven, straight from the gates of hell—

Charlie threw back his head and laughed. He watched in fascination as the proud minx rode out of town. Now, there was a female with spit—a female who would be feisty and fun, a pure challenge to tame and master.

And wild as a tigress in bed. The very thought made Charlie's hand tremble on his mug as a ripple of excitement coursed through him. This was the girl he'd been looking for, all right.

With a grin, Charlie lifted his mug. "Mr. Maloney," he drawled softly, "you got yourself a deal."

Chapter 4

Kate's temper was hotter than the noonday heat when she, her father, and the two cowhands finally crested the last rise and approached the prosperous Bar M ranch nestled in a valley three miles north of Round Rock. The air was thick with the scents of sun-baked grass and newly mown hay.

Kate's smoldering green eyes scanned the familiar landscape—the big house with its limestone exterior and pitched tin roof, the old oak and pecan trees shading the house, the familiar outbuildings, the clumps of cedar and prairie grass dotting the rocky landscape. A sparkling stream cut a path down the hillside behind the house and curved in front of it. Longhorn cows grazed on the rolling prairie to the east. In one of the three large corrals, two wranglers were training freshly broken mustang ponies.

Kate realized that home should be a welcome sight after the hellish weeks she'd spent at Mrs. Eberhard's boarding school, her stint in jail, and three rough days on the trail. Instead, she felt little joy at the prospect of returning to the house where she'd been born. She was still furious at her father for refusing to listen to her, and for arranging for her to marry some odious old toad.

Kate felt miserable, as well—exhausted, sore, and filthy. Her bottom ached from the long ride, and her skin was chafed and sunburned. She'd spent the entire journey in the same dress—the brown calico Sheriff Wilson had given her. She was beginning to feel as if she'd been buried in the torn, filthy frock. Despite her gloom at returning home, Kate did welcome the thought of a good, hot bath and a long nap in her feather bed upstairs.

The four riders slowly descended the hillside and crossed the small wooden bridge fording the stream. As they pulled up to the front porch, a plump, middle-aged Mexican woman emerged from the house, her dark eyes aglow. The woman wore a nut-brown homespun dress and a white apron streaked with flecks of *masa*. Her thick, braided hair was pinned around her pleasant face in a coronet.

"*Catelina*, you are home!" she cried.

Her spirits heartening a bit, Kate smiled at the kindly Mexican woman who had raised her. Conchita Gonzalez had always considered Kate a daughter, just as Kate had always thought of the gentle housekeeper as a second mother. Unfortunately, though, the woman had been little help in Kate's constant battles with her father, since Conchita had invariably been caught in the middle.

The housekeeper paused before the riders, staring at Kate's hands, still bound to the saddle horn. She turned indignantly to her boss. "Señor Jeb, *qué pasa*? You bring your own daughter home trussed up like an animal?"

Jeb grunted self-consciously as he heaved himself off his horse. He knew Conchita was a wonderful housekeeper, and she did have a way with Kate, although even she couldn't control the little hellion. Still, Jeb deferred to the woman as much as possible, not wanting to risk losing his capable, trusted housekeeper.

"Now, Chita," he said, awkwardly removing his hat. "You know how stubborn Kate can be. She tried to bolt on us, and we had no choice but to tie her up—for her own protection. You wouldn't have wanted her to run off and end up captured by one of them renegade Injun bands, would you?''

''*Madre de Dios!*'' Crossing herself, Conchita glanced at Kate. Only Conchita could look beyond the girl's mask of chilly disdain to see the deep hurt inside her.

Turning back to Jeb, she asked, ''You will untie her now, señor?''

Jeb went over to Kate's horse, took out his knife, and carefully sliced the rope binding her wrists.

In an instant, Kate jumped down from her pony and defiantly faced her father. ''I'm not going to thank you for cutting me loose, Pa, because you known damned well I'd rather be hung at sundown than be back here with you!''

''It's mutual!'' Jeb barked back. ''And cease your profanity, daughter!''

''I'd be only too glad to take myself—and my profanity—elsewhere!''

''Hah!'' Jeb retorted. ''The long and short of it is, no one this side of hell wants you—except for the geezer I managed to bribe into marrying you.''

''Bribe?'' Kate was outraged. ''Why, you snake!''

Jeb shook a finger at Kate. ''Watch your language, or I'll see you gagged! Furthermore, you even try to vamoose, and you'll be horsewhipped!''

Kate was about to reply when Conchita stepped between the two. ''Señor Jeb, Señorita Kate! Enough, now. Señor, you and your daughter are both trail weary and filthy. This is no time to discuss such matters. The señorita needs a bath—''

''Yeah, and a good scrubbing out of her mouth with lye soap wouldn't hurt none, either,'' Jeb snarled.

''Señor, please,'' Conchita said, wrapping a pro-

tective arm around Kate's rigid shoulders. "Señorita
Kate is a young lady now."

Jeb snorted. "This so-called young lady burned
down a boarding school and damn near required me
to mortgage the ranch to spring her worthless hide
from the calaboose!"

While Kate continued to glare at Jeb, Conchita
drew herself up proudly. "If she did such a thing,
I'm sure she had good reason."

"Yeah, I sure did!" Kate put in.

Ignoring his daughter, Jeb angrily waved off his
housekeeper's protest. "Conchita, you've always
been blind as a beggar where Kate is concerned. If I
was you, I'd see to it that she stays in the house.
Now get her inside."

"I want to go see Diablo first," Kate put in defiantly.

"That devil horse?" her father scoffed. "I'm selling him off for crow bait the first chance I get."

"You do that and I'll kill you!" Kate declared.

"You leave the house and I'll wring your little
neck," Jeb shot back. He turned to one of the cowhands. "Miguel, you take the first watch on the
porch. If Kate so much as sticks her nose out that
door, you have my permission to throttle her."

When Miguel grinned sheepishly and ambled off
to the porch, Conchita protested, "Señor, what are
you doing? Locking up your own daughter like some
sort of prisoner?"

"She *is* a prisoner," Jeb shot back. "Are you forgettin' that I just sprung her from the hoosegow?
And there ain't no way I'm letting her hightail it out
of here until I get her married off."

"Married off?" Conchita exclaimed. "What is all
this nonsense about married off and geezers?"

Jeb was about to reply when suddenly, his hat
sailed off in the path of a whizzing bullet. While
Kate and Conchita gasped in horror, Jeb bellowed

out orders to everyone to take cover. Diving behind a nearby tree with Conchita, Kate caught sight of her father's old enemy, Spuds Gilhooley, streaking across the prairie to the south of them, making one of his frequent east to west raids. As usual, cantankerous old Spuds was crouched low over a swift horse, his gun spitting out bullets faster than a striking snake. Kate grinned to herself at the sight.

Once the firing ceased, Jeb emerged from behind a holly bush. "Goddamn Spuds Gilhooley!" he roared. He drew his mighty Colt Dragoon and fired six rapid shots at the retreating rider.

Kate could only shake her head as she watched Spuds make it to safety. She'd always been amused by her father's boundary dispute with Gilhooley. Their feud had long been much more show than substance; of the thousands of rounds that had been fired over the years, nary a one had actually contacted human flesh. Privately, Kate was sure that both men savored their ongoing battle too much ever to shoot to kill, and she often wondered why they even bothered to dodge the bullets in the first place.

Watching her father pick up his hat and push his finger through the gaping hole, Kate said spitefully, "Too bad Spuds didn't aim a mite lower, Pa."

Jeb's features darkened to a menacing red. "Get that brat in the house, Chita!"

As Conchita grasped Kate's arm and dragged her out of harm's way, Kate's frustration was at the boiling point. She wondered why her hateful words to Jeb brought no real feelings of vindication.

"Damn! Damn! Damn!" Kate cried.

Inside the house, Kate's rage was such that her outflung arm had sent a vase of sunflowers hurtling off the gateleg table. Now, she stared, horrified, at the mess she'd made on the parlor floor—a huge puddle strewn with shards of glass and drenched flowers.

"Conchita, I'm sorry," she said, sinking to her haunches and picking up a ragged piece of glass. "I was mad as blazes at Pa, but that gave me no call to do this. I know how you love your flowers."

Conchita rushed over. "*No es problema, chica,*" she said gently. "Now give me that before you cut yourself. Go on upstairs and I'll bring up water for your bath. You must soak off that trail dust, and have a long nap."

Swallowing the lump in her throat, Kate braved a smile and handed Conchita the shard. "I—I didn't break somethin' of Ma's, did I?"

"Oh, no, *mi corazón,*" Conchita said, reaching out to brush a wisp of dusty hair from Kate's eyes. "It was only an old canning jar. This is no tragedy. Go on upstairs and I'll see to this."

"Thanks, Conchita." Biting her lip, Kate moved through the parlor, noting the familiar furnishings— the horsehair sofa and braided rug, the massive stone hearth with its large keystone, and the old flintlock rifles hanging above it. For the most part, the room was cold, masculine, free of embellishments except for a few pieces of furniture Kate's mother's family had brought over from Ireland. Kate felt a poignant loss as she gazed at the delicate mahogany breakfront, with Margaret Maloney's English china tea set and Sheffield silver pieces displayed inside. Then her gaze moved to her mother's Windsor rocker, next to the fireplace, its red velvet cushions faded by years in the bright sunlight.

Taking a deep breath, Kate inhaled the familiar scents of the room—the mustiness which clung to the old furniture, the spiciness of pomander balls, the pungence of her father's pipe tobacco, and, from the distant kitchen, the spicy aroma of Conchita's *menudo* stew simmering on the stove. Kate smiled ruefully. At least she had a hearty supper to look forward to—

Imagining herself and her father glowering at each other over that supper table, she sighed. She trudged up the steep stairs to the second floor and walked down the narrow corridor. Her room at the end of the hallway appeared just as she'd left it. The plain bed was covered by a snow-white coverlet which matched the lace-trimmed curtains at the window. A colorful rag rug graced the smoothly sanded puncheon floor. The huge old walnut wardrobe gleamed softly in the noonday light. On the dressing table sat another canning jar spilling out its bounty of sunflowers as if in welcome.

Bless Conchita's heart, Kate thought. Then a wave of melancholy and fatigue overwhelmed her; she sank into the soft feather bed and began unbuttoning her dress.

What was she to do? she asked herself, pondering the dire fate Pa had in store for her. Clearly, she had to get out of here—and soon.

Even as Kate was plotting her course of action, Conchita swept in carrying a bucket of steaming water. Setting down her heavy load, she glanced askance at Kate. "*Chica*, you're too filthy to be sitting on that bed—I scrubbed the coverlet just yesterday," she scolded. She pulled the old tin tub from behind the dressing screen and poured the water into it. "Just throw everything on the floor while I fetch more water."

Nodding in acquiescence, Kate stood and dusted off the coverlet. She stripped off her remaining clothing as Conchita made four more trips with warm water. When Kate finally stepped naked into the filled tub, Conchita scooped up the girl's filthy clothing and left the room.

The warm water felt heavenly against Kate's abused skin. She scrubbed herself with a soft cotton cloth and a cake of Conchita's rose-scented soap. By the time the housekeeper returned to help Kate shampoo her hair, she was so relaxed that she was actually humming a strain of one of her favorite songs, "Black-Eyed Susan."

Scrubbing the girl's scalp with skilled fingers, Conchita smiled with motherly pride. How happy she was to have her Catelina back. If anything, the girl had grown lovelier over the weeks of absence. Her young charge was a striking beauty, her cameo face perfect in every detail—the large green eyes, straight nose, high cheekbones, and full mouth. Even chafed and sunburned, Kate's skin glowed with youthful exuberance. Conchita made a mental note to apply her homemade aloe balm to the raw areas.

Yet Conchita well knew that Kate's outward loveliness hid an inward hurt and need that the girl's father had never assuaged. Too bad Señor Jeb had never been able to see Kate's good qualities—the stalwart spirit and loyal heart hidden beneath all those layers of fierce Irish pride.

At last, Conchita murmured, "Now, Catelina, tell me all that has happened to you."

Kate smiled at Conchita's use of her Spanish name. She told her friend of what had occurred in Nacogdoches—of Mrs. Eberhard's cruelty, of how she had felt impelled to burn down the boarding school . . . of how she had subsequently been thrown in jail.

"*Sangre de Cristos!*" Conchita exclaimed at last, crossing herself. "I can't say I blame you for acting as you did! And what did Señor Jeb have to say about all this?"

Kate's eyes darkened in outrage. "As usual, Señor Jeb was not even willing to listen to his daughter."

Conchita clucked to herself as she poured the rinse

water over Kate's thick black hair. "Oh, *mi hija*, I'm sorry. I don't know what it is with the two of you, always fighting like wild badgers. Señor Jeb was so different when Señor Margarita was alive—"

"And he's never quit blaming me for her death," Kate added bitterly.

The Mexican woman sighed and turned to take towels from the dresser. As Kate stood, Conchita wrapped one towel around her wet body and began blotting her hair with another. "You know, *hi ja*, I'm in a bad position, always caught between the two of you. I respect Señor Jeb and know he's a good man at heart. Still, with you—"

"He's never had a whit of patience," Kate finished.

"And you have never tried his patience?" Conchita asked gently.

Kate sighed as she took the linen nightgown Conchita handed her. "The point is, Pa don't care about me at all."

"Then why did he come after you in Nacogdoches?"

Kate shrugged into the gown. "Just his stubborn pride, I guess. He couldn't let me disgrace the family name. Besides, he's dead set on punishing me by marrying me off to some old coot he has lined up."

Conchita's eyes widened. "Ah, yes. What is this loco business about you being promised in marriage?"

"Ask Pa. It ain't loco according to him. He swears up and down that he's gonna see me hitched up to some old codger with gout, rheumatism, and rotting teeth."

Conchita gasped. "Surely Señor Jeb was jesting."

"It sure as Sunday didn't sound that way to me. And frankly, I ain't planning to hang around long enough to find out."

Conchita's hands flew to her face. "*Chica*, please, you mustn't try to run away!"

"You gonna tell Pa on me?"

"You know me better than that, *hija*. Just promise me you'll stay and try to work things out."

"And you know better than to ask that of me," Kate returned.

Conchita heaved a great sigh as she led Kate to the dressing table. She brushed out the girl's thick, tangled hair and applied the balm to her chafed face and neck. Then she moved over to the bed, drawing back the coverlet. "Sleep now, *hija*. Please don't do anything hasty. I promise I'll speak with Señor Jeb on this matter."

"Thanks, Chita," Kate murmured, climbing into the bed. Watching the housekeeper leave the room, she didn't believe for a moment that Conchita would have any effect on her iron-willed father.

Though Kate was exhausted, she found sleep elusive. Shifting about on her narrow bed, she inhaled the warm, honeysuckle-scented breeze and listened to the familiar sounds of a shutter rattling, a horse nickering in the distance. After a while, she opened the drawer on her bedside table and pulled out her mother's old rosary. Holding the strand like a treasured talisman, she watched the light play over the lovely ebony beads.

Eighteen years ago, Margaret O'Herlihy and her family had been new immigrants to Texas when Kate's father had all but plucked the eighteen-year-old beauty off a boat in Galveston. Within a week of meeting her and her family, Jeb had made a bid for Margaret's hand. The two had been wed three days later at Saint Mary's Church in Galveston, and, almost a year to the day afterward, Margaret had died in this very house, bearing Kate.

Kate's eyes stung at the thought. She'd often sneaked into her father's room to stare at the small portrait of her mother on his dresser. Margaret had been beautiful, and Kate knew she resembled her ma.

As a child, Kate had been insatiably curious about her dead parent, but her father had brushed off her questions. Luckily, Conchita had remembered much about Margaret, and had told Kate of her mother's piety, her kind spirit, and her lovely red hair and green eyes.

Growing up motherless had not been easy for Kate.

She remembered her first day at Round Rock's small public school, back when she'd been only six years old. The schoolmarm had been nice, but ten-year-old Jimmy Turner had teased Kate ruthlessly about being born without a mother. He'd told the other children that Kate had been hatched in a cabbage patch, and when Kate had attacked him, the schoolmarm had made them both stand in corners. Kate remembered swallowing back sobs as she'd muttered endlessly, "I *do* have a ma! I do!" When recess had come, Kate had fled the schoolyard and run all the way to the town cemetery, to prove to herself that she did indeed have a mother. She'd stood before her mother's grave, sobbing, her young voice entreating a dead woman, demanding to know why Margaret had left her.

Her father had found her there three hours later. When Kate had refused to budge, he'd forcibly dragged her away. That once, for some unknown reason, he hadn't spanked her, not even when she had flailed out at him with her fists. Later, at home, Kate had sobbed in Conchita's arms.

Now, Kate again watched the beads catch the light. Even though Margaret had been Catholic, Kate's father had come from a long line of Irish Presbyterians; after Margaret died, Jeb had raised Kate a Presbyterian, and she'd always felt this was a betrayal of her mother's memory.

She remembered his cruel words from an hour earlier: *No one this side of hell wants you.*

"You wanted me, Ma, didn't you?" Kate whispered. "I know you wanted me."

As a tear trickled down her cheek, Kate slept . . .

Spuds Gilhooley was chuckling to himself as he galloped back toward his ranch. Spuds was pleased as punch that he'd managed to shoot off Jeb Maloney's hat without blowing a hole through his asinine head. As far as Spuds was concerned, the feud between them grew more interesting with each passing day.

Spuds guided his horse through a gap in the wire fence that separated this edge of Maloney's spread from his own. He himself had clipped the wire an hour earlier, to gain access to Maloney's land. He assumed the Bar M outriders would have the gap fixed before nightfall. He shrugged. No matter. It was an ongoing game—a fence cut here, a cow rustled there, shots fired that never quite hit their mark.

Spuds Gilhooley and Jeb Maloney had never liked each other. Five years ago, the two had been the first ranchers in Williamson County to fence in their ranges with the new Meriwether smooth wire invented at New Braunfels, in an effort to keep each other out and their cows in. But their feud had escalated over water rights, when the South Creek, originally on Gilhooley's spread, had shifted its boundaries onto Maloney's property.

Most of the other ranchers in the vicinity were open-rangers who lived in peaceful coexistence with their neighbors. All were bewildered by the continuing feud between Maloney and Gilhooley, especially since both men had other sources of water on their land. But for Spuds, it was a matter of principle. Maloney considered the creek his, while Spuds well knew it belonged to him—lock, stock, and every damned barrel of water to be had.

He'd get his creek back yet. If bullets couldn't convince Jeb, then he might be able to get to the man through his hellion of a daughter, now that Maloney had brought the girl back from boarding school. . . .

Chapter 5

In the tack room at the Bar M, Jeb Maloney was talking with his ranch foreman, Walker Dennison. Jeb felt particularly at home at his scarred desk in the cluttered old room.

"Much happen while I was away?" Jeb drawled.

Walker's lanky form was stretched out in a rawhide chair. "You mean other than Spuds Gilhooley shootin' up the range?"

"That sidewinder," Jeb cursed. "He took some pot-shots at us when I brung Kate back. He borryin' our stock again?"

Walker shrugged. "The usual. Between him, the prairie wolves, and the Comanche, we lost half a dozen more *cimarrones*—"

"Thievin' redskins! I was sure them Injuns would be layin' low after Rip Ford chased their hides clean across the Red River."

"I allow the redskins are gettin' scarce in these parts," Walker commiserated. "But we still got the gall-durned renegade bands to reckon with—and the Comanche moon a' comin'."

"Tarnation."

Walker cleared his throat. "So how's Miss Kate?"

"Ornery as ever."

Walker chuckled. "I'm relieved to hear you got

48

her out of that scrape in Nacogdoches. She ever tell you why she burnt down that there schoolhouse?"

"Naw. Neither did I ask her."

"You still aimin' to marry her off to that bounty hunter?"

Jeb took a deep draw on his cigar. "Yep. I'll be goin' to town tomorrow to talk with Durango and line up the Bible-puncher."

Walker whistled. "And what does Miss Kate have to say about this?"

Jeb smiled in vindictive pleasure. "It ain't her place to say nothin'. Still, that gal's fit to be tied—and about time."

Walker coughed. "You don't think she's a mite green to be handed over to a *buscadero* like Durango?"

Jeb snorted. "It's Durango you should frettin' over, not my hellion of a daughter."

Frowning, Walker stood and picked up his hat. "No offense, boss, but I hear tell Charlie Durango once cut a man down on the streets of Fort Worth— without even blinkin'."

"So what are you saying, man?" Jeb snapped.

"I'm just saying there ain't no kindliness in a man like that."

Jeb snorted. "It ain't kindliness my daughter needs. And furthermore, why don't you mind your own goddamned business?"

Walker clapped on his hat. "Sure, boss. It bein' Saturday evenin', guess I'll mosey on into town and stir up a poker game."

"If you're ridin' for town, would you do me a favor?" Jeb asked.

"Sure."

"Find Charlie Durango at the saloon and tell him I'll be lookin' him up tomorrow after church, to make the final arrangements for the weddin'."

After Walker left, Jeb strode over to the window,

gazing through the dusty pane at the frisky mustang ponies dancing about in the corral. What he wouldn't give to be as young and feisty as one of them fresh-broke *remuda*.

Jeb smiled. Now Dora Mae Fuermann, she fired his blood. He was looking forward to seeing his widow lady tonight. He had missed her over the past days, he realized. Now, his heart lifted at the thought of eating Dora's tender beefsteak and laying with her in her snug bed. Dora was the first woman he'd taken a shine to since he'd lost his precious Margaret almost eighteen years ago . . .

Then there was Kate. Jeb ground his jaw. Why hadn't his daughter taken more after her ma and less after him? Jeb wasn't particularly proud of himself regarding the constant state of warfare between himself and his sole offspring. Indeed, the obvious hatred Kate harbored for him often made him feel blue.

But Jeb was also a man at his wit's end. He could think of no remedy for his problems, other than handing Kate over to Durango. Obviously, the girl was miserable here with him, and he could seek no permanent happiness with Dora until Kate's situation was resolved.

He could only hope that Charlie Durango would succeed where he had failed.

Charlie Durango sat at the Round Rock Saloon clutching a winning poker hand, a plump prostitute perched on his knee.

Ever since seeing Kate Maloney for the first time, Charlie had been in a jubilant frame of mind. He'd already won twenty dollars off his three crusty poker companions, and, from the way pretty Mabel Purvis kept bucking against him, he was being offered another juicy jackpot for free. Mabel had descended on him the minute he'd stepped through the saloon doors. Though he feared he might drown in her cheap perfume, he'd felt himself growing harder as the afternoon had progressed. Yet Charlie knew it was not this lusty whore who stirred him so, but the memory of a pretty Irish filly he would soon take to wife.

"Well, Durango?" one of his companions prompted. "You gonna show yer hand or just paw that there Cyprian?"

While Mabel emitted an outraged squeal, Charlie grinned and laid down his three aces. The other men cursed their foul luck and threw in their hands. Mabel chortled her delight and smacked Charlie on the mouth. Then he turned at the sound of a throat being cleared. He stared up at a lanky man with thinning brown hair.

"You Charlie Durango?" the man asked awkwardly.

"Yeah. Who wants to know?"

The newcomer extended his hand. "I'm Walker Dennison, foreman of the Bar M ranch, Jeb Maloney's spread."

Charlie shook Walker's gnarled hand. "So what can I do for you?"

Walker shifted his weight. "I'm just here delivering a message. The boss says to tell you he'll—uh—be lookin' you up tomorry, after church—you know, to make arrangements for the hitchin'."

"Swell," Charlie said.

While the other men muttered to one another, Mabel uttered a gasp of dismay. "You fixin' to wed old Jeb Maloney's gal?" she asked Charlie with a full-lipped pout.

"Yep," Charlie drawled back with a grin.

"Sugar, I hear that filly's a real hellcat," Mabel warned.

"Well, maybe I'm a hellcat-tamer," Charlie replied with a wink. Watching one of the other men

get up, he added to Walker, "Care to join us for a
round, pardner?"

"Don't mind if I do." Walker was chuckling as he
took the vacant chair across from Charlie. He nodded toward Charlie's impressive winnings. "Looks
like you already got Lady Luck corraled for the afternoon, friend."

"Lady Luck and Mabel Purvis too," the whore
added, smirking.

While the other men laughed, Charlie grinned to
himself as he felt Mabel squirm against him once
more. If she thought she was gettin' him in the sack,
though, she was wrong. Later, a swift slap on the
rump would send this line gal off to go sulk and
peddle her wares elsewhere.

As for Charlie, he was saving it all for a comely
little spitfire he intended to have warming his bed
by Tuesday.

He picked up his new hand and grinned at the
full house. Hot damn! He couldn't seem to stop
winning.

At ten p.m., Kate Maloney stood at the window
of her room, staring grimly at the silvery landscape
below, watching her father gallop off to the north
on his fancy Sunday horse. Kate was certain that Jeb
was bound for Widow Fuermann's house, and that
he'd likely not return until close to dawn. She was
hardly shocked by her father's behavior, for she had
long suspected that he and Dora Fuermann were
lovers.

Indeed, she felt relieved, for she knew that the
time had come to make her escape. She had already
dressed in boots, denim trousers, and a matching
jacket. Her hair was pinned beneath her wide-
brimmed cowboy hat. No use drawing attention to
herself as a woman traveling alone, she mused.

She thought over the last few hours. Supper had

been a strained meal down in the kitchen. Afterward, Jeb had escorted Kate upstairs, stripping the covers from her bed and locking her in for the night.

Kate laughed at the memory. She knew that Jeb's precautions had been spurred by the fact that twice before, she had torn up her sheets, knotted the strips together, and lowered herself from her room on the makeshift rope. Jeb doubtless thought he'd outmaneuvered her this time.

But he couldn't have been more wrong. He'd forgotten about the stout lengths of hemp upon which Kate's mattress rested in the bedframe. Kate had already dismantled her bed and had tied the half dozen lengths of rope together. Then she'd moved the bedframe to the window, tied one end of the rope securely to the post, and had lowered the rest out the window. Now, she stared at the end of the rope, which dangled a good six feet above ground. Yet Kate had solved this problem as well, by shoving her feather tick out the window; it lay below, waiting to break her fall.

Taking a deep breath, Kate grasped the rope, climbed out the window, and began lowering herself. She gasped sharply as she felt the rope begin to give; her heart hammered wildly as she heard the bedframe screech against the floor, then felt it cinch up tighter against the window frame. Heavens to Betsy!

Kate paused for a moment with both feet braced against the side of the house, then she shimmied downward. At the end of the rope, she looked down and frowned. Taking another bracing breath, she swung outward and released the rope—

Despite the fact that she landed squarely on the tick, Kate hit the ground with a bone-jarring thud, tumbling hard on her bottom. Ignoring the razor-sharp pain knifing her from foot to hip, she got up quickly and hurried toward the front of the house.

Inside the darkened parlor, Kate tiptoed over to her father's gun cabinet. With only the moonlight streaming through the windows to guide her, she spent several frustrating moments picking the lock with a hairpin. Meeting with success at last, she opened the door and extracted a Hawken rifle and a Colt Texas with gunbelt. After strapping on the pistol, she stuffed extra ammunition for both guns into her pockets. If she met up with any renegade Indians out on the trail, she'd be prepared.

Proceeding to the pantry, she grabbed a knapsack and loaded it with essentials—dried *frijoles*, jerky, bacon, cornmeal, and coffee. She then pilfered the necessary cooking utensils. Tying her bounty securely inside the sack, she left the house and crossed the yard to the barn.

Inside, she opened the gate to Diablo's stall and feasted her eyes on the magnificent black stallion. A year ago, she'd found the animal running with a herd of wild mustang ponies. Small yet noble, Diablo was a throwback to the blooded horses of the *Conquistadores* that had roamed the Texas prairies for centuries.

Diablo regarded his mistress with head held high and nostrils flared. When he stepped forward, rubbing his face affectionately against Kate's arm, she grinned and stroked his flank.

"Miss me, boy?" she whispered, reaching for his blanket.

Kate worked quickly, saddling and bridling the horse. All the while, she spoke softly to him. "Pa sure as Sunday didn't bring you out to Nacogdoches for me to ride home. Oh, no. Ain't no one on this ranch you cotton to but me. Why, if he'd a brung you along, we'd a'been across the Red River by sundown, right, old boy?"

Diablo whinnied in agreement.

Kate secured her knapsack and shooting iron to

the saddle then grabbed her canteen from its hook on the wall. She led Diablo from the barn. "As if I'd ever let Pa go and sell you," she murmured as she walked the horse across the yard. "We're two of a kind, boy. Renegades, the both of us."

At the well at the side of the house, Kate drew a bucket of water for her horse, then filled her canteen. After Diablo had drunk his fill, she mounted him and cantered up the hillside. The trail she took would soon converge with Stagecoach Road, and her plan was to follow this public trace all the way to Fort Worth. There she would look up her mother's old cousin. She would have to pray that Cousin Sophie would take her in.

At the top of the hill, Kate turned to take one last look at the ranch house. "*Adios*, Pa," she murmured ironically. Then, with a squeeze from her muscled thighs, she nudged Diablo into a gallop. The mighty horse seemed to fly over the hillside and into the shimmering shadows of the valley below.

At last Kate felt truly alive, liberated, galloping down the wild, silvery brush-country, free as the wind and the moonlight . . .

Chapter 6

Sunrise found Kate camped near a small creek thirty miles north of Round Rock; she was eating a breakfast of crisp bacon and cold *sopaipillas*.

Sitting on a smooth rock with her plate in her lap, Kate kept a wary eye on the landscape. Beyond her, a mild morning breeze was just stirring the prairie grass; half a dozen buffalo grazed indolently on a gentle rise.

Last night, Kate had ridden hard beneath the full moon, taking the Stagecoach Road well past Georgetown, not stopping until she was certain she had put a good head start between herself and Pa. She hadn't bothered to try to cover her tracks—an impossible task at night—but today, she would lay out a false trail or two.

It wasn't just her Pa's certain pursuit that gave Kate pause. Unfortunately, her escape route took her straight through the center of the *mal pais,* or bad country—the vast, grassy plains of Texas that the renegade Comanches considered their own.

Last night, only hours after she'd escaped from the big house, Kate had passed too close for comfort to a band of renegade Indians. She had heard the sounds of their drumbeats and chanting, and had glimpsed the distant glow of their campfires. She had suspected that the men were having one of their all-night *peyote* ceremonies.

Thank God Diablo did not spook easily! As soon as Kate had spotted the encampment, she'd dismounted and led her horse quickly and quietly past the danger. Once the sounds had faded, she'd mounted the stallion and had ridden hard for two more hours.

Kate shuddered at the memory. September was almost here, the time of the feared Comanche moon, when fierce warriors streaked black paint on their faces and took to the vengeance trail against Texas settlers. Over the years, Kate had heard her share of horror stories concerning atrocities committed by the Comanche against homesteaders, about women being forced into white slavery. If anything, the Indians were even more riled now that the Rangers and U.S. Cavalry had officially expelled them from Texas.

Kate broke up camp and saddled Diablo. As she cantered her horse down the trail, she smiled as she imagined her father's reaction when he found she had flown the coop. She had at least two days of hard riding ahead of her, and Pa would be on her trail quicker than flies on a buffalo chip, she reckoned. But with any luck, she'd reach Fort Worth by sundown the day after tomorrow, and she could then seek out Cousin Sophie.

Kate frowned. Would her mother's cousin take her in? She'd only met the woman once, back in '53. Sophie Harper had come through Round Rock with some friends; all had been en route to Austin for a ball to honor Sam Houston's re-election to the U.S. Senate. A forthright widow, Sophie had seemed a kindly enough sort to Kate, but had acted rather cold and standoffish around Jeb. From some of the woman's comments, Kate had allowed that Sophie likely blamed Jeb for her mother's death.

Thus, Kate hoped that Cousin Sophie would be

the perfect person to stand between herself and her father, when Jeb came to fetch her. But first, she'd have to outrun Pa—not to mention, arrive in Fort Worth with her scalp intact!

At the very thought, Kate grimaced and urged Diablo into a high lope. Lord knows, she wouldn't breathe a comfortable breath as long as she was out here alone in the dangerous Texas brush.

"Damnation!" Jeb yelled.

At six a.m., he was standing in Kate's room, staring at the damning length of rope that marked her escape route.

"Why didn't I recollect about them dad-blamed bed-ropes!" he cursed, banging his fist on the windowsill. "I should have used 'um to tie that brat to the bedpost, that's for damn sure!"

"Señor, *que pasa?*"

He turned to watch Conchita sweep into the room with a breakfast tray; a look of alarm creased her plump features as she noted Kate's absence.

"You may as well feed that there grub to the buzzards, Chita," Jeb said in disgust. "Kate's hightailed it."

"Oh, *por Dios!*" Conchita exclaimed, setting down her tray and rushing over to join Jeb. She glanced downward at the dangling end of the rope. "I hope Señorita Kate did not hurt herself when she jumped to the ground."

"Hurt herself, my butt," Jeb grumbled. "She won't be walking for at least a week after I get my hands on her!" His gaze narrowed on the housekeeper. "You know anything about this, Chita?"

"Why, Señor Jeb!" Conchita scolded, turning to him haughtily. "Would I encourage Señorita Kate to run away from home? With renegade Comanches loose out in the hills?"

"You might or you might not," Jeb muttered.

"But neither would you tell me what that crazy filly was aimin' to do." When Conchita would have protested again, Jeb waved her off. "Aw, to hell with it. I might as well forgit church and go break the news to Kate's intended. Let her future husband track down that she-wolf."

At Jeb's astonishing words, Conchita balled her hands on her hips. "Señor, I fear you are *loco*. Señorita Kate told me of your plans to marry her off to this geezer. How can some grandpapa with gout and rheumatism hope to chase down Señorita Kate?"

Jeb chuckled and hitched up his pants. "That's just a tale I told my daughter to put the fear of God in her."

"Shame on you, Señor Jeb." After glowering at Jeb a moment, Conchita heaved a grateful sigh. "Then you did not arrange for Miss Kate to marry, after all?"

Jeb grinned. "Oh, I arranged for her to get hitched, all right—but to a man with enough grit to keep 'er in line."

"And who is this man?" Conchita asked suspiciously.

"The bounty hunter, Charlie Durango."

Conchita emitted a shriek of horror, followed by a barrage of expletives in rapid Spanish. Finally, she demanded, "You are giving my *bebé* to this—this *pistolero*?"

Jeb's face darkened with anger. "Chita, Kate brought this on herself by being so dad-blamed ornery. 'Sides, Durango's a straight shooter. He's aimin' to retire soon, and he gave me his word that he'd treat the girl proper."

Conchita's dark eyes implored Jeb. "Oh, Señor Jeb! It is not right that you try to force Kate to marry this man. On the memory of Señora Margarita, I beg you to reconsider!"

Yet Jeb's granite features didn't waver. "That gal's

made her bed—and now, by damn, she's gonna lay in it!''

Leaving Conchita to gape after him in consternation, Jeb strode from the room, and slammed the door.

Charlie Durango sat in the dining room of the Stagecoach Inn, finishing off a hearty breakfast of beefsteak, grits, and strong coffee. He was looking forward to meeting with Jeb Maloney later today and getting everything set for the wedding. A simple ceremony before a judge or preacher would suit him just fine. And, as anxious as Jeb had seemed to marry off his daughter, Charlie doubted Maloney would be cooking up any elaborate fandangos.

A pair of jaundiced mustangers ambled past Charlie's table, slanting him curious glances as they headed toward the door. Charlie grinned to himself. Ever since Maloney's foreman had looked him up at the saloon yesterday, he'd drawn curious stares everywhere he'd gone. Evidently, as the man who was about to wed Kate Maloney, he'd become something of a local legend overnight.

That Kate Maloney must be some gal, he mused, if the mere prospect of his marrying her made the locals sit up and take notice. He'd waited for the girl long enough, that was for damn sure. He'd hung around Round Rock for over five days now, and the old restlessness still hadn't gripped him. He smiled. He must be ready to give up his wandering ways, all right. Indeed, he couldn't wait to meet up with this headstrong filly—

Charlie's reverie was abruptly shattered by the sound of the restaurant door banging open. With a frown, he watched barrel-chested Jeb Maloney stride in, huffing out streams of smoke and looking mad as a charging bull.

"So there ya be, Durango," Jeb drawled, heading

straight for Charlie's table. He unceremoniously tossed his hat on top of Charlie's empty plate and heaved his bulky form into the chair across from him. "I been lookin' for you all over town."

"Good morning, Mr. Maloney," Charlie said, extending his hand.

Jeb waved it off. "You sure the hell ain't gonna be feelin' sociable once I tell you what your fiancée went and did."

Charlie scowled. "What she gone and done?"

"She's hightailed it outta here, that's what she done," Jeb informed him.

Stunned, Charlie fell back in his chair. "She— what? Where'd she'd go?"

Jeb flung a hand outward in exasperation. "You tell me, Durango. All I know is, she stole a sackful of vittles, two guns, her horse, and skipped town in the middle of the night."

"But why?"

Jeb heaved a disgusted sigh. "Cause she don't want to marry you, mister, that's why."

For a moment, Charlie was too flabbergasted to reply. "She give any reason?" he ventured at last.

Jeb shrugged. "Said she'd sooner be hitched up with Satan in red longjohns than wed you."

"She said that?" Charlie asked, his expression still bewildered. He scratched his jaw. "What the hell did you tell her about me, anyway, mister?"

"Why, nothin'," Jeb responded innocently. "I didn't even tell her you name." Absorbing Charlie's suspicious glower, he added, "Hell, I warned you Kate's a mite contrary."

"So you did, neighbor." Charlie crossed his arms over his chest, and his expression grew deeply abstracted. "Well, I guess that does it, then."

"Does what, son?"

"She don't want to marry me, so that's about the size of it."

"You mean you're jes' givin' up?" Jeb bellowed.

"A man hadn't oughta got to bulldog and hogtie his own bride," Charlie grumbled.

"So you're jes' gonna let yourself become the laughingstock of the whole town?" Jeb demanded.

Charlie frowned darkly. "What do you mean, laughingstock?"

"Why, everyone hereabouts already knows you're my Kate's intended," Jeb put in slyly. "Now, you want 'um all to hold that she's plumb left you standing at the altar and made a jackass outta you?"

Glaring at Jeb, Charlie didn't reply.

Jeb chewed on his cigar. "Look, son, it ain't you she's riled at. It's jes' that the girl ain't never minded her pa worth a durn. That don't mean she won't make you a goodly wife. And don't forget that one day, the Bar M will go to Kate's husband—"

"I told you before, mister—and I'll tell you again—I don't want your dad-blamed land," Charlie put in angrily.

"Sure, son, sure," Jeb said. "But the question is, do you want my daughter?"

Charlie sighed, his features softening a flicker. "I seen her yesterday," he admitted, "when you brought her through town with her hands hitched to the saddle horn. I allow the girl's a looker."

"She is that."

"But from what you're saying, she's also ornery as a polecat stuck in a briar patch," Charlie continued morosely.

"That too." Unwittingly, Jeb grinned.

Just as spontaneously, Charlie grinned back. "Yeah, I reckon I still want her."

Wearing a huge smile of relief, Jeb reached across the table and pumped Charlie's hand. "Good decision, son."

"What do you want me to do, then?"

"Why, track her down, of course," Jeb said vehemently. "And you ain't got a minute to lose, neither. I reckon she's got an eight hour start on you, and from the direction of her tracks, she's headed straight for Injun territory."

"Damn," Charlie muttered, feeling an unaccustomed catch in his throat at the thought of lovely Kate being subjected to the tender mercies of a Comanche raiding party.

"What do you want me to do when I find her?" Charlie asked softly.

"Son, you do whatever pleases you. Wallop her good, if you've a mind to. Just so long as you save what's proper for your wedding night. And don't forget that the Bible-puncher and me'll be waitin' fer your return."

Nodding decisively, Charlie stood and clapped on his hat. "Then I'd best quit jawin' and hit the trail," he muttered grimly.

Charlie bought the necessary supplies for several long days on the trail, then rode out of town on Corona. By now, it was mid-morning, and already, the late August heat beat down upon him in blistering waves.

Out at the Bar M ranch, Charlie easily picked up Kate's trail at the side of the barn. He guessed her initial strategy would be to put distance between herself and the ranch. Later, she might try to lay a false trail and cover her tracks. From what Jeb had told him previously, the girl was an expert horsewoman and clever as a fox. But Charlie, a master scout, would not be fooled. As far as he was concerned, the girl was as good as caught.

He scowled and lit a cheroot as he galloped his horse down the hillside. He remained confused as to why the girl had gone and run off. Surely she hated her pa, but marrying her daddy's choice had to be preferable to sashaying straight through the heart of Indian country just days before the Comanche moon.

Evidently, Kate Maloney didn't see it that way. Once he caught up with the little hellion, he'd have a mite of gentling to do.

He grinned as he remembered Jeb advising him to wallop her good. As far as Charlie was concerned, there was more than one way to tame a wild cat.

Chapter 7

⟨⟨⟩⟩

"Damn! Damn! Damn!'' Kate cried.

Just an hour after she'd started out that morning, Kate crouched next to *Diablo* in a stand of cedar, her expression crestfallen as she carefully examined the horse's injured foreleg. The flesh was bruised and already swelling.

It had happened in the twinkling of an eye. One minute, Diablo had been galloping along, fast and free as the wind. In the next instant, he had stumbled into a gopher hole and gone lame.

Kate's only consolation was that the horse hadn't broken his leg. The fetlock was strained all right, but she'd seen worse. With proper care, he might recover in a few weeks. This was most fortunate, since Kate would just as soon shoot herself dead as to kill her beloved stallion.

But the hell of it was, she couldn't ride him anymore—if she did, he'd surely go lame permanently. Her choices were grim ones—either to set Diablo free, or to walk him all the way to Ft. Worth. Either choice would make her a sitting duck for renegade Indians.

Muttering another curse, Kate took off her hat and wiped her sweaty brow. She wasn't turning back, that was for damn sure. Though this area of Texas was sparsely settled at best, perhaps up ahead, she'd find a farmer willing to take Diablo in trade for a fit mount. Kate hated the thought of parting with her horse, but Diablo wasn't up to riding the brutal hundred or so miles they still had left to go, and she could always return for him later.

Rifling through her knapsack, Kate found a dishtowel, which she quickly ripped into strips. She wrapped the cloth about the horse's sprained foreleg as tightly as she could. And perhaps she would come across a river up ahead; a mud pack might help that sprain.

Kate led the horse for several more miles, pausing once so both of them could drink at a small spring. With Diablo limping so badly, their progress was slow and arduous at best. Toward mid-afternoon, she was about to stop for a meal when suddenly, she heard the sound of hoofbeats approaching from behind her. Rats! Was Pa on her trail already?

Kate backtracked slightly, taking shelter in a stand of scrub oak toward the top of a rise. She tethered Diablo to a nearby tree and took out her rifle. She moved to the edge of the stand, raised her rifle, and pushed back her hat. From the sound of the hooves, she figured the rider would crest the butte to the south of her at any minute now. It could be Pa, or perhaps a homesteader, or even a renegade Comanche stalking her.

If it were Pa, could she really shoot him? The thought brought an unaccustomed, aching sadness to her heart. Hell, she could for damn sure scare him off, perhaps even graze him—

Every muscle in Kate's body tensed as she watched the rider appear over the rise. Why, it wasn't Pa at all, but a lanky stranger in dark clothing, shot-gun chaps, and a wide-rimmed black hat! This man wasn't no hayseed from the hills, that was for damn sure. He had the look of a Ranger or a bounty hunter. He rode with studied grace, like the lithe, beautiful animal beneath him, and she suddenly hated the thought of shooting this man.

But there was no doubt in Kate's mind that the man was trailing her. Why else would he be riding in this direction alone, and hell-bent-for-leather? So, Pa had resorted to hiring *pistoleros* to drag her home? She'd have to give this man a mite of discouragement, just as she would have given Pa.

Still, fair was fair, she thought. She couldn't just dry-gulch the stranger without first giving him warning.

Her rifle raised, Kate cautiously emerged from the stand of trees. "Hold it, mister!" she called out in her most menacing tone.

He didn't stop!

"Damn it, mister, I said halt right there!" she yelled.

He kept right on a'comin'!

Kate murmured a very unladylike expletive, took careful aim through the sight, and squeezed off a shot. Ahead of her, the stranger's palomino whinnied and double-shuffled. An instant latter, the *pistolero* flew off the back of his mount and landed flat on the ground.

Hell and Halifax, she'd up and killed him!

Setting down her rifle and taking out her Colt, Kate left the cover of trees and walked warily toward the still form in the valley ahead of her. As she stalked through the tall buffalo grass, she neither heard nor saw a spark of life coming from the fallen *pistolero*. A few moments later, she stood staring down at him.

Damn, but he was a good looker—long and lean, with a dark, handsome face and thick black hair. She looked at the creeping stain of red on his shirt and grimaced. He appeared to be deader than a doornail. His eyes were shut tight, and she couldn't detect a hint of movement.

With a frown, Kate shoved her pistol into her waistband and knelt beside the man she had killed. She leaned over and placed her ear against the *pistolero*'s chest—

An instant later, Kate was flat on her back on the ground, pinned beneath a body hard and tight as whipcord. Her pistol was yanked from her trousers and tossed away, and a Colt Dragoon was shoved up under her nose.

Defenseless and terrified, Kate stared up into the blackest, most remorseless male eyes she had ever seen in her life.

"I didn't kill you, mister!" she yelled.

"Do I look like I'm dead?" the stranger yelled back.

Kate's blood was boiling as she stared up at the ruthless, implacable stranger whose hard body pinned hers to the ground. "Do you mean to say you was playin' possum all this time like some lowdown Injun?"

"I was trying to avoid meeting my Maker was all."

"Why, of all the dirty, rotten—"

"Dirty and rotten? After you ambushed me and practically blew my shoulder clean off?"

"Mister, I never dry-gulched you," Kate argued furiously. "I gave you fair warning. Can I help it if you're too dad-blamed stupid to—"

"Stupid!" the stranger roared.

"Yeah, stupid."

"Well, who'd take seriously a warning from a runt like you?" he barked back.

"Runt? How dare you call me that, you bone-headed jackass!"

At her scathing insult, something frighteningly lethal flashed in the stranger's dark eyes, and his thumb moved to the hammer of his pistol. "You got some mouth on you, kid. And furthermore, you ain't in no position to be criticizing, boy."

"Boy? I ain't no—"

But before Kate could finish, the stranger holstered his gun, ripped off Kate's hat, and stared flabbergasted at his captive. His flint-hard gaze flicked over the riotous black curls pinned on top of her head, then narrowed accusingly on her delicate face. "So it's you."

"Yeah, it's me."

"I was wondering why some greenhorn kid took a shot at me. Now I know."

"So now you know. Who in blue blazes are you?"

For a charged moment, the two continued to glare at each other, both breathing hard. Kate felt half-dizzy, crushed beneath this powerful, menacing stranger; Charlie felt just as bewildered about how to deal with the spiteful female he had just bull-dogged.

"I said, who are you, mister?" Kate repeated angrily.

Staring down at his defiant captive, Charlie continued to hesitate as he recalled the hateful things this headstrong girl had already said about him, her future husband. He hadn't expected to capture the girl quite so quickly, and now, he definitely had a tiger by the tail. But Lord, she was a looker! He studied her pretty face, with its snapping green eyes, upturned nose, stubborn chin and petulant mouth. Some bit of caution prompted him to say simply, "Your pa hired me to fetch you home."

"Well, it figures," she said in disgust. "So you're some no-account bounty hunter, are you? Would you mind gettin' the hell off me, you big bully?"

Not taking his eyes off her for a moment, Charlie drew back. Kate was off like a shot—rolling over and scrambling to her knees. In mid-scramble, her calf was seized in a steely grip, and, to her humiliation, she was yanked, face down, to the dirt. She landed with a bone rattling thud.

"Let me go, you mad dog!" she screamed, struggling in earnest.

Not daunted in the least, the stranger dragged Kate to a nearby log, flung her face down across his lap, and rewarded her struggles with a sharp slap on the behind—

Kate was so horrified that she froze, both her face and her rear end burning—

"Your choice, lady," the stranger drawled, his hand poised above her bottom. "You gonna lay still or am I gonna blister your little butt?"

"Oh!" Kate shrieked. "I might know you'd resort to brute force!"

"My pleasure, ma'am," he drawled back.

"You beast!"

Charlie chuckled, staring down at the red-faced female lying across his lap—and especially at her saucy, rounded derriere clad in that tight-fitting denim. Lord, how he'd love to fill his hands with that tempting female rump. She did fire his blood, this gal, and it looked like taming this little filly was going to be a might easier than he'd allowed.

"You gonna lay still?" he repeated.

"Do it look like I'm bucking, mister?" Kate snapped back. "I value my backside as much as the next person."

Still grinning, Charlie reached into his pocket for a length of strong twine. The movement brought the first twinge of razor-sharp pain to his wounded shoulder. He grimaced, gazing down at the small bullet hole and the creeping red stain on his checked shirt. Funny, he hadn't even felt the pain until now, though he vaguely recalled a burning sensation as the bullet whizzed clean through his flesh. Damn the little baggage for shooting him. When this hellion had first confronted him, ordering him to stop, he'd assumed she was an overzealous farmboy out hunting. He hadn't thought for a second that he—or rather she—would actually pull the trigger and stop him flat in his tracks . . .

Live and learn, Durango, he scolded himself, feeling grudging admiration for the spitfire. It was rare for anyone to get the slip on Charlie Durango. Oh well, he'd survived much worse before. Once he hogtied this vixen, he'd tend to his wound.

Charlie bound Kate's hands behind her with secure knots, then proceeded to do the same with her feet.

"What the hell do you think you're doin', mister?" Kate demanded.

"Hitchin' your hands and feet, so I can carry you home."

"Why, of all the no-good, miserable—"

Before Kate could heap more insults on Charlie, he lunged to his feet with her slung against one hip. Uttering a pained grunt, he strode quickly toward Diablo in the stand of trees ahead of them.

"What are you doing now?" Kate asked, even as the blood continued to pool in her face.

"You sure do jaw a lot, even for a female."

"Answer my question, damn it!"

"Yes, ma'am," he drawled back with elaborate courtesy. "I'm taking you to your horse, so I can hoist you over him."

"Why, you no-good skunk!"

The stranger's reply was a dry laugh.

Panic edged Kate's voice. "Look, mister, you can't throw me across Diablo. The truth is, he's up and gone lame on me."

The stranger hesitated, staring ahead at Kate's horse. He spotted the makeshift bandage on the animal's foreleg. Muttering an annoyed curse, he pivoted about and carried Kate back to his own mount. An instant later, she felt herself being hurled, facedown, across his saddle.

"What the Sam Hill are you doing now?" she demanded.

"Carrying you home on my horse."

"What about Diablo?"

"Don't you ever shut up?"

"No."

"One thing at a time, lady," he said tiredly.

Kate's outrage over her own mortifying position was soon forgotten as she watched the stranger stride around to her side of the horse and unsheathe his rifle from its scabbard. "What's that carbine for?"

"What do you think? I got to shoot your horse, lady. We can't leave him here to die."

All at once, Kate's entire world flooded with red. "Mister, you touch one hair on Diablo's hide and I swear, I'll bury you."

Charlie's gaze flicked back to Kate, taking in her red face and ferocious mien. For a woman in her position, she sure was a feisty little beggar. Despite himself, he found her razor-sharp words giving him pause. "Lady, you done admitted it yourself. Your horse has plain gone lame—"

"That's temporary," Kate retorted. "Diablo stumbled into a gopher hole, is all. He'll be fine in a few weeks, if we favor his foreleg."

"In a few weeks? If we favor his foreleg?" Charlie repeated. "Hellfire and damnation, lady!"

Drawing a breath of pure frustration, Charlie stared ahead at the magnificent stallion tethered to a tree. The animal was pawing the ground with his wounded foreleg. To Charlie's experienced eye, the situation looked far more serious than this slip of a girl had claimed.

"Damn it, lady," he uttered angrily, "from the way he's favoring that leg, it's for sure canon broke—"

"Is not!" Kate interjected. "Diablo's got a strained

fettock is all, and it'll be fine if we give it time and care.''

Charlie's eyebrows shot up; he was impressed, despite himself. ''So you know that much about horses, do you, sister?''

''Yeah—and it's one helluva lot more than you know about spit.''

Charlie fought a grin. He stared again at the wounded animal. The thought of killing such a prime specimen of horseflesh did needle his conscience, but at the moment, other, more pressing concerns motivated him. Life and death matters.

''Lady, have you gone plumb loco?'' he asked Kate. ''Even if that stallion has just got a strain like you claim, we either got to walk him all the way back to Round Rock—a good four days on the trail— or we got to leave him here. Either way, we're all three gonna be dead by sundown.''

''What do you mean, dead by sundown? You sure do talk in riddles, mister.''

''Riddles, my butt. Haven't you ever heard of the Comanche moon?''

''Heard of it? Mister, I was reared beneath it. And I passed right by one of them renegade bands on my way out here. But if you're such a clumsy coward that you can't outsmart a few Injuns half-loco on *peyote*—''

All at once, Kate was hauled violently off the horse. With both hands and feet tied, she barely managed to maintain her balance as she stared up at her enraged captor.

Charlie shook a finger at his infuriating charge. ''Lady, if you were a man, and up and called me a coward like that, you'd be pushing up daisies right now.''

''Then it's a good thing I'm a woman, huh?''

''Woman? I'd say you're a she-devil straight from hell.''

''And I'd say you're right on the money.''

By now, Charlie was so riled, he could only glare at the maddening female. Finally, he heaved a harsh breath and said, ''Lady, that damn horse has got to be shot. We both know it.''

Kate faced him down with all the vengeance of hell burning in her eyes. ''You shoot him, mister, and I'll see you dead. I don't care if it takes me the rest of my life.''

''Goddamn it!'' Charlie exploded.

Leaving Kate to totter on her bound feet and glower at him, Charlie began to pace. His shoulder was now throbbing mercilessly, and he was beginning to feel nauseated, half-dizzy. Hell, he'd probably lost a good pint of blood, he was smack in the middle of Indian territory, and he was stuck with some crazy woman who had taken a shine to a lame horse.

He glanced warily at Kate as he moved. He was beginning to understand why her pa had wanted to unload this little shrew, and he was questioning his own sanity for ever agreeing to Jeb Maloney's mad scheme. He was thirty years old, and already, this little pissant had him plumb wore out.

Then, unwittingly, he grinned. Lord, she did look a sight, standing there glaring daggers at him, with her bosom heaving and her hair all askew, tumbling loose from its pins and falling in crazy waves about her face and neck. She was small, but right shapely, too. Full of pride and mettle, this gal was surely more trouble than a badger with a stubbed toe, but the hell of it was, Charlie still wanted her. Indeed, he burned to wipe the pout off that impudent mouth of hers. He bet she'd be hot as sin when they finally wrestled it out in the sack. And all his instincts told him that if he shot her horse, their future together would be doomed.

Charlie returned his rifle to its scabbard, strode up

to the little witch, and glared her down. "All right, lady, here's the deal."

"Yeah?" she retorted, sounding as full of prunes as ever.

"I'm dressing this here shoulder you near shot-off. Then I'm tending your horse's lame foreleg."

"And then?"

"Then I'm cuttin' you loose."

Kate's delicate eyebrows shot up. "You are?" For the moment, she was too startled to be angry.

"Yeah, I'm cutting you loose," Charlie repeated heatedly. "Then you're walking that horse clean back to Round Rock and I'm following you."

All at once, Kate was suspicious. She didn't for a moment mind walking Diablo back to Round Rock, if it would save her horse's life. Still, the stranger's deal sounded almost too good to be true. "So what's the catch, mister?"

Charlie unholstered his Colt and cocked it. "The catch is, you try anything, sister, and I'm firin' first and askin' questions later."

"You gonna shoot me or the horse?" Kate taunted.

Charlie smiled, and his smile was so frightening that, suddenly, Kate was glad he hadn't answered her.

Chapter 8

For the next half hour, Kate sat on a boulder with her wrists and ankles bound, soberly watching her captor. First, he tramped up the rise to fetch Diablo. He led the stallion back to the small valley where Kate sat, then loosened the bandage on the horse's foreleg and examined his fetlock.

Watching the stranger, Kate felt more than a little grudging respect for him. Indeed, she was amazed that he would actually tend to her horse before thinking of himself—even though his own shirt was soaked with blood.

Next, the stranger removed his bloody shirt and checked kerchief. Kate winced at the sight of the ugly, oozing bullet hole she'd inflicted high on his left shoulder. She tried to tell herself that it served him right for tracking her, but, somehow, this thought brought no real sense of triumph or moral vindication.

She watched him wash his wound, then gather wood to build a fire. Despite herself, Kate soon became captivated by the sight of him—especially his bare, sinewy chest with its covering of crisp, dark hair. A collection of faded scars crisscrossed his torso, front and back, accentuating his fearsomeness; this man was obviously a seasoned veteran, having survived many a fight. She studied his lean waist and narrow hips. He'd removed his chaps, giving her a good view of his long legs and the hard muscles that rippled powerfully against his denim trousers as he strode about. Then, there was that wicked-looking bulge at the front of his trousers. Oh, Lordy, if Conchita knew where her eyes were straying now! Yet something about the way he moved kept drawing her gaze to that forbidden territory.

Seeing the blatant evidence of his maleness made her mouth grow dry. As he leaned over to gather kindling, his trousers hugged his tight buttocks, and Kate observed the muscle play in shameless fascination. After he stacked the wood, she watched him hunker down to start the blaze. She studied his well-sculpted face with its broad forehead and deep-set eyes, the straight nose and grim, no-nonsense mouth. With the dark line of whiskers along his strong jaw and the penetrating quality in his near-black eyes, Kate had to admit that this man possessed a raw animal magnetism that would surely set a weaker female to swooning.

Not that *she* was feeling all that strong at the moment! Unbidden, a flush heated her cheeks as she recalled the feel of his strong body pinning hers to the ground. She could even remember the smell of him—the salt of the trail, the essences of leather and tobacco, and a duskier scent, keenly male. To her chagrin, these unsettling memories set her pulses to stirring . . .

She stifled a wince as she watched him stick the tip of his Bowie knife into the blaze. She dreaded the moment when he would cauterize his wound. He'd not be feeling too kindly toward her then, she mused ruefully. In the meantime, she decided she might as well explore the territory a bit, see what she could find out about this man her pa had hired. A little knowledge might well give her just the edge she needed to escape.

"You a *pistolero*, mister?" she asked conversationally.

He shrugged as he stared at the snapping fire. "I prefer to call myself a bounty hunter. I used to be a Ranger."

Kate betrayed no sign of trepidation, but her spirits sank at this revelation. Everyone in Texas knew of the fearsomeness of the Rangers. They were a loosely organized band of hired cutthroats, and the record of their ruthlessness was unparalleled. She might well be up the creek with this character.

"How'd you come to know my pa?"

He shrugged. "We met at the saloon in Round Rock."

"And he just up and hired you to bring me home?"

"Yep."

"So what's he offering you to carry me back?"

The stranger plucked a piece of grass and lazily chewed on it. "I prefer to keep that between him and me."

Kate's chin came up. "Whatever he's offering you, I'll do you one better."

He laughed. "Oh, will you?" He looked her over slowly, insultingly, in a way that made her skin prickle. "Thanks, darlin', but I prefer to take my ease with females who got somethin' sweeter 'n pistols in their britches."

Kate's face burned at his bald insult, even as his impudent words stirred her on another level. "I wasn't offering you no roll in the pasture, stranger," she spat out.

He grinned, revealing even white teeth. "Now that's a relief, honey, since it's for damn sure I'd end up with a knife in my back come sunup."

By now, Kate's temper was boiling, but she wisely resisted hurling more well-deserved invective at this infuriating stranger. She watched him pluck his knife from the blaze and stand. She pulled a hideous face as he laid the red-hot tip against both his entry and exit wounds. Within the space of a few seconds, she saw the stranger reel, stagger, drop the knife, then heard him bellow a string of blue curses that would have made the devil blush.

Ten seconds later, he was still wobbling on his feet, his features white beneath his tan. "You want me to say I'm sorry I shot you?" she asked him sweetly.

Stifling a groan, he glared at her. He picked up his discarded shirt, rending the cloth with his teeth. Discarding the bloodied sections, he began efficiently tearing the rest of the blue checked material into strips. "Don't bother, honey, for you for damn sure wouldn't mean it."

Kate shrugged. "What are you doing anyway, tearin' up your shirt? Won't you be needing it?"

"I've a fresh one in my saddle bags," he replied. "I'll use these strips for bandages for me and your horse." Nodding toward Diablo, he added tersely, "That was a damn sloppy job you done of bandaging him."

"Oh." Though his words spurred a stab of guilt, Kate managed to finish waspishly, "And this from the man who wanted to shoot him."

"Lady, I still want to shoot him," the bounty hunter snapped back as he continued to rip the cloth. "But if you're foolhardy enough to insist on keepin' that animal alive, then you should at least have wrapped that leg proper to give him a fighting chance."

"Oh. Well, all I had was a dishrag," Kate argued, feeling even more contrite as his words hit home. Though she hated to admit it to herself, it was kind of this man to tend Diablo's injured foreleg. "You need some help?"

He laughed without humor as he wound a strip

of cotton around his shoulder and arm. He grimaced. "No offense, lady, but you've already given me more help than I can stand."

She frowned. "What's your name, anyhow?"

Charlie glanced at her sharply. He hesitated a moment, then recalled Jeb Maloney's claim that he hadn't even told Kate the name of her future husband.

"Well?" she urged impatiently.

"Charlie Durango," he muttered. Watching her face closely and seeing no hint of recognition, he added with a nasty smile, "And you're Kate Maloney, right?"

Kate knew there was no point in denying it. He already damn well knew who she was, and was only trying to needle her. "Do you know you could be hung for kidnaping me this way?" she asked haughtily.

He rolled his eyes as he strode to his horse and took a blue chambray shirt from one of his saddlebags. "I ain't kidnaping you, lady. All I'm doing is returning a runaway child to its pa."

"A runaway child?" Kate cried indignantly. "I ain't no child."

He shrugged into the shirt. "You sure couldn't prove that by your actions. The fact is, you're a female, sister, and bound to obey your daddy. And have you asked yourself what the law might do to you for shooting me without call?"

"Without call? You were tracking me, mister."

Buttoning his shirt and tucking the tails into his pants, he ambled back toward the fire. "There ain't no law says we can't use the same trail. I hadn't done a thing when you up and blew me clean off my horse."

Kate was becoming exasperated. "So you're just taking me back to my pa, no questions asked?"

"That's the deal."

"Did Pa tell you I hate his guts?"

At her spiteful words, Charlie's jaw tightened and his expression grew strangely shuttered. "That's between you and him, lady."

Kate was silent for a long moment, chewing her bottom lip. At last, she asked, "You know what he's planning to do with me, don't you?"

A muscle twitched in his cheek. "I reckon I do."

Kate's green eyes shot sparks at Charlie. "Ain't you got no conscience? Are you just gonna take me back to be married off to some old coot with a glass eye, a peg leg, and a club foot?"

Charlie was so stunned, he could only stare at Kate. It occurred to him vaguely that there must be a contradiction somewhere in the outrageous terms she had used, but for the moment such subtle distinctions were buried beneath a mountain of amazement and disbelief.

Where in hell had this girl learned such ridiculous lies about him, her future husband? A peg leg and a club foot indeed! Damn, but he was glad he'd decided not to tell her who he really was! He sure as Sunday better learn more about this fix he was in before he revealed the truth.

"Well, stranger?" the girl demanded.

"That's about the size of it, lady," he drawled, turning and striding toward her horse.

Twenty minutes later, after Charlie had carefully rewrapped Diablo's injured foreleg, Kate led her horse down the trail. Studying the bounty hunter's handiwork, she had to admit he had done a great job of bandaging the horse, using both her strips and the ones he'd torn from his shirt.

Her captor rode behind her on his palomino; she could feel his cold gaze boring into her back as she walked, as if daring her to defy him. Kate had a feeling she may well have hit a granite wall with this

Durango character. Yet, she was determined not to let him take her back to Pa trussed up like some prize turkey. She'd never been one to give up a fight easily, and she wasn't about to change her ways now. Indeed, she was concentrating fiercely on what new tack she should take with him when she stumbled over a root in the trail and nearly took a spill.

"Hey, easy," he called out to her.

Regaining her footing, Kate turned to glare up at him. "Don't tell me you care what happens to me, bounty hunter?"

He rode up beside her and spoke in a cutting hiss. "Lady, I don't give a damn what happens to you. I just want to get you back to your pa, unload you, and collect my pay. I can't do that if you go lame like your fool horse."

"Then you might have to shoot us both, huh?"

He flashed her that evil grin again, and again she was glad he didn't answer.

"You really don't have a conscience, do you, stranger?" she spat out, turning away and resuming her trek down the trail.

Behind her, Charlie ducked his head to avoid a branch. "I find havin' a conscience don't pay in this business."

"Then you're as much of a coward as my pa."

Kate heard a low, blistering curse, then Charlie rode up beside her and seized her by the scruff of her neck. "Lady, I told you to watch who you're calling a coward," he snapped, propelling her forward and causing her to stumble again.

Yet, as she steadied herself on her feet, Kate was grinning, confident that she was getting to this hired gun a little. "So you're no craven, eh?" she taunted.

"Lady, it's a job. It ain't nothin' personal."

"They why don't you tell me what you'd call a man who'd leave a defenseless girl at the mercies of an old skunk with gout, rheumatism, and rotting teeth?''

Charlie blinked at her. He couldn't figure out what mystified him more—these continuing, ridiculous descriptions of himself, or the idea of Kate Maloney being defenseless. ''Sounds like a pretty even match to me,'' he drawled.

''It's cruel and unusual punishment, and you know it,'' Kate argued back. ''Furthermore, I understand the old derelict is blind as a bat and his head is so bald, you can flat fry an egg on it on a hot day.''

''Do tell,'' Charlie mocked, though inwardly he was appalled.

'' 'Sides, I hear half the county takes to the hills when the old codger breaks wind.''

Charlie was rendered speechless.

Kate continued, obviously relishing every word. ''They say he belches worse than a mud bog and smells like he never made it to the outhouse.''

''Is that a fact?'' Charlie managed.

''Yeah, they said he made it to the necessary once and created such a ruckus he plain blew off the door.''

''Who told you all of this?'' Charlie demanded, suddenly ravenously curious, despite himself.

She shrugged. ''Why, it's common knowledge in these parts. Plus, they say no sheep in the county is safe around him.''

''Damn,'' Charlie muttered, totally flabbergasted.

''Yeah, and he bit a dog once and drove it plumb mad,'' Kate went on with relentless enthusiasm. ''They had to shoot the poor beast—''

''Which beast?''

''Why, the dog, you idjut. Damned fine sheep dog, too.''

Charlie couldn't resist a grudging grin. ''Tell me,

does your intended have horns, a tail, and carry a pitchfork?''

She chuckled. ''No, but you're gettin' the general idea.'' She turned to gaze up at him in challenge. ''So what are you going to do about it, bounty hunter?''

''Do about it?'' He shrugged. ''Nothin'.''

''Nothin'!''

''Lady, I'm just taking you back to your pa. The rest is between you and him.''

Kate balled her hands on her hips and glared up at him. ''Don't give me that load of manure, stranger. I don't care who the hell you think you are, or what job you're out to do. You know damned well what my pa intends for me, and that makes you no better than a lowdown''—she thought fiercely for a minute, then finished self-righteously—''accessory after the fact.''

''Shit, lady,'' Charlie groaned. ''Give it a rest.''

''Like hell I will. Here you are, leavin' me at the mercy of a geezer from hell, and you have nothin' to say about it?''

''I'd say my sympathies are with the man.''

They continued down the trail, with Kate still spouting every malicious slur she could think of—and still getting nowhere with the hard-bitten bounty hunter. When hurling lies regarding her future husband gained her no ground, she concentrated on attacking Charlie Durango's attributes outright. With every step, her gibes grew more preposterous; with every step, his visage grew more unyielding.

She scoffed at his intelligence.

He tipped his hat.

She maligned his character.

He clucked to his horse.

She cast aspersions on his ancestors.

He chewed a twig.

She questioned his sanity.

He questioned it, too.

She scorned his looks.

He spat tobacco.

She insulted his horse.

He pulled his gun.

By late afternoon, Kate's tongue was literally hanging out, and she was beginning to realize she was in quite a pickle. Here, she had thought *she* was stubborn. But this bounty hunter was obviously sharp as a whip, with a will as inpenetrable as steel. His only soft spot seemed to be his horse. When she'd called his handsome palomino a "broken down nag," he'd damned near shot her. That tack had clearly gotten her nowhere, however. If she couldn't find some way to get around this man, she was certain to be taken straight home and wed off to the fossil Pa had lined up for her.

Obviously, since defying Charlie Durango had gotten her nowhere, perhaps she should try sweetening him up some instead. She flicked her calculating gaze back at him, taking in his long legs with their hard saddle muscles, the sleek lines of his torso, the granite edge of his jaw, the piercing quality of his black eyes, even shaded beneath the brim of his hat. She studied the obdurate line of his mouth and wondered suddenly, outrageously, what it would feel like to have those ruthless lips claiming hers.

Kate turned away hastily, shamed and horrified by her own wayward thoughts. Then she realized, just as quickly and disgracefully, that she was going to have that kiss—have it and use it to her advantage. While Kate had never before stooped to feminine wiles, like most women, she was aware that such tactics worked—leastwise, that was how most women in Round Rock got their husbands or sweet-

hearts to run and fetch and fawn over them all the
time. Normally, Kate considered such manipula-
tions contemptible; but right now, she was desperate. Perhaps when they stopped for the night, she
could try to soften up Charlie Durango a bit . . .

As they went along, Charlie was thinking about
Kate, too, and wondering what was going through
her scheming brain. Though her insults toward him
were to be expected, he remained appalled at the
things she had said about her future husband—
supposedly, sight unseen. How in the hell had her
''intended'' become such a monster in her eyes? Had
Jeb Maloney poisoned Kate's mind against him?

But that made no sense. If the rancher was indeed
dead set on marrying off his daughter, why would
he shoot himself in the foot by turning Kate against
the man he'd chosen? After meeting Kate, Charlie
could certainly understand Jeb Maloney's desperation to unload this brat.

Perhaps it was just Kate's hatred of her pa that
prompted her to spout such lies. He watched her
strut down the trail in front of him, her head held
high, her impudent behind swinging from side to
side, taunting him. Damn, what a pistol!

One thing was for certain. Right now, telling Kate
who he really was would be tantamount to tying a
noose around his own neck. Thank God he'd been
smart enough to keep his peace earlier. He'd have
to find out a lot more about this hotheaded gal before he chanced spilling the beans. . . .

Chapter 9

Before dusk, they stopped to make camp near a stream shaded by huge cottonwoods. Under Charlie's watchful eye, Kate unsaddled the horses and watered them at the creek. Charlie rubbed down both animals and rewrapped Diablo's foreleg, poulticing the swollen fetlock with mud. Then he built a small fire and prepared them a supper of beans, corn dodgers, and strong coffee.

The sun was sinking toward the western horizon when they sat down to share their repast, sitting on opposite sides of the fire. Charlie eyed the prideful spitfire across from him. Kate had taken off her hat and unpinned her hair, and, with her thick, untamed curls falling about her face and shoulders, and the light of the fire snapping in her green eyes, she looked exotic and beautiful.

"Mind telling me somethin'?" he asked.

She shrugged. "That depends."

"Where was you headed when I captured you?"

She shot him a resentful glance. "To my Cousin Sophie's place in Fort Worth."

"Who's she?"

"My ma's relation."

"And you didn't think you were being the least bit foolhardy, trampin' straight through Comanche territory all alone?"

With a murderous scowl, Kate tossed the dregs of her coffee into the fire. "Mister, I was doin' just fine till you come along."

Charlie was quiet for a moment, thoughtfully lighting a cheroot. Watching him take a deep draw, Kate was tempted to ask for a smoke herself. But she knew better.

At last, he asked casually, "How come you and your pa don't get along?"

That question pricked Kate's pride. Her first thought was to tell this character to go straight to hell, that her relationship with her pa was none of his damned business. Then she reminded herself of her scheme to get on Charlie's good side. He was even making the first move—a stroke of luck, when she thought about it.

With a sigh, Kate set down her empty plate. She braced her forearms on her raised knees. "My pa feels a woman is good for two things."

"And what might they be?"

"Having babies, and obeying her husband."

Charlie chuckled.

Kate's eyes blazed at him. "I might 'a known you'd be of a similar mind, bounty hunter."

He held up a hand. "Did I say I agreed?"

"No, but I could see it in your eyes."

He shook his head with good humor. "Why don't you just tell me more about you and your pa."

Kate picked up a twig and stabbed at an ant crawling too close to her trouser leg. "We never could abide each other, is all. My ma died bearing me, and I don't think Pa's ever quit blaming me."

"Hey, I'm sorry," Charlie said sincerely.

She shot him a withering look. "I don't need your sympathy, stranger."

He raised both hands in a gesture of surrender. "Whatever you say."

Kate glowered at him for another moment, then

stared abstractedly at the fire. "There's not much else to tell. From the time I can remember, all my pa did was send me to this school and that school. He never did try to rear me himself."

Listening to the girl, sensing the deep hurt behind her words, Charlie wisely resisted offering additional words of sympathy. "I suppose some men just don't cotton to raising children."

Kate tossed her stick into the underbrush. "I wouldn't know. But it's for damn sure my pa never cottoned to me."

A slow grin spread across Charlie's face. "And you never gave him no trouble, right?"

Unwittingly, Kate smiled. "No more'n I've given you today."

Charlie threw back his head and laughed, and for an instant Kate felt an odd kinship with him.

Afterward, they were silent for a long time, listening to the snapping of the fire, the bubbling of the creek, the low cooing of mourning doves. A slight evening breeze was stirring, rustling the leaves of the cottonwood trees and wafting the scent of earth and wildflowers over them.

Kate glanced at Charlie, watching him flex his sore shoulder. He had favored his left side all day, she recalled, but didn't appear badly injured. She considered asking him about his wound, then quickly decided that this would only raise his hackles. Still, she mustn't give up on her scheme to cajole him. She decided to try a different tack.

"What about your kin, stranger?" she asked.

The handsome lines of Charlie's face tightened. "My folks settled here in the late twenties, joining Austin's original colony. They were massacred by Comanches when I was four years old. After that, I was reared by my grandpa."

"Hey, I'm sorry." To her surprise, Kate found herself sincerely repeating his earlier words.

Now it was Charlie who shrugged, belying his own pain. "I made out all right."

"You sure must hate the Comanche."

Charlie's expression grew tense, brooding. "I'm not saying I cotton to the redskins, but it was their land first, you know." He took a long draw on his cheroot. "I've done my share of Indian fighting with the Rangers over the years—but it was always just a job for me, not a grudge."

She shook her head at his astounding attitudes. "Is that what I am to you, stranger? Just a job?"

A glint of devilishness gleamed in his dark eyes. "I'd have to say you're a mite more of a job than fighting Injuns—and a heap better looking."

Kate had to bite back the smile that pulled at her mouth. While she still bitterly resented being this man's captive, she had to admit that this bounty hunter could be a charmer when he wanted to. She found herself feeling more curious about him.

"What brought you to Round Rock in the first place?" she asked. "I mean, I can't recall hearing of you being in the area before. Were you on the trail of some desperado?"

He shook his head. "I was just passing through, between jobs. My friend Sam Stockton told me I could stay at his hunting cabin."

"And then you met my pa."

"Yep. I reckon you know the rest."

Kate frowned, sensing that there was more behind his words than he was willing to reveal. But she resisted the urge to delve further into his motives, not wanting to arouse his suspicions this early in the game. Watching him stand and pick up the frying pan, she rose and dusted off her britches. "Mister, I was wondering. Could I go wash up in the crick?"

He glanced at her suspiciously. "You wouldn't be aiming to give me the slip, would you, sister?"

She shook her head and tugged at the filthy collar of her shirt. "It's just that this here trail dust is driving me crazy."

He set down the frying pan, picked up his rifle, and nodded. "All right. Let's go."

Kate's eyes grew huge. "B-but you can't be aimin' to come with me!"

He laughed. "You don't actually think I'm such a fool that I'd let you go off to the creek alone?"

"But . . . I can't bathe with you . . ." Watching his grin widen, she blurted, "Look, I'll sing."

He appeared astonished. "You'll what?"

"I'll sing while I'm bathing. That way you'll know I'm within shouting distance."

He stared at her in perplexity, then set his rifle down against a tree. "Very well, lady, you sing. But make it good and loud, or I'm coming straight after you."

Kate nodded and started off down the trail.

Charlie's voice stopped her. "One more thing. Leave your shirt, britches, and boots behind."

She whirled, her face crimson. "You can't be serious."

He grinned, crossing his forearms over his chest and rocking on his bootheels. "Oh, yes I am." He winked at her wickedly. "I reckon you won't get too far in your unmentionables, sister."

Rage boiled inside Kate. She wanted to claw this arrogant cad's eyes out, to call him every vile name she could think of. Yet she knew that if she were to escape, she had to play the game his way. Choking back half a dozen scathing rejoinders, Kate removed her shirt, trousers, and boots, and tossed them all in a heap at Charlie's feet.

Afterward, standing in just her bloomers and camisole, Kate's visage was trembling, if proud. She glared at her maddening captor. "You satisfied now?"

Charlie's gaze roved over the shapely, irate female standing before him with hands balled on her hips. Her defiant stance and ruffled female feathers only increased her allure. His heart thudded and a hot twinge of lust seared his loins.

Lord, she looked ripe and blushing as a June bride, dressed in that lacy underwear! Damnation, but she was put together fine. He could trace the outline of every delectable curve and valley on her shapely little body—the creamy neck and straight shoulders, the impudent breasts, the tiny waist and well-curved hips. There was even a tiny blue bow between those two upthrust breasts, as if to tempt a man to unbind those ripe globes and explore further. Many a female would cower in mortification to be in her position. Instead, Kate Maloney faced him down with unmistakable spunk and mettle. He realized that what he felt for her went way beyond lust to a sense of keen admiration.

A telltale catch edged his voice. "You do look a sight, darlin'."

Muttering a curse, Kate turned and started toward the creek.

Charlie grinned in pure pleasure as he watched her pretty behind bob down the trail. "Don't forget to sing now, honey," he called after her.

Through gritted teeth, Kate began a loud, off-key rendition of "The Yellow Rose of Texas." At the creek, she turned west to put some distance between herself and her captor. While she moved gingerly due to the rocky terrain and her own bare feet, she sang louder with each step she took.

Now what was she going to do? she wondered. She was in a fine fix. As the bounty hunter had pointed out, she was in no shape to go anywhere in just her underclothes, especially with no shoes.

Kate realized that her only hope would be to get the slip on Charlie, grab her clothing, and steal his horse. Oh, damnation, stealing his horse! Wouldn't that just roast his chops? She shuddered as she remembered him pulling his gun on her earlier today, when she'd insulted Corona. Nevertheless, she refused to abandon her scheme. She recalled where he'd left his rifle, propped against a sycamore tree. If she could just circle back around through the woods and grab that gun before he spotted her . . .

Still proceeding west, Kate sang steadily for a few minutes, then decided it was time to make her move—

She was just diving into the trees when she landed squarely against a rock-hard body—

"Hellfire and damnation, woman, are you flat trying to kill me?" Charlie Durango bellowed, gripping Kate's arm with one hand as he rubbed his aching shoulder.

"You were spying on me!" she accused furiously.

"And you were fixin' to hightail it," he shot back.

"Was not. I was headed into the woods to answer Mother Nature's call."

He laughed. "You were aiming to circle back and get the drop on me."

"Was not!"

"My, my, if you ain't a feisty little firecracker," he mocked. "Didn't you say you wanted a bath? Perhaps a little dip in the stream will cool off that temper a mite."

And before Kate could protest, Charlie heaved the indignant female into his arms, took three long strides to the creek, and summarily dumped her in the shallow water. She landed on the bumpy creek bottom with a mighty splash and an indignant yowl.

"Satan's drawers!" Kate shrieked, staring murder up at Charlie, and flinging clumps of cold, wet hair from her eyes. Her bottom smarted from her rough landing, and her pride rebelled at the indignity of her position.

Meanwhile, Charlie looked down at her and laughed. His shoulder was smarting like hell from lifting the girl, but he reckoned the pain was well-worth feasting his eyes on her now. "You still want to try to get the drop on me, honey?" he taunted.

Kate heaved herself to her feet and glowered at the insufferable bounty hunter. Then her rage turned to fear as she watched Charlie's dark gaze flick over her with hot, riveting lust. She looked downward and was horrified to see every inch of her charms revealed through the wet, transparent linen of her undergarments.

She covered herself as best she could. "Quit gawking at me, Texan!"

"But you're such a fetching eyeful." The husky catch in his voice, the bald hunger in his eyes, confirmed it.

"May we please go back to camp?" The water had been cold, and Kate was trembling all over, her voice shaking.

"Not so fast." His voice sounded even raspier as he stepped closer. His smile was more frightening still. "You broke the rules, so first I've got to wallop you."

"You what?" Kate was outraged. "After you just dumped me in the creek?"

"Why don't you just take your medicine like a man," he teased.

Kate stamped her foot in impotent fury, sending new waves of water sluicing over her. "I ain't no man."

He looked her over and whistled. "Honey, I noticed." He reached for her arm.

She recoiled. "You ain't gonna wallop me in my underwear!"

He chuckled. "You sure ain't putting on your britches first."

Kate was mortified to the depths of her soul at the

thought of being thrown across the stranger's lap again, with her all-but-naked bottom in the air.

"Please, you don't have to hit me," she begged at last. "I—I apologize."

"You what?" he exclaimed, his eyes dancing with laughter.

"You heard me the first time, mister."

He leaned back against the tree and lazily crossed one boot over the other. His stance was indolent, yet every bit as threatening as before. "So, you admit you were trying to hightail it?"

"What else could you expect of me?"

He grinned at her. "Get out of that creek and come here."

Trembling with fear and frustrated anger, Kate did as he bid, all the while keeping a wary eye on Charlie. She paused before him, dripping and humiliated, and he again looked her over with a thoroughness that curled her toes. She tried to face him down bravely, but her trembling lower lip revealed her vulnerability.

When he spoke, the softness of his voice sent a shiver down her spine. "You deserve a good blistering, all right. But I might just settle for a kiss instead."

Rage banished Kate's fear. Shaking a fist at him, she spat, "*You* might settle? Mister, you can go kiss a—"

But, before Kate could finish her seething protest, Charlie hooked an arm around her neck, dragged her up against his steely frame, and pressed his mouth to hers.

Never before had Kate felt a man's lips on her own. At first she tried to wrestle away, but she might as well have tried to force her way past a brick wall. She knew she should be infuriated by Charlie's impudent assault, that she should fight like a cornered wildcat. But, to her surprise, she found that being kissed by this bounty hunter was quite pleasant. Her outrage faded before her fascination with new and provocative sensations.

Charlie's mouth felt hot and urgent on hers, demanding a response she somehow hungered to give. The whiskers along his jaw abraded her soft flesh in a deliciously sensual way. His body felt warm and alive against her own. His kiss tasted of coffee and fierce desire, and, unwittingly, a moan rose in her throat—

Charlie heard her woman's call and answered it. His arms came tightly around her, binding her to him, molding her softness against his strong frame.

Kate felt her toes leave the ground, felt her hips lock against the heat of Charlie's loins. To her horror, she could feel the hard length of him rise up between them. Sudden, riveting visions of barnyard creatures mating flooded her mind, and she thought she might die of mortification—

But Charlie just went on kissing her as if he might never stop.

Strange longings exploded inside Kate. Even in the heat, she found she was shivering, the pit of her stomach going all achy, and her nipples tightening against the bruising pressure of Charlie's chest. Somewhere in the back of her mind, she knew she was behaving wantonly, brazenly giving in to her enemy. She knew she should shove away this insolent cad—

But surely that would mean being thrown across his lap and walloped, and this alternative was far more pleasurable.

All at once, nothing mattered to Kate but the new, irresistible yearnings within her. She felt as hungry as a newborn lamb frolicking in its first spring meadow, as ravenous as a bee sampling its first taste of nectar. Her lips softened beneath Charlie's, and she reached up tentatively to stroke his shoulder.

Hearing him groan, she realized her error and slipped her arms around his waist instead. She heard him moan contentedly, and she shuddered as his thumb stroked the base of her spine.

Feeling the sweet shiver that seized her, Charlie grew bolder, teasing Kate's lips apart, then pressing his hot tongue in and out of her mouth—tantalizing, audaciously. Kate's entire world reeled, and she tried desperately to pull away from her own shattering response. But Charlie was relentless, pivoting and pressing her back against the tree, blocking her escape with his unyielding body and ruthless lips. With both hands holding her face, he took all the time in the world to finish mating her mouth with his own.

When he finally pulled back, Kate took a sharp breath and stared up at him. He was breathing raggedly, too, and gazing down at her with that same near-black intensity that knotted her stomach and made her heart beat at a dizzying tempo.

Kate could bear the tension no longer. "You get what you wanted, bounty hunter?" she taunted.

He chuckled. "No complaints. How 'bout you, ma'am?"

She shrugged, tossing damp hair from her eyes. "Beats being walloped, I reckon."

He laughed heartily. "You keep acting so agreeable, honey, and maybe next time I'll teach you how to kiss me back."

"Oooh!" Kate couldn't decide whether she was more angered or insulted. "I thought you said you had no complaints."

He grinned and reached down to toy with the blue ribbon between her breasts. She gasped. "Oh, I liked the taste, all right," he drawled huskily. "But I'm a man who's used to devouring the whole pie."

Watching him tease his errant finger into the opening of her camisole, Kate choked on a shameless whimper. Why couldn't she force herself to slap his hand away? Why instead was she consumed with jealousy at the thought of him gorging himself on someone else's pie?

Finally, she managed a terse, "Unhand me, bounty hunter."

At her breathless order, Charlie moved back and looked her over again, staring at the wetness from her camisole that had seeped into his own shirt. He whistled low under his breath. "I'd say you've been washed but good now. We'd best head back to camp."

Back at camp, the two awkward strangers washed up the supper dishes as the sun went down. Afterward, they unrolled their bedrolls on opposite sides of the dying fire.

Charlie glanced at Kate and said in a clipped voice, "You'd best spread out your bedroll next to yonder tree. I'm tying you up for the night."

"Is that really necessary?" she protested.

"Yep."

Tossing him a mutinous look, Kate stomped off with her blankets and flung them down next to a cottonwood sapling. Once she had laid down, Charlie came over and knelt beside her, gently but firmly tying her wrists. As he worked, he seemed to be making a deliberate attempt to keep his gaze from sliding over her underwear-clad body. He secured the knots to the tree trunk on a long thong, then threw a coarse woolen blanket over her.

As he prepared to leave, she snapped, "You know, mister, this ain't the best country for a body to be hogtied and defenseless. What am I supposed to do if a snake sidles up to me in the middle of the night?"

He winked at her. "Guess that depends on the snake."

"I was talking 'bout a copperhead or a rattler, not a viper from hell like you."

"Just call out for help, honey," he said affably. "I'm at your service."

"Well, what a comfort."

He gazed down at her, his smile taking on a grim tautness. "Before you think about tryin' to escape again, may I remind you that there are Indians loose in these hills?"

Kate tossed her head defiantly. "I ain't no idjut."

He chuckled, but his tone sent a chill down her spine. "I'm relieved to hear it. 'Cause if you should try to give me the slip again, I'm gonna see that you live to regret it, darlin'." As she glanced up at him sharply, he added, "And it won't be with a kiss this time."

Then, whether contradicting himself or not, he leaned over, caught her chin roughly, and took her lips in a brief, hard kiss that said in no uncertain terms that he considered himself the boss.

As Kate watched him stand and stride off, tears burned her eyes—tears of anger at herself because she knew she should hate him, and somehow she couldn't. Oh, she hated the bounty hunter who had captured her. But the man who had kissed her . . . that was a different matter altogether.

Kate watched him recline on his bedroll with his back to her. She glared at him until it was too dark to see. After she calmed down a bit, she realized she couldn't really blame Charlie for tying her up for the night, not considering her earlier escape attempt. She lay awake in the darkness for a long time, staring up at the starry heavens and reliving her moments with him at the creek. The memories made her tingle all over, made her face burn with humiliation and her heart pound crazily.

Kate had discovered something about herself

down by that stream—something she wasn't sure she liked.

She had discovered something about Charlie Durango, too. And now, she knew she held the key to her own freedom.

Across from Kate, Charlie, too, found sleep elusive. He was a man in pain, and the greatest source of his agony was hardly his wounded shoulder. His manhood ached and throbbed mercilessly, burning for the female solace that his male conscience hadn't allowed him to take.

He felt half-feverish, whether from his wound or from lust, he wasn't sure. All he could think of was the feisty little siren who was now his captive, and how he'd come within a hair's breadth of shoving her up high against that tree, shredding her flimsy underwear, and embedding himself to the hilt inside her. Kate was a seductive little witch all right—and she damn well knew how to use her charms to drive him plumb loco. While he harbored serious doubts about her motives, one thing he did know was that she had responded to him down by the stream. Damn, she had been hot! Even now, a torrent of desire seared him as he remembered her sweet lips trembling and parting beneath his, her nipples puckering against the sinfully wet cloth of her camisole, her arms trembling about him.

Charlie's innate sense of fairness told him it wasn't right to make love with this woman until she knew who he really was. Yet his lurid fantasies would give him no peace. She was his, yet she was forbidden. It was exquisite torment.

He groaned and rolled over, trying unsuccessfully to find a comfortable position on the hard ground. He'd get Kate safely home all right, but whether he'd get her there intact was another matter. His good intentions notwithstanding, he feared she might well leave her virginity behind somewhere on the trail.

Chapter 10

Sunrise found Kate and Charlie off again. Kate led Diablo down the trail and Charlie followed her on his palomino. Toward midday, they stopped near the ford of a river to water the horses, and ate a modest meal of jerky and biscuits.

Flexing his sore shoulder, Charlie stared at Kate. She was sitting across from him, on a path of sun-dappled ground near the riverbank, daintily nibbling a cold biscuit, her wild black hair fluttering about her face and shoulders. The sight of her thrilled him, and he was glad she'd worn her hair unbound again today. Her hat had protected the creamy skin of her face, although the tip of her nose was slightly sunburned. Part of him longed to rub salve on that cute little raw patch and kiss it better.

He wondered what she was thinking. While she appeared placid, he didn't trust this wayward girl for a minute. He knew she was still intent on escape. Nonetheless, she looked tired; he could see lines of fatigue on her face. Had she gotten any rest last night? he wondered. He took solace from the possibility that she might have felt every bit as restless and tormented as he had.

"Sure you're up to walking that horse for three more days?" he asked casually.

She stared at him in defiance. "Don't doubt it for a minute."

He sighed. "You know, I'd be willing to spell you, walk your horse a while, and let you ride Corona, but you'd be off like a shot."

To Charlie's surprise, Kate laughed. "You're right, mister," she said, getting to her feet and brushing off her trousers.

After packing up, they forded the river and continued down the trail in the merciless heat. Frequently, Kate had to remove her hat and wipe the sweat that was forever trickling into her eyes. A passing stagecoach showered them both with dust, increasing her misery. At times, Kate did doubt her ability to walk Diablo all the way back to Round Rock, and as the day lengthened, the horse seemed to favor his lame foreleg more and more. She began to fear that, by the time they arrived back home, her mount would be lame permanently. Still, every time Kate glanced back into Diablo's huge, soulful brown eyes, the thought of the alternative—letting Charlie shoot him—was unbearable.

Kate was trudging up a rise when Charlie cantered up on Corona and extended his hand.

Pausing in her tracks, Kate stared up at him in perplexity. With the wide brim of his hat shading his eyes, she couldn't read his feelings. "What's this for?"

"Hand me those reins and get up here," Charlie said gruffly. "You're plumb wore out."

She eyed his sweaty mount; Corona was snorting and kicking up dust with his foreleg. "What about your horse?"

Charlie shrugged. "You don't weigh more'n a handful of feathers. Slow as we're going, it ain't gonna hurt Corona none if we double up. Hell, we'd be riding double anyway if you'd allowed me to shoot your mount."

After a moment's hesitation, Kate gratefully handed Charlie Diablo's reins. He tethered the reins to his saddle horn, then easily pulled her up behind him on his horse.

As she slipped her arms around his waist, she heard him clear his throat, then warn hoarsely, ''You make a move for my gun, sister, and your backside's gonna hit the dirt quicker 'n you can wink.''

Unwittingly, Kate chuckled. ''Yes sir,'' she acknowledged with mock gravity.

Kate felt supremely grateful for Charlie's kindness as they continued at a slow but steady pace. Much as she hated to admit it, she was beginning to like and respect this bounty hunter. Of course, he was taking her back to Pa, and she should despise him for that; yet on another level she realized, as he had already told her, that he was only doing his job. And it was certainly pleasurable riding so close to him, feeling the hard muscles of his back ripple against her breasts, inhaling the male scent of him. Unbidden, memories of the kisses they'd shared yesterday came back to haunt her, and she realized she felt sorely tempted to repeat that little episode—

Lord have mercy, what was she thinking? This man was her captor, her enemy, and here she was, lusting after him like some mare in heat! Besides, the two of them were alone out on the trail. If she let Charlie kiss her again, there was no guarantee that he would stop before he had his way with her—

Did she want him to? The wicked thought both tantalized and appalled Kate. She realized her feelings were in chaos. On the one hand, she knew it might be wise to sweet-talk the bounty hunter a bit, so she could win his trust and then give him the slip. On the other hand, she didn't know whether she could trust herself not to get caught in her own trap.

Could she face doing that with Charlie?

She smiled. Even if it came to that, surely bedding down with this handsome bounty hunter would be a heap more pleasant than the alternative—sharing a mattress with the old coot Pa had lined up for her. Hell, the geezer was probably too feeble to close the distance between himself and a young wife.

She would risk it then, she decided. She would try to sweet-talk Charlie into dropping his guard. But, if worse came to worse and she couldn't give him the slip . . . If the Texan ruined her, then so be it. When they arrived back in Round Rock, she would simply tell Pa. Like any outraged parent, he would feel duty-bound to fetch his shotgun and force Charlie to the altar.

Kate grinned at the thought. Indeed, the realization was almost dizzying. Wouldn't that be rare! she mused with vengeful pleasure. She would win; she'd get to defy Pa and choose her own husband! It would almost be worth the price of giving up her independence—and her virginity.

Of course, that would be *only* if she couldn't give Charlie the slip, she mused self-righteously.

Her mind made up, Kate pressed her cheek against Charlie's back and dozed . . .

In front of her on the saddle, Charlie stiffened as he felt the tips of Kate's firm breasts slide against his back, felt her warm sweet breath raise gooseflesh on his nape. As she sagged against him, her hands at his waist relaxed slightly, the fingers slipping innocently yet provocatively lower. He emitted an agonized grunt, hastily moving her hands out of harm's way and bemoaning the painful constriction of his trousers and the throbbing, relentless torment in his loins.

Brilliant move, Durango, he chided himself. It wasn't enough to have temptation along on the trail;

he had to have the seductive little siren right here in the saddle with him.

At least he had the satisfaction of knowing that she hadn't gotten any more rest last night than he had. Even now, he was sorely tempted to pull them over beneath a shade tree and spend the rest of the afternoon in a much more pleasurable fashion. After all, the girl was *his*—signed, sealed, and delivered by her pa. The idea of Kate belonging to him—whether she knew it or not—sent a reckless thrill coursing through him and made his heart pound hungrily. If he took his due a step or two ahead of the preacher, who was to say it was wrong?

Then his conscience rose up to needle him, reminding him that the girl had had no say regarding her own fate. He wondered what kind of man Jeb Maloney was, to entrust his daughter to a stranger this way. Maloney had no doubt spent more time selecting lumber for his outhouse than he'd spent choosing a husband for his daughter. How could Maloney know he wasn't placing the girl at the mercies of an unscrupulous scoundrel, a man who would not hesitate to exploit the situation—

A man like himself. Charlie groaned, realizing he did not like this image of himself, or confronting the naked truth this way. Already, this wisp of a girl had him wishing he could be more than he was.

Kate's hands slid lower again, and, with a wince, Charlie once again shifted her fingers higher on his waist. It was going to be one helluva long ride back to Round Rock.

Some time later, Kate jerked awake as Corona lurched to a halt; she heard Charlie curse and felt the muscles of his back grow rigid. Sitting up, she glanced at the rise ahead of them and gasped in mingled fear and revulsion—

On the rocky knoll stood the charred, smoldering

ruin of a peddler's wagon. Shredded cloth, broken
bottles, and other plundered merchandise littered
the landscape. Horrified, Kate craned her neck to
see. The wagon looked hauntingly familiar.

Her arms tightened about Charlie's middle. "What
on earth . . . ?"

"Comanches," he muttered grimly. "I figured
we'd be seeing their handiwork sooner or later."

While Kate shuddered in trepidation, Charlie dismounted and unsheathed his rifle. When she started
to follow him, he scolded, "No. You stay put and
watch the horses while I scout around."

Kate slid to the ground and nervously gathered
the reins of both horses. "Sure, Charlie."

Striding off, he added ominously, "By the way, I
wouldn't be tryin' to escape just now if I was you."

She gulped.

Huddling next to the horses, Kate figured that
Charlie was trying to shield her from whatever horrors lay ahead. She could see a slight haze of smoke
rising from the other side of the wagon, and the re-
volting smell of scorched meat filled the air. Surely
the Indians hadn't . . . ? She fought back a spasm
of nausea at the gruesome thought and glanced worriedly at the surrounding woods. As Charlie had
warned, this was certainly no time to try to escape,
with renegade Indians possibly still hovering about.

Hearing the cry of a bird, she glanced upward.
Buzzards were circling in the cloudless blue sky, a
portentous sight. Her stomach clenched even more
violently.

Kate stared at the burned-out wagon again, at its
large wheels and the few specks of peeling red paint
that remained on its sides. Deep despair seized her.
Sweet Jesus, she knew this wagon!

"Shit!"

Hearing Charlie's revolted curse from the other
side of the wagon, Kate could take no more. Drop-

ping the reins, she rushed toward the scene. Rounding the wagon, she shuddered. Staked out on the ground was a hideous sight—the burning raw flesh of a human body, or what remained of it. The corpse was still smoldering, flies were buzzing about, and the stench was overpowering—

Nausea hit Kate in a massive blow. Reeling, she dashed for the bushes and quickly emptied the contents of her stomach.

A moment later, she felt a gentle hand on her shoulder. "Easy, honey, easy," Charlie whispered. "Did I tell you to stay away? Why'd you have to go and look at that?"

Kate's horror and revulsion were such that she felt no shame that Charlie had seen her vomiting. She straightened and thrust herself into his arms, trembling and sobbing. "Oh, Charlie, why'd they have to go and do that to him? Skinning that poor man alive, and burning him, and—"

"Easy, honey," Charlie repeated helplessly, holding her tight and rubbing her back. "It don't do no good to think about it."

She pulled back, her tear-ravished face meeting his. "But—but I think I know that man, Charlie. I'm almost certain he's the peddler, Aloysius McCoy. I'd recognize his wagon anywhere. He used to come around the ranch and sell Conchita his wares."

"Damn. Kate, I'm sorry," Charlie murmured, brushing a tear from her cheek with his thumb. Hearing *Diablo* whinny down the trail, he cleared his throat. "Look, honey, you'd best go grab the horses before this smoke and the stench plumb spooks 'um. I'll bury Mr. McCoy."

Kate nodded tremulously. "Do—do you think that Comanches have spotted us?"

Charlie shook his head. "If they had, we wouldn't be standing here right now."

Acknowledging Charlie's pronouncement with a

grimace, Kate did as he bid. By the time she returned with the horses, Charlie had unstaked the corpse and shrouded it with some of the discarded cloth. Kate watched the horses while Charlie dug a shallow grave and buried Mr. McCoy.

Afterward, Charlie came up to her, removed his hat, and wiped the sweat on his brow. "Kate . . ." His gaze moved to Diablo. "You know we'd make much better time if you'd let me—"

At once, she moved to shield her horse. "No way in hell, Charlie Durango."

He sighed explosively. "So be it." He nodded toward the grave. "Reckon we should say something over him?"

She shook her head violently. "Let's just go. I think Mr. McCoy would understand."

A grim silence gripped them as they rode on. Kate kept reliving the horrors of their harrowing discovery. Her sole solace was the memory of Charlie holding her so tenderly and calling her "honey." Indeed, his comfort had been much too sweet . . .

That evening, they camped in a small hollow shaded by mesquite and scrub oaks and sheltering a bubbling spring. Neither had much appetite for the supper of beans and bacon Charlie prepared. Nightfall found them both sipping coffee. Kate stared at the fire, while Charlie sat with his rifle in his lap, warily eyeing the surrounding trees.

"Why'd they have to be that way, the Comanche?" she asked him at last. "I mean, I've heard my share of horror stories about them over the years, but to actually see . . ."

Charlie gazed at her across the flames, seeing the hurt and disillusionment in her beautiful young eyes. Remembering her trembling in his arms earlier today, and the fierce, protective feelings that had surged in him, he wished he could somehow banish her pain. It saddened him to realize there were grim realities in life that he just couldn't shield her from, just as it stunned him to discover the depth of his developing feelings for this headstrong beauty.

"The Comanche culture is different from our own," he began thoughtfully. "Their braves think nothin' of torturing their captives, or even burning them alive. They'd expect the same from us if they was captured."

She shook her head. "Why can't they just be peaceable, like the Alabamas and the Coushatas?"

He gazed off at the rising moon. "The Comanche have always been fierce warriors, just like their brothers, the Kiowas."

She gestured in frustration. "But why'd they have to go and kill Mr. McCoy?"

"I reckon they wanted his goods. To them, it's just the spoils of battle."

"So he got skinned alive for a half-dozen shiny pots, some bolts of cloth, and a few bits of jewelry? It ain't fair! Mr. McCoy didn't do nothin' to them."

"I reckon that's not the way they see it." Charlie sighed and tossed another log on the fire. "You ever heard of the Council House Fight?"

Kate frowned. "Sounds vaguely familiar."

Charlie nodded. "I reckon you weren't even born then, and I was still just a kid. It happened back in 1840, in San Antonio."

"Were you there?" she asked tensely.

He shook his head. "No, but I heard a lot about it from the old timers in Jack Hays' company of the Rangers. During that summer, President Lamar's Indian commissioners arranged a truce with the Comanche chiefs. All the chiefs came to San Antonio for a big peace powwow; they even brought along their wives and a young white captive, Matilda Lockhart. The Comanches aimed to turn Matilda over to the Texans as a gesture of good faith."

Kate stretched toward him with forearms braced

on her knees. "Oh, yes, I think I remember hearing about her. So what happened?"

He stabbed at the fire with a twig. "Seems Matilda had been raped and tortured by the Comanche, and her body was badly mutilated. When she told the Texans about the horrors she had endured, and how the Comanche still held a number of other white captives . . ." Charlie shook his head. "Well, the authorities pretty much went loco on the spot. They up and decided to hold the chiefs for ransom until all the captives were returned."

"Can't say I blame them," Kate muttered.

Charlie laughed ruefully. "Then you know nothing about Indian traditions. To a Comanche, violating a truce is unthinkable. When the Texans moved to surround the chiefs, they resisted violently. Most of the chiefs were killed. The Comanche have been on the warpath against the Texans ever since."

Kate shook her head. "So they think nothing of raping and torturing their captives, but they draw the line at breaking a truce?"

"It's not just that," he continued seriously. "Kate, this entire war has been about stolen land and broken promises. All along, the government has talked out of two sides of its mouth, promising the Comanche land on the one hand, then stealing it away for the settlers on the other. No self-respecting Indian could ever stand for such a violation of his honor. When you cut to the heart of the matter, that's what has caused most of the Indian aggression over the years."

"But the tribes have been officially removed from Texas now."

"True, but the renegade bands are still on the warpath. I reckon that poor peddler ain't the only one who's gonna feel the brunt of their vengeance before it's all over."

Kate shivered as they both fell soberly silent, listening to the snap of the fire and the distant croaking of a bullfrog. At last she dared to ask Charlie the question that had gnawed at her for hours. "What we saw today . . . Was it that way with your kin? I mean, I hope the Comanche didn't . . . ?" She gulped. "Were you there, Charlie?"

He shook his head, but Kate could see the sadness gleaming in his dark eyes. "My parents built their homestead near San Felipe. When I was four, they left me with Grandpa and went off to town for supplies. That's when it happened."

Kate's fingernails dug into her pantsleg. "Did they suffer?" Quickly, she added, "If you don't want to talk about it—"

He held up a hand. "That's all right."

Thinking back, Charlie felt warring emotions surging inside him—remembered anguish, and a peculiar feeling of warmth that this defiant girl actually seemed to care about his past tragedies. He spoke in a low, tense tone. "When I was older, Grandpa told me about it. Guess the Comanche wanted the supplies my folks had bought in town, and I reckon my folks resisted. Pa took an arrow through the heart. He must have gone first. As for Ma—Grandpa said she must have put up quite a fight, for the braves slit her throat on the spot." As Kate gasped in horror, he added grimly, "Usually, the Comanches take white women captive, as slaves and breeders."

Kate glanced away in acute discomfort. "I've heard that they do that. And I'm really sorry about both your parents."

"I reckon you are," he acknowledged tightly.

She gestured passionately. "But what I still don't understand is, how can you not despise the Comanche? I'd think you'd want to shoot every Indian in sight."

His fingers clenched about the stock of his rifle.

"Perhaps you wouldn't feel that way if you'd seen some of the things I have over the years—squaws and Indian children butchered, villages plundered and burned. There's been wrongs on both sides, and I allow there's just too much bitterness in this Indian war for me. Especially in the last two years, both the Cavalry and the Rangers have been out to massacre the Comanche at any cost. That's why I quit scouting redskins for the government."

Kate regarded Charlie curiously, thinking of how much more of life he'd seen than she had. She realized he was a strange, fascinating man—a loner who resisted even the extra baggage of bitter memories. "How long did you fight the Indians anyway?"

"I started almost ten years ago."

Kate was stunned. "Ten years! Hell, mister. You must be pushing thirty!"

He chuckled. "As a matter of fact, I turned thirty in June."

She smirked at him, rather relieved to have the mood lightened between them. "You don't look too long in the tooth for your advanced age."

"Thanks for the compliment, ma'am," he drawled. "And you don't look too feeble for a mouthy sixteen-year-old kid."

"Seventeen," she protested.

"I stand corrected, ma'am."

For a moment, they laughed and shared a feeling of camaraderie. "So you don't fight them Indians no more?" Kate continued.

Charlie shook his head and stoked the fire. "These days, I prefer just tracking outlaws, turning them in and collecting my pay."

"That's what you're doing with me," she pointed out with sudden resentment. "Turning me in for the bounty."

"Only you ain't going back to jail," he teased.

"Ain't I?" she challenged.

He sighed explosively and reached for the coffee-pot, emptying out the grounds. "Look, sister, don't start up again. I'm taking you back to your pa, and that's final."

"And you don't care at all that you're ruining my life?"

"Lady, you wouldn't have a life a'tall if I hadn't come along," he said ruthlessly. "Your sweet little wig would be dangling from a scalp pole right this minute."

At the grisly image, Kate shuddered and glanced away, and Charlie instantly regretted his harsh words.

A tense silence lingered. Watching Kate jump slightly at the distant, ominous sound of a coyote howling, Charlie said placatingly, "Look, Kate, I'm sorry for runnin' at the mouth so crudely. Don't fret overly about the Comanche. The closer we get to Round Rock, the less likely they are to threaten us. By tomorrow afternoon, I reckon we'll be out of their territory. After that, one more night on the trail ought to do it."

Kate nodded, relieved that they were moving away from Indian territory, but still much-sobered at the prospect of returning to Round Rock. She was no closer to her goal of escaping Charlie, and the Comanches were a most unwelcome complication.

Chapter 11

That night, both of them were tense and slept little. Even though her wrists were again tied, Kate was certainly exhausted enough to rest. Yet, following their nightmare of finding Aloysius Mc-Coy's body, she found herself jerking awake at every sound, fearful that renegade Indians could be lurking behind every tree or bush. She observed that Charlie was restless, too, tossing about on his bed-roll across from her and keeping a hand on his rifle all night long.

The next day as they rode double down the twisting trail, both of them were bone-weary and taciturn. Kate kept falling asleep against Charlie's back, and then she'd jerk awake as one of the horses neighed, or a bird called out from a tree.

That evening, they camped in a small, secluded hollow, and both felt somewhat revived after a supper of beans, bacon, and strong coffee. After they cleared up the dishes, Kate watched Charlie roll a smoke. Licking her lips in anticipation, she at last dared to ask, "May I have one?"

His eyebrows shot up. "You smoke?"

She shrugged. "I like to take a drag now and then."

He lit the cigarette and handed it to her with a grin. "Why not?"

Kate savored the taste of the tobacco as Charlie
rolled and lit himself another one. There was something very intimate about having her lips touch the
same spot on the paper where his had been. There
was also something treacherously companionable
about sharing a smoke with him. She realized that
their harrowing experience yesterday had bonded
them somehow, and she found this realization both
fascinating and frightening. The truth was, she
didn't want to feel close to Charlie Durango; she
remained determined to betray him and win her
freedom.

"Where'd you learn to smoke?" Charlie asked after a moment.

"Behind the barn, just like anyone else."

He laughed. "Most females wouldn't be caught
dead behind the barn with the boys."

Kate shrugged. "I ain't a'feared of no menfolk. In
fact, one summer when I was home from boarding
school, I had a smoking contest with six farmboys."
She took a deep draw and grinned. "I turned 'em
all blue."

"I believe it," Charlie said ruefully.

"But don't get the idea that I'm loose," she added
primly. "There's been many a scoundrel who's
made that mistake before and lived to regret it."

Charlie looked her over slowly. "You didn't seem
to find me too unpalatable the other evening,
honey."

She blew out an elaborate smoke ring. "I reckon
I was just enjoying myself. I don't know where
there's a law that says only menfolk can enjoy kiss-
in' and such." She slanted him a feisty look. "If I
hadn't a'cottoned to a smack or two, do you really
think I couldn't of knocked you on your heels,
bounty hunter?"

Charlie threw back his head and laughed. "Katie,
if you don't beat all."

As Kate continued to enjoy her smoke, Charlie snuffed his out, drew out a pack of cards, and began casually shuffling them.

"Why don't you deal, bounty hunter?" she asked.

His dark eyes danced with mischief. "So you gamble, too?"

"I've played a hand or two in my time."

"But don't get the idea that you're loose, right?"

She smirked. "You may be dense, bounty hunter, but you're gettin' the general idear."

"Do you always win at poker, too, like you done at smokin' contests?" he teased.

She shot him a look of pure challenge. "I might just win my freedom from you."

"Oh, honey," he said gravely as he dealt the cards. "That's one thing I'd never put on the table."

They played a few hands of five card stud, using matches as poker chips. The score was three to two in Kate's favor when her turn again came up to deal. She was concentrating fiercely on her shuffling when an owl swooped down from a high limb directly above them. As the huge bird dove within inches of their heads before it soared off, Kate started, sending a cascade of fifty two cards shooting into the air.

Her display was comic, yet Charlie's expression couldn't have been more sober as he reached out and touched her hand. "Hey, easy Kate. It was only an owl taking off to go huntin'."

She shivered and began grimly gathering up the cards. "I guess after yesterday, I'm still about ready to pop my cork over them Injuns."

"I know. But I figure we're just about out of Comanche territory by now. Besides," he went on in a lighter tone, "if we do meet up with any renegades, I figure you and me can handle them."

Unwittingly, she smiled. "Do you now?"

He winked at her. "From what your pa told me, you'll probably roast them all at the stake."

Kate chuckled, despite herself. "So my pa told you I burned down the boarding school?"

"Yep," Charlie replied.

"I warrant he didn't tell you why," she continued, her chin coming up slightly.

"Nope, he didn't."

She crossed her arms over her chest in a familiar, defensive attitude. "That's 'cause he don't never listen to me."

Charlie was silent for a long moment. Then he whispered, "I'm listening, honey."

Kate glanced over at him. He had reclined on his elbow with his long legs crossed; he looked sleek and muscled and magnificently male. The intent gleam in his dark eyes made her heart leap. Lord, he was such an appealing man—and doubtless, equally dangerous!

Fighting her own traitorous response to him, she shrugged her shoulders and replied, "You don't want to know."

"Sure, I do."

To Kate's surprise, she found herself spilling out to Charlie the entire story of Mrs. Eberhard's cruelty and her own subsequent, rash actions. He listened to her account in fascinated silence, not even stopping her to ask a question.

When Kate finished her tale, she stared at Charlie uncertainly. He was still regarding her with a mixture of amusement and amazement, though she felt certain that criticism was bound to follow. Actually, she had to admit that her story of unholy retribution sounded pretty awful, even to her own ears.

After a moment, she spoke tentatively. "Mrs. Eberhard—she was a battle-ax straight from hell, all right. But what I did—burning down her boarding school—that was pretty bad, huh?"

To Kate's astonishment and delight, Charlie threw

back his head and laughed. "Hell, honey, if it'd been me, I would have shot the old bitch."

For a moment, Kate stared at Charlie in utter disbelief. Then she laughed too, laughed until her eyes teared and she was sure her sides would split. She felt so close to Charlie in that moment, and she realized that she'd never before known anyone like him. She had expected outrage and condemnation from him, but had received understanding and kinship instead. She realized with awe that Charlie Durango was the first person she'd ever met who accepted her just the way she was. Maybe it was because they were so much alike, she thought—both of them loners, and fiercely independent.

But then, she didn't want his acceptance, or his approval, she added to herself with angry reproach. She wanted to snare this bounty hunter in his own trap, to exploit his feelings in order to escape, just as he was exploiting her to collect his bounty. Damn it, she mustn't let her softer feminine nature get in the way!

Still, outwardly, she played along with the mood of congeniality building between them. "You know you're a strange man, Charlie Durango."

"Strange in what way?"

"You're hard as nails, just like my pa. But you don't seem to mind the way I am."

He shrugged. "I just happen to admire a woman with spunk."

"And you wouldn't want to change me?" she challenged.

"Naw, I wouldn't want to change you." With a solemn grin, he added, "That's up to your pa."

Kate glanced away with sudden resentment and the magical mood between them evaporated.

After playing a few more hands, they retired for the night. Charlie again bound Kate's wrists, securing the thong to a nearby, sturdy juniper bush. The exhaustion of the last day and a half overtook her, and she drifted deeply to sleep.

The middle of the night found Kate caught in the grip of a hideous nightmare. Savage Indians had staked her out on the prairie and were about to skin her alive and set her afire. Watching the braves circle her with their painted faces and wickedly sharp knives, she screamed and screamed, until her terror was smothered by a brutal hand—

"Kate! Kate! Hush now, honey. It's Charlie."

She awakened to find herself clutched in Charlie's arms beneath the full moon. His hand was clamped hard on her mouth; her heart was pounding so fiercely, she feared it would burst.

"You gonna stop screaming now?" he asked her gently, his dark features taut with worry and alarm. "I don't mean to hurt you, honey, but I can't have you waking every Injun in a hundred square miles."

Kate nodded tremulously, and Charlie released her mouth.

"Oh, Charlie, it was awful," she sobbed, gasping for breath. "The Indians had captured me. They were gonna skin me alive and burn me. My hands and feet were tied—"

"Damnation!" Charlie cursed, reaching for his knife. "No wonder you're having nightmares, with your hands tied like this . . ." He quickly cut her wrists free.

Heedless of the fact that she was dressed only in her underwear, and he wore just his trousers, Kate flung her arms around Charlie's neck and clung to his bare chest. "It wasn't the bindings on my wrists, Charlie. It was what we saw yesterday. I've tried not to think about it, but I guess it finally caught up with me."

"I know, darlin'. I know." Gently, he caressed her back.

"Oh, Charlie, hold me," she whispered.

"I ain't going nowhere, honey."

Indeed, feeling the sweet sobs and shudders seizing Kate, Charlie was lost. His heart ached for the anguish and terrors this innocent girl had known, both yesterday on the trail and tonight during her nightmare. He knew he couldn't banish the harrowing images from her mind forever, but at least he could offer her some comfort . . .

His arms tightened about her, and he buried his face in the dusky silk of her hair. Lord, she felt so soft, so sweet, so heavenly. She smelled of wildflowers and the crisp spring where they had both washed up before supper. The ripe curves of her breasts tantalized his bare chest, and her damp face was pressed trustingly against the hollow of his throat.

An unfamiliar emotion tugged at Charlie's heart. Kate was such a contradiction. The girl/woman he held in his arms was brave and defiant, yet vulnerable and fragile, too. She maddened him, she fascinated him. More than anything, she made him want to shield her from all harm forever. Though he knew it was wrong, he had to have more of her.

"Look at me, sugar," he coaxed.

When Kate turned her beautiful, tear-streaked face up to him, Charlie could take no more. He leaned over and smothered Kate's lush lips with his own. When he tasted her tears, he wanted to drown in her. He thrust his tongue deeply into the warm nectar of her mouth.

Kate moaned, kissing Charlie back with all her being. Oh, how she needed him tonight, right this minute! Her nightmare had been hell, and Charlie's kiss was the blessed salvation that would let her tortured mind forget. As their tongues plunged, ravished and mated, sweet, savage yearnings consumed her. She felt giddy all over—every inch of her alive and hungry for Charlie. As he clutched her ever closer, her nipples tautened against the rough pressure of his chest, and she rubbed her chemise-clad breast against him in shameless invitation—

With a fierce, possessive movement, Charlie pulled Kate astride him, setting her knees widely apart on either side of his hips. He kissed her as if he wanted to climb inside her—and oh, Lord a'mighty, he did!

Kate was captivated by Charlie, losing herself in the wonder of his nearness, the scorching wildfire of his kisses. She ran her hands boldly over the planes and textures of his muscled back, loving the tremor that seized him at her touch. Her womanly center was pressed baldly against his bulging manhood, yet she felt no shame, only fiercest excitement. When his strong hands gripped her bottom and guided her against him more tightly, she reeled with delight. She could feel pangs of arousal deep within her, like bold, relentless fingers, making her throb and ache for him . . .

"Oh, Kate," he whispered, leaning over to nibble on her bare shoulder. "Kate . . . God, woman, you do fire my blood."

Kate responded by nipping his lower lip wantonly, even as she arched her hips against his. Charlie murmured a rough endearment and stroked her breasts. At the erotic stimulation, she panted ecstatically, and he rewarded her with a savage, deep kiss. His loins thrust against her with a provocative rhythm that shocked and enthralled her. All at once, Kate knew it would be the most natural thing in the world to have him bury his vast hardness deep inside her. Indeed, she wanted him to, badly. Fascinated by the thought, she drew her fingers down his chest, then lower, past his waist . . .

To her surprise and disappointment, Charlie shoved her out of his lap almost roughly. For a moment, they knelt facing each other on her bedroll, both breathing hard. Charlie looked so tense that Kate was surprised he didn't snap in two right before her eyes.

She reached out to stroke the rough texture of his jaw. "Charlie—"

After snatching her hand away, he held her at arm's length, his hands trembling on her shoulders. "Kate . . . Honey, we've got to stop."

"But why?" she asked in bewilderment.

"Why?" He pulled his fingers distractedly through his hair. "Lordy. Don't tell me I've got to learn you how babies is made now."

Kate giggled. "Charlie, I was reared up on a ranch."

Charlie frowned at her. "Well, I'm relieved to hear it." His gaze narrowed. "I think."

She stared up at him dreamily. "Charlie, would you marry me?"

"What?" He appeared stunned and highly agitated. "What makes you go and ask a fool thing like that?"

She shrugged. "I was just wondering."

"Well, what a thing to be just wondering," he retorted indignantly. "So you up and ask me, like you'd say, 'How's the weather?' "

She chuckled. "Somethin' like that."

He glowered at her. "Do you go around asking every man you meet if he'd marry you?"

"No." She grinned. "You're my first."

For an unguarded moment, he grinned back at her. Then his expression darkened with suspicion and he shook a finger at her. "This is all about your pa, ain't it? You're bound and determined not to accept the man he chose. You just can't let him tell you what to do, can you?"

"Well, can you blame me?" As his scowl deepened, she smiled coyly and added, "Besides, you ain't bad to look at, even if you are pushing thirty."

"I *am* thirty! And if you ain't the most exasperating female I've ever met."

"You haven't answered my question," she teased.

Charlie crossed his arms over his chest and set his chin stubbornly. "The answer is no. I ain't interested in helping you win no battles with your pa."

Now Kate was indignant, too. "Then why did you go and kiss me and pull me into your lap just now? You were as bold as a bull in season. I was sure that at any minute you was gonna unhitch my drawers and have your wicked way with me."

Charlie's jaw dropped, and he blinked at Kate. "Tarnation, woman. Do you up and say any blamed thing that comes to your mind?"

She nodded. "Pretty much."

He threw up his hands. "Well, if this don't beat all."

"You still ain't told me why you kissed me like that," she said with a pout.

He smiled nastily. "Didn't you say you was raised up on a ranch? And didn't you call me a bull in season? So tell me, does the bull go fetch the preacher before he takes out after a biddable heifer? Or do I have to spell that out, too?"

"Oh, you no-good sidewinder!" Furious, Kate shoved him away. "Get the hell out of my sight."

"My pleasure." He pushed her down and began binding her wrists again.

"You brute!" she cried, struggling with him. "I might'a known you'd tie me up again."

He subdued her easily, straddling her as he wound the thong around her wrists. "You want to share my bedroll, honey?" he sneered.

"I ain't no two-bit whore, Durango," she spat at him.

To her surprise, Charlie gripped her shoulders,

and his eyes blazed with indignation. "I never said you was no whore, Kate."

"No! You only said you wanted to have your way with me without benefit of marriage!"

"And you didn't want to take advantage of me a'tall, did you now, woman?" he accused hotly.

"Oh, leave me be!"

Having finished his task, Charlie cursed under his breath and strode off to his bedroll.

Kate blinked at tears in the darkness. She cursed herself a fool for ever opening her big mouth to Charlie without thinking.

Sure, she'd felt close to him when he'd comforted her following her nightmare. But that was no excuse to go plumb loco and ask the man to marry her—even if wedding this stranger would spite Pa. The fact was, she'd left herself wide open to having her pride stomped in the dirt, and Charlie Durango had tramped all over her feelings with both boots.

Well, she wouldn't make the same mistake twice, that was for damn sure. She had to remember the type of man Charlie was—obviously, not the marrying kind. He was a bounty hunter, a no-good tumbleweed, the kind of man used to long trails and loose women. If she let him have his way with her, to him she'd only be one more notch on his bedpost. Hell, the man didn't even own a bedpost!

And why should she want to marry him, anyway? His kisses might be hot, sweet, and delicious, but marriage was forever. Marriage would mean being saddled with that no-good saddle tramp for life, having his young'uns, scrubbing his floors, and cooking his meals. A pack mule probably had a better life, when she thought about it.

Kate realized that just a few, seductive moments in the moonlight had almost made her lose sight of her own priorities. Charlie wasn't her friend—he was her enemy. Charlie wanted her pa's money—she wanted her freedom. Any action she took which strayed from her goal would only defeat her own purpose.

So, if she kissed Charlie again, it would be only to secure his trust, to get him to drop his guard. If she brought up the subject of marriage again, it would be strictly to achieve her own ends—namely, escape.

This was war. And there was no place in war for the treachery of romantic feelings . . .

Chapter 12

The next morning, Charlie was terse and uncommunicative around Kate. He was so impatient to get them back on the trail that he actually yelled at her as she washed out the coffee pot at the spring. With great restraint, Kate managed not to hurl the potful of cold water in his face.

Moments later, as Charlie pulled Kate up behind him on his palomino, she studied his grim expression and wondered what was stuck in his craw. Obviously, her questions about marriage last night had put him off.

At least she now knew the lay of the land between them. She mulled over her options morosely as they plodded down the trail. At the rate they were going, they were bound to reach Round Rock before noon tomorrow, and Charlie had already made it clear that he wasn't going to help her. Oh, he wouldn't mind bedding down with her, but he'd feel no obligation to marry her afterward. The scoundrel!

Kate knew that her only remaining choice was escape. A needle of fear pricked her at the thought. After glimpsing Aloysius McCoy's fate, could she really be such a fool as to venture forth on her own again?

Yet she'd managed to evade the Comanches before, her more independent nature reminded her.

And surely McCoy had made himself a sitting target by going straight down the public trace in his fire-red wagon, with all his valuable merchandise dangling about to tempt the Indians. After all, the Comanche had yet to bother her and Charlie. If she just took care, perhaps even plotted her own trail, surely she'd be safe.

She nodded to herself in grim resolution. Would she let fear keep her from doing what she must? Could she let Pa win? Never!

Then practical considerations flitted to mind. Getting away would not be easy. She'd have to give Charlie the slip, and probably steal his horse, as well. She shuddered at his imagined response. He set such store by that horse. Hell, he spent at least an hour each evening currying Corona. He'd be mad enough to spit fire when he discovered that she'd up and turned horse thief.

And would it be fair to leave Charlie alone on the trail, with only her own lame horse? Could she even bear to leave Diablo with him? Could she trust Charlie not to shoot the stallion out of spite?

Maybe it wouldn't be so bad for Charlie, she rationalized. If she gave him the slip tonight, by then they'd be well out of Indian territory. They'd also be close enough to Round Rock that he could either walk back to town, or buy himself another horse at a nearby farm or ranch.

Then she would simply have to pray that he wouldn't come after her! Of course, if her plan worked, she'd gain a big head start on him. Still, if he should catch up with her, she feared his retribution more than she feared the savage Indians.

But the first problem remained, how would she give Charlie the slip? Remembering their romantic tryst in the moonlight last night, Kate felt her face bloom with high color. She knew the bounty hunter wanted her, even if he wasn't prepared to give her his name. Still, his desire for her was her only weapon now, and she would use that weapon to her ultimate advantage.

As to the particulars, she had all day to ponder . . .

Charlie, too, was lost in deep thought as they proceeded down the trail. His moments with Kate in the moonlight last night had thrilled him deeply, but her callous words afterward had cut him to the quick. She'd seemed to reduce the magic between them to little more than breeding rites, and she'd even admitted that she would consider marriage with him only to get even with her pa.

What a vengeful little vixen this girl had turned out to be! Short days ago, Charlie had felt determined to have Kate on any terms. But now the rules had changed. He'd scoffed at her offer of marriage, because he refused to become a pawn in her game of revenge against her pa. Like anyone else, he wanted to be wanted for himself.

Could he ever truly win Kate's love, her respect? Maybe not, but he would for damn sure have her on his own terms.

Charlie smiled as he thought of the maddening truth Kate would discover as soon as they returned to Round Rock. Ultimately, retribution would be denied her. For he would turn the tables on this feisty female, and then true revenge would be all his . . .

Toward mid-afternoon, they left the wide prairie and moved back into the gently rolling terrain closer to Round Rock. The woods abounded with game— foxes, squirrels, deer, and boar. Charlie shot a wild turkey for their supper and tied the bird to his saddle straps.

They stopped for the evening next to a beautiful, clear branch of the San Gabriel river. The shallow waters were shaded by river willows; a lovely small waterfall cascaded from a rocky ridge. Fat dragon-flies buzzed at the waters, and the air was thick with the crisp scent of the river and the duskier smell of damp vegetation.

Kate was entranced by the scene. She plucked and cleaned the turkey while Charlie built a fire. He then skewered the bird with a sharp branch and sus-pended it above the flames by balancing the branch on rocks he'd stacked on either side of the blaze.

While the tantalizing aroma of roasting wild game filled the air, Kate went to the river and gathered wild watercress and onions. Back at camp, she knelt on the ground, rummaging through Charlie's saddle bags for rice.

He seemed to have everything but what she needed—a tin of tobacco, a sack of beans, a cake of soap, and even a bottle of liniment. Then, to her surprise and apprehension, her hand closed on her own pistol!

Kate's heart beat explosively at her discovery. She was pondering what she should do when she heard a male voice.

"Lookin' for somethin', darlin'?"

With her fingers still gripping the pistol, Kate stared up the long, hard frame of Charlie Durango. He was gazing down at her with dark eyes keenly focused; his firing hand was poised close to his holstered Colt.

Kate gulped. "I was just hunting for fixins' for supper."

Charlie hunkered down beside her and reached inside the saddle bag. Kate barely had time to snatch her fingers away before he grabbed her Colt and pulled it out. Holding the pistol barrel-down, he asked with soft menace, "Lookin' for this, Kate?"

She shook her head violently, her wide, guilty eyes meeting his.

"You ain't much of a liar, honey," he drawled.

"I was looking for rice!" she retorted.

He chuckled dryly, reaching into the bag and pulling out a small packet. He tossed the bag into her lap. "You'd best ask next time, Kate, before you go rifling through my things," he warned.

As Charlie stood, shoved her gun into his belt and strode off, Kate pulled a nasty face at his retreating back. Damn! She hadn't realized he'd kept her gun in his saddle bags all this time! If only he hadn't spotted her at that critical moment, she might have gotten the drop on him—

Then she sobered as second thoughts assailed her. She remembered glimpsing Charlie's fingers poised so close to his gun. Doubtless, he could have drawn his pistol and shot her quicker than she could have pulled her own trigger. She shuddered. The last thing she needed was to get into a shootout with Charlie Durango—she'd be sure to come out on the losing end. Her only hope was to escape him by stealth—

Or by seduction. She smiled grimly as she remembered the plan she'd concocted while out on the trail today. She'd best be about it.

Kate cooked up the rice, flavoring it with the wild onions and watercress. Charlie complimented her on her cooking as they ate their hearty supper. The wild turkey was roasted to perfection, and the coffee Charlie made was rich and strong. After they ate, Charlie rolled cigarettes for them both. They puffed away contentedly, then washed up the dishes in the river.

Once everything was tidied, Kate took the cake of soap they'd used for the dishes and approached Charlie. He sat with his back propped against a tree, smoking another cigarette.

"Think I'll go down near the waterfall, take a bath, and wash out my clothes," she told him casually.

He regarded her with mingled surprise and suspicion. "You gettin' all gussied up just to go back and see your pa?"

She shrugged. "After three days on the trail, I'd just like to feel clean."

He grinned, then cleared his throat. "If you're washing all your clothes, what are you gonna wear afterward?"

She smiled. "I thought about your shirt. You know, it could use a scrubbing, too."

His eyebrows shot up. "You gonna wash it while you're wearing it?"

"Why not?"

Grinning ruefully, Charlie stood and snuffed out his smoke. He unbuttoned his shirt and handed it to her. She felt an unsettling blush heat her cheeks as she stared at the beautiful, tanned lines of his chest. His muscles rippled under skin that gleamed like polished bronze, and the hair dusting his chest and arms was crisp and dark. Moving her gaze upward, she noted that he no longer wore a bandage, and his gunshot wound was healing nicely. No thanks to her, she mused ruefully. His neck was strong and corded, and the heavy coating of whiskers along his jaw lent him a dangerous air.

A quizzical smile lit his face at her perusal. "Maybe when you're finished, I'll wash up, too," he said softly.

Kate shrugged with bravado. "Suit yourself."

As she started down the trail, he scolded, "Don't venture too far away from camp now. You wouldn't try to give me the slip again, now would you, honey?"

She slanted him a defiant glance over her shoulder. "Not if you agree not to watch me."

He chuckled. "You got a deal."

Kate walked down toward the deeper end of the river and undressed behind a bush. After she'd removed all her clothing, she donned Charlie's shirt.

She restrained a shiver as the rough chambray rubbed against her bare breasts. Wearing his shirt seemed so intimate—it was almost as if Charlie himself were touching her. Indeed, she could smell his essence on the shirt—tobacco, sweat, and pure man.

Kneeling next to the water, Kate wet her clothing then scrubbed everything vigorously on a flat boulder. After rinsing the garments and hanging them out to dry on bushes, she waded into the waist-deep water with soap in hand, still wearing Charlie's shirt. The sand on the river bottom felt wonderful against her toes, and the cool current flowed deliciously against her bare thighs. She glanced about with a smile. The sunset was beautiful, the waters liquid gold and leaf-dappled. The waterfall was a feast for her eyes as it poured down from the cliff and flared outward in a rainbow of light; the sound of it was sweet music to her ears. In this pastoral setting, she felt her taut nerves beginning to relax.

Humming a chorus of Foster's "Oh! Susanna," Kate wet herself from head to toe, lathered her hair, scrubbed Charlie's shirt, then soaped her body. After rinsing off, she was feeling gloriously refreshed until she looked up to see Charlie standing on the bank staring boldly down at her—

"Charlie Durango, you no-good skunk! You promised not to watch me!"

He chuckled as he crossed his arms over his bare chest. "You sounded like you was having so much fun down here, darlin', that I decided to join you."

"You snake!"

"Hell, honey, I just want to be clean, too."

Kate gulped as she watched Charlie unbuckle his gunbelt, lay both shooting irons down on the ground, then begin unbuttoning his trousers. "You're not going to—"

His purely wicked grin stopped her in mid-sentence. "If I was you, Miss Kate, I'd be lookin' the other way."

Smothering an indignant cry, Kate did as he bid. Oh, he was such an infuriating scoundrel! Even if he was placing himself just where she wanted him to be right now. A moment later, she heard him splash into the river, moving ever closer—

"You want to scrub my back, sugar?" a husky voice asked.

Her heart pounding, Kate turned to see Charlie standing next to her, looking unspeakably sensual with water dripping from his muscled arms and bare chest. His thick black hair curled wetly about his face and the nape of his neck. His eyes were sharply focused, dark as onyx as they studied her. Lord! He looked as charming, purposeful, and lethal as the devil himself!

In a squeaky, faltering voice, she protested, "Just because I came down here to bathe doesn't give you call to—"

His throaty chuckle interrupted her. "You started this, Kate. Either you scrub my back, or I might just insist on another kiss."

"Oh, you villain!" But as he laughed and turned his back to her, she dutifully ran the soap over his strong, corded muscles. His skin felt so fine beneath her fingertips that she realized she felt sorely tempted to kiss his smoothly textured shoulder.

Heavens to Betsy, what was wrong with her? She warned herself that this was the man she planned shortly to betray—yet the admonition had little effect on her wayward senses. Struggling to distract herself, she began to soap his hair—

A moment later, Charlie howled in pain and turned to her, squinting. "Damn it, woman, you plumb got soap in my eyes!"

He hastily dipped his head beneath the surface, and Kate chuckled at the sight. He came up glowering and spitting out water. "You did that on purpose!" he accused.

"Did not!"

He grabbed the hand that held the soap. "If you don't do a better job of soaping my front, I'm gonna dunk you but good."

Kate gulped as she looked down the hair-covered expanse of Charlie's chest, to where the river shielded the rest of his charms from view. She knew he was utterly naked beneath the water, and suddenly, the thought of touching his front so intimately made her shiver.

"Why all of a sudden am I your slave?" she protested.

He laughed. "Honey, I'll be glad to soap you down any time—front, back, and in between." He wiggled his eyebrows devilishly. "Especially there. Just take off that shirt, and let's make us some suds."

At his audacious offer, Kate's face burned, even as excitement raced along her nerve endings. "No way in hell, Durango!"

"Then you'd best get busy soaping me, 'cause I ain't leavin' this pond until I'm scrubbed right good."

Gritting her teeth at the maddening rogue standing next to her, Kate realized she was trapped. Yet maybe he was trapped, too, her more calculating nature added—*if* she played her cards right.

Drawing an unsteady breath, she drew the cake of soap tentatively down Charlie's chest, over his thick muscles and rough tufts of hair. At her touch, Charlie's breathing quickened and his dark gaze flashed to her face; the stark intensity of his expression made her dizzy.

As she moved the soap toward his stomach, she gasped as her hand brushed something hard, long, and smooth.

"Lower, honey," he whispered.

Even as Kate glanced up at him in horror, Charlie grabbed her hand. The soap went floating off as he guided her fingers to his erection. Kate gasped, both appalled and fascinated. She watched Charlie's dark face duck toward hers, and then her senses reeled with his scorching kiss—

Charlie's lips coaxed, seduced, and mastered hers. When her lips unwittingly parted on a soft gasp, he stole her breath away, boldly sucking her tongue deep inside his mouth. Kate staggered against him, a lightning bolt of sensuality shooting straight through to her womanly center. Sweet heavens, she could not bear it! Charlie was kissing her with ravishing, violent hunger, all the while holding her hand tightly against his throbbing shaft.

At last Kate wrenched her mouth away from his, staring up at him with mingled desire and fear. Charlie smiled back, his eyes gleaming with dark sensuality. "Come closer, sugar," he coaxed. "There's a part of me that's just bustin' to meet a part of you."

Kate shook her head vehemently and somehow managed to snatch her fingers free from his tantalizing manhood. She held her arms protectively about her breasts and shivered.

Charlie frowned as he sensed her trepidation. "Hey, honey, I didn't mean to spook you."

"Well, you sure as hell could have fooled me."

His expression darkened to one of utter solemnity, and he reached out to stroke her cheek gently. "I wouldn't try to force nothing on you, Kate."

She bit her lip. "Charlie, would you please just leave me be?"

"Sure that's what you want, honey?"

She nodded.

He sighed resignedly. Moving off, he found the soap, which had gotten snagged in some onion sprouts near the bank. He returned, placing the cake in her hand. "Scrub real good now," he teased with a lascivious wink.

As he turned to leave her, she cleared her throat noisily. "If you leave your trousers and socks on the rock, I'll scrub them out." As he raised his dark brows at her, she added primly, "You can wash out your own drawers."

He winked at her. "I don't wear no drawers."

Kate blushed crimson. "You got somethin' else to wear back to camp?"

"You mean you wouldn't want to watch me prance about in the altogether?"

"That's exactly what I mean." Kate's voice trembled on the outraged words.

He chuckled. "I've got another pair of trousers in my pack."

"See that you put them on."

"Yes, ma'am," he said with a mock salute.

Kate tried to look the other way as Charlie left the pond. But as he climbed out of the water, she couldn't seem to help herself—she stared shamelessly at the gilded muscles of his back, the sinewy lines of his taut buttocks and long legs. Heavens, he was a magnificent man! Remembering how she'd held his swollen shaft in her fingers—recalling how she hadn't really wanted to pull away—she felt shame and a fierce, primal excitement storming her senses. A tenacious need had settled between her thighs, a hot aching that she knew the cool river waters could never extinguish. Only one man could quench that—and, for her own good, she'd best get as far away from him as possible!

Kate was still feeling giddy when she moved over to the rock to scrub and rinse Charlie's trousers and socks. With trembling fingers, she hung his garments to dry next to hers. Dusk was falling by the time she headed back to camp in Charlie's still-dripping chambray shirt.

Charlie turned as she entered the clearing. He wore a clean pair of tan trousers. His chest was still bare and his hair curled damply around his face. His gaze roved over her in the wet shirt and he whistled. "Damn, to be in that shirt right now . . ." As she flushed and glanced away in embarrassment, he stroked his rough jaw. "Bring me that soap, honey. Reckon I'll shave while there's still some light left."

Moving closer tentatively, Kate was surprised to watch Charlie pull a comb from his pocket. "Looks like you could use this."

"Thanks," she muttered.

They exchanged the items, and Kate hurried off. She spread out her bedroll, sat down, and combed out her hair as she warily watched him shave. He slanted occasional furtive glances her way.

Kate still wondered at the sensual moments they'd spent together in the river. Actually, that interlude should fit in well with her overall scheme—if she could remain cool-headed enough not to succumb to her own invention!

As he shaved, Charlie was also thinking of his moments with Kate in the river. He'd stunned himself with his own audacity, and he hoped he hadn't scared the girl off for good. But she'd looked so fetching standing there with his wet shirt clinging to her ripe curves. Her nipples had been so tight, as if begging for his mouth, and he'd known by the way she'd shivered and gasped that she had wanted him. He'd longed to pull her to the mossy bank and cover her with himself, burying himself in her tightness until she cried out for mercy.

When she'd soaped him with her tantalizing fingers, it had been more than he could bear. But pressing her hand to his . . . Well, that had been a mite too bold, perhaps.

Charlie realized he'd been without a female far too long. There had been a sweet young filly, Rosa, back at Lupe's Cantina in San Antonio, who granted her favors only to him. But he hadn't visited the pretty barmaid in a month of Sundays.

Kate was different, of course, he reminded himself. She was the woman he would wed.

Would it be such a crime to sample her charms first? The idea tantalized him, distracting him so that he nicked himself with the razor. He cursed vividly and rubbed his stinging flesh. When he finished, he dried his face and stared at Kate in the deepening dusk—

She was seated cross legged on her bedroll. Scrubbed clean, her face was a vision—delicate and beautiful, the skin rosy-hued. Her damp hair curled in vibrant waves around her face, neck, and shoulders. His shirt, also still damp, outlined her shapely breasts and tiny waist—the tails shielded the lovely, forbidden territory between her thighs. Her legs were long and supple, the flesh pearly white. Even her toes looked delectable enough to chew on!

Damn, but she was fine . . . Suddenly, it didn't matter to him whether or not she might be taking advantage of him to win some point with her pa. He just wanted those lovely bare legs wrapped tight around him.

Catching Charlie's gaze, Kate stood, walked over, and awkwardly handed him back his comb. "I'm finished now."

His hand caught her wrist. "Are we finished now, Kate?"

Dropping the comb, Kate stared at him. Charlie caught her chin in his strong grip and gazed down at her trembling mouth and vulnerable expression. The air between them seemed to sizzle with sensuality.

Weakly, she protested, "Charlie, don't—"

"Damned, if you ain't too sweet to resist."

Charlie leaned over and kissed her again. The heat of his lips swamped her; the scent of soap filled her senses, along with the smoothness of his freshly shaven cheek rubbing against her own. As she kissed him back tentatively, she felt a shudder seize him; she heard a groan rise in his throat. But before his arms could move to envelop her, she jerked away.

They stood staring at each other for a charged, wary moment. An owl hooted in the distance; Charlie glanced off at the western horizon.

"Reckon night will fall any minute now," he said in a tight voice. "Guess I'll have to tie you up, Kate."

She shot him a pleading glance. "Charlie, please can't we sit by the fire and talk for a few moments first?"

He hesitated a moment. "I reckon it won't do no harm," he conceded at last.

For a while, they sat on opposite sides of the fading fire, stealing glances at each other. Soon, the tension became unbearable to Kate. "Talk to me, Charlie," she murmured.

He raised an eyebrow. "What do you want me to say?"

She shrugged. "Oh, I don't know. Tell me about the desperadoes you've tracked down in the past."

His expression grew guarded. "What about them?"

"Tell me how you got started bounty hunting."

He frowned. "It ain't a pretty story."

"Please, I really want to know."

He was quiet a moment. "I got started about five years ago, in San Antone. I'd gotten in the habit of visiting a certain señorita there, in her *casita* just off Market Square."

"Did you, now?" Though her words were casual,

Kate was astonished by the jealousy that suddenly flooded her.

"Yeah." Charlie's expression grew grim, his voice cold and flat. "Only one day, when I come acallin', I found her on the bed beaten to a pulp, with a knife sticking out of her back."

"Oh, my God!" Kate gasped. "Who did it?"

Charlie sighed, stretching toward her and resting his arms on his raised knees. "A bastard by the name of Wild Eyed Willy. One of the neighbors had seen him hightailin' it outta there. Anyhow, the company of Rangers I was with had just broke up, so I did me some investigating on my own. Come to find out old Wild Eyed Willy was wanted for rape, murder, and bank robbery in three different states."

"My God! So what did you do?"

"It took me over three months, but I tracked the varmint down, killed him, then turned him in for the bounty." Charlie grinned. "Lordy, did he stink by the time I turned him in to the Federal Marshal in Fort Worth. After that, word got out that I would do any job, no matter how dirty, for the right price, and lawmen began looking me up. That's pretty much how I've supported myself these last five years—aside from a few junkets of Indian fighting with the Rangers."

"So you kill men for the reward money?"

He glanced at her and said coolly, "Dead or alive, it don't make no never mind to me."

The coldness of his tone and the hard glint in his eyes, sent a shiver down Kate's spine. Sometimes, it was so difficult to understand Charlie Durango. Right now, it was hard to believe there was any gentleness in this man—it would be impossible, in fact, if she did not already know better. For this man had listened to her sympathetically, had comforted her tenderly, had kissed and held her. Still, after hearing his account, she couldn't help but think twice about her own plans to cross him.

"How does it feel to kill a man?" she asked quietly.

He snapped a twig in his hand, and his eyes blazed with an emotion she couldn't quite identify. "It don't feel like nothin', cause it ain't nothin' being killed." Watching her flinch, he added, "I ain't never shot a man who didn't deserve to die, Kate. They've all been like Wild Eyed Willy—mongrels who come out of nowhere, killing and raping and plundering the land. The one I just turned in—the Hondo Kid—he up and slit his own parents' throats for the gold coins buried under their floorboards. You think I shed a single tear when he swung from the gallows in Fort Worth?"

"You sound very bitter," she said.

He tossed the pieces of the twig into the fire. "Maybe I just see things like they really are. I ain't lived no sheltered life."

Her chin came up. "And you're saying I have?"

"Compared to me, yes."

Kate glanced away. She couldn't deny his words. Frowning, she murmured, "You must have loved her a lot."

"Loved who?"

She stared at him. "That woman back in San Antonio. The one who got you started bounty hunting."

He shrugged. "I've always said what's right is right."

"So you're a man committed to justice, not revenge?"

He smiled enigmatically. "Let's just say I know about as much about justice as you know about revenge."

Unwittingly, she smiled back. "You still didn't tell me if you loved that woman."

His dark eyes twinkled. "How come you're so interested?"

She feigned a wounded air. "After your behavior at the pond, you can ask that?"

"There have been many women, Kate," he said with a shrug.

"And you want me to be just another one."

He stared at her. "Sugar, if you think you're just another woman, come over here and we'll clear that up real quick."

She glanced away, secretly fascinated. In a shaky voice, she said, "You can say that, Charlie Durango, but a tumbleweed like you can't do no more than kiss and run."

To her surprise, he laughed, lacing his fingers together behind his head. "Now, what would you know about a tumbleweed like me?" He winked at her. "I might just be full of surprises, darlin.' "

"Then why don't you surprise me," she put in impulsively.

"Meaning what?"

She stared him straight in the eye. "Why don't you just let me go?"

Wearing an expression of utter disgust, Charlie heaved himself to his feet and brushed off his trousers. "I might have known this was a'comin'—again."

She struggled up to face him. "You say you have a sense of justice," she argued passionately. "Well, you can't think that what you're doing to me is right."

"Damn tootin', it's right!" Charlie retorted, waving a finger at her. "You're just a spoiled brat who's gotten way too big for her own britches. Jeb Maloney is your pa, and you're bound to obey him."

She balled her hands on her hips. "And am I bound to marry a man I hate?"

A muscle worked in his jaw. "You ain't never

even met that man. Are you gonna start spouting them ridiculous lies again? Well, don't bother, sugar, 'cause I ain't listening.''

"Charlie, please let me go,'' she pleaded.

"No.''

They stood facing each other in the darkness, both breathing hard, totally at odds with each other. In the distance, a coyote began to howl.

At last, Charlie crossed over to her side and roughly took her hand. "Kate, it's time. You know I've got to tie you up for the night.''

"Charlie, please don't,'' she begged.

He gestured in frustration. "Just what are you suggesting as an alternative?''

She stepped closer, looking up at him with wide-eyed innocence. "I could sleep with you.''

Charlie groaned, looking down at the glorious creature standing before him, her angel perfect features and wild, curling hair outlined in the soft moonlight. "Damn, but you're good,'' he murmured cynically. "One minute, you beg me to let you go, then when I flat refuse, you sidle up to me like some filly in heat. Do you take me for an idiot, woman?''

"No,'' she murmured sincerely. "I just don't want to be tied up again.'' Licking her lower lip with deliberate sensuality, she added, "Besides, if you're holding me, how could I escape?''

Charlie groaned, reaching out to stroke that lush, wet underlip with his index finger. "If we play this little game, Kate,'' he warned tightly, "you know damn well exactly how it's going to end.''

Despite his admonition, she moved even closer, reaching out to touch his bare arm. She felt the muscles jerk beneath her fingertips. "Please, Charlie,'' she cajoled, "if you tie me up, I'll have nightmares again.''

His eyes blazed with the heat of uncertainty, and

his fists clenched at his sides. "Damn it, Kate, that's not playing fair."

"But it's true and you know it."

"Tarnation, woman!"

She edged closer. "Please, just hold me tonight. Trust me this once." Watching his nostrils flare, she added plaintively, "But I can't give myself to you. That I can only do with the man I marry."

Charlie shut his eye against the vision of femininity enticing him beyond all reason. His features were seized in a fierce struggle. "Kate . . . woman, you're askin' too much."

She edged even closer. "Charlie, you can't want me to suffer in the darkness, to be frightened again . . ."

He opened his eyes and stared down at her; his lungs filled with her tantalizing scent. His gaze settled again on that lush, delectable mouth, on those velvet lips he so hungered to ravish and bite and devour. Her innocently expectant expression practically ripped his gut to shreds.

Yet he knew a will of steel dwelled beneath that guileless facade. He attempted a stern scowl. "Why should I trust you?"

" 'Cause I'm askin' you to," she purred, moving so close that her breasts rubbed his chest. "Please, can't we call a truce—just for tonight?"

Mumbling a defeated curse, Charlie pulled Kate into his arms, burying his face in her freshly washed hair. "All right, then, Kate. You win. Just for tonight."

Chapter 13

⌒◯◯⌒

Charlie took Kate's hand and led her to his blankets, and they reclined together in the moonlight. He stared at her intently for a moment and, when he spoke, his first words surprised her. "If you try to give me the slip tonight," he murmured in a soft, menacing tone, "I'll blister your butt."

She laughed. "You mean you're not man enough to control one headstrong seventeen-year-old girl?"

That comment brought a grin flashing to his face. "Are you woman enough to handle me?" As she chuckled, he reached out and touched the button between her breasts. "Shirt's dry now," he murmured.

At his provocative words, his touch, the mood between them changed as abruptly as with the sudden flaring of a wildfire. Indeed, Kate could barely hear Charlie over the thundering of her own heart. He looked so irresistible lying next to her, with the moonlight shining in his thick black hair and outlining his rugged features. Irresistibly, her gaze moved down to the hard bulge straining against his trousers. "I reckon it is," she murmured.

Charlie's hand clutched her breast through the chambray. A gasp escaped her. Moving closer, he pushed her down on her back and began purposefully unbuttoning the shirt.

"Charlie! You promised!"

His hand slipped beneath the shirt to caress her breast. She caught a sharp breath of keen arousal and delight.

"You laid out the rules, Kate," he whispered, "but my cooperation don't come without a price. I've just got to have another taste of you, woman."

The bud of her nipple sprang to life against his rough fingers as he leaned over to kiss her. His mouth was hot and sweet—his tongue bold. When she bucked at the indescribably erotic sensations, he covered her supple body with his hard, lean frame.

Kate thought she'd died and gone to heaven. Charlie's body felt warm and solid on hers; his rough, muscled chest abraded her breasts deliciously, and his kisses were deep and drugging. Her tongue vied with his as she kissed him back and tasted every texture of his warm mouth. She felt bereft when he pulled his lips away. But then his hot lips traveled down her throat, nibbling and tormenting, making her break out in shivers. His hand closed over her breast, and his mouth took her nipple, his teeth tugging gently.

Kate cried out and thrust her fingers through his hair. She'd never before known such deep, riveting pleasure. Charlie tantalized each breast in turn, wetting the nipples with his tongue then sucking provocatively. Kate could barely lie still. Then his hands grew impatient, yanking her shirt apart, sending the lower buttons flying; his fingers slipped into the sweet curls between her legs.

"Charlie!" she gasped, overwhelmed by fear and desire.

"Shhh! It's all right, honey." He moved with slow deliberation, his finger dipping and teasing until she relaxed. He pulled back, kneeling between her spread thighs and holding her open to him. She felt exposed and vulnerable, yet equally powerless to fight him. When he stared down into her eyes, she could barely breathe; the stark need in his gaze rooted her to the spot.

He found the tiny, aching nub of her desire and stroked it expertly. She cried out, chewing her underlip in helpless frustration. He watched her eyes dilate with desire; her lips slide open on a gasp; her perfect breasts rise and fall, the nipples so hard and tight. His gaze slid lower, to her flat belly and the tantalizing cleft of her femininity. "My God, you're so incredibly beautiful," he whispered, his fingers growing ever bolder.

Shockwaves of rapture exploded inside Kate and her thighs clenched against Charlie's knees. He moved higher between her thighs, relentlessly holding her open to him. She panted, writhed, and tossed her head. Her entire being became focused on the hot, exquisite tension building in the aching core of her. Within seconds, she was moaning and moving against his hand. He smiled, slowly pressing a finger inside her; she bucked and cried out, biting her own hand.

Charlie gloried in every second. Damn, but she was so hot, so wet, so snug! He pressed into her ruthlessly, in and out, deeper and tighter, until she sobbed and shuddered beneath him. "That's it, sweetheart—give yourself over to me," he coaxed. "Don't fight it."

When she climaxed with a raw cry, he took her mouth roughly, smothering her gasps and drinking in her tears. She threw her arms around his neck and clung to him. Absorbing the convulsions seizing her sweet, slender body, Charlie felt his manhood stiffen to agonizing readiness. He knew that if he had any decency, he would leave this girl alone. But he was beyond redemption, totally obsessed with the idea of joining himself with lovely Kate. He longed to take her with his mouth, to bury his lips

in her dewy depths until she begged him to stop.
Then he reminded himself that this was her first
time. Just being filled with his teeming length would
be enough of a shock for her. Later, he could school
her in the darker intricacies of rapture.

Charlie pulled back to free his swollen manhood
from his trousers. Glimpsing his intent expression,
watching his determined fingers move, Kate at last
panicked. She already felt far too close to Charlie,
devastated by the shattering climax he'd wrenched
from her body. He'd made her feel things she'd
never felt before, made her long to be his forever.
She knew that if she gave herself over to him completely now, she'd never get free of him, physically
or emotionally.

"Charlie, no!" she managed in an alarmed voice.
"This ain't right. You know we ain't never gonna
marry!"

The word "marry" at last penetrated Charlie's
mind. Breathing hard, he stared down at his sweet,
vulnerable captive. He *was* going to marry this darling girl, but she didn't know that. She was right
that to proceed now would be wrong. He couldn't
take her with a huge lie hanging between them.
When he told her the truth, she'd be mad enough
to kill him; but in time, she'd recover, and they could
make love together in all honesty.

With a groan, Charlie refastened the buttons on
his trousers, then fell down on the blanket beside
Kate. He pulled the folds of his shirt together to
cover her nakedness. He positioned his arm protectively around her middle.

"Charlie?" she asked tentatively.

"Sleep now, honey," he said gruffly.

She turned trustingly into his arms. He stared
down at her beautiful, moonlight-washed face and
thought he would die of frustration and the piercing
desire that still blazed within him.

For him, there would be no rest. For him, it would be a long, long night.

In the middle of the night, Kate awakened to find Charlie gone. She sat up, then gasped as she spotted him standing at the edge of the clearing. ''Charlie? You all right?'' she called out softly.

''I'm fine, sugar.''

''What are you doing up?''

He laughed. ''Couldn't sleep. I kept dreaming I'd sprouted a totem pole and was walking around with no place to hide it.''

Kate grinned. ''You rascal!''

''You should have seen the looks I got—especially from the ladies,'' he added wickedly.

''Liar!''

Chuckling, he moved toward her, and she saw the moonlight glint off a metal flask as he raised it to his lips and took a sip.

''What are you drinking?'' she asked.

He sat down on the blanket beside her, and the scent of the liquor on his breath wafted over her. ''Redeye whiskey. Want some?''

She grimaced, shaking her head. ''So you couldn't sleep, huh?''

He ruffled her hair, then planted a sloppy kiss on her cheek. ''Yeah, and you're the lady who knows why.'' He took another swallow.

''Sure you should be drinking that stuff so fast?'' Kate asked with concern.

He shrugged. ''We're out of Comanche territory. I don't reckon I've got to sleep quite so light anymore.'' Setting down the flask, he abruptly wrestled her to the ground. She giggled in delight as he straddled her. ''Besides, I've only got to keep an eye on you now, baby.'' Giving her a wicked wink, he leaned over and kissed her.

Kate shoved Charlie away and pulled a face. "Yuck! You taste awful!"

"If you took a sip, we'd both taste the same," he teased with another wink.

"Quit corrupting me, Durango, and go to sleep!"

His hand pawed her breast. "Sure I've corrupted you enough for one night, Katie gal?"

"Charlie!"

He chuckled with good humor and rolled off her, pulling her into his arms and tucking her head beneath his chin. Within a minute, both were sleeping soundly.

Kate couldn't remember the exact moment when Charlie rolled away from her. But, near dawn, she awakened to the loud sound of his snoring and glanced over to see him lying on his back, dead to the world.

Here, at last, was the opportunity she'd prayed for, her one chance for escape! Yet, to Kate's dismay, she found she felt reluctant to leave him. She realized that, over the past days, she'd come to like and respect Charlie Durango a lot. Not to mention, desire him! Her face bloomed with high color as she recalled their kisses last night, and how he'd pushed her over the edge into a torrent of ecstasy she'd never before experienced. Charlie could be an exasperating devil at times, but he was also a potent, powerful, irresistible man. Guilt and recrimination gnawed at her at the thought of doing such a low-down, rotten thing to him—

But then, what was Charlie planning to do to her? Hadn't he made it clear all along that he was determined to do his job, no matter what the cost to her? And when she'd called his hand in the moonlight last night, hadn't he all but admitted that he would never offer her his name? How sincere could his advances truly have been?

All of which meant that she'd eventually end up married to the old coot, and Pa would win. This being the case, what choice did she have but to run for her life?

Filled with terrible resolve, Kate got stealthily to her feet. In the faint pre-dawn light, she tiptoed down to the waterfall and retrieved her clean clothing, quickly dressing behind a bush. While her underwear was dry, her trousers and shirt were still damp. But at least the garments felt bearable against her skin.

Back at camp, once she'd donned her boots and hat, she saddled Corona with her own tack and took her pistol from Charlie's saddle bags. She left Charlie his own Texas rig and saddlebags, musing ruefully that these items would be of little help to him without a horse. Battling her guilty conscience, she untethered Diablo, checked the wrappings on his leg to make sure they were still tight, then sent him off with a sound swat on his rump.

"Go home, boy," she called softly after the stallion. Watching him trot off, his gait faltering but stronger than yesterday, Kate wondered if he'd ever make his way back to the ranch. Sorrow lanced her heart. Diablo had always been half-wild, and he would more likely join a band of mustangs. At least he'd be free, and, she hoped his leg would heal.

A bleak, overcast day was breaking when Kate knelt next to Charlie and placed his neatly folded shirt beside his sleeping body. She tried to swallow the painful lump in her throat. Charlie looked so peaceful, so handsome and trusting lying there, with a slight shadow of whiskers across his jaw and his arms flung outward on either side of his bare chest. She gently kissed his brow, feeling rotten to her very soul. Charlie didn't even stir.

"Charlie, I'm sorry," she whispered, wiping a tear with her sleeve. "But you gotta understand—I gotta be free. I can't do Pa's bidding this way.'' With a catch in her voice, she added, ''Please, don't come after me.''

A moment later, Kate rode quietly into the dawn.

Chapter 14

By late morning, Kate had ridden well back onto the plains. She avoided the public wagon trace and made her own trail whenever possible, traveling close to the protection of brush or cedar brakes.

Corona proved to be an excellent, fast mount, although guilt continually gnawed Kate that she had stolen the palomino from Charlie. She cringed every time she imagined his reaction when he awakened and found she had given him the slip. Where was he now? she wondered. Had he made his way back to Round Rock? Or had he already found another horse and started after her?

A slow drizzle began to fall, making Kate's journey arduous and miserable. Despite the cover of her hat, water began to trickle down into her eyes. She felt wretched, with her clothing clinging to her body like a cold, clammy second skin.

Just after noon, she stopped in a thicket of chaparral and ate a lunch of bacon and biscuits. A small herd of bison grazed on the grassy plain to the west of her.

Kate was about to leave the shelter of her stand of scrub oak when she glimpsed a frightening sight. A band of Indian braves, about a dozen in number, had appeared on the western horizon, advancing toward the buffalo on their pinto ponies. The mere

sight of the braves made Kate's heartbeat quicken
with terror. Watching the men quietly surround the
buffalo, Kate grabbed Corona's reins and retreated
deep into the stand of trees. She tethered the horse
to a branch and stood warily watching the scene.
She'd seen only a few Indians during her lifetime.
But from the small, squat bodies of the braves, their
broad, blunt-featured faces, their near-naked bodies
and horsemen's leggings, she very much feared they
were the dreaded Comanche.

Kate gritted her teeth in helpless fear and frustration. What rotten luck! Her stomach lurched sick-
eningly as she recalled the atrocities the Indians had
committed against Aloysius McCoy. Granted, these
braves seemed to be hunting for food, not for white
victims; yet she might well be stuck here for hours—
if she was fortunate enough not to get caught.

She watched the Comanche close in on their prey,
then begin their blood-curdling yells. The buffalo
stampeded, the braves chasing them into a small
barranca to the south. Once the mighty beasts were
trapped in the shallow gorge, the braves began killing them with their arrows and wickedly long lances.
Some of the massive bison had to be stabbed three
or four times before they succumbed. Sickened, Kate
turned away from the slaughter, yet the wind carried the nauseating stench of animal blood, as well
as the mingled cries of man and beast. Corona whi-
nied at the smell, and Kate talked to him soothingly,
terrified that he would give away their hiding place.

Once the buffalo had been slaughtered, Kate
watched a group of women appear from beyond the
horizon in their fringed buckskin dresses. While the
men howled their victory cries and ate the buffalo
entrails in celebration, the women began skinning
and butchering the animals. Though everyone
worked quickly, it was a good two hours before all

the hides, fat, and meat were collected and loaded on pack animals.

By mid-afternoon, the last of the Indians had disappeared over the western horizon. Kate watched vultures swoop down on the awful, bloody carnage the Comanche had left behind on the prairie.

Once she was as certain as humanly possible that the coast was clear, Kate ventured out of the grove of oaks, leading Corona. She cautiously mounted him, then headed north, away from the direction the Indians had taken. At first, she risked only the slowest trot, but as she crested the first rise, she nudged Corona into a full gallop.

Suddenly, two braves seemed to appear from nowhere, closing in on Kate on either side. Terrified at the sight of the savage warriors with their near-naked bodies and merciless features, Kate applied her crop to Corona, trying desperately to outdistance them. Corona made a valiant effort, but the Comanches, skilled horsemen for centuries, quickly closed on her. The brave on her left snatched the reins from her hand.

Kate lashed out at the Indian with her crop. The brave on her right yanked the crop away from her as the man on her left hammered his fist into her jaw with such force that she fell off her horse, and blessedly, lost consciousness . . .

At noon, Charlie Durango was cussing a blue streak as he trudged up a steep rise with thirty pounds of saddle slung across his shoulder and a slow rain drenching him to the skin. He was heading south, back toward populated areas, in the hope that he might find a farm or ranch where he could buy himself a horse.

It had been one devil of a morning. First, he'd awakened at dawn with a splitting hangover; then he'd discovered that Kate Maloney had given him the slip and stolen his horse.

He'd called himself a fool three ways to sundown. Every time he remembered how Kate had pleaded with him in the moonlight, begging him to trust her and seducing his cooperation with her treasonous kisses, bitterness rose in his throat like bile. How could he have allowed himself to be bamboozled by that two-faced schemer? When he caught up with her—and he would—he'd exact a retribution she would never forget.

For there was no way Charlie would go back to Round Rock without her and admit defeat to Jeb Maloney. Hell, the girl had stolen his horse—hanging was too good for her.

Then he groaned as he thought of how, even now, Kate was riding straight through Indian territory, smack in the middle of the Comanche moon. He realized he was using his anger as a shield to hold at bay the terrible fear that she could be captured by Indians, tortured—or worse. The sooner he started after her, the better—even if he did intend to beat the willfulness out of her hide once he found her.

On the crest of the knoll, Charlie gazed down at a one-storied log farmhouse nestled in the valley below. An aging sodbuster sat at the center of the dog run, smoking his pipe; several frisky horses roamed the corral to the west of him.

Good, Charlie thought. An outpost of civilization, at last. He had enough cash on him to buy a new mount, and then he would hit his own vengeance trail against Kate Maloney.

Kate awakened to a nightmare. Every inch of her body hurt from her jarring fall to the ground, and her head was swimming. But her physical malaise was nothing compared to her outright terror as she stared up at the two fierce Comanche warriors loom-

ing over her. She couldn't restrain a panicked cry at
the sight of them. Wearing breechclouts and leggings, the men argued over her in their foreign
tongue interspersed with a few words of Spanish.
The two looked much alike with their broad faces,
huge hawk noses, and straight black hair. Both men
wore eagle feathers in their hair and strings of bear
claws around their necks. Kate idly wondered if they
might be brothers. While the men were small, they
were massively muscled, their legs and torsos hard
and brown.

As Kate watched in trepidation, one of the men
shoved the other away, then hunkered down beside
her, his features harsh and pitiless. The vile odor of
buffalo grease and his unwashed body assailed her
as he reached out with stubby fingers and ripped at
her shirt. At once, she slapped him hard across the
face. For a moment, the Comanche seemed too
stunned to react. Then his features contorted in rage;
he backhanded Kate viciously and, even as she
screamed, he grabbed her savagely by the hair and
pulled out his knife. Just as Kate realized with sickening clarity that she was about to be scalped, she
heard the sound of the other man laughing. Both
Kate and the angry brave stared at the other man in
amazement. He rocked on his heels and pointed at
Kate saying, *"Tejana Nenuhpee."*

At these words, the brave restraining Kate made
a harsh, guttural comment and hurled her violently
to the ground. He stood and stared down at her with
awe and fear. The other man approached, and the
two resumed their squabbling. Occasionally, both
men would wave their arms or point at her, and
Kate was certain they were arguing over which one
of them would scalp her. While she understood next
to nothing of what they said, she was able to make
out, from words being repeated, that the brave who

had almost scalped her was called, "Piava," while the other one was named, "Paha Yuca."

After a few more moments of bickering, the two men seemed to reach an agreement. They laughed and slapped each other across the shoulders. Then both men turned back to Kate, kneeling on either side of her, their expressions cautious but determined.

Suddenly, Paha Yuca grabbed Kate's shoulders, and Piava again tore at her shirt. Desperation filled Kate like bile. She realized that the braves intended either to rape her now, or to drag her back to their camp naked, as she'd heard the Comanche did with white captives. In either case, her only hope was resistance—

She kicked, scratched, and fought the braves viciously, all the while shrieking obscenities at the top of her lungs. She had heard that Indians feared crazy people, and her ploy seemed to work. Within a few seconds, both men drew back, their expressions perplexed. Piava pointed to his head and said meaningfully, "Loca."

But Paha Yuca merely shrugged and went to his pony. He returned with a length of rawhide rope and knelt next to Kate. When she again resisted, he slammed her across the chest with both fists, hurling her to the ground and knocking the breath out of her. As she lay terrorized, unable to breathe, Paha Yuca quickly bound her wrists. Just as Kate finally recovered her breath with a gurgle of agony, Paha Yuca yanked her to her feet and dragged her off toward his pony. As she stumbled along, she watched Piava take Corona's reins and stride off to his own horse.

At his pony, Paha Yuca mounted with rope in hand, leaving about ten feet of rope between the rump of the animal and Kate. He tied his end around the high pommel of his crude, Spanish style saddle.

A physical dread filled Kate as she realized that the braves intended to drag her back to their camp.

They wasted no time. As the two Indians trotted off on their ponies, Kate hurried along behind them, her wrists afire from the cruel jerking of the rope, her heart galloping with terror. She tried to keep a level head, even as panic threatened to flood her mind, leaving nothing but madness.

If the braves continued at this pace, she might make it to their encampment alive. But she knew that if Paha Yuca broke into a gallop, she would be doomed, dragged all the way to their camp—across cactus, over rocks, through branches.

When the braves broke into a canter, Kate still somehow managed to keep up—running for her life and breathing in desperate gulps. All the while, she frantically scanned the ground rushing past her feet for rocks and gopher holes, knowing that just one stumble would spell almost certain death. The two braves did not even glance back in her direction as they laughed to each other and rode along—obviously, they cared not at all whether she lived or died. She knew they were treating her this way to break her spirit, as a first step in subjecting her to slavery.

Such was Kate's obsession with staying alive that she wasted little time thinking of what horrors might lie ahead for her. Soon, her wrists were bloodied, the pain from the ropes excruciating. Her sides and her legs cramped in agony with each leap she took across the prairie. Her heart was thundering at a dizzying pace, and each breath stabbed her lungs with the force of a huge, sharp knife.

The two braves finally slowed down a bit when they approached the Comanche village. Feeling relieved to be spared for the moment, Kate drew in huge, ragged gasps of air and studied the encampment ahead of them. The village was nestled among a stand of mesquite trees near a stream. She spotted about twenty tan tipis, some painted with symbols or scenes. Around the village, braves, squaws, and children milled about, while horses and dogs roamed at will.

When the two braves entered the camp, most of the other Indians came forward to stare at Kate curiously. The stench of the village was unbearable, a nauseating mixture of smoke, unwashed bodies, human and animal excrement, and rotting meat.

Somehow, Kate managed to keep her mien proud and her roiling stomach under control as she stared back at the many hostile faces surrounding her. She remembered hearing once that white captives who defied the Indians seemed to fare somewhat better—if they weren't killed outright. The Comanches did respect strength.

While Kate was trying to assess her new surroundings, a heavyset woman came forward. Wearing a buckskin dress and copper beads, the squaw started shrieking at Paha Yuca and pointing angrily at Kate. Kate wondered if the woman was one of his wives. If so, she was no doubt in deep trouble.

The woman continued ranting at Paha Yuca, but when he only grinned, the fat squaw charged at Kate, hitting her savagely across the side of the head with a hide scraper. While half-stunned by the blow, Kate nonetheless screamed her outrage and hit the woman back, slamming her bound hands across the squaw's face. The squaw howled in agony, and Kate heard the braves around them laughing as the woman again charged Kate, beating at her head with the hide scraper. Kate was trying her best to fend off the vicious blows when her bound hands were abruptly yanked forward and she hit the ground with a painful thud.

To Kate's horror, Paha Yuca galloped about the campsite, dragging Kate behind him. He hooted his victory yells while the other braves cheered him on.

Since most of the ground was cleared, Kate didn't
suffer as badly as she would have out on the plains.
Still, the bumpy ride was agonizing, her wrists on
fire, her hands and arms feeling as if they were being jerked off of her body. The rest of her was bru-
talized by the hard, uncaring earth and the many
small rocks and twigs in their path. Brambles and
sharp bushes seemed to reach out and snatch tufts
of her hair as they passed. Kate actually felt grateful
when Paha Yuca finally reined his horse in and cut
the tie binding her wrists to his saddle. Leaving her
hands still bound, the brave picked her up, slung
her over his shoulder, and stalked off. He hurled her
down on a stack of hides next to a tipi and proceeded to tie her feet. When the woman Kate pre-
sumed was his wife again came forward, yelling
invectively and waving her hide scraper, Paha Yuca
grabbed her arm and dragged her away. Several
times in the next few minutes, the irate woman again
shouted at Kate, and even spat, yet Paha Yuca's
watchful eye kept her from attacking outright.

Thus began a period of several long hours for
Kate, beneath the cruel sun. By now, her head was
throbbing mercilessly, her body ached all over, she
was caked with dirt and debris. Her throat was raw
and she was dying of thirst. She knew that escape
was impossible, bound as she was and surrounded
by this hoard of Indians.

Trying to put off harrowing thoughts of her own
fate, she observed the camp life surrounding her.
The women were the most diligent, tending pots of
stewing buffalo meat, nursing infants, working hides
with their sewing awls, or gathering wood. In front
of a nearby tipi, a group of young girls were string-
ing bead necklaces and playing with homemade dolls.
A troop of wild, naked boys raced through the camp
with a pack of howling dogs at their heels. With
child-sized bows and arrows, the boys mimicked the

hunting and warfare of their fathers. The men made great ceremony of tending the horses, but mostly stood about talking and glancing frequently in Kate's direction. Doubtless, they were speculating on her fate, she mused ruefully. While she assumed she was to become the slave of Paha Yuca and possibly of Piava, too, she had no way to be certain of her future—if she even had one. Off to the west, the tall scalp pole, with its many grisly war trophies, was a constant reminder of the hatred the Comanche held for whites.

Toward evening, another band of Indians, about ten in number, rode up. Everyone in the camp rushed forward to greet the newcomers. The visiting group seemed to be composed of two large families. The two husbands took an immediate interest in Kate, gathering over her and bickering with Piava and Paha Yuca. From the sign language the four exchanged, Kate guessed that the braves were bidding for her as their slave. When one of the men went off and returned with two beautiful pinto ponies, Kate's worst fears were confirmed. She didn't know whether to be relieved or disappointed when Paha Yuca responded negatively to the brave's offer.

Soon, Kate's throat and tongue were so badly parched that both felt swollen. She watched the women serve the men their meal of buffalo meat, wild berries, and *piñones*. Afterward, while the women and children ate leftovers in the background, the men took out their pipes and gathered about the fire, smoking, talking, and laughing. Kate knew that soon one of her captors was bound to take an interest in her. At the very thought, she yanked her hands and feet ineffectually against the tight bindings of rawhide, cursing when she succeeded only in bringing more excruciating pain to her wrists. Damn—if not for these bindings, she might escape.

At a distracting flash of light, Kate glanced upward. She watched lightning streak across the sky, followed by the loud boom of thunder. At least some rain might fall in her aching mouth or soothe her battered body—

Her momentary relief turned to terror as she watched the woman who had beaten her earlier creep toward her with a wickedly sharp rawhide awl. After glancing warily over her shoulder, the fat squaw drew closer to loom over Kate, her eyes burning with malevolence. She spit at the girl, striking her full in the face. Kate glared murder at the woman as the squaw raised her awl. Just as Kate realized she was about to be ripped to shreds, another woman stepped between her and her attacker. Kate's rescuer grabbed the squaw's arm to restrain her, and the two women argued quickly and intensely in their tongue. Kate was able to catch both of their names. Her tormentor was named "Tonacey," while he rescuer was called "Naduah." Kate recognized Naduah as one of the newcomers. After a brief, fierce discussion, the one called Tonacey threw down her awl, spat at the ground, and stalked off.

The other woman also walked off. Then she returned with a drinking gourd filled with water. Avoiding eye contact, the woman knelt beside Kate and handed her the gourd. Balancing the gourd in her bound hands, she began gulping frantically, and the squaw grabbed the cup back. Kate panicked until the woman murmured some soothing words in Comanche and returned the gourd. Still, the woman did not look directly at Kate, but she soon realized that the squaw was only trying to prevent her from becoming ill from drinking the water too fast. She finished slowly, handed the woman the empty gourd, and said gratefully, "Thank you."

At last the woman looked her in the eye, and Kate

gasped. While the woman's face was brown and heavily lined, and her hair was dark and greasy, she had the blue eyes of a white woman! She was clearly no Comanche!

"Please!" Kate cried desperately, gripping the woman's sleeve. "You're white. You must help me!"

But the woman shook her head in violent fear and hurried off.

Kate rested her head on her bound fists as the hopelessness of her situation began to sink in. Never in her life had she felt so tempted to break down and bawl. If only she hadn't been so headstrong and defiant, she would be home by now. Oh, she'd be battling like a demon with Pa, and she might even end up married to the old coot, but at least she'd be safe, and alive.

She thought of the timid but kind white slave who had just come to her rescue. Was that to be her fate twenty years from now? Would she be beaten, humbled into becoming a faceless squaw for some savage brave?

At last, she dared to think of Charlie and a lump rose in her throat. She remembered his sweet kisses—kisses she might never know again—and the cruel way she'd deceived him. If she was ever lucky enough to see him again, she would kiss his boots, beg his forgiveness.

"Oh, Charlie," she sobbed. "I've been such a dang fool. Please—please help me."

Toward sundown, Charlie was riding hell-bent-for-leather on the roan gelding he'd bought earlier that day. Following Kate's tracks out onto the wide prairie, he spotted the buffalo carnage that had obviously been left behind by a band of Indians. "Damn!" he cursed, at this evidence that Kate had

wandered smack into the path of a band of renegades. "Damn! Damn! Damn!" he repeated.

Keeping a wary eye out for Indians, he galloped
over the next rise. There, he discovered two sets of
prints from unshod horses hooves converging on
Kate's tracks. He reigned in his horse and studied
closely the signs of the struggle that had followed—
the trampled grass, the indentations in the dirt.

Charlie groaned, his gaze lifted to beseech the
heavens. Hell and high water, the girl had up and
gotten herself captured by Indians, no doubt renegade Comanches. There would be the devil to pay
before he got her out of this fix—

If she was still alive. The very thought shook
Charlie to the core of his being. She had to be alive.
She just had to be. Otherwise, he'd never have the
satisfaction of shaking the living daylights out of the
little idiot once he found her. Surely, after all he'd
endured, the Good Lord would not deny him that
pleasure.

He eyed the tracks going off to the west—three
sets of horses hooves, one set of boots. His best
guess was that two braves had captured Kate, and
that they had pulled her back to their camp on a
rawhide lead. Had they stripped her first, as they
usually did with white captives? The fact that she'd
kept her boots on was some consolation. Yet had
she managed to run all the way to their camp, or
had they viciously dragged her across the prairie?
At these thoughts his stomach gave a sickening
lurch.

Charlie lit a cheroot in an unsuccessful attempt to
calm his raging nerves. He tried to map out his strategy. He knew it was foolhardy, perhaps even sui-
cidal, to try to take on an entire band of Indians
alone, but he didn't see what other choice he had.
If he rode for help, by the time he returned Kate
could be raped, tortured, killed; the Indians could

have picked up and moved. . . . The endless, appalling possibilities wracked his mind.

At the sight of jagged lightning overhead, Charlie glanced upward. Ominous skies loomed above him; thunder was booming. He sighed. He'd best hit the trail, before a gully washer obliterated all the tracks.

Still, some rain might be helpful in covering his approach once he spotted the Comanches. He knew his only hope was to track Kate to the Indian camp, then try to steal her away under cover of darkness . . .

Chapter 15

Kate's nightmare continued. A slow rain began to fall; she opened her mouth and caught what drops she could. While at first, the rain felt good against her parched flesh, she soon became drenched and miserable, unable to wipe the moisture that was forever trickling into her eyes and down her face and neck.

The kindly white squaw did not come again, no doubt due to fear of possible reprisals from the Indians, and Kate spent much time wondering about the good Samaritan who had mercifully brought her water.

At sunset, Paha Yuca returned with a glowering Tonacey and three giggling young squaws. Standing over Kate, the brave and Tonacey again exchanged heated words, and Paha Yuca was once again compelled to restrain his wife from attacking Kate. When Tonacey was at last chastised into seething silence, Paha Yuca cut Kate loose. As she rubbed her smarting wrists and eyed the Indians warily, Paha Yuca turned to the three other women and issued what was obviously a string of orders. When he pointed at Kate, then nodded toward the nearby tipi, the three younger women again convulsed in laughter.

After Paha Yuca stalked off, the three squaws dragged Kate inside the tipi. Tonacey followed with arms crossed over her chest, still scowling formidably.

While Tonacey watched grimly, the three squaws began stripping Kate of her clothing. Kate tried to fight, but these women seemed much more determined than the two braves who had captured her earlier that day. Two of the women calmly held Kate down while the third pulled off her boots, trousers, shirt, and even her underclothes. Once Kate was completely nude, the women drew a fringed and beaded doeskin dress down over her head; Kate found the garment surprisingly soft against her skin. Matching, fringed doeskin leggings were pulled on to cover her calves and feet. The women then greased and braided her hair, placed a rawhide band around her head, and stuck in two eagle feathers. A necklace of copper beads was placed around her neck. As a final touch, the squaws streaked her face with red paint. Kate had a feeling she looked about as appealing as a trussed up turkey—and that the fate awaiting her would be equally pleasant.

Kate guessed she was being readied for some type of ceremony—probably to become one of Paha Yuca's wives, or so Tonacey's fierce frown would seem to attest. Even now, she could hear the sounds of chanting and drumbeats coming from the center of the encampment. She realized dismally that escape was impossible with these four women guarding her. Anyway, she was sure Tonacey would welcome an excuse to strangle her.

Soon, the giggling trio led Kate from the tipi. As they wended their way past the other lodges, she noted that the rain had stopped, and a balmy darkness had fallen. She was pulled to the campfire at the center of the village, where the men sat in a circle with their pipes and jugs of mescal liquor.

Spotting the women, Paha Yuca and an old man wearing some sort of ceremonial headdress got up and approached them. Paha Yuca grabbed Kate's arm and motioned for her to follow him; the two trudged behind the old brave to the fire. As the elderly man turned to face them, Kate studied his weathered features, flowing white hair, heavy silver and copper jewelry, and elegantly fringed buffalo robe; she judged him to be some sort of Comanche chief, either civil or ceremonial.

As the other braves solemnly watched, the old chieftan began chanting and signing over Kate and Paha Yuca; several times, he waved his ceremonial rattle. Occasionally, the other braves beat their drums and joined in the refrain. Lightning began to flash and thunder to boom, adding an eerie, otherworldly quality to the ritual. Kate glanced at the fierce-featured warrior standing next to her and barely stifled a gasp of dismay.

When the ceremony was finished, a whoop went up from the other braves. Paha Yuca grinned at the sound. Then he dragged Kate off to his tipi, to the ribald cheers of the others.

By now, Kate was convinced that she had just endured some sort of marriage ritual, and that Paha Yuca would rape her. But back at his tipi, the taciturn brave surprised her by throwing her down on a pallet of buffalo hides and retying her hands and feet. Then he left—she assumed to rejoin the other men.

Kate lay in the darkness, listening to the sounds of the drums and male revelry, struggling uselessly against her tight bonds. From the bawdy sounds coming from the campfire, she assumed the men were now passing around their *peyote* buttons and mescal liquor. She figured that sooner or later—probably when he became sufficiently inebriated—her new ''husband'' would seek her out to sate his lusts.

Rain began to fall again, pelting against the tipi in

hard droplets and trickling down through the smoke
flap at the top. Kate began to fear that the men
would soon seek shelter.

"Oh, Charlie," she murmured distraughtly.
"Where are you?"

Charlie had endured a frustrating couple of hours.
Tracking Kate and the Indians had not been easy in
the fading light, especially with the rain obscuring
their tracks. More than once, he'd lost the trail en-
tirely and had been able to find it again only through
sheer willpower and a generous dose of luck.

Fortunately, after sunset, he picked up the sounds
of chanting and drums, and was able to follow the
din the rest of the way to the Comanche encampment. When he at last spotted the lights of the Indians' fires, he paused on a rise overlooking the
village and grimly surveyed the scene.

At least a dozen braves were gathered about a
large fire at the center of the encampment; their
bodies, outlined by the flames, cast huge, sinister
shadows on the tipis surrounding them. From the
loud sounds of their revelry, Charlie figured they
were in the midst of one of their *peyote* ceremonies.
If the Comanche remained true to character, then
later in the night, some of the young men would
probably streak their faces with black paint and stage
a war dance. Afterward, the braves would leave to
hunt for white victims to torture and kill.

As for finding Kate, Charlie realized he might be
best-served to wait until later, when the night waned
and the braves had either passed out or left. In the
meantime, where was she? And how would he
eventually find her? There was no visual evidence
of her, and it would be nearly impossible to steal
into the encampment undetected, then search
through two dozen tipis.

And where was Corona? If he could locate his

horse, that, at least, would prove that Kate was also likely somewhere in the village.

Charlie tethered his roan gelding to a scrub oak, then warily crept toward the village. He slipped into the group of mesquite trees near the stream, where many of the horses roamed freely. At last he spotted Corona, tethered to a river willow. A relieved sigh escaped him; surely Kate was somewhere in the encampment.

The horse nickered at Charlie's approach, and he spoke to the animal soothingly. He located the horse's tack on the ground nearby. Removing the rawhide thong the Comanche had used to tie the horse to the tree, he saddled and bridled the stallion, securing his reins to a low branch. The horse would be ready when he returned with Kate.

Charlie crept to the edge of the trees and continued to watch the braves in the clearing. One of the younger warriors had seized the scalp pole, and several braves with blackened faces were now dancing around it, chanting and working up a frenzy of bloodlust. In the background, other men were smoking pipes or drinking mescal liquor. Charlie reckoned that the war party would soon leave—cutting down the ranks of his enemies and increasing his own chances of success—and survival.

As time passed, Charlie's frustration mounted because he still hadn't spotted Kate. He'd seen only a couple of squaws serving the men. He assumed the rest of the females were sleeping in the tipis with the children.

Soon, half a dozen of the braves howled their Comanche yells, mounted their ponies, and rode off into the night. Several others remained by the fire. Charlie could only hope that they would all soon fall asleep. Then, perhaps he could hunt for Kate with some degree of stealth.

When all but a couple of the braves had nodded

off, Charlie realized that now was the best opportunity he would have. Using trees for cover whenever possible, he stole toward the tipis. At the first one, he drew back the flap and stared inside by the light of the full moon. He spotted a squaw and two small children asleep on a pile of hides. He gently replaced the flap and methodically went on to the next tipi, wondering how long his luck would hold out before he was captured or killed.

As he reached for the next flap, a hand seized his shoulder, and his blood turned to ice . . .

Paha Yuca dreamed his *peyote* visions by the fire. He was soaring high in the clouds, a mighty eagle surveying a vast, grassy plain filled with buffalo and other fine game. His spirit soared wild and free with the bird, blessed by the gods with *puha*, the strongest spiritual medicine.

Then he spotted his mate gliding below him. With a wild cry, he dove toward her . . .

Paha Yuca awakened to the sound of thunder. He shook his head, struggling to clear the confusion of his drug-induced sleep. He glanced about. The other warriors dozed, and the fire was dying out. His loins ached, and he knew the time had come to visit his new wife.

He smiled to himself in grim satisfaction. His brother, Piava, wanted nothing to do with their white captive. Piava had claimed the *tejana* was *loca*, an evil specter sent by the cannibal owl to slaughter brave warriors at night. But Paha Yuca had recognized the *tejana* as a creature of spirit, like the mighty eagle's mate.

Perhaps this one would bear him a son. His other four wives had not. Sadness filled his heart at the thought. While he hungered to choose his favored mate from among his own people, sometimes the white captives were more fertile. His friend Peta Nawkohnee, chief of the Nawkohnees, had two fine sons by his white wife, Naduah. Paha Yuca would pray to the spirit god for two such splendid offspring.

Paha Yuca staggered to his feet and went off toward his tipi . . .

A split-second after he felt the arm on his shoulder, Charlie whirled, simultaneously drawing his knife. He locked his elbow around his attacker's neck and brought the knife blade up to the throat of his nemesis.

To his astonishment, he found that he held a squaw—a middle-aged female who implored him with fearful, and curiously pale, eyes. He quickly dragged the woman behind the nearest tipi.

"You're white," Charlie hissed, still holding the knife to her throat.

The woman nodded convulsively. "I help."

Charlie eyed the white squaw skeptically. From her aged appearance and the stilted sound of her speech, she had been with the Indians for some time. The Comanches of the plains were notorious for converting white captives to their way of life, and this woman's offer of help could well be a trap.

It could also be his only hope of getting Kate out of here alive.

"Do you know where the white woman is?" he asked.

"Paha Yuca tipi," she said.

"Where?" he asked.

"I show."

But as she started off, Charlie restrained her, pressing the knife meaningfully against her throat. "If you're trying to trick me, woman, I swear I'm gonna slit your throat—then I'll kill your husband and your children, too. Do you understand?"

"I no trick," the woman said, and for some reason, Charlie believed her.

She led him quietly past the smaller tipis. Then, when they approached a towering lodge with a painted scene of an eagle about to grasp a rabbit in its talons, the woman abruptly halted in her tracks and lifted a hand to Charlie in caution. Pulling back, he caught a glimpse of a young brave staggering toward the tipi.

The woman pulled Charlie behind an adjacent lodge, and he looked down into her fearful face. "That Paha Yuca?" he asked.

She nodded. "He go bride."

Charlie groaned. "You mean Kate's his wife now?"

She nodded.

"Shit." This was just grand, he thought. Kate had up and married an Injun.

The woman glanced anxiously at the tipi, then back at Charlie. "You no hurt Paha Yuca?"

Charlie sighed, then showed the white squaw the blunt end of his Bowie knife. "I'll just knock him over the head with this, if it's all the same with you. From the way he's staggering, it won't take much to put him out for the night." When she only frowned at him in confusion, he added, "I ain't gonna kill him—all right?"

She nodded.

Charlie eyed her skeptically. "You're not going to start caterwauling soon as I walk off, are you?"

She shook her head, and for some reason, Charlie again believed her.

"Thanks," he muttered as he crept off.

Inside the tipi, Kate quaked in horror as Paha Yuca staggered inside. She watched him fumble with his breechclout. Just as he dropped his loincloth, lightning flashed across the open flap to the tent, illuminating the brave's swollen shaft and casting huge shadows across the buffalo skin walls—

"Oh, my God!" Kate cried.

An instant later, Paha Yuca groaned and collapsed on top of her . . .

Charlie had stepped inside the tipi right after Paha Yuca had dropped his breechclout. He heard Kate's frantic "Oh, my God!" then he slammed the Indian over the head with the butt of his knife. He nodded to himself in grim satisfaction as the Comanche crumpled to the ground.

"Kate?" he whispered. "Kate, you in here?"

"Charlie!" came a familiar voice, half hysterical with relief and gratitude. "Please, get this big brute off of me!"

Charlie knelt and rolled the Indian off Kate. An instant later, he pulled her into his arms. Her hands and feet were bound and she was trembling fiercely. Quickly, he skimmed his hands over her doeskin-clad body to make sure she was unharmed. His fingers came to rest on one of her long, greased braids.

"Hear you're married now," he muttered dryly.

"Please, Charlie, untie me and let's get the Sam Hill out of here," she implored in a tense whisper. "I'm just so glad to see you again!"

"Are you?" The words were laced with bitter irony, but Charlie nonetheless quickly cut her bonds. Tensely, he asked, "Did that Indian—"

"No. But he was about to—"

"I figured as much. All right, let's hightail it."

"My clothes!" she cried.

They found her clothing balled up in a corner of the tipi. "Bring everything along—you can change later," Charlie directed.

Outside the tipi, they were shocked to see the white squaw awaiting them, holding Corona by his reins. She handed the horse over to Charlie and said urgently, "Go—hurry."

Charlie smiled gratefully at the woman. "You can come with us, you know."

She shook her head. "I stay here."

"I understand," Charlie said. He quickly mounted the horse and offered Kate his hand.

"Thank you," Kate said to the woman as Charlie pulled her up behind him.

A moment later, as the white squaw watched solemnly, the two rode off into the night.

Chapter 16

⌒⌒◯◯⌒⌒

Charlie and Kate rode fast and hard beneath the full moon. He led the way on Corona, while she followed on a roan gelding he told her he had bought from a farmer. Rain pelted them, soaking them to the skin. Kate realized that the downpour was surely a stroke of luck, since the rain would quickly obliterate their tracks. Nevertheless, she was soon so miserably soaked and exhausted that she kept her eyes open through sheer willpower.

She knew Charlie was furious with her. He'd been tight-lipped and terse ever since he'd rescued her. She realized that once they reached a place of safety, he would deal with her, and she dreaded that reckoning to her soul. She almost wished she'd remained a captive of the hostile Indians. What daunted her the most was knowing in her heart that there was no excuse for the lowdown way she'd deceived Charlie, and that she well-deserved whatever punishment he meted out.

Following her ordeal, she also desperately needed human comfort, and she knew Charlie would not offer it to her now. Her eyes stung as she realized that she wanted Charlie's respect and esteem more than anyone else's, and that she may well have ruined herself forever in his eyes. Why she so badly needed the regard of this bounty hunter who had captured her was something that still, in large part, eluded her.

As the rain ceased and dawn began to paint the landscape with its pale pink and yellow hues, Kate stared at the alien grasslands surrounding them. "Where are we?" she asked Charlie.

"Heading east."

"East?" Kate repeated, flabbergasted. "But home is south."

"Yeah, and it's straight through Comanche territory," he retorted sternly. "We'll be taking the roundabout way back."

"Oh." Kate had to admit to herself that his logic made sense.

"Besides," she heard him drawl, "you and me got a couple of things to settle, lady."

His words were so softly ominous, they sent a chill straight through her. She studied his remote expression, the features set hard as stone beneath the brim of his hat. She restrained a shudder. If anything, Charlie was even angrier at her than she'd thought. Anxiety lanced her anew regarding the confrontation that drew closer with each passing mile.

Kate decided to make a stab at more pleasant conversation. She braved a smile at her forbidding companion. "That woman who helped us back at the village—she was white."

His frown did not waver. "I reckon she was."

"It was good of her to help us."

"Sure as Sunday."

"But she didn't want to come with us."

Charlie shrugged. "I'm not surprised. If that was who I think it was, she's been with the Comanche for over twenty years now."

Kate was astounded. "Who do you think it was?"

"Cynthia Ann Parker."

"Cynthia Ann Parker!" Kate gasped. "I've heard

of her and her brother being captured many years ago. And you really think that was her?''

"Yep. Back when I was scouting Indians with the cavalry, several of the men talked about her having been seen from time to time. Rumor is she's married to some Comanche chief and has several children by him.''

Kate tried to digest these revelations. "Still, I can't imagine her wanting to stay with the Comanche.''

"I hear tell her family's still holding out hope for ransoming her back." A trace of bitterness edged his voice. "But do you really think most whites would welcome her back into their midst, after she's been a squaw for all these years?''

This harsh reality saddened Kate. "I hadn't thought—''

Charlie's rueful laughter cut her short. "Hell, honey, you ain't been doing much thinking a'tall, far as I can tell. If I hadn't come along when I did, it wouldn't have been long before you'd a been toting around a papoose or two.''

Kate shuddered. Though Charlie's words were cruel, they were also true, and she was feeling too miserably guilty to become angered by his gibes. Indeed, she grimaced at the sober images his words evoked, and at the bitter sarcasm in his tone. Her attempt to smooth things over between them had failed dismally, she realized. He was not about to forget or forgive her betrayal—not that she could blame him.

"You know, I didn't want to marry that—that savage,'' she managed to tell him at last. "I wasn't offered a choice, Charlie.''

He glanced at her sharply, then tugged down the brim of his hat. "You made your choice when you run away,'' he said without sympathy.

They fell into a tense silence, while Kate struggled to get up the nerve to ask the terrible question that had been gnawing at her all night. "I—I'm not really married, am I, Charlie?" she asked, gulping.

He laughed shortly. "Now there I wouldn't worry. Ain't no court in Texas gonna honor the ravings of some medicine man waving his rattle over you."

She heaved a huge sigh of relief. "Then I can just forget about it?"

"Yeah, I reckon you can. That part, anyhow."

"But you can't forget it, can you?" she added morosely.

When he clenched his jaw and rode on in silence, she had her answer.

Dawn had flooded the landscape when Charlie grabbed Kate's reins and pulled her mount to a halt at the bottom of a shallow gorge lined with shrunken trees and a few clumps of prairie grass. As he glanced about warily, she inhaled the fresh scents of cedar and rain-washed air.

"Reckon we'll hole up here for a while and get some rest," Charlie said wearily. "With all the rain, I don't see much chance of the Comanche tracking us this far."

With a grateful nod, Kate dismounted and slid to the ground. She tottered on her feet for a moment, feeling lightheaded and exhausted. Her head hurt and her wrists throbbed. She still wore the wet doeskin dress, which clung to her skin in the warmth of morning. She noted that the garment was now streaked with blotches of red dye, and she figured the rain had washed away the ceremonial paint the squaws had put on her face. Her hair was still braided; she drew off the headband and eagle feathers, then loosened the tight pigtails with a sigh. Combing out the coils with her fingers, she sorely wished she had a bar of soap to wash away the buffalo grease. She was just thinking that she should change into her other clothes, when she absorbed the heat of an angry male gaze focused on her.

Charlie stood across from her. He had tethered the horses and removed his hat, and was watching her solemnly. His arms were crossed over his chest, and every inch of his tall body seethed with lethal menace. After a moment, he turned to his horse, taking a length of rope from the saddle. He approached her with implacable intent hardening his expression.

Kate gulped as he neared her. Whether he intended to tie her up or beat her, she did not know. Her heart skidded crazily, and she backed up against a cedar tree.

"Charlie, I'm sorry," she said miserably.

"Are you?" His tone showed no hint of softening as he stood before her, breathing hard and glaring down at her. "What are you sorry for, Kate? Sorry you deceived me? Sorry you stole my horse? Or are you just sorry you got caught?"

She wrung her hands. "I'm sorry for it all."

He laughed cynically. "I'll just bet you are—especially the part about gettin' caught. Right, honey?"

His words were filled with such cutting bitterness that she winced. She watched him slap the length of rope against his hard thigh. The sight of it prompted new fear.

"You gonna beat me?" she asked in a rising voice.

"Now that's a fitting idea," he replied nastily. "But I reckon beating's too good for you." He moved closer, and his hot breath seared her cheek. "Are you aware that they hang horse thieves in these parts?"

Kate was horrified, her eyes growing huge. "So this is all about your horse?"

He stared her down with eyes blazing. "Stealing a man's mount is a damn serious matter, Kate."

She gazed wide-eyed at the rope. "You ain't gonna hang me!"

"I fancy hanging's too good for you, as well," he drawled with contempt. "Think I'll just turn you over to your pa. Let him deal with you."

Then, before Kate could protest further, Charlie pulled her down to the ground and prepared to tie her hands. Abruptly, he stopped, gazing intently at the scabbed-over wounds on her wrists. His gaze flashed up to meet hers, and something violent flared in his eyes.

"Did the Comanche drag you back to their village?" he demanded.

"Y-yes," she answered tremulously.

"Goddamn it, woman!" he exploded. "How you managed to keep from getting your fool self killed is beyond me."

Muttering another blistering curse, Charlie took a handkerchief from his pocket and ripped it in two, then gently bandaged Kate's wrists. He reached for the rope. "If you weren't such a heartless little liar, I wouldn't have to do this—but damn it, I can't risk having you run off again," he muttered grimly as he bound her hands loosely with the rope. Securing the knots, he shot her a look of murderous warning. "You pull at them ropes, Kate, and I promise you it's gonna hurt like hell. You try to give me the slip again, and that's not all that's gonna hurt like hell once I'm through walloping you."

"Please, Charlie, you don't have to tie me up like this," she protested, fighting tears. "I've learned my lesson. I swear I ain't going to try to escape again."

Charlie's bitter laughter dashed her hopes. His face remained impassive as he secured her bound wrists to the trunk of the cedar tree. "You're asking me to trust you again?" he sneered, getting to his feet. "Hell, honey, don't bother."

She gulped as she stared up at him, looming so

tall and powerful above her helpless body. "Why are you so mad at me?"

"Why?" he repeated with a furious wave of his hand. "Because you hornswoggled me, woman. You lied to me like a whore fleecing a drunken green-horn."

"Can you blame me?"

"Hell, yes, I can!" His expression was murder-ous. "Just because you don't cotton to your pa gives you no call to steal my horse and deceive me like some two-bit Cyprian!"

"Damn it, Charlie, will you stop about the horse?" she cried in desperation. "I told you I was sorry! I know I was wrong to lie to you that way."

He sank to his knees beside her and spoke with vehement passion. "Were you? Was this one of your lies, too?"

And, to Kate's astonishment, Charlie tangled a hand in her hair, brought her face up to his, and slammed his mouth brutally into hers. His kiss burned with lust, anger, need, and hurt, and when his hot tongue ravaged her mouth, Kate reeled with emotion and helpless desire. Her heart ached for the hurt she had caused him, and her throat throbbed with welling tears. She tugged powerfully at the rope binding her, sending shafts of white-hot agony shooting through her wrists. Yet she was heedless of the pain, obsessed with her need to throw her arms around his neck, beg his forgiveness, comfort him, hold him to her forever.

After a moment, he pulled back, his eyes still hot with anger and recrimination. His hand moved down her trembling throat, then boldly clutched her breast. A gasp escaped her, yet she knew there was no love or tenderness in his touch, only a desire to demean her.

"Charlie, please," she whimpered.

"Please?" he mocked. "Is this more of your sweet-talk, Kate? More of your lies?"

"No, I swear—"

Yet Kate was stunned to silence as Charlie forced his knees between hers, spreading her thighs just wide enough to let her know she was completely in his power. He looked down into her huge, panicked eyes and smiled.

"What, no more silken seduction?" he taunted. "Aren't you going to tempt me with your kisses, trap me with your body, like you done the last time we were together? Are you going to enjoy it this time as much as you loved making a fool of me?"

"Charlie, I didn't intend—"

His knees edged ruthlessly higher. "It's not so much fun when your hand is called and your skirt is raised, is it, honey?"

As Kate lay bound, helpless beneath him, tears flooded her eyes, and a riot of emotion lanced her heart—anguish, regret, fear, and a powerful, appalling sexual heat. She knew there was nothing to stop Charlie from driving himself into her, right here and now. Yet all her instincts told her this was wrong— this was not making love, but a cruel and barbaric animal revenge.

She spoke convulsively. "Charlie, I never meant to hurt you."

But he was beyond hearing her, crazed by his own hurt and rage. " 'Trust me, Charlie,' " he mimicked cruelly, forcing a hand between her thighs. " 'Hold me tonight. But I can't give myself to you. That I can only do with the man I marry.' "

"Charlie, I—"

Kate's heartbroken apology was smothered by another violent kiss. This time, he fell on her with his hard, unyielding body, and at that moment, Kate's overstrained emotions gave way and she began to sob—

Charlie pulled back at once, staring down at her stricken face. "God, Kate, I'm sorry," he said, reaching for his Bowie knife.

She continued to cry heartbrokenly.

He cut her wrists free, and she looked up to see tears in his eyes. He tossed the knife aside and caressed her cheek. "Precious, please don't cry. I really am sorry."

Kate lurched upward and threw her arms around his neck. "I'm sorry, too," she sobbed.

At her wrenching sorrow and the shudders seizing her, Charlie could have broken down and bawled right there with her. He clutched her trembling body tightly to him. "God, I'm acting like such a bastard," he admitted with a catch in his voice. "It's just that you scared the living hell out of me, darlin'. I thought you were dead, scalped—"

"I know," she admitted, wildly kissing his neck. "I was such a danged fool. And I was scared, too. So scared I'd never see you again."

"Oh, Kate." Deeply touched by her heartfelt words, and feeling intense guilt for having been so mean to her, Charlie kissed Kate's tear-streaked cheek. But by now, the emotion welling in Kate was beyond control. She grabbed Charlie's rough face in her hands and brought his mouth down hard on hers. He groaned, struggling to restrain himself against the dizzying assault of her lips. But when her tongue plunged inside his mouth, his restraint crumbled and he kissed her back hungrily, stroking expertly with his own tongue, tasting every heavenly recess of her mouth. They devoured each other with wanton kisses until both of them were lost in a whirlpool of passion. Charlie pulled the bandages from her wrists and kissed the wounds tenderly. Kate's innocent body writhed against his, and his hand stole to her breasts, squeezing the firm globes lovingly.

Somehow, he managed to pull back from the sensual madness consuming them both. "Kate—honey, we shouldn't," he said miserably.

But she was a tigress, pulling him to the ground and coiling her long legs around his waist. "I want to, Charlie. I want you."

An agonized sound escaped him. He stared down at her, and found himself drowning in the look of surrender sculpting her beautiful face. "God, honey, you don't know what you're saying—or doing," he somehow managed.

"Yes, I do." Her hand slid down to his trousers, and she gripped his hardness wantonly. As his fervid gaze shot up to meet hers, her green eyes implored him. "I want you to be my man, Charlie."

At her brazen touch and provocative words, Charlie's loins hardened in an agony of need. His heart was thundering, and his breathing was so sharp and ragged, he feared his lungs would burst. He considered himself as decent as the next man, but he was no saint. And the willing, irresistible female in his arms could well have driven the loftiest saint to mortal sin. Hell, he was going to marry the girl anyway, he rationalized, if she didn't get them both killed first. After all the torment she had put them both through, he longed to make her his forever, and there was only one way.

Finished fighting himself and her, Charlie claimed Kate's lips again, this time moving with slow, steady seduction. She ripped at his shirt, and her fingernails clawed his smooth flesh.

He grabbed her hands. "Sugar, if we go too fast, I'm for sure gonna hurt you," he warned.

"I don't care," she said recklessly, tugging the shirt off his body and brazenly kissing his bare chest.

Charlie moaned as her tantalizing lips and tongue roved over his smooth flesh. "Oh, God, sugar. That feels so good."

Kate's seductive, uninhibited kisses drove him mad. He pulled open her dress and stared at her lovely bare breasts. They were small and perfect, beautifully rounded. He touched his mouth to a rosy nipple, tasting a riot of seductive delights—salt, sweetness, and pure woman. He chuckled in satisfaction as he heard her sharp cry of pleasure.

"You like that, darlin'?" he asked, running his tongue over the taut tip.

"Oh, yes," Kate breathed, holding his head tightly to her breast.

Lying beneath Charlie's hard body, Kate was swamped by yearnings so powerful, she could not begin to comprehend or deny them. The roughness of his face felt heavenly on her breast, and when he tugged at her nipple with his teeth, the womanly core of her throbbed and hungered for the hard length of him pressing so deliciously against her.

Most of all, Kate longed to bridge the painful gap between them, and she knew that the only way to do so was to have him inside her, really inside her, until they were truly one.

She ran her fingertips over the satiny muscles of his back, then felt a shudder grip him as her hand moved to the buttons on his trousers.

He drew back and stared at her. "Kate—"

"Please, Charlie," she murmured, boldly unbuttoning him. "I thought I was going to die back there. I want to feel alive, and the only time I feel that way is when I'm with you."

She found his hardness and freed him, stroking him boldly. A mighty shudder seized him, and he closed his eyes in an agony of pleasure.

She stared at his manhood in unabashed fascination, her mouth going dry at the beautiful sight of him. "My Lord, you're so big, so hard." She couldn't repress a grin. "Hell, honey, you got even that Injun beat—"

"I *what?*" he demanded, suddenly wild-eyed and alert.

She stared up at him earnestly. "Charlie, when I said you arrived in the nick of time, I wasn't just shootin' the breeze."

He groaned.

"But don't worry, darlin', you coldcocked that Indian before he could—"

Charlie buried his face against her neck and laughed at her apt descriptions.

"Besides," she continued, clutching him tightly with her fingers, "I done learnt my lesson. You're the only man for me."

She heard his sharp intake of breath, watched his nostrils flare, felt his manhood grow hard as stone in her hand.

His voice drifted down to her, raw and hoarse. "This changes things, you know."

"I know."

His eyes opened, and his hands roughly gripped her face. "It's you and me now, Kate."

"I understand."

"Do you?" His expression was almost violent with passion. "You got me so crazy from wanting you, I don't know my backside from the moon. But I swear, girl, if you're lying to me again, I'm gonna wear you out three ways to sundown."

She looked up at him with wide, trusting eyes, her lips sweetly parted. "I'm not lying to you, Charlie," she breathed. "I'm yours."

Her ardent declaration was more than he could bear. He ravished her lips in a long, deep kiss. He shucked off his trousers, then gently pulled the doeskin dress and leggings from her body. His eyes devoured her nakedness. God, she was so lovely! She had a slim figure, girlish yet curvaceous. Her breasts were high and proud, the nipples taut with desire; her belly was flat and smooth, her legs long and slender; the lush black curls at the joining of her thighs enticed him beyond human endurance. Her skin was soft and luminous as pale pink satin. He traced a pathway of pale bruises across her midsection, where her lovely body had been cruelly dragged across the ground and, for a blinding moment, rage burned brighter than his need for her. The very idea that some savage Indian might have raped her lush innocence unleashed a torrent of desire and possessiveness within him.

He drew his fingertips down her body, delighting at the shudder that seized her. "Woman, you're so beautiful," he said in awe, burying his face against her smooth belly, kissing the bruises.

Kate gloried in the shameless intimacy, in the feel of Charlie's wet mouth against her stomach. She held her arms out in unabashed invitation, and he fell on her softness, kissing her until their teeth ground together.

His fingers moved boldly between her legs, finding her aching pulse and stroking it. He heard her shudder and gasp, felt her wetness on his fingers and could take no more. He pressed the hard tip of his arousal against her tight portal.

A moment later, he looked down into her feverish, pain-filled eyes. His loins were near bursting now, but the gentleman in him forced him to give her one last chance to back out. "Kate, are you sure?" he asked.

Kate stared up at him. Poised above her, his naked body appeared bronzed and magnificent against the red morning sky. His eyes were black as pitch, deeply dilated with passion, fiercely focused on her. His manhood strained high and thick against his belly, and the sight of it, the thought of having him plunder deep inside her, took her breath away.

He was so beautiful, Kate thought achingly. And

so tender. Her man. He was about to burst with desire for her, yet he held back, for her sake.

When Kate pushed Charlie back to his knees, he was certain she'd decided to stop. Then joy filled his heart as she quickly followed him, straddled him and wrapped her arms around his neck.

She boldly pressed her womanhood against his hardness and smiled at him in sultry invitation. "Let me," she whispered.

Charlie threw back his head and laughed, and in that moment, he realized that he loved this woman. She was just like him—a loner, fierce and proud— yet she was giving herself to him. Her she was, perched small and vulnerable above him, about to experience a woman's first pain, yet she welcomed him with spirit and humor. He leaned over and nibbled her throat, placing his hands at the small of her back.

"Take me, sugar, I'm yours," he whispered back.

She began sinking onto him, her movements bold yet inexperienced. At his barest penetration, he heard her startled wince, felt her tight flesh squeezing about him like a hot, pleasurable vice. Bless her heart, she was trying so hard to be brave. He ached to help her through this, and knew he mustn't prolong the torture.

Meanwhile, she was struggling to sink herself deeper. "Charlie, I can't—"

"Too late for that now, sugar," he teased roughly at her ear. "Trust me. Just for a moment. Then it won't hurt, I promise."

"I trust you, Charlie."

At her sweet words, he almost exploded then and there. He whispered a ragged apology and locked his arms about her waist. Kate pressed downward, assisting his efforts even as he drove upward forcefully. She shuddered, crying out, but she held him, not pulling back one iota, not even when he rammed himself inside her. Buried in the tight heaven of her, Charlie knew he was causing her discomfort, yet she had let him, wanted him to, and he loved her all the more for it. He stared into her tumultuous eyes, gently nipped her trembling mouth, and stroked her breasts. When she sobbed in pleasure, he could not seem to help himself; he clutched her buttocks and he eased himself in deeper. This time she did buck at the unbearable rapture, and he pulled her back to him tightly, letting her feel him to her womb, glorying as her slender body absorbed the shock of his size.

Above him, Kate had reeled at Charlie's sudden move and the blinding intensity of having him inside her. But the sharp flash of pain was quickly replaced by a profound and more exquisite aching. She was so full of him, strained to the limit, and it felt so good to know at last that he was completely hers. She realized in that moment that she loved him, that she wanted nothing more than to spend the rest of her life with him, and this realization brought tears to her eyes. She had never seen anything more beautiful than his face right now, so fiercely filled with desire for her. She had never felt anything more glorious than his hands at her spine, holding her to him so possessively.

For the longest moment, they didn't move, Charlie locked inside her as tightly as a root anchored deep in the earth.

"Oh, Kate," he whispered, raggedly at last. "Darling, I'm sorry I had to hurt you. I want to show you pleasure now."

She trembled and touched her lips to his rugged jaw. "I know. And I want more," she whispered.

Charlie kissed her, a deep, mating kiss. Kate kissed him back wantonly, nipping his lips and running her tongue over his smooth teeth. Gently, he lowered her to the ground. With a tortured groan, he began to move inside her, penetrating her thoroughly with each jarring stroke. Kate gasped in mingled surprise and wonder, digging her fingernails into his shoulders. When his mouth took her breast, sucking greedily, the bliss was indescribable; her hips arched in response. He stroked her with his thumb as he began to move harder and faster. An agonizingly pleasureable seizure began to roll over her. Then he pinned her to him as he plunged powerfully and deeply. Kate tossed her head, gasping for each breath, unable to bear the sweet torture. She felt her senses shredding apart as Charlie came to rest inside her with a last, powerful thrust.

A moment later, he collapsed on top of her, covering her face with wild kisses.

Chapter 17

They slept in each other's arms until well past noon, and when they finally did awaken, they were shy as two strangers together. Charlie kissed Kate's cheek and smiled at her, and she smiled back tremulously. He got up, reaching for his pants and shirt. Studying the magnificent lines of his legs and buttocks, she recalled those muscles tightening, growing hard as rock beneath her fingertips as he thrust into her. Even the memory made her gasp and draw a hand to her aching belly.

Charlie seemed to have other matters on his mind. He fetched Kate her clothing, then went off to check on the horses. She dressed quietly beneath the sheltering branches of a scrub oak. By now, the sun had climbed high in the sky. The day was humid and bright, and the scent of wet, baking prairie grass was thick in the air. In the background, a mockingbird's call trilled out, accented by a rattling of wings as a covey of quail soared up from the grasslands into the vast heavens.

As Kate pulled on her pantalets and trousers, she still felt twinges of soreness from her fierce lovemaking with Charlie. She felt besieged by a torrent of emotions—tenderness, love, vulnerability, and fear. Making love with Charlie had meant the world to her, but she couldn't help wonder if it had meant as much to him. After all they had endured and shared together, she'd expected a little more from him afterward than just being handed her trousers.

Perhaps that was proper protocol as far as he was concerned. Charlie was so much older and more experienced than she, as his skilled lovemaking had demonstrated. She shivered as she recalled him stroking her so expertly, even as he drove into her so hot and hard. This man was evidently a connoisseur of women, knew how to ply a female as a master musician might his instrument. He had made her feel shattered yet reborn both at once. He had taken her out of herself and into him, something that had never happened to her before; a remolding of her heart and spirit that made her feel very exposed to him. Yet could she really trust him with her feelings? Had the mating touched and transformed him as profoundly, or had his passion sprung merely from carnal need, from the anger and fever of the moment?

Once she was dressed in her shirt, britches, and boots, Kate stepped toward Charlie, watching him tighten the double cinches on Corona's saddle. His serious expression seemed to confirm her worse fears. It was almost as if the storm of passion between them had never occurred. How could he act so detached and unaffected now? Her feelings were exactly the opposite. Still, Kate had no regrets—even if Charlie was pulling away. What on earth was stuck in his craw?

As he worked on the horse, Charlie was wrestling with his own torn feelings. Making love with Kate had rocked him to the depths of his being. God, she had been so sweet, so willing in his arms, even when he had hurt her. He reeled at the memory of taking her virginity and plunging into her tight depths, even as she kissed him with such abandon and moaned into his mouth. It was as if she'd been made for him, an angel sent straight from heaven to be his woman. He knew now that he loved this headstrong girl, but could he really trust her? Had she given herself to him for some ulterior motive? The girl had deceived him before, and might well do so again.

While he didn't regret their lovemaking, Charlie feared they might have succumbed to their desires too soon. Hell, Kate didn't even know who he really was. Once she did find out that he was the man her pa had chosen, she might well use his own feelings as a weapon to get revenge on both him and her father.

He heard her clear her throat awkwardly, then her anxious words drifted over to him. "Charlie, what's wrong?"

He turned toward her. Lord, she looked so beautiful, standing there, batting those huge green eyes and licking those lush lips, still bruised from his kisses. While the sight of her slammed him like a fist in the gut, he managed to maintain a stern facade.

"Why should anything be wrong?" he asked offhandedly.

As usual, Kate cut straight to the heart of the matter, speaking with a defiant twist to her mouth. "Damn it, Charlie. You've never played games with me before. Don't start now."

He sighed and faced her squarely. "All right, then. I just don't know about you, Kate. You're a mighty hard woman to figure out."

She appeared stricken, and was twisting her slender fingers together nervously. "What do you mean?"

He scowled, steeling himself against her vulnerable expression. "Well, one minute you're all lovey-dovey, saying whatever I want to hear. Then the next minute, you turn on me. You done it once—maybe you'll do it again. Makes a man wonder what you're really up to."

She stepped closer, reaching out to touch his rigid shoulder. "You're still mad at me, aren't you? For deceiving you and running away? You still don't trust me."

Her nearness and the sweet, womanly scent of her were driving him wild, bombarding his senses with memories of their fevered lovemaking. Still, he managed to hold at bay the tempest of emotion battering his heart. "After all you done, Kate, you tell me."

"What do you want to know?" she asked miserably.

"I want you to tell me why you bedded down with me."

Her face grew crimson. "Because I wanted to," she said in a small voice.

"So, you wanted to," he replied dryly. "Then are you going to hit the hay with the next stranger who happens to strike your fancy?"

His crude words infuriated and hurt her. "How can you say that, Charlie Durango? You know damn well that you were my first."

He paced off a few steps, his face set in bitter lines. "Yeah, I was your first. But does that really change anything?"

"What do you mean by that?"

He turned his flint-hard gaze on her. "What else do you have on your scheming little mind?"

She gestured in exasperation. "What are you talking about? There's nothing else I could want from you."

"Oh, isn't there?" he challenged. "You want your freedom, don't you?"

She balled her hands on her hips. "Yes, I do. But we both know you ain't gonna give it to me."

"You're damn well right there."

"And you already told me you ain't gonna marry me," she added petulantly.

He crossed his arms over his chest. "And you don't think what we just done changes anything?"

"Does it change anything for you?" she snapped.

"What if you're carrying a young-un?" he roared.

Kate was utterly perplexed by his anger. "What if I am? Damn it, Charlie, why are you so riled at me? You told me you won't—"

"What I meant was, I ain't gonna marry you just so's you can get even with your pa," he ground out.

"Oh." Kate glanced away guiltily.

"And that's what you really want, isn't it, Kate?" he pursued, striding toward her. "You're hellbent on defying your pa, not to mention escaping the old codger he has lined up for you. So tell me what's different."

Staring at the impassive stranger looming before her, absorbing his hurt, angry expression, Kate vacillated for an agonizing moment. Considering her behavior over the past days, she couldn't blame Charlie for having such terrible doubts, and she knew that only she could reassure him now. At last, she swallowed her pride and looked at him with her heart in her eyes. "I'm different, Charlie. I want to marry you now."

His features softened at her words, then hardened again. "Oh, you do? Why?"

"Because I really want to," she admitted wretchedly. "Not to get even with Pa—or to escape the man he wants me to marry."

"Why should I believe you?" he demanded.

At his unrelenting ruthlessness, hot tears flooded her eyes, and she stamped her foot. "Oh, you bastard! How can you not believe me, after I just—after we—"

The sight of her so close to tears was too much for Charlie. Mentally cursing himself, he said gruffly, "Aw, honey, come here."

Kate flew into his arms, coiling herself about him

like a tight whip and practically knocking them both over in the process. Soon Charlie was laughing, tottering with her in his arms.

"Hot damn, woman!" he exclaimed, still struggling to keep his balance. "When you want something, you flat go after it."

She grinned. "Sure do."

"Yes, but you're about to pitch us both down in this here gulch."

"So what if I am?" All at once, Kate was deadly serious, locking her arms tightly around his waist. "I want you, Charlie."

"You do?" he asked with a catch in his voice.

"Yes. For always. And I ain't letting you go."

"You ain't?" He stared at her earnestly. "So you really want me?"

She nodded. "Do you want me, Charlie?"

"Oh, yeah." He pressed her bottom against his loins and stole a kiss so hot and dizzying that they both almost toppled over.

Afterward, Kate's expression was breathless, yet heart-wrenchingly solemn. "Do you want me for your wife, Charlie? You know, to have and to hold, and all that?"

His grin seemed wide enough to split his face. "I allow I'm crazy, but I do."

"Why?" she asked dreamily.

"Why?" He pondered that for a moment. "I reckon we're two mavericks, sugar, and we deserve each other."

"We probably do." She bit her lip. "And you're ready to settle down?"

His hands tightened on her bottom. "I fancy I am. But you have to be doing this for me, Kate, not because you're determined to spite your pa."

"I'm doing it for you, Charlie, believe me."

He looked pleased as punch as he set her on her

feet, but his tone held a steely menace. ''Woman, if you're giving me a bum steer again—''

''I ain't, Charlie.''

''Promise?''

''Promise.'' She shot him a surly look. ''Besides, you didn't make one bit of this easy. Do you think I enjoy humiliating myself this way?''

He winked at her. ''Sure hurts going down, don't it, Kate?''

She frowned suspiciously. ''What?''

''Swallowing all that pride,'' he drawled.

Instantly irate, she punched him in the shoulder. ''I wouldn't do it for anyone but you, Charlie Durango.''

He caught her close and thrust himself brazenly against her. ''Do what?''

Fighting a smirk, she shoved him away. ''You rascal.''

Charlie laughed, but his expression was deadly serious. ''So we're really gonna get hitched?''

She nodded.

''You ain't just saying this to get in my good graces—''

''What good graces?'' she flung at him.

He slapped her behind playfully. ''Woman, you may get that blistering yet.''

She chuckled. ''Naw, I reckon that's not how you'll be giving me my saddle sores.''

Charlie howled with ribald laughter. ''Katie, with a mouth like yours, the sooner we make an honest woman out of you, the better.'' He took her hand and nodded firmly. ''All right, then, honey. We'd best head home and tell your pa.''

Chapter 18

Charlie and Kate rode quietly across the prairie, occasionally exchanging shy smiles or a few words about the passing landscape. Kate felt relieved that the chasm between them had at last been bridged. Her life had changed radically during the last twenty-four hours, she mused. She'd been captured by hostile Indians and had even been married to one according to Comanche law. Then Charlie had rescued her and made her his. She felt no shame that they had made love without benefit of marriage. For she knew now that this man was her equal, her destiny. She knew he was the man she loved. Only Charlie was strong enough to tear down the barriers of pride that she'd erected all her life to shield her heart. Only he could touch her where she was most vulnerable, and, while on one level this scared her, on a deeper level she knew she trusted him.

At the back of her mind was also a flicker of spiteful pleasure that she'd get to win in her war against Pa, that she would now marry a man who was not of his choosing. She didn't particularly like herself for this streak of vindictiveness, and she knew that Charlie would wear her out if he ever learned of her guilty secret. Still, she couldn't help but feel that this turn of events served Pa right.

While she was feeling very comfortable with Charlie on an emotional level, on a purely physical plane, the long ride soon had Kate shifting about uncomfortably in the saddle, a not-so-subtle reminder that she'd crossed the portal from girl to woman only a few hours ago.

Charlie, watching her grimace and squirm about, grabbed her reins, pulling her mount to a halt. He winked at her solemnly. "Saddle sores, honey?"

Outraged, Kate took a swipe at him, missed, and nearly fell off her horse.

Charlie chuckled as he gripped her arm and steadied her in the saddle. "You could always come over here and ride with me," he teased.

"Then we'd never get home," she quipped back.

He handed her the reins with a grin. "Reckon we'd best slow our pace, or you'll be flat done in by our wedding day."

Kate tossed her curls defiantly. "The day you do me in, Charlie Durango, is the day pigs sprout wings."

Charlie's humor-filled eyes beseeched the heavens. "Lord, if you ain't the most outspoken woman I've ever met."

"Yeah—and now I'm all yours, bounty hunter."

Charlie's deep laughter echoed over the prairie.

They rode on more slowly, stopping at noon for a brief meal on a vast plateau covered with Black-eyed Susans. Toward late afternoon, they arrived back at the same clearing where Kate had given Charlie the slip two nights ago. A young family—obviously settlers, with their prairie schooner—were camped there, near the San Gabriel river.

At their approach, the man stepped toward them with his rifle braced against his chest. He was tall and fair with rugged features; he was dressed in a sweat-stained shirt and dusty trousers.

Kate and Charlie halted their horses at a safe distance. Charlie nodded toward Kate and whispered behind his hand. "Let me do the talking, now."

"Yes sir," she responded mockingly.

"Good day, friend," the man called out in a thick Scottish brogue.

"Afternoon," Charlie replied, tipping his hat.

"Where you folks bound?"

"Round Rock."

Stepping closer, the man glanced at Kate. "That your wife?"

Charlie turned toward Kate with a proud smile. "Naw, she's my intended. She up and got herself carried off by Comanches, and I had to go rescue her back."

While the man looked taken aback, Kate seethed in silent outrage at Charlie's audacious remark. Meanwhile, the man's wife stepped forward. She was a pretty, plump blonde in a brown homespun dress and matching bonnet. She was holding an equally plump baby girl; two towheaded boys trailed behind her, studying the newcomers warily.

The woman glanced at Kate in keen compassion. "How terrible for you," she murmured. "Did the Indians have you long, dear?"

"Only a few hours," Charlie replied, again answering for Kate. "No harm done." He winked at Kate. "She's fit as a fiddle and ripe to get hitched."

While Kate continued to glower at Charlie, the woman turned awkwardly to her husband. "William . . ." she began with a hint of reproach in her voice.

The man named William set his rifle against a tree and cleared his throat. "Would you folks care to join us for the night? There's plenty of room for you to camp, and the wife's making up a quail stew."

While Kate drank in the succulent aromas filling the clearing and realized she was starving, Charlie nodded. "That's right neighborly of you folks."

The man nodded back. "Safety in numbers, you know," he said gruffly. With a hint of reproach, he added, "Besides, it appears to me that you two could use a chaperone."

"Or a preacher," Charlie put in drolly. "You folks didn't happen to carry one along in your cedar chest?"

A titter of nervous laughter rippled over the group as Charlie slid to the ground and helped a still-glowering Kate to dismount. The blonde man strode up to Charlie and offered his hand. "I'm William McLaughlin. This is the wife, Betty, and our boys, Will Junior and Ben. Betty's holding our wee one, Cora Marie."

After shaking William's hand, Charlie introduced himself and Kate to the others. Then, while William helped Charlie tend their horses, Kate helped Betty with supper. The matron was kind and talkative, and Kate found she enjoyed the feminine companionship. She particularly loved holding the baby, little Cora Marie, who waved her rattle and cooed up at her. Kate remembered Charlie's comment from earlier that day—"What if you're carrying a young 'un?"—and she realized with joy and awe that she loved the idea of bearing his child.

"My dear, again, I must tell you how sorry I am about your ordeal," Betty murmured as she added wild onions to the stew and turned the stick bread browning over the fire.

Kate shrugged. "It wasn't so bad. I got pretty well shook up when the Comanche dragged me around their village—"

Betty crossed herself. "Oh, blessed saints!" She glanced in horror at Kate's scabbed-over wrists. "Is that why you have those terrible gouges?"

"Yeah, but don't fret yourself—they're healing just fine."

"Well, thank goodness. Still, I must put some of my salve on those wrists later."

"That's kindly of you."

Betty's expression was deeply sympathetic as she added, "What else happened, dear?"

"Well, the Injuns painted my face and made me someone's squaw—"

"Good heavens!"

"But, luckily, Charlie happened along before things really got out of hand," Kate continued seriously.

Betty's hand fluttered to her breast. "Why, all of that sounds pretty well out of hand to me." In an intense whisper, she added, "Tell me, those heathens didn't—"

Kate waved her off. "Naw. Charlie don't cotton to that sort of shenanigans—certainly not from redskins."

The two women shared a conspiratorial laugh. Then Betty glanced at Charlie, who was standing near William and offering him a cheroot. "He seems a fine man, your Mr. Durango."

A proud smile lit Kate's face. "That he is."

"Was it difficult escaping the Indians?"

Kate shifted the baby and smoothed down her blonde curls. "Not too bad. A white woman helped us, back at the village."

"You don't say!"

"Yeah. Charlie says she's been with the Comanche for over twenty years. We tried to get her to leave with us, but she refused."

"Why, how tragic. You know, the Indian problem here was one of the main reasons I didn't want to come to Texas in the first place."

Kate frowned. "Why'd you folks come here, anyhow?"

Betty drew a heavy breath. "Well, according to William, our farmland back in Tennessee was pretty well worn out. I must admit that our harvest grew more scarce and stunted each year. But, like I said, I didn't want to risk starting over here." She shrugged and stirred the stew. "But then, William is my husband, and his word is the law."

Kate eyed the other woman with a skeptical frown. "I see."

"At any rate, William has a cousin here who helped us secure a homestead."

"Where?"

"It's south of here, near New Braunfels."

Kate nodded. "A lot of people come to Texas for reasons just like yours. And don't worry yourself overly about the Indians—you should be fairly safe as long as you stick around civilized folk."

"But isn't Round Rock civilized?" Betty pursued. She flashed Kate a kindly smile. "Pardon me if I'm prying, dear, but I can't help but wonder how you came to be captured by Indians in the first place."

Kate chuckled as little Cora grabbed one of her fingers and began chewing on it. "Oh, it was really my own fault. You see, I ran away from home."

"You what?"

As Betty listened in fascinated silence, Kate related how she had run off to disobey her pa, how Charlie had tracked her down, how she'd thoroughly defied him, and how they'd ultimately fallen in love. She prudently left out the fact that she and Charlie had consummated their love several steps ahead of the preacher.

"Why, my dear, I do admire your spirit," Betty commented when Kate had finished. The matron's face was flushed with fascination. "Why, I could never dream of flouting William's wishes that way. Did you drive Mr. Durango quite past his patience?"

Kate laughed at Betty's apt description. "Well, let's just say I figured out not too long after I met

Charlie that he was either gonna marry me or murder me.''

As the two women convulsed in laughter, the men came up to join them, the two boys trailing behind. William regarded his wife sternly. ''What do you two ladies find so amusing?''

The two women exchanged guilty expressions before Betty smiled at her husband. ''Oh, Miss Maloney was just telling me the most amusing anecdotes about life in Texas.''

''Was she, indeed?'' William replied, shifting to a challenging stance. ''Perhaps Mr. Durango and I would like to hear these clever stories.''

''Yeah, honey, fire away,'' Charlie encouraged with a wicked grin. ''You know how I just love a tall tale.''

''Oh, hush, you two,'' Betty scolded in her most motherly tone. ''Miss Kate's been through enough without you men giving her a hard time. Now, take the boys to the creek, and all of you get washed up. Kate's going to serve up your plates while I nurse Cora.''

''Yeah, honey, serve away,'' Charlie teased.

Kate made a face at him as he and the other males strode off. She was tempted to gather a fistful of onion sprouts to hurl at Charlie when he returned, but realized she could never be so rude to their kindly hostess. She served up plates of stew and stick bread while Betty sat against a nearby tree, nursing the baby and humming to her. The sight of the fat baby suckling so contentedly at her mother's breast filled Kate with strange stirrings. Then she looked up to see that Charlie had returned and was gazing down at her tenderly. As she stared at his freshly scrubbed face and damp hair, her heart thumped wildly. She was stunned by the depth of her own response.

Her hands trembled as she handed him his plate

and a cup of coffee. He thanked her solemnly and
sat down next to her. The male scent of him wafted
over her, further inflaming her wayward senses.

The men dominated the dinner conversation, talking about such mundane matters as Sam Houston's
return to the governorship, horse ailments, the price
of livestock and crop forecasts, and whether or not
there'd be a war on the slavery issue. Still, for Kate,
the atmosphere of the meal was charged as Charlie
kept staring at her again and again. Sometimes, she
caught him gazing at the baby with that same tenderness in his eyes.

After everyone had eaten their fill, as the boys
dozed by the fire, William pulled out his harmonica
and began playing haunting Scottish ballads—"Annie
Laurie" and "Coming Through the Rye." Charlie offered to hold the baby while Kate and Betty washed
the dishes.

"I think your bride-to-be might appreciate a bath,
as well," Betty commented tactfully to Charlie.

"Sure, take all the time you want, ladies," Charlie
replied. He stared down at the curly haired moppet
sleeping in his arms. "This little filly and I are gettin' along just fine."

The two women laughed as they went off to wash
the dishes. After all the pots, plates, and utensils
had been dried and put away, Betty led Kate over
to the covered wagon. The gate at the back was
open, and there was a wooden chest on it. Betty
opened the chest, took out a towel and a nightgown,
and handed both to Kate. "I want you to keep the
gown," she murmured.

Standing there in the fading light, Kate gasped
with pleasure as she examined the lovely garment.
It was exquisite—straight-lined, handsewn out of
handkerchief linen, with a pleated front and lace
trimmed cuffs and neck.

"I can't take this," she told Betty. "It's far too precious and delicate. I'd be afraid to wear it."

"Nonsense," Betty replied as she took a cake of rose-scented soap from the chest. "Every bride needs a trousseau. I sewed that gown myself, and I want you to keep it as my wedding present to you."

Kate beamed at Betty's thoughtfulness. "Oh, how kind of you. Still, you don't have to—"

"I *want* to, my dear," Betty interrupted firmly. "Now let's have our bath while the light's still good."

Kate thoroughly enjoyed bathing with Betty down at the river. The rose soap smelled marvelous; she made generous use of the bar, washing the grease from her hair and the grime from her body. The setting sun cast a molten glow over the waters, and the air was thick with the sweet scents of greenery. The sounds surrounding her were so soothing—the tinkling of the distant waterfall, the croaking of frogs, the rustling of leaves in the breeze.

Afterward, as the two women dried themselves and dressed behind some bushes, Betty confided, "William said you can sleep with me and the children in the wagon tonight. He'll sleep with Mr. Durango by the fire."

"But I can't split up your family!" Kate protested.

Betty rolled her eyes, her expression scandalized. "My dear, it's the only proper way. What else are we to do—let you and Mr. Durango sleep unchaperoned out in the clearing?"

Kate couldn't argue in the face of such logic. Once she was dried and dressed in her gown, she hung her wet towel on a bush, donned her boots, and dutifully followed Betty back to the wagon. Betty again opened the chest. She replaced the soap, took out a small jar of salve, and gently rubbed the soothing balm over Kate's wrists. As Kate thanked her, Betty handed her a lovely mother-of-pearl hairbrush. "Why don't you climb on in, brush out your hair, and go to sleep, dear. You look done in."

"Thanks," Kate murmured gratefully.

As she hopped into the wagon with the brush and settled onto the feather tick, she watched Betty pull another cake of soap from her chest. "I'm going to go relieve Mr. Durango and get Cora settled for the night. I may as well take this sandalwood soap to the menfolk so they can bathe, too. Lord knows when we'll find another nice clear river like this one."

Watching Betty walk off in her robe, Kate began brushing out her hair. Her locks smelled so clean, scented by the crisp river and the rose soap, and she glorified in feeling truly fresh for the first time in days. She studied the interior of the wagon. The small tick had been reserved for sleeping, and she could tell that there was just enough room for her, Betty, and the children. The rest of the wagon was crammed with trunks, boxes, a Singer sewing machine, an old Windsor rocker, a huge family Bible. All were cherished items, Kate knew, and she wondered how many other treasures had been left behind in Tennessee, lost forever to Betty.

That poor, dear lady, Kate thought. Betty hadn't wanted to leave her civilized home at all, yet she'd dutifully obeyed her husband and had trudged off with him to the wilds of Texas.

When Kate married Charlie, he'd surely expect that same kind of blind obedience. Hell, they weren't even hitched yet, and already, Charlie was talking in her place and ordering her about, bold as brass. Did she have it in her to become the docile wife he'd surely expect?

She frowned as additional second thoughts assailed her. Charlie had claimed he was ready to settle down, but he hadn't offered any specifics. Once they were married, she'd be subject to his control.

What if he went back on his word and decided to drag her all over creation, just as William was doing with Betty? Much as Kate railed at the injustice of the laws and customs that made women virtual chattel of their fathers and husbands, this was the harsh reality she'd soon be facing.

Kate knew she was a headstrong woman. She knew she was not one to belabor a decision. She'd taken a real shine to Charlie Durango, had made love with him, and had decided on the spot that she wanted him for her husband. But she hadn't really considered all the implications of her rash actions. Had she gotten herself in a terrible pickle through her own recklessness? Had she sold her entire future for a few sweet kisses?

The thought made her toss about on her tick. This was damn serious, this marriage business. Her talk with Betty had certainly confirmed this. Wedding with Charlie would mean a real commitment. It would mean giving up her independence and following her man, as Betty had done.

Her ma had followed her pa, had obeyed him to her death. Was this what she wanted? To lose herself in someone else? To give up all her own choices?

Grim defiance rose in Kate, and she considered telling Charlie that the whole deal was off. Then she remembered his devastating kisses, thought of sweet little Cora again, imagined having Charlie's baby growing inside her . . .

Kate rolled over with a painful gasp. Heat twisted in her belly, a treasonous desire to have Charlie close to her, loving her again. She pounded her fist on the pillow in rage and confusion and helpless desire. Hell, she didn't know what she wanted anymore!

Hours later, Charlie found himself unable to sleep beneath the wide Texas sky. The night was clear, a thousand stars blinking at him from the vast heavens. Yet none seemed as dazzling as the sweet girl asleep in the wagon just a few feet away from him, the lovely siren now frustratingly forbidden to him. He couldn't keep his mind off Kate, or off the hunger for her that blazed in his loins.

Seeing her with that baby . . . Oh, she was so fine! That's just how he wanted his Kate—barefoot and pregnant. The girl was a mite wild, and having his young'un in her belly might calm her down a bit.

Then he grimaced as he thought of the truth she would find out about him tomorrow. She'd likely kill him when she discovered what he'd done, how he'd withheld his true identity from her.

He heaved himself to a sitting position, resting his forearms on his knees. Despite the cool bath he'd taken earlier that evening, he felt hot all over; his entire body seethed with frustrated passion. He might well lose Kate tomorrow, but he could have her tonight. He groaned in tormented pleasure at the thought of taking her bare breast in his mouth and sinking himself deeply inside her. Oh, those sweet little gasps coming out of her—he had to hear them again, had to watch her come apart in his arms. And he was ruthless enough not to mind one bit if he got her pregnant. Hell, once she found out the truth, he'd need all the ammunition he could muster.

His mind made up, he donned his boots, got up, and strode over to the wagon . . .

Kate was deeply asleep next to Betty and the children when a sharp tug on her foot awakened her. She started, glancing up to see Charlie standing at the opening, shirtless and staring down at her.

"Charlie, what on earth are you doing here?" she whispered tensely. "You'll wake everyone up."

He didn't move, his gaze focused fiercely on her. "Come over here, darlin'."

Kate obediently crawled toward the opening, taking care not to waken the others. As she knelt next to the raised gate, Charlie reached inside, gathering her gown up around her bottom and grasping her about the waist.

"Charlie!" she hissed, even as hot lust shot through her at his brazen touch.

"Shhh!" he scolded, pressing his fingers to her mouth. "Now, Katie, I'm gonna pull you out, and I want you to wrap your legs around my waist. We're taking us a bit of a walk, and I ain't gonna have you steppin' on no brambles to mar them pretty feet."

Kate was mortified. "B-but, Charlie, I ain't got no drawers on."

He chuckled. "I noticed."

He was grinning with pure devilishness as he hoisted Kate out of the wagon. She coiled her arms around his neck as she shifted against his hard torso. She had no choice but to wrap her legs around his waist as he had directed. When she did, her gown hiked up scandalously, gathering about her waist. Charlie smothered her protest with a hard kiss and a menacing pinch on her behind; his hands gripped her bare bottom firmly, and her feminine cleft slid straight into his cold belt buckle. She gasped in an agonizingly pleasureable response.

"Where are you taking me?" she managed to pant as he started off with her.

He laughed huskily. "Straight to heaven, sugar."

Chapter 19

❦❦❦

Safely away from the wagon, Charlie paused for a moment and kissed Kate. It was a hot, heavenly kiss, seething with lust and torrid virility. His tongue plundered her mouth; his fingers dug into her soft bottom, increasing her shattering arousal. Her senses swam in his wonderful scent—the sandlewood soap, the crisp fragrance of the pond, and a duskier essence, pure man.

Kate clung to him like a drowning woman; she had never known dying could be so pleasant.

When he started off again, she panted for breath. The stimulation against her most sensitive parts became more acute with each firm step Charlie took. Most women couldn't have spoken in the face of such blinding sensations, but Kate was always one to speak her mind.

"Do you think I'll make you a good wife, Charlie?" she managed.

"What a question!"

"Well, do you?"

He laughed. "I'd say it's gettin' better every minute."

"I won't be obedient, like Betty," she asserted.

"Did I say I wanted a wife like her?"

"She didn't want to leave Tennessee, but she did so when her husband told her to."

"And so she should have."

"Well, I wouldn't have!"

Charlie stopped in his tracks and glowered at her. "What do you mean?"

"I mean, if my husband asked me to leave Texas, I wouldn't do it."

His frown grew fearsome. "And what's so great about Texas? Far as I can see, you don't give a tinker's damn about your pa, and I sure don't see what else is holding you here."

She lifted her chin stubbornly. "Texas is my home, is all."

Charlie laughed derisively and started off with her again. "Spoken like a true tenderfoot who's never been anywhere else in her damn life."

"I ain't no tenderfoot! And furthermore, when you were ordering me about earlier today and speaking in my place, I didn't like it one bit."

"Oh, you didn't, did you?" he demanded.

"No!"

Charlie grinned. "Well, ain't that a cryin' shame."

"Oooh!" she seethed. "You're so exasperating! And I guess you think you're gonna boss me around like that after we get hitched?"

He considered that for a moment. "Yep," he replied with daunting confidence.

"Oh! You're impossible!"

"Not at all, darlin'," he countered smoothly. "Truth to tell, I'm a right reasonable man. But when push comes to shove, I'm gonna be the husband in this here marriage. So, either you're gonna mind me, or I'm gonna blister you."

"Well, that's a fine system!" she blustered.

Charlie only shrugged. "It's been working since the dawn of time, far as I can tell. Someone in the family has to wear the pants, and it sure as Sunday ain't gonna be you."

"Then I've changed my mind! Take me back! I don't want to marry you!"

This mutinous outburst stopped Charlie in his tracks again. He scowled ferociously at his bride-to-be. "Honey," he said sternly, "you and me made ourselves a deal, and if you're aimin' to back out now, you're crossing the wrong man."

His ominous words and the savage glint in his eyes gave Kate pause. She gulped in trepidation and quickly decided to try a new tack. Stroking Charlie's rough jaw, she began in a more cajoling tone, "Honey—"

"So it's honey now, is it?" he drawled cynically.

She grinned. "Yep. Well—um—honey, I'm just tryin' to point out that maybe neither of us has given this marriage business enough thought."

"Oh, you are, are you?" he snapped.

"Yeah. And maybe we should call it off before—"

"Call it off?" he cut in angrily. "And if you're carrying my child, are you gonna call that off, too?"

Kate stifled a groan as Charlie strode on, shifting her slightly in his arms and deepening the mind-bending stimulation between her thighs. "Charlie . . ." She paused to shudder, and her voice came out hoarse and breathless. "If you're plannin' what I think you are, then that's not gonna help my chances none."

"You're right," he taunted cheerfully.

"Damn it, Charlie Durango, take me back!" she ordered, near-panicked by the longings consuming her.

He slapped her behind. "Hush up, now, before you wake the dead. You think I want to spend the rest of the night arguing with a pissant like you? I got much more serious business in mind."

"I said, take me back," she hissed through gritted teeth.

"I said no," he returned agreeably. Even as she

glared daggers at him, he added wickedly, "It's sparkin' time, sugar."

Kate groaned with a mixture of exasperation and pleasure.

Next to the stream, Charlie at last set her on her feet. By now, Kate was so aroused, she felt dizzy. As she struggled to catch her breath, she watched Charlie shuck his boots, then unbuckle his belt. Irresistibly, her gaze slid lower, becoming riveted on his generous endowments. Desire stormed her anew.

Charlie winked at her as he began freeing the hard bulge straining at his trousers. "Now that's a mighty fine gown, Miss Kate. If you don't want it ripped, I'd suggest you take it off."

"Go to the devil!"

He tossed his trousers down on top of a bush. "Kate," he said with deliberate impudence, "either you're gonna quit being so ornery and take off that gown right this minute, or I'm gonna strip it off you and beat your little butt."

Kate stamped her foot, even as her senses reeled at the sight of his magnificent nakedness, his firm, distended manhood. "Oh, you brute! You mean you'd force me to—"

He laughed. "Honey, I'm not forcing you to do a thing but quit lying to us both. Hell, I near burnt my fingers undoing my belt buckle."

Kate's vision swam with red. "Why you—"

Kate attacked him with fists flying, but Charlie merely caught her close against his hard, naked body and kissed her. Waves of tormenting arousal slammed through her at the feel of him, so hot and rough and ready against her soft body. A mortified protest died in her throat, and she sagged in his arms.

He pulled back and began undoing her gown. His voice held a steely tone. "Katie, we got ourselves a deal, and there's gonna be no backing out. Tomorrow I'm gonna take you home, then we're gonna get hitched up as soon as possible. And tonight . . .'' He paused to pull the gown from her body, then drew her fingers firmly to his solid erection. ''We're gonna make us some serious love.''

His fiercely passionate words and the hot feel of him in her hand destroyed the last vestiges of Kate's control. The cool night breeze felt divine against her bare skin, deepening the flames of her ardor. ''Sure, Charlie,'' she breathed, stroking him wantonly and pressing her aching breasts shamelessly against his hair-roughened chest.

Charlie groaned and caught her closer. ''I want to take my time, drive you crazy.''

''You think I'm not plumb loco now?''

Chuckling, Charlie drew Kate down with him onto a log, setting her on his muscled thighs. He nudged her lips apart in a gentle, titillating kiss that was purest torment; his hand tenderly stroked her aroused breasts. Kate whimpered and reached for him blindly, caressing his sinewy chest, his flat belly, then gripping his thick, rock-hard arousal. Moaning ecstatically, she took his hand, pressing his fingers against her throbbing center. His fingers danced and probed there, exciting her deeply. Within seconds, she had surged to her knees on the log. Straddling him, she struggled unsuccessfully to take his teeming hardness inside her.

Charlie tensed against her and pulled his lips away. He drew in a seething breath. ''Hold on, sweetheart. You're a fresh-broke filly and I don't want to hurt you—''

''And you're a rampaging stallion and I'm eager to ride.''

''Sweet Jesus, woman!'' His voice was hoarse, tortured. ''We got to ease into this a bit.''

Charlie nudged her to her feet, took her hand,

and led her out into the cool water. Kate looked around them in delirious joy. The river was gorgeous, rippling in the wind and dappled with silver. The waterfall played its sweet music in the background.

When they were in up to their knees, Charlie leaned over and kissed her again. She thrust herself at him brazenly, but he only chuckled and held her at arm's length. "Slowly, sugar," he teased, easing her closer, inch by tormenting inch.

This time, Charlie began his assault with his tongue, running it delicately over her face, her neck, and then her lips. Kate's entire body broke out in gooseflesh. She slammed her mouth hard into his and drew on his tongue. She glorified in the tortured sound escaping him.

They seemed to stand there forever, their mouths locked, their hot, aroused bodies barely touching. The stimulation was unbearable for Kate. Charlie slid his fingers slowly, tantalizingly through her hair as his tongue drew unhurried, erotic circles inside her mouth. Just when Kate was sure she was going insane, when she was squirming away from him out of pure frustration, Charlie cradled her face in his hands and deepened his kiss, taking her mouth with rough, bold hunger. He pressed a knee between her thighs and rubbed her provocatively until she moved with feverish need against him. Leaving her gasping, he leaned over and caught her nipple between his teeth, wetting the tight aureole with his tongue. Kate went wild, bucking fiercely; his arms locked about her waist to hold her still as he sucked the tip of her breast deeply into his mouth.

A moment later, he found a long, barely submerged boulder and pressed her down on her back. She trembled and gazed up at him.

"There, sugar," he said wickedly, kneeling between her spread thighs and running his hands over

her breasts, her belly. "My God, you're so beautiful, and to think you're all mine. Just lie back a while
and let me do the work."

Kate had never known such sweet torment. She
lay with several inches of cool water sluicing over
her, and the heat of Charlie's hands and lips driving
her insane. She stared up at the sky, with its full
moon and thousands of stars. She gazed at the cur-
tain of greenery lining the river like dark lace. She
stared up at the face of the man she loved, at his
fierce features and eyes as fathomless as her desire
for him. She felt his fingers slip boldly between her
thighs—

Yes, this was heaven.

And that was before Charlie pressed his mouth to
her wet breast, even as he continued the teasing torment with his fingers. Kate's back arched and her
entire being went achy and hot. She tangled her fingers in Charlie's thick hair as he tantalized each of
her breasts. When he thrust two fingers inside her,
she gasped at the exquisite pressure. His lips slid
down her slick belly, and lower. Then he moved off
the rock and knelt in the water, pulling her hips to
the edge of the boulder, spreading her thighs and
leaning over—

Ecstasy crashed inside Kate in riotous waves as
Charlie kissed her curly mound and teased her with
his tongue. Even as he wet her, the waters of the
pond continued to slide over her—cool, primal,
erotic.

"Charlie—you're gonna flat drown," she gasped
somehow.

"That's the idea, sugar," he replied devilishly.
Nonetheless, his hands slipped beneath her bottom,
raising her to his eager mouth—

"Oh, Charlie . . ." Kate felt no shame as he
pressed his lips between her spread thighs, and
showed her all the intricacies of a different kind of

passion. She panted and clenched her fists as his tongue did a slow mating dance against her throbbing nub. He took his time, sucking one moment, nibbling the next, or merely teasing her with hot, darting strokes. He drove her to a peak of unbearable sensation and pushed her relentlessly into a shattering climax. Kate cried out, her entire being throbbing and careening as he held her pinned to a peak of delight.

She was limp as a ragdoll when Charlie lifted her up and away from him. "I don't want to crush you, sugar," he whispered.

He reclined on his back on the boulder, bringing her body astride his. A split-second later, he plunged himself to the hilt inside her tight flesh.

Kate cried out as the night whirled crazily about her. Charlie felt so hot, so solid, so deep inside her, yet she accepted him eagerly, sinking onto him, desperate for all the passion and love his body could pour out.

Beneath her, Charlie's features were twisted in an agony of need. "Oh, Kate . . . darling Kate," he whispered. "Woman, you feel so good."

Indeed, never in his life had Charlie Durango known such blinding pleasure as he did at this moment, buried in the hot, snug sheath of the woman he loved. Kate looked so beautiful sitting astride him, opening herself to him in a position of complete trust and vulnerability. His hands reached upward to clutch her firm breasts, his thumbs and forefingers pinching the tight nipples slightly. He gloried in her raw cry. When he looked into her beautiful eyes, and saw the mindless surrender reflected there, he felt himself growing hard as iron inside her. All his control spun away into the night. His fingers dug into her bottom and he showed her how to roll her hips and arch into his thrusts. The resulting torrent of white-hot ecstasy made them both cry out.

Charlie branded Kate with hard, convulsive thrusts that rocked her being. She responded in a frenzy of uninhibited movements and wild sobs. The climax storming over them both was quick and violent. Kate felt herself tightening about him, then going soft and liquid as he surged powerfully to rest, pouring his seed inside her. He pulled her lips down to his for a fevered kiss. Their hearts thundered together in the wild, spinning night.

It seemed an eternity before their breathing, their frantic pulses, returned to normal. Charlie reached up, pressing the flat of his palm against her lower belly. His words were raspy, uneven. "Woman, we'd best get hitched soon. The way we're going, you will be carrying my child come autumn."

"I know," she murmured, and a small gasp of misery escaped her.

He frowned. "Kate? What is it, honey? Don't you want my young'un?"

"Sure, I do," she whispered sincerely.

"Then what is it?"

"I can't really put it into words right now."

Kate turned her face away, ashamed of the lie she'd just told Charlie. In truth, she could put what she felt into words—but how could she say to this man she loved that she belonged to him now, and yet a big part of her still rebelled against his domination? How could she say anything of the kind, especially with him still buried deep inside her, and stroking her so tenderly?

Charlie's hand reached up to grasp her chin, turning her toward him. "You frettin' about going home tomorrow?"

"Yes, maybe that's it."

To her surprise and confusion, Charlie gently lifted her off him, then sat up at the edge of the boulder. Kate sat up next to him, studying his abstracted scowl and watching him idly move a hand through the water. His sheer physical beauty staggered her, and she reveled at the way the moonlight outlined his rugged features. The wind surged, ruffling his hair and the leaves of the dark tree limbs stretching above him. An owl hooted in the distance.

"You sorry for what we done?" he asked at last.

"Oh, no," she replied quickly.

"That ain't quite how it sounded to me."

At the hurt in his voice, Kate felt miserable. "Charlie please. I—I'm glad that we—"

"Are you?"

She nodded solemnly.

His gaze grew heated. "Then show me."

Without hesitation, Kate leaned over and latched her mouth onto his manhood.

Charlie uttered a guttural sound of mingled surprise and agonized arousal. He tangled a hand in Kate's hair as she moved her lips and tongue up and down, mimicking his earlier kisses.

"You learn quick, sugar," he said tightly.

"Not as quick as you move," she replied, glorying as she felt him thicken against the assault of her lips and fingers.

"Lord, that feels so good." Both his hands tangled violently in her dark locks as he held her face to him. "I love your hair. It's soft as silk and smells so damned good."

"Now that's an odd thing to be saying at a time like this." Kate chuckled, drawing her tongue lower. "What else do you love, Mr. Durango?"

"Your mouth . . . your breasts . . . your. . . . My God, woman!"

Kate was suddenly pulled off Charlie. "Hey, it's still my turn!" she protested as he pressed her down on the boulder.

Charlie laughed in sheer delight. "Your turn, hell." He knelt between her spread thighs, pulled her legs toward him, and hooked her knees high over his arms.

"Charlie!" A gasp escaped her as he locked their bodies deep and tight.

"Kate?" he queried tenderly.

"Don't stop," she breathed hoarsely, her fingernails digging into his hard thighs. "Please, don't ever stop."

"Oh, darlin'."

Her words unleashed a tempest of passion in him. Kate felt herself being carried away on an all-consuming tide. Charlie felt hot as a Texas summer, hard as steel, deep as her very soul. The pleasure would have been unendurable had it not felt so right.

His strained words drifted down to her. "Still having second thoughts, Kate?"

At that moment, such coherent distinctions were beyond her. But somehow, she managed to protest, "You get to have all the fun."

"Are you so sure?" Charlie withdrew, then hammered himself into her again, hard and sure.

Kate's overstrained senses could bear no more. She began to move against him, taking him greedily, crying out when his fingers stroked her.

What was fun when one had mind-shattering ecstasy?

Before the night was over, Kate had her turn, too, pushing Charlie down on the boulder and exploring his body at length, at will . . . By the time it was all over, she was so limp that he had to, dress them both. She felt exhausted, sore, and utterly sated when he carried her back to the wagon. After she slid onto the tick next to Betty, after she watched the man she loved stride off into the night, she heard the matron by her side chuckling.

"My dear, I do admire your spirit," Betty McLaughlin said.

Even after the heavenly hours with Kate, sleep still eluded Charlie Durango. He stared up at the black heavens and thought about her. He loved his feisty, headstrong girl with each moment that passed, yet their troubles were far from over. Kate might wed him, but she was determined not to mind him.

Not that he had really expected to hold a spunky filly like Kate on so tight a rein; part of the fun of loving her was the continuous battle of wills between them. But when all was said and done, and his gold band was on her finger, he was going to have to be the husband and she was going to have to be the wife. He would make his vow to provide for her, and she would make her vow to obey him.

Only Kate didn't see things that way. He'd known a few tornadoes more agreeable than she was.

Beyond that, two other stumbling blocks remained in their path, and Charlie knew that each could spell disaster for their relationship. First, Kate would soon find out that he was the man her pa had chosen as her husband. They might never survive that obstacle, but even if they did, a second barrier every bit as threatening loomed before them—

How in the hell would he tell Kate that he was taking her to live in Denver?

Chapter 20

Jeb Maloney sat in Dora Mae Fuermann's cozy
kitchen, eating a rich breakfast of grits and fat
German sausages. He glanced about in approval at
the homey room. Blue chintz curtains adorned the
spotless windows; matching potholders hung from
pegs on the walls. The pie safe was filled with baked
goods—pies, cookies, and breads—and fresh vege-
tables were already laid out on the dry sink to be
added to the succulent stew that would simmer on
the stove all day. Herbs and spices were strung up
to dry on a rack overhead, and the room teemed
with sweet, aromatic, and pungent smells.

Finishing his repast with a contented sigh, Jeb
leaned back in his chair, patted his ample stomach,
and stared at his ladylove, who stood across from
him, stirring a huge pot of soup bones at the cast
iron stove. Dora Mae Fuermann was a lovely
woman, thirty-five years old, blonde and pleasingly
plump. Today she wore a crisp blue and gold calico
dress and a starched, lacy apron. Even with the
strands of gold hair slipping free from her tight bun,
and the gloss of sweat on her rounded face, she was
a fine sight of bustling domesticity.

Jeb had always secretly admired Dora, even when
she was still wed to Franklin Fuermann. After Frank
had died of the wasting disease two years ago, Jeb

had waited the requisite year, then had begun courting the comely widow.

Jeb had expected Dora Mae to fall at his feet. After all, his ranch was ten times the size of the modest Fuermann homestead, and Dora had no man to care for her. Jeb had had grave doubts that she could make it on her own—

He'd been stunned and grudgingly impressed to find that the widow Fuermann had hardly fallen apart over the death of her husband. On the contrary, Dora had proved to be a highly independent, resourceful businesswoman. Soon after Frank's death, she'd rescued two itinerant drunks from the local saloon, sobered up both men, and convinced them to work her spread. While the ranch was being made profitable again, Dora had paid the hands' wages and provided for her own essentials by selling her wonderful baked goods, stews and soups, to the cafe in town. Even after the ranch had become profitable again, she'd continued to supply the restaurant, and had set aside a nice nestegg for herself.

In time, she had consented to begin seeing Jeb, and before long, the two had become lovers. Yet, to Jeb's surprise, when he had proposed marriage, Dora had put him off. She was not at all sure she wanted to give up her ranch, or her independence.

He'd persuade her to his point of view before long, he mused with determination. Kate's situation was likely to be resolved soon, and Jeb had a hankering to start a new life. For years, he'd grieved over his beloved Margaret, but now he was ready to get hitched again. Indeed, last night had given him a wonderful taste of what married life could be like. Usually, after making love with Dora, he went home; but this time, they'd fallen asleep in each others' arms. Jeb had forgotten how heavenly it could be to awaken next to the woman he loved, and he wanted to savor that pleasure for the rest of his life. He fully intended to straighten this stubborn woman out and set a date for the hitchin' with all due haste.

First, though, he'd have to get Kate wedded off, he thought grimly. And he'd have to deal decisively with Spuds Gilhooley. Jeb sighed. Spuds had really become a nuisance of late, salting Jeb's well and taking pot-shots at several of the ranchhands.

Dora left the stove with her coffee pot, moved over to Jeb's side, and poured him a cupful. "May I get you anything else, dear?" she asked, pouring a half cup for herself.

Jeb took a fond swat at her tempting rear. "You can set down that kettle, put your pretty self in a chair, and talk to me."

Laughing, Dora swept off to set the coffeepot back on the stove. Jeb watched her, admiring the sway of her hips and the crisp fullness of her calico skirts. She moved back to the table, sat down, and smiled at him.

"Any news of Kate?" she asked.

Jeb shook his head with a frown. "No, but if anyone can fetch that girl home and straighten her out, it's Charlie Durango."

Dora looked skeptical, her brow knitted as she lifted her pottery cup. "Jeb, I just don't like the fact that this man's a bounty hunter. And do you really think that Kate will just accept him as her husband?"

Jeb scratched his jaw thoughtfully. "Durango may not give her a heap of choice." As Dora gasped, he added sternly, "Now, darlin', I'll allow that Durango's a tough, ruthless man. But he's also a straight shooter. Don't you think I checked him out?"

Dora sighed. "I'm sure you did. Still, there's bound to be terrible gossip in town, when the two of them ride in from the hills without a chaperone."

Jeb shrugged. "That can't be helped, and my daughter has only herself to blame. What was I supposed to do? Send a passel of nuns out to Injun territory to fetch that holy terror home?" Jeb took a gulp of coffee. " 'Sides, any gossip in town will be all to the good, far as I can see. It'll only make the hitchin 'bout as easy for Kate to escape as the hangman's noose."

Dora rolled her eyes at Jeb's droll humor. "But what about this Mr. Durango? How can he know so quickly that he wants Kate for his wife?"

Jeb grinned. "Honey, it only takes one look at a pretty filly for a real man to know his mind."

Dora laughed. "Jeb Maloney, you're a devil!"

"Naw, honey, I'm just a man who knows what he wants," Jeb teased with a solemn wink. "As for Durango, he's seen the girl once, and it's plain as day he's taken a shine to her. He'll be retiring soon, and needing a wife." Jeb contentedly hooked his thumbs at his waist. "Yep, I reckon he'll lay down the law to Kate."

"I wish I shared your confidence," Dora put in ruefully. "I'm not even sure they'll make it back home safely. Aren't you worried about your daughter, off all alone in Indian territory?"

Jeb shrugged. "I've a mite of sympathy for the Comanches, but no, I ain't frettin' overly about that vixen of mine."

Dora sighed. "Jeb, Kate is seventeen. Have you ever thought of just letting her run her own life?"

Jeb hooted in derision. "The last time I let that she-devil run her own life, I found her rotting in the hoosegow in her unmentionables, playing poker and smoking a cigar."

Dora couldn't resist a grudging smile. "She's quite an independent woman, your daughter."

"And so are you, Dora Mae. I allow, sometimes you're as ornery as Kate." Jeb reached across the table and squeezed her hand. "You know, you're a fine one to be frettin' about gossip, after what we done last night, falling asleep in each others' arms. We'd best get hitched as soon as possible, honey. It's bound to get around town that we've been makin' time together.''

Grinning, Dora waved him off. ''Who's to gossip about a couple of middle-aged loners like us? Certainly no one here on my spread. Hermann and Jose are both tight-lipped and devoted to me. They've seen enough of life not to be shocked by anything. And I simply refuse to believe that your lovely housekeeper would ever say a word against either of us.''

Jeb's eyes implored the heavens. ''Woman, why are you being so contrary about this? You'd be so much better off if we married and merged our two spreads—''

''But I don't want my ranch swallowed up by the Bar M,'' Dora cut in passionately. She set down her coffee cup and stared him in the eye. ''You've got to understand something, Jeb. When Franklin died, I was devastated. I'd never even thought before of making it on my own. Then I decided I must pull myself up by my own bootstraps, since no one else was going to step in and rescue me. That experience taught me that I must never depend on a man again.''

''That attitude is foolish and prideful,'' Jeb scolded.

''Jeb, it's the way I am.''

He heaved a frustrated sigh. ''And what we've been doing, darlin' . . .'' He cleared his throat in acute discomfort. ''What if there's a young 'un?''

Dora blushed and smiled. ''Oh, Jeb, I'm sure I'm too old. Besides, during all those years with Franklin, and then with you, I've never conceived. I've always feared I may be barren.'' Biting her lip, she added quickly, ''I hope you aren't disappointed—''

Jeb waved her off and laughed heartily. ''Are you

funning me, woman? After raising up Kate, do you honestly think I'm hankering for another hellion to kick my butt into the hereafter?'' Watching her blanch, he continued, ''Now don't fret, darlin'. After all, such matters is best left with the Almighty, ain't they? Let's leave the decision in His hands. In the meantime, don't you think it's about time we asked for His blessing?''

Dora wagged a finger at him. ''Jeb Maloney, you're a determined man.''

''Well, darlin'?'' Jeb's grin was wide.

Dora's answering smile was full-dimpled. ''Shouldn't you be getting back to the ranch?''

Muttering an exasperated curse, Jeb set down his empty cup. ''Yeah, darlin', I reckon you're right. I've got a crew finishing up my new well, after Spuds Gilhooley poisoned the last one. Now if that jackass don't shoot me off my horse on my way home—''

''Oh, Jeb!'' Dora put in worriedly, reaching out to squeeze his gnarled hand. ''I nearly had apoplexy when you told me how the two of you had that shoot-out across your watering hole last week. Can't you and Spuds settle your range war?''

Jeb crossed his arms over his massive chest and frowned. ''Well, honey, water rights is pretty basic, and it would help a heap if the South Creek would quit shilly-shallying and decide which way it wants to run. Most of that creek now crosses my property, but you'd think Spuds owns the whole damn thing, kit and kaboodle, the way he keeps shooting at my cows and outriders. He's also rustled several of our head and altered their brands with his running iron. He's nothing but a lowdown brand artist.''

''And you can't share the creek with him?''

Jeb shrugged. ''I'd be willing to, honey, just to end this mess, but try to convince Spuds of it.'' He stood, pecking her cheek. "I'd best mosey along now, darlin'."

She rose and winked at him. "Come back soon."

"Just try 'n stop me," Jeb drawled with a grin.

Kate and Charlie were approaching the Bar M ranch, cantering over the rolling hills in the sweetness of the September morning.

Kate glanced at Charlie riding next to her, admiring his handsome face and muscled body, the easy way he rode in the saddle. Memories of their beautiful lovemaking stirred her senses, and pride filled her heart.

Their ride this morning had been most pleasant. Indeed, an hour ago, they'd stopped in a small, tree-shaded hollow, and had coupled together quickly and fiercely. A tremor seized Kate as she recalled the intensity of those passionate moments. It had been as if both of them felt threatened by their return to Round Rock, as if they both needed to reaffirm their love and commitment one last time.

Kate felt happier than she would have expected regarding her return. She did love Charlie, and she no longer rebelled so much at the prospect of marrying him. If she had to take a husband sooner or later, she supposed Charlie was about as prime a candidate as she could find. Besides, she could still savor her secret victory in winning over Pa, couldn't she? It would also be good to see Conchita again. Wouldn't Chita have fun planning her wedding? And perhaps Diablo would be waiting for her at home—how she prayed that her stallion had found his way back!

Yet at the back of Kate's mind still dwelt niggling doubts. Charlie was a charmer, but he was also a ruthless, determined man; he'd made it clear that he intended to wear the pants in the family, clearer still that he expected to bend her to his will.

Kate had fought just such a battle with her pa all her life. Jeb Maloney had scoffed at Kate's independence, had tried to control her with his ironclad domination. Now, was she merely trading one taskmaster for another?

Did she have a choice? She smiled ruefully. If only Charlie weren't such a good kisser and sweet-talker! And so much fun! He could have her convulsing in giggles one minute, then threaten to blister her the next. She definitely had a tiger by the tale in her handsome bounty hunter, she mused. Being head-over-heels in love with him didn't help one bit, either. She had a sinking feeling that by the time it was all over, Charlie Durango was going to flat wheedle her into getting his way . . .

As they rode along, Charlie was also thinking of their return. He was deeply worried about how Kate might react when she discovered that he'd withheld the truth from her. His only real hope was that he might take Jeb Maloney aside for a moment, and convince him not to tell Kate immediately that he was the man Jeb had chosen.

On the other hand, if he couldn't prevent Jeb from spilling the beans . . . Heaven help him!

Charlie stared at Kate riding beside him. She looked so lovely, yet so preoccupied, with that tight little frown marring her lovely brow. He wondered what she was thinking. When they'd stopped an hour ago and made wild, reckless love in the shady hollow, she had clung to him almost desperately. Lord, it had been so sweet! Yet it saddened him to think that she felt so threatened about returning home—and quite possibly, about marrying him . . .

Indeed, Kate's spirits were sagging a bit as they crested the last rise and approached the large farmstead in the valley below. Everything appeared normal, although she was surprised to see two hands digging a new well behind the house. How odd. Had the old well dried up?

She glanced at Charlie. "You want to stay with us at the ranch?"

He smiled. "Thanks, sugar, but all my gear is still out at Sam Stockton's hunting cabin. Reckon it would be best if I headed on back there—after we get things settled with your pa, of course."

Kate nodded, sobered at the thought that she and Charlie would soon be parted, if only for a short time. As they continued into the valley, she spotted her pa galloping up from the east, and her mood hit bottom. She watched Jeb dismount in front of the house; he then stood near the porch with a hand shading his eyes, watching them approach.

Charlie and Kate slowed their ascent and exchanged uncertain glances. "Well, I reckon this is it," she remarked tremulously.

Charlie frowned. "Reckon so. Honey, why don't you let me do the talking?"

"You always want to speak for me, don't you?" she said resentfully.

He smiled. "I'm just trying to spare you any unpleasantness with your pa, darlin'."

Kate shrugged. "Sure. Be my guest."

A moment later, they rode up to the house. Charlie quickly dismounted, then helped Kate off her horse. Jeb strode forward eagerly to greet them. "Well, ain't you two a sight for sore eyes," he drawled, offering Charlie his hand.

Charlie shook Jeb's hand and spoke forthrightly. "Mr. Maloney, you and me got some talking to do."

Jeb's guarded gaze flashed to his daughter, then back to Charlie. "What do you mean? Something wrong with Kate?"

"No, she's fine." Charlie shifted uncomfortably from boot to boot. "It's just that you and me—"

The sharp retort of a whizzing bullet stopped

Charlie in mid-sentence. As Charlie and Kate ducked and glanced about wildly, Jeb Maloney spotted his nemesis riding toward them from the east, with rifle raised. He stamped his foot in rage. "Goddamned Spuds Gilhooley! He's regular as the southbound stage! Now come on, you two, git in the house!"

Charlie grabbed Kate's hand, and the three made a dive for the house even as more bullets flew. Inside, Charlie helped Kate to a place of safety next to the far wall. He and Jeb grabbed rifles, then hunkered down by the front windows and returned Spuds' fire. Kate huddled near the fireplace, hands over her ears. She winced as a window shattered across the room, sending a spray of glass into the room. She wondered idly where Conchita was. When Spuds pulled his antics, the Mexican woman usually came out screaming rapid invective in Spanish.

After several tense moments, the firing at last ended. Charlie and Jeb got up warily, stepped outside, and made sure the coast was clear before striding back inside. While Jeb replaced their rifles in the case, Charlie came over to help Kate to her feet. "You all right, sugar?"

She nodded. "Looks like things ain't changed much around here."

Jeb came over to join them, staring at both of them with an expectant frown.

Kate turned to Charlie, lifting her chin. "I want to tell him," she said.

"Tell me what, daughter?" Jeb demanded suspiciously.

Kate stared steadily at Charlie, and he in turn threw up his hands in a gesture of defeat.

Kate took Charlie's hand, then turned proudly to Jeb. "Pa, I hate to disappoint you, but I've decided to marry Charlie here."

To Kate's confusion, Jeb threw back his head and

laughed. ''Now, why should that news disappoint me, daughter? Why, I'm pleased as punch that you've at last come to your senses. What could make a father prouder than to know his daughter has accepted the man he has chosen as her husband?''

Chapter 21

There's going to be a murder. That was the first thought that penetrated Kate's spinning mind. Her rage was so blinding that she couldn't see. Then she spent a wrathful moment wondering who she was angrier at—Charlie, or her pa . . . or herself.

That decision was quickly made. Even as Charlie held up a hand and said lamely, "Now, sugar . . ." Kate made a dive for him. She yanked his gun out of his holster, and the two struggled over it. In the end, Charlie managed to wrench the pistol away from Kate—but not before she had fired two bullets through the floor.

"Goddamn it, woman!" Charlie roared, his features white as he reholstered his gun. "You near shot off my foot! It's a wonder you didn't kill us both!"

Kate slapped him hard across the face. "You bastard! You lowdown, dirty, lying skunk!"

"Now, honey," Charlie said, rubbing his cheek. "I didn't lie—"

"And neither did you tell me the truth! You let me think that our getting hitched was all my idea, you miserable rotten scoundrel. And all the time, you were the one Pa chose!"

"You didn't tell her?" Jeb interjected. He appeared fascinated.

"You!" Kate exclaimed, whirling on her pa. "You're a bigger snake than he is. You told me I was marrying some geezer with gout, rheumatism, and a glass eye."

"Rotting teeth," Jeb corrected with a grin.

"You told her *that*?" Charlie put in, staring flabbergasted at Jeb.

Jeb hitched up his britches self-importantly. "The gal deserved a good scare after the stunt she pulled." He nodded decisively at Kate. "Spout off steam if you wish, daughter, but you're sure as blazes gonna get hitched—to Charlie Durango here. Make no mistake about that."

Jeb's arrogant directive poured fuel on the flames of his daughter's resistance. "As far as I'm concerned, the wedding's off, and you can both rot in hell!"

Jeb laughed, while Charlie paled by several shades.

Kate continued to face down her father vengefully. "Where's Conchita?"

"It's Saturday. She's gone off to town for supplies."

"Tell her I want to see her soon as she gets back." She bit her lip. "What about Diablo?"

"What about him?"

"I—I gave him his head, sent him home. Did he ever make it back to the ranch?"

Jeb shrugged. "I ain't seen hide nor hair of that devil horse."

"Damn it." Appalled to find herself fighting tears, Kate made a dive for the stairs.

Charlie rushed after her, grabbing her arm. "Honey, I'm sorry. Look, we'll straighten this out and find your horse. Please, you gotta let me explain—"

Kate jerked her arm free. "There's nothing to explain, you lousy son of a bitch!" she hissed. "You and my pa have had your joke on me, haven't you? So why don't you both just go have a good laugh?''

"Sugar, it wasn't that way. Not at all—''

Kate trembled in fury. "Don't call me sugar! And get the hell out of my sight! You come around again, Charlie Durango, and, by God, I'm gonna kill you!''

Kate stormed off up the stairs, leaving Charlie to groan as he stared helplessly after her.

He heard Jeb chuckle behind him. "The gal'll come around in time.''

Charlie whirled on Jeb. "No thanks to you. How could you tell her such terrible lies about me?''

Jeb waved him off. "Come on now, son. I swear the girl likes you, or she wouldn't be so riled.''

Charlie rolled his eyes. "If that's liking me, I'm sure as hell not gonna survive her ever loving me. Damn it, why did you have to go tell her I was the one—straight out like that? Why couldn't you give it some time?''

"Hell, son, I thought you'd already filled her in.'' Jeb laughed and strode over to the sideboard, picking up a decanter of whiskey. "Looks like you and me could use a drink.''

"Now that's the first thing you've said that makes any sense.''

The two men took their drinks, sat down, and eyed each other warily.

"So what do we do now?'' Charlie asked.

Jeb took a slow sip. "Give the girl some time to cool off.''

"Now, why didn't I think of that?'' Charlie said sarcastically. "You know, she's gonna run off again, first chance she gets.''

"Then we'll just have to see that she doesn't get that chance, won't we?'' Jeb asked slyly.

Charlie slammed his drink down on the table. "Why do you have to be so mean to her?''

Jeb glowered back at Charlie. "So I'm the villain

now? Do you have any idea of the grief that brat has caused me over the years?''

"Kate told me you've always blamed her for her ma's death," Charlie accused hotly. "I'm beginning to think it's true."

"That's a bunch of bull!"

"Is it?" Charlie got up and began to pace. "I wonder. You know, she's got feelings, too, just like anyone else. Kate may put on a fine show, but inside, she's fragile as glass."

"Fragile, my butt! That gal is tough as rawhide."

"Do you ever give her a chance?" Charlie continued furiously. "Do you ever even listen to her?" He turned on Jeb. "Do you know that German bitch out in Nacogdoches all but killed those girls? Do you even care? How much do you know about your own daughter?"

For once, Jeb Maloney was rendered speechless.

"Now she's never gonna marry me," Charlie continued morosely. "Just because I'm the one you chose. She's got her pride, and she got it straight from you. If you hadn't poisoned her mind about me, we mighta had a chance. But now . . ." About to explode with helpless frustration, Charlie kicked over a basket of wood. "Hellfire and damnation!"

"Come on, son, calm down," Jeb interjected irritably. "You ain't gonna solve nothin' by bustin' up the furniture."

Charlie threw himself in a chair and glared at Jeb. "Then you tell me what we should do."

Jeb smiled. "If you want to go upstairs right now and straighten her out, that's fine by me. I'll even throw in my razor strap."

Charlie shook a finger at Jeb. "There's enough bad feelings here already. I ain't gonna force that girl to marry me, and that's final."

Jeb scowled. "You know, there's gonna be talk,

once it gets around town that you two rode in from the hills, unchaperoned.''

Charlie ground his teeth. All at once, it occurred to him that Jeb Maloney hadn't even bothered to ask about their journey, or about whether they'd encountered any hardships or dangers along the way. All the man appeared to care about was his reputation in the community, and getting Kate off his hands. Charlie's meager respect for Jeb was slipping rapidly.

"I said I ain't forcing her," he repeated in a lethally soft voice.

Jeb shrugged. "Suit yourself. I still say, give the girl some time—or a good blistering—and she'll come around."

Charlie hooted derisively and lit a cheroot. "Give the girl some time, and she'll shovel us both six feet under."

Upstairs, Kate had thrown herself across the bed and was sobbing her heart out.

She should have known! Oh, what a fool she'd been! She'd let that no-good bounty hunter deceive her and make a mockery of her feelings! She'd fallen in love with Charlie Durango and had stumbled straight into her pa's trap, blind as a bat! Now Pa and Charlie were no doubt laughing themselves silly downstairs!

What hurt the most was knowing that *she* had allowed this to happen. In the final analysis, she had only herself to blame. She had let Charlie charm her, steal her heart away, and win her trust. Heaven help her, she had loved every minute of it! Then he had ruthlessly shattered her trust forever.

Now, if she knew anything about her pa, he was going to try his best to force her to marry Charlie. Once it got around Round Rock that she and Charlie had ridden in alone, the local gossips would jaw their heads off. And what if Charlie told her pa that they'd become lovers? She groaned. If Pa didn't kill Charlie first, he'd grab his shotgun and march them both off to the altar.

Well, damn it, she wasn't going to stand for it! Wiping her tears with her sleeve, she got up and walked over to the window. She frowned as she spotted her father's handiwork. Pa had nailed several stout boards across the window, leaving only slight gaps for ventilation. Kate laughed ruefully. She might be able to kick the boards out, but not without making one hell of a racket that was bound to give her away.

Tarnation. Pa had thought of everything. She was a prisoner in her own house. She'd no doubt be kept locked in up here until she consented to marry Charlie.

Kate clenched her fists and ground her teeth. She'd find a way to get around both of them yet! Surely Conchita would help her, once she learned how low Pa had sunk. She'd run away, and—

Where would she go? Remembering her fate as a captive of the Comanche, Kate shuddered. She could not be so foolhardy as to ride north again—

Suddenly, she smiled as she recalled Betty Mc-Laughlin's words when the two of them had said goodbye this morning. The kindly matron had invited Kate to come visit them any time in New Braunfels. Perhaps she'd fare better heading south this time. She could stay with the McLaughlins until she figured out what she should do next.

How would she get there? She'd have to steal one of Pa's horses, she reckoned. Oh, where in the Sam Hill was Diablo? If only her favorite horse had found his way home, she'd feel so much better about her own chances now. The stallion's disappearance only deepened Kate's depression.

One thing was for certain—Diablo was much more free at this moment than she was.

To the west of the Bar M ranch, Spuds Gilhooley was chuckling to himself as he rode toward home. An expression of vengeful pleasure sculpted his face as he recalled Jeb Maloney, his daughter, and the stranger making a dive for the big house as he rode past with his gun blazing. Hadn't he rattled their hocks!

Then a frown drifted in. While Spuds felt as determined as ever to get his creek back, as always, Jeb Maloney was proving to be a stubborn adversary. Only last week, when Spuds had attempted to water some of his head at the South Creek, he and Jeb had shot it out for almost three hours on opposite banks of the watering hole. Indeed, one of Maloney's bullets had taken an inch of flesh off Spuds' left arm. He still had the hole to prove it.

Now Maloney had his daughter back again, that little spitfire Kate. And there was that stranger hanging around—probably some no-account shadow rider Maloney had hired to track the girl down.

While Spuds knew from local gossip that Jeb and his daughter hadn't gotten along well for years, it was also clear to him now that Maloney set great store by that gal. Why else would the man go to such lengths to bring her back after she'd run off?

Spuds stroked his grizzled jaw and grinned. Maybe there was more than one way to skin a skunk, he mused.

Chapter 22

"**O**h, *Pobrecita, pobrecita*," Conchita lamented.
Two hours later, Kate sat huddled on her bed next to Conchita; the motherly woman had wrapped an arm about Kate's shoulders. Kate had sobbed out the entire story of her ordeal to her friend, leaving out only the fact that she had made love with Charlie.

Conchita was stunned and sympathetic. "To think of all you went through, *chica*," she said, squeezing Kate's hand. "Being chased down like a lowly outlaw, then captured by Indians. After all this, you come home to find that your father has played this dirty trick on you."

"Chita, I've got to run away again," Kate announced. "Will you help me?"

Conchita hesitated. "What about this Charlie Durango? How do you feel about him?"

Kate shrugged. "I've known worse scoundrels, I suppose. But I'll never trust him again, not after the way he betrayed me with Pa."

Conchita nodded. "I'm sorry."

"Well?" Kate pressed. "Will you help me?"

Conchita hesitated. "*Corazón*, you know how I try not to interfere between you and your father—"

"But look what he gone and done!" Kate cried. "What would my ma think of all this?"

Conchita gasped and quickly crossed herself. *"Por Dios! Señora* Margarita would turn over in her grave."

"So why ain't you helping me?" Kate implored. She squeezed Conchita's hand. "You know, Chita, there comes a time when a body has to make a stand."

At last Conchita nodded dismally. *"Sí,* you are right. This time *Señor* Jeb has gone too far." As Kate lit up with vengeful pleasure, Conchita held up a hand. "But there's a condition, my friend. I'll only help you if you promise me you'll stay far away from the *mal pais* this time."

Kate laughed bitterly. "Believe me, I've learnt my lesson. I'm heading due south and staying in civilized areas, well away from the Comanches."

Conchita snapped her fingers. "I know! You can stay with *mi madre* in Austin! I'll write down the address for you."

Kate nodded eagerly. "We also met a nice family out on the trail. They were headed to live in New Braunfels, and the wife invited me to come visit them any time."

Conchita gazed at Kate sadly. "Are you sure all of this is necessary, *mi amiga?*"

Kate drew her hand to her heart. "I swear on my ma's memory, Chita. There's no other way."

Supper was a somber meal for Kate, her father, and Conchita down in the kitchen. While Kate had bathed, washed her hair, and put on a fresh dress, her attitude toward her father was coldly disdainful throughout the meal. Luckily, Jeb made no further mention of her marrying Charlie—if he had, Kate was fully prepared to claw his eyes out. She assumed that Charlie had gone back to the hunting cabin where he was staying—not that she really cared, of course.

After dinner, just as Kate had feared, her father locked her in her bedroom for the night, throwing the outside bolt. Seething with resentment, she changed into a fresh shirt, trousers, and her boots, packed a small carpetbag, and laid a warm jacket and a hat across her bed. Then she paced for hours by the light of a candle. Conchita had promised to help her escape, and the two women had agreed that they couldn't make their move until late at night. When Kate had tried to discuss specifics, the Mexican woman had said simply, "Leave this in my hands, *chica*."

During the lonely, frustrating hours that followed, Kate found her thoughts turning to Charlie. She hated him for his betrayal, but she missed him, too. Though she'd sent him packing in no uncertain terms, in the back of her mind was a gnawing hurt that he'd given up on her so quickly.

It was past midnight when Kate at last heard a key turning in the lock. She waited expectantly, biting her lip as the bolt slid back and the door creaked open. Then, with intense relief, she watched Conchita slip into the room.

"Conchita! Well, it's about time," Kate said.

"Shhh!" Conchita scolded back, holding a finger to her lips. "Don't forget that *Señor* Jeb is asleep in the next room. I had a most difficult time sneaking in there and getting these keys out of his trousers."

Kate smiled, taking the ring from Conchita. "Don't worry, I'll sneak these back into his room before I leave, so he won't know for sure how I got sprung. What about downstairs?"

"*Señor* ordered Pepe to guard the house tonight. But do not fret—I brought him three cups of coffee laced with brandy, and now he's sleeping like a baby out on the front porch."

"Oh, Conchita, what would I do without you?" Kate hugged her tightly.

The two women moved apart. Conchita frowned worriedly as she watched Kate don her jacket and hat. "Do you have everything you need?"

Kate nodded, picking up her carpetbag. "I've packed a couple of changes of clothing, as well as a few dollars I've saved from my allowance. I'll be fine."

Conchita lifted an eyebrow. "I wish I shared your confidence, *chica*. It worries me sick that you're leaving this way—stealing off like a thief in the night. Couldn't you hide in one of the line shacks—at least until dawn?"

Kate shook her head. "Can't risk it. Pa might catch me there."

Conchita sighed and handed Kate a small piece of paper. "Here is *mi madre's* address in Austin. Her *casita* is just a few blocks to the east of Capitol Square."

"Thanks, Conchita." Kate studied the address and pocketed the slip. "Don't worry, I'll likely be there long before first light."

"You'll let me know?"

"I'll write you as soon as possible. I'll send my letter General Delivery, care of the Oatts store in town. That way, Pa won't know where I am."

Conchita touched the girl's arm. "Kate, how are you going to support yourself, with no family to care for you?"

Kate shrugged. "I'll find work somewheres."

"But for a young woman in your position, there's really nothing, except—"

"I'll make out," Kate assured her proudly.

Conchita's eyes were deeply troubled as she hugged her charge one last time. "*Vaya con dios, mi hija,*" she whispered.

"You take care, too, Chita." Kate hugged Conchita back, then slipped from the room. Outside, next to her father's door, she set down her carpetbag and listened intently. Hearing the muffled sounds of Jeb's snoring, she opened the door and crept into her father's room.

She stood for a moment staring at him. Jeb Maloney lay on the big double bed in his nightshirt, a beam of moonlight outlining his massive body. He was sound asleep and snoring loudly. Spotting his trousers laid across a chair, Kate tiptoed over and carefully replaced his key ring in the pocket.

She stared at her father for one last time, strangely wishing she could feel something more for him. Why did they always have to be so at war with each other?

Kate slipped from the room.

On the rise overlooking the ranchhouse, Charlie Durango sat on Corona, smoking in the darkness and waiting for Kate to make her move. He'd known it would be only a matter of time before she gave her pa the slip again, and this time, he fully intended to be one step ahead of his feisty little fiancée.

Events he'd witness over the evening had only confirmed his suspicions. The Mexican housekeeper had come out on the porch several times, bringing coffee to the ranchhand who had pulled guard duty there. Charlie had a feeling that coffee had been heavily spiked, for now, the man lay sprawled back in his chair, his rifle propped across his knees and his sombrero pulled down over his eyes.

Charlie reckoned that soon Kate would appear.

He was beginning to understand Kate's antipathy toward Jeb Maloney. The man was a block-headed idiot without one whit of tact. If only Jeb had restrained that tongue of his for five minutes after they'd arrived . . . Now, he had them all in a fine pickle. For it would no longer be enough for Charlie to convince Kate that he was the right man for her. He'd have to convince her it didn't matter that he was the one Jeb Maloney had chosen.

And to Kate, it would always matter.

As a flicker of movement caught his eye, Charlie straightened in his saddle. He smiled as he watched Kate appear, streaking out from the back side of the house. She was dressed for the trail, had a carpetbag and a rifle in hand, and was heading for the barn.

It was about time to make his move—

Then Charlie started as he watched another shadowy figure emerge from behind the house and begin to stalk Kate. Even from a distance, Charlie could tell that the man was rangy, bow-legged, and familiar.

"Shit," Charlie cursed, throwing down his cheroot and clucking to his horse. This varmint's appearance was an unexpected and dangerous complication.

Could he make it to Kate in time?

Spuds Gilhooley smiled to himself as he followed Kate toward the barn. He had figured it would be only a matter of time before Maloney's daughter tried to hightail it again—and he'd been right. Two hours ago, he'd left his horse tied to a tree just over the northern rise and had sneaked down to the back of the Maloney big house. He'd waited in the shadows near the back door for Kate to appear—an uneventful time, except for his having to knife-kill a drowsy copperhead that had wanted to cozy up to him.

Then, the girl had slipped out the back door, not even seeing him in the shadows. The little hellion was playing right into his hands! He would kidnap little Miss Kate and ransom her for just the prize he wanted—

The South Creek.

Watching the girl enter the barn, Spuds crept steadily toward the doors. It was critical that he get the drop on the girl, that he not be seen.

Taking a position behind one of the doors, Spuds lifted the butt of his pistol and thoroughly relished his coming victory as he waited for Kate to emerge . . .

In the barn, Kate saddled up a large yellow horse. Nutmeg was not as fleet a horse as Diablo, but he was docile, responsive, and tireless. She secured her rifle in its scabbard and hung her carpetbag and two empty canteens from the saddle. She knew she'd have to fill the canteens at the new pump behind the house. Pa had mentioned over dinner that Spuds Gilhooley had salted their old well, and that the two of them had engaged in a three-hour-long gunfight last week. Kate shook her head ruefully. She supposed Spuds and Pa would plow each other under sooner or later. It was a tossup as to which man was more ornery—

Kate was leading Nutmeg from the barn when abruptly, her hat was yanked off from behind. Even as she tried to whirl to face her attacker, a large burlap grain sack was yanked down over her head and everything went black—

Kate fought valiantly, kicking and screaming at her unknown assailant. But she was soon rendered helpless as the sack was firmly tied beneath her knees and she was heaved over someone's shoulder like a sack of potatoes. Fighting became impossible, as the bag was tight and her arms were pinned against her body. Worse luck, she doubted her muffled cries could be heard as far away as the house.

A moment later, she was thrown face-down across a horse and felt someone mounting behind her. A man—she could feel the hard muscles of his thighs. Oh, god, who had kidnaped her? Was it Charlie—or perhaps someone much more dastardly, like Spuds Gilhooley?

Kate sneezed violently. The rough fabric of the burlap tickled her nose and smelled of dust and grain. But, thank God, she could at least breathe, since whoever had captured her had cut several small slits near the top of the sack. The holes were big enough to allow air to pass, but not large enough that she could really see anything beyond a bit of denim and a glimpse of a dusty boot.

The horse leaped forward into the night. Kate's very bones were jarred as they galloped along. She squirmed violently, letting out a yelp of discomfort and indignation. At once, a hand slammed down hard on her bottom.

Kate froze. Hot indignation practically choked off her breathing. Hell's bells, this was enough! Whoever this bastard was, she was flat gonna murder him!

Chapter 23

H alf an hour later, Kate felt the horse skid to a stop. Her captor dismounted, rolled her off the saddle and across his shoulder, and strode off with her.

She heard a door creak open. Three more steps, and she was thrown down on what appeared to be a mattress. She heard footsteps move off, listened to the hiss of a match, and then a lamp was lit—she could see its wavering glow through the slits in the burlap.

The bed squeaked as someone sat down beside her. The knot beneath her knees was undone, the sack slowly pulled off her.

For a moment, Kate was disoriented, shaking her head and blinking at the brightness. Then she looked around. She appeared to be in a small, rustic cabin. On the bed next to her sat—

"Evening, sugar," Charlie Durango drawled.

"You!"

With fingernails bared, Kate made a dive for Charlie's throat, but he was too quick for her, tumbling her down on the mattress, grabbing her wrists, and pinning her to the bed with his hard body. His dark face loomed above hers in the wavering light.

Lying there helpless beneath his muscled frame, Kate screamed out every obscenity she could think of. Charlie listened in grim silence, with only the twitching of a muscle in his jaw betraying his exasperation.

At last, Kate could think of no further invective to hurl at him, and she merely glowered at him, her face hot and her chest heaving.

"You finished?" he asked softly.

"Drop dead!"

"You gonna listen now?"

"Go to hell!"

"Damn it, Kate," Charlie muttered. "You can have your choice. Either I'm gonna gag you and tie you to this here bedpost—and you can just lay there while I explain things—or we can talk this out quietly, like two adults. In either case, you're gonna listen, woman."

Kate glowered at him for a fearsome moment, her bosom heaving.

"Well, Kate?"

"Fine," she snapped.

Charlie stared at her suspiciously, then moved off her. The instant his weight was lifted, Kate sprang to her feet and made a dive for the door. She was seized about the waist so abruptly and forcefully that she almost lost her wind, her face purpling. An instant later, she was flung back down on the mattress, and an enraged Charlie again loomed over her, pinning her to the bed.

"All right!" she cried. "I give up!"

"You try that again—" he warned.

She shook her head and retorted nastily, "You don't have to finish. I've no hankering to be hogtied. I'll listen."

After scowling at her for another menacing moment, Charlie got up, crossed the room, and sat down on a straight chair. Kate sat on the side of the bed, smoothing down her disheveled hair and glancing about warily. They were in a one-room log cabin with a cedar roof. The room was sparsely furnished, with a bed, a table and chairs, and a dry sink. The floor was composed of rough puncheons, and a huge stone fireplace, complete with cast iron tripod and pots, added a touch of warmth to the scene.

She turned back to Charlie, biting back a wince at his formidable expression. "Where are we?"

He shrugged. "This here is the hunting cabin owned by my friend, Sam Stockton. He told me I could stay here while I'm in Round Rock."

"And does he approve of your stealing females away from their beds in the middle of the night—and spiriting them off here?"

His jaw tight, Charlie leaned forward, lacing his long fingers together. "You were gonna run off again, weren't you?"

"So what if I was?" she flung at him.

Charlie cursed under his breath. "Woman, didn't you learn nothin' the last time? Are you hellbent on gettin' yourself raped, scalped, or worse?"

"That's a matter of opinion!"

"Bullshit," Charlie retorted. "If I hadn't shown up tonight when I did, you would have hightailed it back out to the hills and gotten your fool self killed this time!"

"So you just up and kidnapped me?"

"Yeah, I sure did. And in the nick of time, to boot. As things turned out, I was only two steps ahead of Spuds Gilhooley."

"You were *what*?" Kate blanched.

Leaning toward her, Charlie drawled nastily, "That's right, darlin'. Spuds was lyin' in wait for you just outside the barn. Luckily for you, I spotted him, coldcocked him, and tossed him out to dry on the woodpile. Reckon he's still there sleepin' it off."

Kate soon recovered her indignation. "So?" she flung at him.

"So," he retorted heatedly, "excepting for me, darlin', you'd be dealing with your pa's worst enemy right now."

Kate's green eyes shot sparks at Charlie. "You're my worst enemy, Charlie Durango—first, for betraying me, and next, for stealing me off like this!"

He sighed heavily. "How else was I supposed to make you listen to reason?"

Kate glowered at him.

"Well, Kate?"

"So I'm listening," she hurled at him spitefully.

He flung both hands outward. "Kate, what are you so riled about?"

She laughed incredulously. "How can you ask that? After you lied to me—"

"I didn't lie," he cut in patiently. "I just postponed telling you the truth for a bit."

She crossed her arms over her bosom and glared at him rebelliously. "Same difference!"

He lurched to his feet. "And what if I had told you who I really was, right from the beginning?"

Staring up at him, Kate was at a loss. "That—that would have been much better."

"Really, Kate?" His voice held cynical disbelief. "What if I had admitted on that first day we met that I was the one your pa chose? You just would have started hating me all the more, sooner."

Kate gulped at that. "I don't hate you, Charlie."

"Don't you?" He stepped closer, the glow of the lamp wavering over him, illuminating his harsh features and the bitter gleam in his eyes. "You hate your pa, so it's for damn sure you're gonna hate any man he likes—"

"Charlie, that's not fair!"

"Perhaps it ain't fair, sugar, but it sure is true. Hell, if I'd a' told you, you would have knifed me in my sleep."

Kate glanced away in acute guilt, unable to deny his words.

Charlie stepped closer, gripping her chin and forcing her tumultuous gaze up to meet his. "It's all about him, ain't it? You can't see nothing beyond how much you hate him. And that's gonna poison your mind about any man in your life—that is, until you find a beau your pa truly despises. Then you'll collar him quicker'n a whore lassoing a greenhorn off the stage."

Kate's face burned at his accurate barb. "That ain't true."

"Ain't it? Then tell me why you hate me so much, Kate."

"Because you—because Pa—"

"See what I told you?" he cut in softly.

Kate lurched to her feet and moved away, so he wouldn't see the hot tears threatening to flood her eyes. "How did all this happen, anyhow?"

"What do you mean?"

She cleared her throat. "How come my pa chose you as—as my husband?"

Charlie watched her thin shoulders tremble, and his heart twisted with sudden sympathy for her. "Sugar, that's not important—"

She whirled on him. "You tell me, Charlie Durango. Now."

Charlie groaned. Coloring the truth would only make things worse, as Kate could always ask Jeb, too, and he had all the tact of a rampaging bull. "It was right simple. Your pa came up to me at the Round Rock Saloon and asked me to marry you."

"Just like that?" she gasped.

"He'd evidently heard of me before," Charlie explained awkwardly. "He'd heard I was aimin' to retire from bounty hunting and needed a bride."

"Yeah—but why did he choose you in particular?"

Charlie stroked his jaw, then glanced at her sheepishly. "Because he thought I was a tough enough man to handle you, darlin'." With a rueful grin, he added, "He was wrong."

Kate had to struggle mightily to repress a smile at Charlie's charming remark. She lifted her chin. "What did he offer you to take me off his hands?"

"Nothin'." Charlie glanced away uneasily.

Kate, not fooled for an instant, confronted him with a clenched fist. "Quit lying, damn it, and tell me what he offered you!"

Charlie sighed. "His ranch, once he passes." Watching Kate's features tighten mutinously, he stepped forward quickly. "I turned him down."

"I'll just bet you did," Kate said scornfully. "You probably wanted my pa's land all along."

"That's not true. You can ask your pa."

Kate shrugged. "It don't matter. If we married, you'd get his ranch anyway, eventually."

"Damn it, woman!" Feeling intensely frustrated, Charlie began to pace. Should he tell her about his gold mine? he mused. Glancing at Kate's face, sensing the hurt buried beneath those many layers of icy pride, he listened to the inner voice that warned him that now was not the right moment.

Instead, he turned to her and said, "Look, Kate, I don't give a damn about your pa's land, or his money. I'm well fixed."

Kate laughed cynically. "You're well fixed? Quit pulling my leg."

"I ain't." Charlie hooked his thumbs in the waistband of his trousers and straightened his shoulders self-importantly. "I tell you, I'm right prosperous. When a man's in my profession, he knows his days trailing outlaws are numbered. I've turned in many a desperado for the reward money over the years, and I've been thrifty."

"Thrifty!" Kate scoffed. "My pa's rich."

"I'm richer," he drawled back.

"Hokum and hogwash." She regarded him skeptically. "And even if it was true, you must want something."

"Yeah, honey," he said softly, starting toward her with a grin. "I want you."

Catching Kate off guard, Charlie pulled her into his arms and kissed her passionately. As always, she reeled at his nearness and the hard heat of his body against hers. Nonetheless, with a strangled, outraged cry, she managed to push him away.

"Oh, no you don't, Charlie Durango!" she cried, throwing him a pouting look. "We can't do this. I'm mad at you—and I'll never be able to trust you again."

"Sure you can, sugar," he coaxed, digging his fingers into her soft behind and yanking her close once more.

Kate's open-mouthed protest was smothered when Charlie kissed her again. She tried to fight him, but Charlie relentlessly assaulted her senses with the provocative thrust of his tongue in her mouth, and the bold stroking of his fingers. When he pushed upward, grinding her pelvis against his hard arousal, Kate gasped, only to whimper when Charlie used the opportunity to deepen the kiss, swamping her protest with his scorching lips and ravaging tongue. Her nipples tightened against his crushing chest, her senses swam with his scent, and hot lust twisted and surged between her thighs.

As Kate stood reeling, disoriented, Charlie planted soft kisses all over her face. Then he began nibbling on her earlobe. "Sugar," he whispered seductively, "don't be this way. I need you so much."

By now, Kate was a mass of quivering gooseflesh,

her protests sounding weak even to her own ears. "Charlie, don't you dare try to sweet talk me. Don't you—"

The rest of her comment was drowned by another drugging kiss.

Kate was panting when she finally managed to push him away again. "Damn it, Charlie Durango! Why do you have to be such a good kisser?"

He grinned and thrust against her devilishly. "That all I'm good at?"

"That, too. Aw, hell."

Trembling with her need of him, Kate grabbed his hand and yanked him toward the bed.

"Hey, sugar, where we going?" he teased.

"Where do you think, you sly devil?" She shoved him down on the mattress and added grimly, "This don't change nothin' now."

"What do you mean?" he asked, frowning as she straddled him.

"You'd best hush, Charlie Durango," she said, reaching for his belt buckle. "I'm in a hurry."

Charlie howled with laughter. Then, watching her deft fingers, he scowled again. "If you think I'm gonna let you have your wicked way with me, then refuse to marry me—"

This time, Kate curtailed his words with a hungry kiss. "Will you kindly shut up, bounty hunter?"

He chuckled, then groaned in agonized pleasure as she stroked him. "You gonna shuck them trousers, woman?"

Kate grinned. "Now you're talkin' some sense." She stood and quickly removed her boots, britches, and pantalets.

Charlie studied her avidly, watching the light flow over her long slim legs and lovely bare hips, and that wonderful enticing place shielded by a swath of raven curls. Damn, she was so fine, with that hot flush of desire on her cheeks and her lips all wet and swollen from his kisses . . .

"The shirt, too," he directed solemnly.

"Yes sir."

Kate came back to him wearing only her lacy camisole, looking hot as sin. When she straddled him again, it was more than Charlie's overstrained senses could bear. Rolling her beneath him, he slipped his hands inside her camisole, gripped her aroused breasts, and impaled her with a deep, sure stroke.

"Oh, Charlie." Kate's fists were clenched against his shoulders, her eyes closed in ecstasy.

"Look at me, darlin'," he whispered.

She did, and Charlie practically exploded at the expression of stark abandonment in her eyes. "You're right—we'll talk later," he muttered, lowering his lips to hers.

A dull pain low in her belly awakened Kate later that night. Gently slipping out of Charlie's arms, she got up, lit a candle, and discovered that her monthly time had come. In a cabinet, she found some clean rags with which to see to her needs. Afterward, she blew out the candle and returned to bed wearing her shirt and pantalets.

Charlie stirred beside her, stroking her back. "You all right, sugar?"

"I'm fine," she whispered.

She felt him getting up. A few seconds later, the light of a lantern spilled over the cabin. She drank in the beauty of Charlie's bronzed, naked body and dark, tousled hair as he moved back toward her. He put the lantern down on a table near the bed, pulled on his trousers, then sat down beside her on the mattress and took her hand.

Gazing at Kate, Charlie was filled with tender emotion. This beautiful girl had made love with him no less than three times before they'd fallen asleep in each other's arms. How he adored her! Now that the fires of her anger had faded, he sensed the time was right for their heart-to-heart talk. He'd tell her about his land in the West, but maybe it would be best not to mention the gold mine yet, he mused. He recalled how she'd scoffed at his claims of wealth. Hell, she probably wouldn't even believe they were going to be millionaires until the gold strike actually came in.

He stroked her tumbled hair and winked at her. "We'll have to get you home before long, honey, else it's going get all over the county that you've run off again tonight."

"I suppose you're right," she said, sitting up.

He reached out to touch her arm. "Kate, before we go, there's something else we've got to talk about—"

She glowered at him suspiciously. "You mean there's something else you've hidden—"

He held up a hand. "Just hear me out before you up and get riled again."

She shrugged. "Very well."

He stared at her earnestly. "Kate, I want you to marry me and come live with me in Denver."

"Denver!" Kate was flabbergasted.

"Yeah, honey. I got some land there, up in the western territories." When she would have protested, he quickly added, "Just think about it for a minute. You could get away from your pa forever. Wouldn't you like that?"

Kate shook her head defiantly. "Hell, Charlie, I ain't even said I'd marry you, not for certain—"

"That's not true," he cut in, glowering. "You gave me your promise out on the trail—"

"Well, that was before I knew, so it don't count."

"Oh, for Chrissakes!"

"Besides, why do you want to drag me off to some Godforsaken place like Denver?"

"Godforsaken?" he echoed incredulously. "Why, it's right beautiful there, darlin'. You should read the letters my partner sends."

"Your partner? What partner?" she asked suspiciously.

Charlie glanced away awkwardly. "Him and me bought some land there together. That's where I want us to live."

"Well, forget it, Charlie," she snapped.

"Why?"

"I don't want to live far away from Texas."

"You don't want . . ." Charlie threw up his hands in exasperation. "Then why in the hell have you been trying to run away from Round Rock three ways to sundown?"

She set her chin stubbornly. "That was different. That was between me and Pa."

"And this move to Denver is between you and me, ain't it, Kate?" he demanded hotly. "It's got nothin' to do with your love for Texas—you just don't want to go off nowheres with me."

"Well, maybe I don't," she argued, her eyes flashing with resentment. "Here, you told me you was ready to settle down, and it appears you ain't nothin' but a tumbleweed, Charlie Durango. First you'll drag me off to this Godforsaken Denver, then, in another year or so, you'll pull up stakes and insist we move somewheres else—"

"That's not how it's gonna be, sugar. We're staying in the Pikes Peak region permanent."

"And how are we gonna afford to live there?"

"I already told you, Kate, I have plenty of money, if that's what's fretting you."

"It ain't just the money, Charlie." Kate got up and walked toward the center of the cabin. "I ain't sure about this. Not at all."

He lurched aggressively to his feet. "Are you saying that after everything that's passed between you and me, you ain't gonna marry me?"

"I'm saying I ain't sure!" she retorted in helpless frustration.

"Well, I'll be hanged." He pulled his fingers through his hair. "What if there's a young 'un?"

Kate glanced away miserably. "There ain't none, Charlie. That's what woke me up."

"That make you happy, Kate?" he asked bitterly.

She turned to him, reeling at the look of hurt on his handsome face. "No, Charlie. But when you think about it, maybe it is for the best. Hell, I don't even know if I'd make you a good wife. I'm too headstrong."

"Why don't you let me be the judge of that?"

"That's just it!" she railed, suddenly angry again. "You want to tell me everything to do. You want to break me like some wild horse."

"Not break you, Kate," he cut in. He flashed her a tender grin. "I reckon you could use some gentling, though."

She balled her hands on her hips. "Whatever you want to call it, Charlie Durango, to me, it's taking over my life. And I'm tired of having men make all my decisions. First it was Pa, always tellin' me to go to this school or that school. Now you're telling me where to go and what to do."

"So we're back to him again?" Charlie asked with thinning patience. He drew a hard breath. "So you ain't gonna marry me?"

She lifted her chin. "Not yet."

Something ominous flashed in his eyes. "You ain't getting rid of me, girl."

Undaunted, she smirked at him. "Did I say I wanted to?"

He drew closer, regarding her intently. "Just what are you suggesting, Kate?"

"A girl likes to be courted," she put in coyly.

Charlie shook a finger at her as realization dawned. "Why, you little stinker!"

"I ain't saying no," she went on primly. "But I ain't saying yes yet, neither."

Attempting a stern expression, Charlie pulled Kate into his arms. "I oughta tan your hide but good. You're bound and determined to make me suffer for all my past sins, ain't you, woman?"

She feigned an expression of demure innocence. "A girl likes to be sure."

Charlie rolled his eyes. "All right, then, sugar. Maybe I'll go along with this. But there's one condition."

"Yeah?" She ran her fingertips teasingly over his chest, and felt a surge of self-satisfaction as she heard his breathing quicken. "What's that?"

He gripped her errant fingers and glared down at her. "You ain't running off again." As she glanced away guiltily, he took her face in his hands. "You do it, Kate, and by God, I will take you over my knee, and—"

"All right, then," she cut in irritably. "But if I don't run off, you've gotta promise to let me make up my own mind."

"Oh, sure, honey," he put in agreeably.

She eyed him dubiously. "Wanna shake on it, then?"

"Shake on it, my butt."

Charlie yanked her close and kissed her until she was dizzy.

Afterward, Kate smiled up at him winsomely. "It's sparkin' time, Charlie. Come and court me."

He swatted her bottom fondly. "You little witch."

As Charlie tried to swoop down for another kiss, Kate pushed against his chest and added, "But this time, it's gonna be on *my* terms."

Charlie threw back his head and laughed.

"Woman, you live your whole goddamned life on your own terms." He turned, picked up her shirt and trousers, and tossed them at her. "Hell, I guess I'd best fetch you home—before I flat murder you."

Chapter 24

On Monday morning, Jeb Maloney and Dora Fuermann were chatting as they walked through the widow's rattletrap hen house, with its many cackling hens and heavy odor of straw and manure. Dora gathered eggs while Jeb followed her with the basket.

"Sorry I couldn't come over yesterday," he remarked to her. "But, like I said, Charlie Durango fetched Kate home."

With a nod, Dora shooed a hen off the next nest and gathered another egg. Setting it down in the basket, she flashed Jeb a worried frown. "You're sure Kate's all right?"

He waved her off. "No harm done, though the girl is mighty riled at the moment. There was one helleva commotion when she hit the house."

"She didn't want to be home, I take it?"

"It's worse than that," Jeb confided. "Seems Durango neglected to tell the girl that he's the one I chose for her husband. When she come home and saw the lay of the land, she flat went loco."

A soft gasp escaped Dora. "But—how did she find out?"

"Why, I told her, of course."

Dora was crestfallen. "Oh, Jeb!"

"Well, how was I to know Durango was so tight-lipped on the subject? Anyhow, now Kate wants nothin' to do with neither of us. When I unlocked her door this morning, she was still pouting and refused to leave her room." He shrugged. "She'll come around in time, though, and marry Durango just to get out from under my roof."

Dora shook her head sadly as she deposited two more eggs in the basket. "Jeb, do you have to be so hard on the girl?"

"Hard on the girl?" he repeated irately. "Why, that little hellion has defied me to perdition and back."

"And you haven't been the least bit proud or unyielding toward her?" Dora chided.

"I'm her pa," Jeb bristled. "It's my job to lay down the law."

Dora shook her head slowly. "I just don't see how anything will ever be resolved between the two of you if neither of you is willing to give an inch. If I know anything about Kate, she's going to refuse to marry this man you've chosen just to spite you."

"Then she can sit in the house until she rots," Jeb said, though an unaccustomed stab of gulit assailed him as he recalled having a similar conversation with Charlie Durango.

"And is this attitude going to help you accomplish your goal?" Dora reproved.

He heaved a mighty sigh. "You've got a point, Dora Mae. What are you suggesting?"

"Only that you try a little patience with the girl."

Jeb rolled his eyes as the two left the hen house.

Outside in the bright coolness, Dora snapped her fingers and smiled at him. "You know, maybe I could give Kate and Mr. Durango a nudge in the right direction."

"What do you mean?"

She continued eagerly, "Well, I was thinking of inviting folks over for a candy-pull after church on

Sunday. The ladies could bring covered dishes, and we could make an afternoon of it." She winked at Jeb. "There's nothin' better for getting young folks together than pulling that hot taffy. Kind of gets them stuck on each other, if you know what I mean?"

Jeb grinned. "Dora, you're a jewel! Why, that's a dandy idea. By all means, start spreading the word around town, and I'll see to it that Kate and Charlie attend."

Dora nodded firmly. "Don't worry, I'll make an announcement at prayer meeting on Wednesday and at choir practice, to boot. We'll have us a good gathering—and maybe Kate will have a change of heart."

Jeb handed her the basket of eggs and pecked her cheek. "Now you're talking, woman. We need to get them young folks hitched, so us old folks can follow them to the Bible-puncher."

Dora threw him an admonitory look. "Jeb, I've warned you that I'm still not ready."

Jeb winked at her. "Could be all you need is a good nudge, too."

An hour later, Jeb strode into the parlor of his home and spotted Kate sitting in Margaret's old rocker near the fireplace. Yesterday, after Conchita had promised to keep an eye on Kate, Jeb had relented and had let her have the run of the house during the day. Just to be on the safe side, he'd kept a ranch hand stationed on the porch.

His daughter was so deeply immersed in a book that she didn't at first notice him. She looked quite fetching this morning in her blue gingham dress, with her thick hair arranged in shiny curls. His heart caught as he noted her resemblance to Margaret.

Then she spotted him standing there and threw him a surly look.

With an effort, he remembered Dora's admonishment to be patient with the girl. "Morning, daughter," he said gruffly.

She shrugged.

"You doin' well?"

A bit taken aback at her father's solicitude, Kate cast him a dubious glance. "I was doin' fair to middling till you walked in."

Jeb ground his teeth. "What's that you're reading?"

Kate held up the book. "See for yourself."

Jeb crossed the room and took the dime novel in hand. "*The Further Adventures of Kid Ransom, Killer Outlaw?*" he quoted irately. "What kind of garbage is that for a young lady to be reading?" He hurled the book into the fireplace.

Kate heaved herself to her feet and faced her father with eyes blazing. "Well, what do you expect me to do around here? You know damned well I ain't the type to be knitting mittens or reading the Good Book. I'm bored silly stuck in this house."

Despite his good intentions toward his offspring, Jeb could feel his temper rising. "And you know the solution to that, daughter. You agree to abide by my wishes, then Charlie Durango can worry about you."

"Well, forget it," Kate hurled at him with a defiant toss of her curls. "I ain't trading one jailer for another."

For once, Jeb felt at a loss. "You find Durango that unpalatable?"

"What I find unpalatable is your runnin' roughshod over my life, with no respect for my feelings."

Jeb hitched up his britches and spoke self-righteously. "It's a man's world, daughter. You'd best get used to it."

"Well, don't hold your breath," she snapped.

Jeb muttered an oath. "Aw, why am I wasting time talking with you, anyway?"

He had turned on his heel and was striding out of the room when Kate hurried after him, grasping his sleeve. "Pa, I want to ride out and hunt up Diablo."

"Forget it," he snapped.

Though it went against the grain for Kate to beg, this time she abandoned her pride. "Please, Pa. You can send a couple of the hands with me. I just have to get him back before it's too late and he goes wild again. I promise I won't try to run off."

"Your promise ain't worth spit, daughter." Watching Kate flinch, Jeb sighed and added gruffly, "Look, I'll tell the hands to keep an eye out for that stallion."

"But that won't work! Diablo won't come to anyone but me!"

Jeb shrugged. "He's better off running the range anyhow. He's always been a renegade."

"Damn it, Pa!"

Jeb shook a finger at her. "Look, if you want to go riding after that horse, you'd best be prepared to stand before the preacher first. After you're hitched, you and your husband can track that outlaw to your heart's content."

Kate crossed her arms over her bosom and set her jaw. "In that case, I'm staying put."

"Suit yourself." Before she could argue further, he added, "By the way, Dora Mae Fuermann's giving a candy-pull on Sunday. You're going, and I'll see to it that Durango escorts you."

"When hell freezes over," she hissed.

Jeb threw up his hands. "If you ain't the most cantankerous female I've ever known. You can't have it both ways, daughter. First you say you can't wait to get out of this house, then you say you won't go to Dora Mae's gathering. It don't matter what I ask you to do, you ain't having any."

"You got that right."

He shook a finger at her. "Well, you're going on

Sunday, if I have to kick your stubborn butt every inch of the way."

Jeb stormed out of the room.

For the next few days, Kate went stir-crazy in the house. She hated being confined, but her pride would not allow her to give in to Pa—even though more and more, she recognized that Charlie Durango was what she most wanted, and in defying her pa, she was really only hurting herself.

The only breaks in her monotonous routine came when Charlie stopped by in the evenings, and the two of them chatted on the front porch. He arrived, sharply dressed and impeccably groomed, bringing Kate a box of chocolates one night and a pretty silk fan the next. He didn't broach the subject of marriage again, but he was so sweet to her both times that she kicked herself afterward for not giving in to him. She realized he was giving her the "courting" she had demanded—and it was kind of fun. In the back of her mind was still the nagging fear that Charlie might be after her pa's land and money, despite his protestations to the contrary. Still, it was hard to resist his charms.

On Wednesday evening, Walker Dennison joined Kate, her pa, and Conchita in the kitchen for supper. Walker and her pa dominated the conversation with ranch business, and Kate scarcely even listened until Walker turned to her.

"Miss Kate, Miguel mentioned seeing Diablo in the south pasture yesterday. Said he tried to get a lasso 'round his neck, but that stallion's plumb gone wild again."

Kate turned desperately to her father. "Pa, please let me ride out after him."

Jeb slowly sipped his coffee. "You already know my answer there, daughter."

Kate was tempted to curse him, but knew this

would get her nowhere. "Look, if you let me ride after him, I promise I'll go to the social on Sunday."

Jeb laughed. "Oh, you're going to the social on Sunday. But if you want to ride after that stallion, then you know damned well what else you have to do—first."

Kate ground her teeth in silent outrage.

Following supper, Kate was in her room sulking when Conchita came up to announce that Charlie had come calling. After touching up her hair and smoothing down her dress, Kate fled gratefully down to the porch.

She spotted him standing near the swing, staring off at the sunset, his hat on the porch railing. He wore a white shirt, dark trousers, a brown leather vest, and a black string cravat. He looked so courtly and elegant, and she could smell the delicious scent of his bay rum.

"Charlie," she breathed with a smile.

He turned to her, his dark eyes lighting as he looked her over. "Evening, sugar. You look right fetching tonight." He stepped forward, kissing her cheek and handing her a furry black ball.

"A kitten?" Kate was delighted by the little creature, with its huge green eyes and piteous meow. She stroked the critter, then chuckled as the kitten purred and wrapped himself around her hand. She grinned up at Charlie. "Where'd you get him?"

"You know Mr. Wharton at the stable?" Charlie explained. "Well, his mouser had a big litter."

She shook her head. "What are you going to bring me next?"

He reached out and playfully touched the tip of her nose. "Oh, I like to keep you guessing." He tugged her toward the swing.

They sat down together, and Charlie wrapped an arm around her. The evening air was crisp and clear, washed with the sweetness of late-blooming honeysuckle. For a moment, they just stared out at the red-gold majesty of the Texas skies, with only the creaking of the swing and the purring of the kitten to disturb the quiet. Kate nestled her head against Charlie's shoulder and realized with a mixture of awe and uncertainty that she'd been looking forward to this moment all day. Why, she'd likely be content to spend eternity this way, snuggling against Charlie, drinking in his scent and absorbing his heat.

She was growing far too accustomed to having this man around, she realized. But somehow, for the moment, that didn't seem to matter.

"Kate," Charlie murmured after a while, "I run into Dora Fuermann in town today."

Kate felt a jab of unease that prompted her to sit up straight. "Oh, yeah," she said sullenly. "Her and Pa's been keeping company."

"Don't you like her?"

Kate shrugged. "She's all right, I guess."

"Anyhow, Dora introduced herself to me in front of the Oatts' store. Seems she's giving a candy-pull on Sunday and she's inviting us both . . ." Feeling her stiffen, he paused. "So you know about this already?"

Her mouth took on a hard set. "Sure do."

"Will you go with me, Kate?"

Kate stared up at Charlie's expectant face. It was on the tip of her tongue to ask if Pa had put him up to this—but then, all of a sudden, that didn't matter, either. "Sure, Charlie," she heard herself reply.

He grinned. "Well, fine. I'll come fetch you before church then?"

She petted the kitten and nodded. "I'll be ready."

Feeling heartened by her acceptance, Charlie studied Kate's lovely face—her pink cheeks and full mouth, her delicate nose and wide green eyes. They'd come so far in their relationship in the past few days, he mused. Yet there was a haunting vulnerability about her tonight, a touching sadness in her eyes.

"Sugar, you look a little low," he murmured.

She flashed him a wan smile. "Miguel spotted Diablo in the south pasture." Her jaw tightened in anger. "That horse won't come to anyone but me, but Pa won't let me ride after him, not until—" Realizing what she was about to say, Kate clamped her mouth shut.

"I see," Charlie put in meaningfully. "So the battle of wills is still going on between you and your pa?" When she didn't answer, he tilted her chin with his fingertip. "Only problem is, it's coming between the two of us, ain't it, sugar?"

Swallowing the lump of guilt in her throat, she managed to face him forthrightly. "Maybe not."

"How's that?"

"Well, when Pa ordered me to go to Dora's party, I told him no. When you asked me just now, I said yes."

Charlie chuckled. "Reckon that is an improvement."

"Reckon so."

Charlie grinned as he watched the kitten chew playfully on Kate's index finger. "You like the critter?"

"Oh, yes. But the poor little thing kind of makes me sad."

"Why, honey?"

To Kate's horror, she found herself fighting tears. "Well, he's so shiny and black, just like Diablo. And all alone in the world, too. Guess I am feeling low, Charlie. I miss my horse."

Charlie squeezed his shoulders. "Ah, darlin', I'm sorry."

His sympathetic words only sent more tears rushing to her eyes. "For Chrissakes," she groaned, wiping her damp cheek with her sleeve, ''I always hated them women who'd bust out crying if they scorched the pudding or ripped a petticoat. I always thought I was stronger than that.''

Charlie solemnly handed her his handkerchief. ''Ah, sugar, don't be so hard on yourself. Sometimes it takes a strong woman to cry.''

She huddled against his shoulder and let the tears flow. ''You think so, Charlie?''

''Why, sure.'' He kissed the top of her head, inhaling the sweet scent of her hair, his own eyes stinging as he thought of how much he loved this woman. So strong she'd fight a man; so fragile she'd cry over a lost horse.

''Maybe he'll come home,'' Charlie whispered.

Her anguished eyes met his. ''He won't. He's free. Why should he?''

As Charlie stared down at Kate's stark, vulnerable face, his very soul ached for the pain she felt. He knew she spoke not just for her horse, but for herself, as well. He brushed a tear from her cheek and smiled at her tenderly. Something within this girl hungered to be unrestrained, to be as wild and untamed as that horse of hers. How could he convince her that she could love him and still be free?

All he knew now was that he wanted to banish that look of sorrow from her eyes forever. He leaned over and captured her trembling lips with his own. Her soft gasp of pleasure made his heart soar with delight. The taste of her tears touched him deeply. He gathered her closer still and nuzzled her ear, whispering endearments.

Somehow, he would win her love. He knew the way to her heart now.

Chapter 25

⌒⟞◯⟞⌒

On Sunday morning, Conchita awakened Kate early, bringing her a tray with hot oatmeal, spicy sausages, and milk. Kate ate her hearty breakfast with a sense of excitement. She and Charlie were going to the covered dish dinner and candy-pull after church today, and at least she'd be getting out of the house. She also had to acknowledge that she was thrilled at the prospect of seeing Charlie again. He'd so endeared himself to her over the last week with his daily courting rituals. He'd come by every evening—each time bearing a different gift—and they'd sat together on the porch swing in the crisp coolness, holding hands, talking, and sharing an occasional kiss. Perhaps today they could even steal a little time completely alone. In anticipation of this, last night she'd taken a long, leisurely bath and had washed her hair with rose-scented soap.

Having finished her repast, Kate selected her clothing for the day with the greatest care, laying out a fine yellow muslin dress and matching bonnet. As she donned her camisole and pantalets and brushed her hair, she watched her kitten frolic about on the bed. She chuckled as the little critter pounced on the pillow and chewed on the pillowcase Conchita had embroidered for her. The little varmint was a real pest and had the entire household in an uproar. Kate had named him "Socks," due to his uncanny ability to steal her father's socks and then either hide them in some dark cranny, or unravel the yarn. Jeb had already threatened to drown the "scrawny rat" several times, and even the usually complacent Conchita had resorted to shrieking when Socks invaded the kitchen, pulling the tablecloth off the table, stealing bacon from the larder, and knocking over the butter churn. Yet Kate defended and protected the kitten tenaciously, even though her bedroom curtains and dresser skirt already bore evidence of his needle-sharp claws. She laughed over his antics and took joy in his company. As far as she was concerned, he was just as he should be, and as she would love to be—wild and free.

Once she was dressed, Kate scrutinized her appearance in the dressing table mirror. The long-sleeved frock fit her nicely, the lace-trimmed boat neckline accenting her rounded breasts, the tight waist accentuating her slenderness. She'd pulled her hair away from her face, pinning the side locks at the back and adding a yellow bow for effect; the rest of her lush black curls cascaded down over her nape and shoulders. She realized ruefully that she looked a prim and proper lady today—a role she'd never before in her life expected herself to enjoy. Yet she knew now that she loved the idea of pleasing Charlie with her appearance. Indeed, she pinched her cheeks for color and dabbed on a few drops of rosewater before she left the room.

Downstairs in the parlor, Kate found her father standing near the front door. Jeb was clean-shaven, wearing his Sunday suit and holding his Bible.

He cleared his throat at the sight of her. "You look right comely today, daughter," he said gruffly.

"Thanks," came Kate's terse reply.

Jeb shifted from boot to boot. "You bringing along a covered dish for the gathering?"

"Conchita said she'd drop off a big pot of *menudo* at Mrs. Fuermann's after she goes to Mass."

Jeb nodded. "Are you and Durango comin' with me to church in our buckboard?"

Kate tilted her chin in a show of independence. "I reckon I'd rather go alone with Charlie."

"But he ain't got no gig to carry you into town."

Kate was poised to reply, but this time, the inevitable argument between father and daughter was postponed by a sharp sound from outside the house, like a pebble hitting the front door. Frowning, Kate swept to the front door, opened it and stepped outside, followed by Jeb.

For a moment, she simply stood on the porch, unable to believe her eyes. "Oh, my God!"

At the base of the porch stood Charlie in his Sunday black suit and hat, white ruffled shirt, and black string tie. He held a huge spray of flowers.

But it wasn't Charlie's presence that stunned Kate. Next to him was Diablo, looking fit as ever, with a huge red bow tied about his neck.

Jubilant, Kate flew down the steps and into Charlie's arms, slamming against him with such force that she almost knocked him down. They were both laughing as he steadied her and leaned over to retrieve the bouquet that had fallen to the ground.

"Oh, Charlie, I can't believe you found him!" Kate turned joyously to Diablo, stretching on tiptoe to throw her arms about his strong neck. The horse nickered and affectionately nudged his face against her arm.

She turned back to Charlie. "How'd you do it?"

He grinned. "Sometimes wild things'll come back to you, if you let 'um do it their way." He winked at her and handed her the flowers. "And if you bring along a lump or two of sugar."

Kate actually blushed at his charming flirtation as she accepted the fragrant flowers. In the meantime,

Jeb had come down the steps. "Morning, Durango," he said, offering his hand.

Charlie solemnly shook his hand. "Morning, sir."

"See you found my daughter's horse."

"Yes, sir."

"Good work," Jeb continued, hooking his thumbs in the pockets of his vest. "Pete'll be bringing 'round the buckboard directly and we'll head on out to church."

Kate turned to him. "Pa, I want to ride Diablo to church." She nodded toward Charlie's horse, which was tethered at the end of the porch. "Charlie can ride Corona."

Jeb glowered at her. "Daughter, you can't ride astride a horse in your Sunday dress."

"There's a side saddle in the barn," Kate reasoned. "I promise I'll use it. Please, Pa."

Jeb groaned. "Aw, what the hell."

"We'll ride real slow and careful like, Mr. Maloney," Charlie assured him.

"See that you do, son. I'll meet you both at the church, then," Jeb replied.

While Kate went inside to put the flowers in water, Charlie took Diablo out to the barn and saddled him. Soon the couple was trotting down the trail for town, Kate riding Diablo sidesaddle with Charlie riding next to her on Corona.

Kate's heart was bursting with happiness as they cantered along. The morning was sweet, clear, and cool, with hundreds of chirping birds singing a chorus in the live oak trees. Her heart was filled with joy and love for Charlie. He was really such a fine man, she mused. On top of his other kindnesses, he'd brought her beloved stallion back—seemingly, no worse for wear.

"He's not limping anymore," she remarked to him as they crested a rolling hill.

"I know," he replied. "He still had that bandage

wrapped around his foreleg when I found him—
Lord, was it filthy. But his fetlock is completely
healed now." Charlie shook his head slowly. "You
should have seen him runnin' out on the prairie,
free as the wind, with the sun gleaming like water
on his back."

Kate bit her lip as she stroked Diablo's silky mane.
"Maybe he wanted to stay free."

"Naw, I don't think so, honey," Charlie interjected. "I think he missed you."

She smiled. "Do you really?"

"Sure do."

She sighed blissfully. "How'd you make him
come to you?"

"Well, it was pretty much like I said. I just whistled, waited, and held out that lump of sugar. Before
long, he just come up to me."

Kate shook her head. "I never thought he'd come
to anyone but me."

"Oh, I got my persuasive powers." Charlie
grinned and edged his horse closer to hers. "And,
come to think of it, I ain't been thanked properly
just yet." He expelled a ragged breath. "Damn it,
woman, but you look tempting."

Kate was all smiles as Charlie took hold of Diablo's reins and pulled both horses to a halt. He carefully lifted her off her saddle and onto his horse. She
smiled and wrapped her arms around his neck as he
lowered his face to hers. For a long moment, they
tasted and teased each other with gentle, fluttering
passes of their lips. Then both of them grew ravenous, automatically deepening the kiss. Kate gloried
in Charlie's clean scent, the wonderful heat of his
mouth on hers.

By the time Charlie finally put her back on Diablo,
she was trembling all over. Both were quiet, basking
in the bliss of their closeness as they started back
down the trail.

Charlie smiled to himself as he studied Kate riding beside him so contentedly, and looking so lovely. He aimed to have her promise again by day's end. He was sure the girl was his already. Just as he'd suspected, the way to this obstinate girl's heart was her horse. Rounding up Diablo had been no mean feat, but it had been well worth it to see his darling Kate smile again. His heart pounded with delight as he recalled the moment when she'd come out on the porch, the look of stark joy in her eyes as she'd come flying down the steps—

To *him*. Kate set great store by her horse, but she'd come first to him, not to Diablo.

By the time they arrived at the small clapboard Presbyterian church on the southern outskirts of town, Jeb's buckboard was already parked off to one side, on the banks of Brushy Creek. Today's service had drawn quite a crowd, Kate judged, glancing at the array of conveyances and horses cluttering the churchyard. A few negro slaves were gathered beneath a shade tree, keeping an eye on the horses and playing dominoes.

Though the service hadn't started, the pews were almost bursting with townfolk when Kate and Charlie stepped inside. Charlie removed his hat, and the two of them glanced about the crowded room, looking for a place to sit. Everywhere, heads turned in their direction—curious matrons with flower-bedecked hats gossiped behind their hands, while inquisitive men with scrubbed faces and pomaded hair craned their necks to see.

Kate suggested that they slip into an empty bench at the back, but Charlie firmly led her toward the front and Jeb Maloney's pew. "We're sitting with your pa," he whispered to her sternly. "Ain't proper otherwise."

Kate gritted her teeth as they pressed forward

through a sea of bobbing heads, fluttering fans, and diverse smells—soap and perfume, bay rum and beeswax, along with the collective pungence of close-pressed bodies. Additional stares and titters of conversation followed them all the way down the aisle. Kate knew that it was already all over town that she had run off and had been dragged back home by Charlie Durango. She was sure the townfolk couldn't wait to glimpse the next chapter in the melodrama of their lives.

Jeb actually smiled as they slipped into the pew beside him and Dora Fuermann. The widow and Charlie shook hands. Dora flashed Kate a smile that bespoke her approval.

The service began soon thereafter, with the singing of ''Bringing in the Sheaves.'' Kate didn't particularly enjoy Reverend Cassidy's sermon, since he was on another of his ''fire and brimstone'' tirades today. The vengeance of hell was not a subject Kate particularly liked to ponder at length, considering her own less than perfect behavior over the years. But she did savor being close to Charlie and holding his hand. After the service concluded with ''Rock of Ages,'' Dora stood up and again invited everyone out to her place for the covered-dish dinner and candy-pull.

As they left the church, several girls Kate's age, as well as some local matrons, rushed up to welcome Kate home and finagle an introduction to Charlie. Kate knew that her newfound popularity had nothing to do with her own doubtful attributes but was based solely on her handsome escort and their fascinating new relationship. Charlie was charming to one and all, and Kate could tell he was a big hit with the womenfolk, from all their simpering and eyelash batting. Biting back her irritation, she maneuvered him out the door as quickly as possible. When they passed by Reverend Cassidy and his wife, Kate dutifully introduced Charlie to the couple. The silver-haired Reverend slanted Charlie a self-righteous look and asked, "Will you two young folks be coming to stand before me soon?" Kate was proud of Charlie and relieved when he replied noncommittally, "You'll be the first to know, sir."

They rode out to Dora Mae Fuermann's ranch, in the midst of a caravan of other wagons and horses. Once they arrived, Charlie tethered their horses to a tree next to the stream. Kate helped the other women set out the food on oilcloth-draped tables in front of the house, while Charlie pitched horseshoes with some of the men. Children were everywhere, the boys playing tag or ball or fishing in the stream, the girls dressing their dolls or helping the women with the meal.

Kate enjoyed helping the other ladies more than she would have thought. When she returned to the kitchen to fetch more food, she paused to chat with Dora and help her slice several loaves of hot bread.

"He seems a very fine man, your Mr. Durango," Dora remarked to Kate.

Kate smiled. "He is, indeed. You know, he brought my horse back to me."

Dora's face lit in pleasure. "Oh, did he? Jeb had mentioned to me that your stallion was lost."

"Yep, he sure was. I was afraid I'd never see Diablo again, but Charlie brought him back this morning—with a big red bow tied around his neck."

"Oh, how romantic!" Dora cried. She set down her knife, a frown drifting over her lovely countenance. "I don't mean to pry, honey, but are you and Mr. Durango planning to tie the knot soon?"

"I reckon we will—leastwise if Charlie has his way," Kate confirmed drolly. She frowned down at the bread she was slicing. "Only, there's a problem."

"Oh?"

Kate's expression grew tight with resentment, and her knife moved with hard, tense strokes. "Charlie wants me to go live with him in Denver."

Dora nodded as she moved off to stir the pot of boiling molasses candy on the stove. "That's the puzzlement of it all, Kate—getting married. The woman always has to give something up in order to gain a husband."

Kate stared at Dora, curious. "What about you and Pa? Are you two getting hitched or not?"

Fighting a smile, Dora moved back to the table and picked up a tray of sliced bread. "I just don't know, Kate. I've got a good life here, though I sometimes think life with Jeb would be better."

Kate rolled her eyes. "Then you must have gone plumb loco. My pa's just about as agreeable as a wild badger."

"But that's not the case at all, Kate," Dora replied firmly. "Jeb hides his best side from the world. You've never seen the more tender, vulnerable aspect of your father's nature."

"Yeah, and you're for sure talking about someone else," Kate quipped.

Dora touched Kate's sleeve. "Honey, how would you feel if your pa and I married?"

Kate shrugged. "Don't make no nevermind to me." Then, observing Dora's crestfallen expression and feeling instantly contrite, she added with a grin, "Hell, you might just soften him up a bit."

Dora laughed. "I'll certainly try my best."

Kate picked up a crock of fresh sweet butter. "Hadn't we better get these things outside?"

"Sure, Kate."

As the two women headed toward the back door, Kate paused, turning thoughtfully to the widow. "Thanks, Dora."

"Thanks for what?"

"For asking what my feelings was." Kate's eyes grew stormy. "Pa ain't never asked me, much less cared how I felt about nothin'."

"He cares, Kate," Dora put in gently. "He just doesn't know how to show it."

Kate was silent, not wanting to contradict the kindly woman. She shifted the butter crock to give Dora a quick, impulsive hug, then went out the door. Dora followed her, smiling.

The two women rejoined the others just as the townfolk were lining up to be served. Charlie returned to Kate's side, holding her hand while Reverend Cassidy offered thanks. As the two of them moved through the line, Kate heard a couple of the men talking about Sam Houston's imminent return to the governorship, and the statewide debate over the slavery question. Kate realized how isolated she had been, wrapped up in her own problems for so long that she really had little idea what was going on in Texas or in the country.

Charlie and Kate heaped their plates with fried chicken, potato salad, *menudo*, and beans, grabbed tin cups of iced tea, then went off to sit on a table-cloth Dora had lent them. The spot they chose was shady, off a bit from the others, beneath a huge oak.

Kate glanced around at the throng of happy townfolk eating and visiting. She flashed Charlie a smile. "You know, as I was growing up, Pa used to have to hogtie me into coming to socials like this. But this is kind of fun."

Charlie had reclined and was resting his weight on an elbow as he regarded her. He set down the chicken leg he'd been nibbling and reached out to stroke her cheek. "If we was married, we could do stuff like this all the time, sugar."

"So you're really ready to give up all them hard trails and desperadoes?" she teased.

"I'm ready to chew on a few chicken legs, watch the clouds roll by, and love you," he teased back.

Though his tender words brought a rush of romantic excitement, Kate felt compelled to add, "In Denver."

He sighed. "It's beautiful there, Kate," he murmured with a wistful look in his eyes. "Mountains so tall you can't see their tops, crystal clear streams, blue furry pines, and quaking aspens."

"You been there?" Kate asked, intrigued despite herself.

"Nope, but my partner's described it in his letters, and he wouldn't lie."

Kate frowned. "I still don't want to leave Texas."

"Damn it, woman, why are you so stuck on Texas? I would think you'd be right relieved to go with me to the western territories 'cause it proves I don't want your pa's land or money."

Kate glanced away guiltily. As the days passed, it became increasingly difficult for her to believe that Charlie Durango could be that mercenary. Indeed, she wasn't completely sure why she still resisted the idea of moving with him to Denver.

When she didn't reply, he asked, "Did you hear the men talking in the line?"

She nodded morosely. "Yep. They're saying that if Lincoln's elected, the whole South is gonna split apart from the North." She glanced at him. "Do you think they're right?"

"I reckon so," Charlie confirmed unhappily. "And if the South secedes, Texas is gonna go with her, despite the fact that Sam Houston is against secession." He gazed at her sadly. "Sooner or later, sugar, there's gonna be a war over this slavery business."

Kate frowned. "You know, Pa and I don't even own any slaves."

"That's not going to matter in the long run,

honey. Many landowners in Texas don't own slaves, but if push comes to shove, they're still gonna side with their brothers in the South."

"So what's the point, Charlie?"

He sat up, took her hand, and spoke intently. "The point is, Kate, you'll be much better off with me in the Pikes Peak region. Hell, it may be years before Congress declares the area a separate territory. If there's a war, it's never gonna spill over that far west. And anyhow, why should either of us have our lives threatened over politics we want nothing to do with?"

Kate bit her lip. "Wouldn't you want to fight for the South, Charlie?"

His passionate gaze flashed to her. "Kate, I've fought all my life. I've tracked down Indians and desperadoes. I've brought to justice scum who'd just as soon knife me in the back as look at me. But I have to believe in the cause I'm fighting for." He picked up a twig and snapped it in two as he glanced at the half-dozen or so negro slaves who'd been brought to the gathering by some of the townspeople. They were huddled together beneath a mesquite tree, eating apart from the others. "Placing fellow human beings in bondage, now that don't sit right with me," he finished grimly.

Kate nodded, realizing again that this was not a subject she'd ever given much thought. She'd been preoccupied with her own situation—perhaps selfishly so.

Charlie turned to stare at her. "All that matters to me now is you and me, sugar. That's it—just the two of us. I'm placing our relationship first."

Kate glanced away guiltily. They both knew she couldn't make the same statement—not yet.

"You know, if we was man and wife," Charlie continued persuasively, "we could wake up each morning, then go off and do what we pleased. You wouldn't have to contend with your pa, or wait for me to come fetch you.''

Feeling slightly uncomfortable that Charlie was pressing so hard, Kate glanced at their hostess, who was laughing as she ladled iced tea for some late-arriving guests. ''Yeah, and if I was an independent woman like Dora Fuermann, I wouldn't have to contend with either of you,'' she asserted with a flash of spirit.

Charlie feigned a wounded expression, placing his hand over his heart. ''But wouldn't you miss me something awful, darlin'?''

She reached out and playfully tugged his hand away, kissing his knuckles. ''Yeah, I would.''

''So what do you say, Kate?'' he teased.

She grinned. ''I say I'm ready for pie and coffee. How 'bout you?''

He laughed. ''Sure, darlin'.''

They went off together, hand in hand.

In an hour or so, the gathering had thinned as parents took sleepy babies and older children home. Most of those who lingered for the candy-pull were younger married couples or single people. Still, at least fifty intrepid souls gathered inside Dora's parlor, dining room, and kitchen for the candy pulling contest. By now, the whole house was redolent with the smell of boiled molasses. The women distributed buttered plates holding huge globs of the cooled candy mixture, and also handed out empty, greased pans to hold the pulled strips.

Once everyone was in position, Dora gave the signal to begin, and the couples dived into the lumps of molasses with shrieks of laughter. The guests had a grand time stretching the boiled candy into taffy strips. No one seemed to care that the pulling process was an incredible, sticky mess. The house seemed to rock with the sounds of giggles and lively conversation.

Charlie and Kate sat apart from the others on a window sill, pulling opposite ends of the stubborn confection. They laughed as the mixture twisted, snarled, and clung to their hands and clothing. When they were at last able to lay the first strip in the greased pan, Charlie grabbed Kate's hand and slowly licked her fingers clean. The ardent look in his eyes and the teasing strokes of his tongue set all of her to tingling. Noticing that a few people were staring at them, Kate tossed him an admonitory glance and grabbed another handful of candy.

Though Dora had baked a cherry pie to be awarded to the couple who pulled the most strips, much of the candy had been consumed by the time the pull ended. It was a content, sated crew that milled about in the parlor, clapping as Dora presented the pie to Sally and Jacob Schultz.

Folks were preparing to leave when Jeb stepped up to the middle of the room and put his arm around Dora. "I think this good woman deserves a big hand for all her efforts today," he declared.

A round of applause and cheers spewed forth from the crowd, and Dora beamed and nodded in response. Afterward, Jeb held up a hand and grinned. "Now, before all of you leave, I got somethin' else I mean to say, so hear me out." He nodded proudly toward Dora and squeezed her shoulders. "Dora here is going to do me the honor of becoming my bride—just like my daughter Kate over there is going to marry Charlie Durango. Hell, we may save the Bible-puncher some trouble and have a double wedding."

Jeb's declaration was heralded with such hurrahs, hand clapping, and foot stomping that hardly anyone in the house at first noticed that both "future brides" were livid.

Kate was the first to break the festive mood by rushing for the door, her expression stricken. Hurling a murderous look at Jeb, Charlie followed close on her heels. As the throng watched in stunned silence, Dora followed suit by glaring at Jeb, turning on her heel, and storming out of the room.

Everyone turned to Jeb, who looked utterly perplexed himself. "Hell, folks," he said lamely, holding out both hands in a gesture of bewilderment. "Guess I was a bit quick on the draw there."

The others shook their heads, mumbled to themselves, and left.

Outside Dora's house, Charlie chased Kate all the way to the oak tree. "Sugar, please," he called out. "Please stop!"

On a rise beneath a huge tree, Kate at last paused and turned to him, her mouth trembling. One look at her shattered face practically tore his guts to ribbons. He pulled her into his arms, and she sobbed against his chest.

"Damn him!" she cried, her fists clenched against Charlie's shoulders, humiliation and frustrated anger welling in her heart. "That should have been my decision! My decision!"

"I know, darlin'." Charlie grasped her face in his hands and looked down into her brimming green eyes. "But you can't let him tear us apart this way."

Kate started to reply, then choked on her tears. Charlie could take no more. With a groan, he leaned over and kissed her with all the love and passion he could pour out, melding his mouth with hers until their teeth ground together. Kate moaned and wrapped her arms around his neck, drawing him possessively closer.

"Oh, sugar." Charlie pressed his lips to her wet cheek. His hands caressed her rounded breasts, then slid down to circle her tiny waist. His voice was shaky, hoarse with desire. "You just got to forget about him. I know he hurt you somethin' awful. But

I need you now. I've got to have you again. I'm about to bust from wanting you."

"Are you?" she asked breathlessly.

"Oh, yes, angel."

"Me, too," she admitted in a tear-filled voice.

"Don't let him do this to us. Please don't," Charlie pleaded.

Charlie kissed her again, his tongue taking complete possession of her sweet mouth. She responded by stroking him with her own tongue and pressing her hips against his arousal. His arms tightened around her. For a long time, they stood with mouths locked, with hungry bodies fitted snugly together amid the sweet smell of the honeysuckle, the drone of the bees.

When at last Charlie pulled back, he spoke thickly. "When are we going to set the date, Kate?"

She looked up at him with love and anguish. "Not now, Charlie. We'll talk on it tomorrow, all right?"

"All right, sugar." Charlie clutched her close and kissed her fragrant hair. He understood. She had her pride, after all.

Back at the house, Jeb was faring much worse with Dora Fuermann. The crowd had left and the widow was pacing her kitchen in a fine temper.

"I've had my doubts about you before, Jeb Maloney," Dora declared furiously, "but today you've gone too far. A woman has a right to know her own mind regarding who she's to wed. And that goes double for your daughter. No wonder Kate doesn't want to put up with the likes of you."

Jeb's expression was crestfallen as he tried to follow her about the room. "But I was just trying to give the both of you a friendly nudge—"

She turned on him, waving a finger in his face. "Well, your little ploy backfired right in your face. Thanks to you, neither you nor Mr. Durango is likely to take a bride any time soon."

Jeb backed away from the charging female. "Dora dear, be reasonable—"

Dora's hand sliced through the air. "You're one to talk about reasonable, after the stunt you pulled. Don't you dare try to darken my door again, Jeb Maloney, until you apologize to your daughter—and to me."

"Until I *what?*" Jeb was stunned.

Dora balled her hands on her hips. "You heard me the first time. Now get out of this house."

"But I'm the girl's father," Jeb blustered. "It's my place to tell her what to do—"

"Just like you're telling me what to do? Well, you'd best think again, Jeb, or there will never be a future for the two of us."

Gulping, Jeb came up and touched her arm. "Dora, you can't be meaning this."

Dora's scornful expression was unflinching. "Yes, I do. Now, you go set things to rights with your daughter. After that, maybe I'll consider hearing an apology from you."

Jeb threw up his hands. "Women!"

He stormed out of the room.

Jeb was just emerging from Dora's house when Pete and Miguel rode up in a cloud of dust.

Pete was the first to spring off his horse and hurry up the steps. He tore off his hat and wiped his sweaty brow with his sleeve. "Boss," he began, panting for his breath, "Spuds Gilhooley must have cut the fence on the west range again. A goodly section is down, and at least two dozen head have strayed onto his land."

"Damnation!" Jeb exploded. "That's all I need, on top of everything else. Two females mad as hornets, and now a Sunday afternoon fence cutting war."

Jeb disgustedly hurried off with the others.

* * *

It was late that night by the time Jeb finally labored up the stairs at the ranch house. Lord, he was getting old. He could not remember a time when he'd felt so weary.

He and his hands had had one hell of a time rounding up the loose cattle and fixing the fence Spuds Gilhooley had clipped. Spuds and his men had fired several pot-shots at them as they'd worked. Jeb and his hands had fired back, but no one had been hurt on either side.

Now he was home. Now this . . .

Jeb trudged along the upstairs hallway in the wan light of a wall sconce. Outside Kate's room, he paused. Women! He'd meant no harm with his announcement today. He'd only wanted to give Kate and Dora a gentle push. Now Dora was furious at him, and so was Kate. And, for the first time in many years, Jeb was having to consider the possibility that he might have been wrong about something.

His eyes misted as he remembered an incident that had happened long ago, when he and his beloved Margaret had first been married. They'd invited the preacher and his wife over for Sunday dinner, and Margaret, a nervous young bride, had burnt the stew. She'd practically been in tears as she served up dinner, though everyone had been gracious. Jeb's heart had gone out to her. Then he'd made some laughing comment about the ruined food—just to lighten up the mood. What was it he'd said? That she might not know how to flip a flapjack, but didn't she smile like an angel?

And Margaret had abruptly fled the room in tears. Later that night, Jeb had apologized—on his knees.

Women.

Jeb opened Kate's door and stepped inside. His

daughter lay in bed beneath the covers. Though her face was in shadow, he could tell by the way she shifted about that she was aware of his presence.

He crossed the room and paused by her bed, clearing his throat nosily. "Daughter, I know I'm a hard man," he began. "It was the way I was reared up. I just don't know any better, and—I don't mean no harm by it."

Kate was silent, and Jeb felt at a loss. He moved away. At the door, he paused a minute. Then he coughed and said, "I'm sorry, daughter."

He quietly left the room.

On the bed, Kate struggled against an aching throat and stinging eyes. Then she turned into her pillow and sobbed.

Chapter 26

The next evening, Charlie again came calling, bringing Kate a boxful of lustrous satin ribbons. They sat on the porch swing together as she sifted through her prizes. Soon she grew quiet, looking down at the heap of riotous colors, and twisting a length of white satin around her fingers.

"Kate?" Charlie nudged.

She looked up at him with moist eyes. "I'm willing to marry you now, Charlie."

"Oh, Kate." Charlie's entire face lit up with joy as he leaned over to kiss her. They shared their bliss for a long moment. Then he pulled back and regarded her quizzically. "You're sure now?"

"I'm sure." Kate got up and moved toward the porch railing. The evening was cool and scented with cedar; she watched a calf drinking milk from its mother on the western hillside. The sight filled her heart with tenderness as she thought of the children she would bear Charlie in the future.

Charlie got up and came over to join her, laying his hand on her shoulder. "What changed your mind?"

She flashed him a smile. "You, of course. And Pa," she added reluctantly.

"Your pa?"

"Yes." Kate's expression grew closed, cautious.

"He came to my room last night and apologized for what he done yesterday."

"Well, I'll be hanged."

"It just kind of took away some of my anger, I guess."

He ducked down to kiss her cheek and placed his hands at her slim waist. "I'm glad."

"We do have to get something straight, though," she added, moving away.

"What's that?"

She turned to face him squarely. "I ain't promising I'll live with you in Denver."

Charlie looked at a loss. Then he said placatingly, "Tell you what, sugar—let's make us a deal. You come with me to the Pikes Peak region, and see it just once. Then, if you can't abide living there, I promise I'll bring you straight home to Texas."

Kate eyed him skeptically. "You really promise?"

He laid his hand across his heart. "May the devil smite me if I'm lying."

Kate had to laugh at his melodramatics. "All right, then. We got ourselves a deal."

Charlie grinned with intense relief. "When you want to set the date, sugar?"

"I don't know. Soon as Conchita can get me a gown made, I reckon. Maybe next Sunday?"

"Sounds great." Charlie squeezed her hands. "Shall we go tell your pa, then?" Watching her frown, he added, "This is our time, darlin', and gettin' hitched is our decision. Just you remember that. Don't let him spoil all the fun for us."

She nodded. "I reckon we'd best go find him."

Holding hands, they stepped inside the parlor to spot Jeb sitting by the fire, reading the *Georgetown Independent*. Crumpling his newspaper and laying it aside, Jeb stood and frowned at them as they crossed the room. "Gettin' too cool for you youngsters outside?"

Charlie and Kate paused before Jeb. "Sir, we got somethin' to tell you," Charlie began.

"Oh?" Jeb glanced from Charlie to Kate.

"Charlie and I are going to get married," Kate announced proudly.

Jeb grinned, but, to their immense relief, he was wise enough not to gloat. "Well, now, ain't that fine," he said diplomatically. "When you two figure to tie the knot?"

Charlie glanced at Kate, and she said, "Sunday, if Conchita can ready me a gown by then."

Jeb nodded. "We'll see that she does."

"There's one thing," Kate added.

"Oh?" Jeb asked.

"I aim to get married in the Catholic church," Kate asserted.

At once the happy smile slid off Jeb's face, and even Charlie looked perplexed. "But, daughter," Jeb reasoned, "we're Presbyterians. I'm sure Reverend Cassidy will be happy to marry you in town after church this Sunday. Then we could invite folks here—"

"Ma was Catholic," Kate put in stubbornly. "I want a Catholic wedding out of respect to her."

Jeb appeared increasingly at a loss, thrusting his fingers through his thinning gray hair. "Daughter, that idea don't set right with me. Them Catholics is a tight-knit herd. They ain't marrying no Presbyterians, lessen it's ordered by the Pope or somethin'. 'Sides, I don't even know any Catholics—"

"You knew Ma. And you know Conchita."

Jeb was poised to reply when Charlie said, "Kate, could we have us a word outside?"

She turned to him sullenly. "Sure, Charlie."

"Sir." With a respectful nod to Jeb, Charlie pulled Kate back outside.

Out on the porch, they both stood silently for a moment. Charlie smoothed down an errant lock on

Kate's troubled brow then stroked a finger across her petulant mouth. "Honey, he's your pa," he said patiently. "It's up to him to plan your wedding. After all, you ain't even Catholic."

"I just want to show respect for my ma," Kate said moodily, clenching her jaw and setting her arms akimbo.

"I know, darlin'. But just 'cause your pa wants us to marry Presbyterian don't mean he's showing no regard for her."

"I know," she muttered, yet her stubborn expression did not waver.

"Tell you what," he went on with an encouraging smile. "Just go along with your pa's wishes, then I promise you we'll find us a Catholic church later that very same day."

She stared up at him, astonished. "But how?"

He drew himself up proudly. "I'm aiming to take us off for a fine honeymoon at a fancy Austin hotel. As soon as we hit town, we'll go find us a priest. Now, I'm not promising he'll wed us again Catholic, but how 'bout if he said a prayer for your ma or somethin'?"

"Do you reckon that would be respectful enough?" she asked wistfully.

"I reckon it would," he replied solemnly.

Kate beamed and hugged his waist, thrilled that he'd taken her feelings into account. "Then, we'll do it. Charlie, you're so wonderful!"

He chuckled and kissed her cheek. "See you don't forget it. If you want," he continued teasingly, "we'll even study catechism and convert."

She waved him off. "Naw, I don't think that will be necessary."

"Then everything's set?"

"Sure."

But even as she spoke, a look of melancholy

drifted over Kate. Noting this, Charlie frowned and asked, "What is it, honey?"

She smoothed out a wrinkle on his shirt. "You know, it just makes me kind of sad."

"What, sugar?"

"Thinking about the wedding." Feeling him stiffen, she quickly added, "Not the marrying part, of course."

"I'm relieved to hear it," he put in drolly. "Then what's making you so blue?"

She sighed, stroking his strong jaw with her fingertips. "Well, you got no kin to stand up with you on Sunday. I mean, your folks was massacred by Indians, and your grandpa passed long ago."

He nodded solemnly. "But you're forgettin' something."

"What?"

He grinned. "I got you."

Kate smiled back.

"It's true, I've been a loner all my life," he continued seriously. "But now I have everything I want. I don't need no one else standing up with me. You're all I want, darlin'."

"Oh, Charlie." Kate could not resist such heartfelt romance. She threw her arms around Charlie's neck and kissed him soundly.

Later that evening, Jeb sat with Dora in her cozy parlor. The two were sipping coffee as they sat on the settee next to a blazing fire.

"Well, it's settled," Jeb announced over his cup. "Kate's marrying Durango come Sunday."

"I see," Dora murmured with a quizzical smile. "What do you suppose changed her mind?"

Jeb coughed and glanced away uneasily. "I apologized, for one thing," he admitted in a strangled tone.

Dora's expression of pleasure grew smug. "You did now, did you?"

He turned back to her, his countenance miserably contrite. "Yes. And I'm saying I'm sorry to you, too, Dora, and praying you'll forgive me."

"I do," she murmured.

"Will you marry me now?" Jeb continued expectantly.

Sadly, she shook her head. "It takes more than fancy words, Jeb. I have to be sure you're willing to meet me halfway on some important matters."

"Such as?"

"I'm not giving up my ranch."

With a groan, Jeb set down his coffee cup. He leaned back on the settee, laying his head against Dora's ample bosom and taking her hand. "Aw, woman. You're going to be the death of me yet. I'll think on it—all right?"

"All right." Her expression serene, Dora squeezed his hand. "You got to go home right away?"

He gave her a devilish wink. "Woman, you couldn't get me out of here with a crowbar."

Laughing, the two lovers headed to the bedroom, hand in hand. Yet Dora's expression was troubled as they lay down in each others' arms on her big feather bed. Jeb was coming around, and would soon offer the compromises that would make him a good husband. But Dora couldn't afford to wait much longer. She had a secret she needed to share with Jeb—and soon.

The rest of the week passed in a flurry of exciting activities for Kate. Conchita was delighted at the news of Kate's coming wedding, and she at once got busy sewing the girl's gown on their Singer sewing machine. Kate suffered through at least three fittings each day.

Now that Kate had consented to marry Charlie,

Jeb no longer kept her a prisoner in her own house. Kate was able to ride Diablo for pleasure again, and even go into town to shop. She also went to visit Dora Fuermann. Dora was thrilled when Kate asked her to be matron of honor on Sunday. The widow also promised to make both of their bouquets with blooms from her garden.

When she was at home, Kate stayed busy taking a thorough inventory of all her things and packing. Charlie had informed her that, after they spent a few days in Austin for their honeymoon, they'd depart at once on their long journey to Denver. It was essential, he said, that they arrive at the Pikes Peak region before the first snows. When Kate had asked whether or not they'd be taking Socks along, Charlie had replied, ''Why, darlin', how could we manage without him?'' Kate laughed each time she thought of this, since already, Socks was doing his best to disrupt her packing, and Conchita had totally banned him from the sewing room.

Kate still had very mixed feelings concerning whether or not she'd be happy in Denver, and she still couldn't figure out why the thought of leaving Texas spurred such tumult within her. As Charlie had pointed out, his wanting to build a new life with her off in the west did prove that he was hardly lying in wait to inherit Jeb Maloney's ranch.

As for Kate's father, he was busy spreading news through town about the wedding. Since the ceremony was to be held on Sunday following church, everyone expected a good turnout. Conchita had already started cooking and baking for the social to be held at their house afterward. Jeb planned to barbecue a side of beef in honor of the occasion.

On Sunday morning, Kate awakened filled with happiness. Hopping out of bed, she glanced out her window to watch her pa drive off to the north in their buckboard. She figured Jeb was on his way to pick up Dora Fuermann. Charlie would meet them at the church later on. Kate and Conchita planned to arrive in town at the end of the service. Pa had excused Kate from church today, because of the wedding and, particularly, due to the tradition that the groom not see the bride beforehand.

As Kate turned from the window, stretching contentedly, the door opened and she watched Conchita step into the room bearing a breakfast tray. The housekeeper beamed at her charge; Conchita was already dressed for the wedding in a handsome gray silk dress.

"Conchita, you look so pretty," Kate murmured.

Conchita set down her tray and rushed forward to hug the girl warmly. "Not nearly as beautiful as you will look in your wedding dress. *Mi hija,* I'm so happy for you." Wiping a tear, she added, "But I'll miss you so, way off in Denver."

Kate nodded. "Charlie promised me that if I don't like it there, he'll bring me home."

Conchita sadly shook her head. "You must follow your man, *chica.* Otherwise, your marriage will be doomed."

Biting her lip, Kate took Conchita's words to heart. She had a feeling the housekeeper was right. But she didn't allow the thought to spoil her jubilant mood. Besides, Charlie was willing to consider her wishes—wasn't that what mattered the most?

After Kate finished her breakfast, Conchita helped her into her many petticoats and then her wedding gown—a lovely confection of satin and lace. Kate admired the lines of the gown as Conchita pinned her curls on top of her head. Long sleeved and tight-waisted, the dress had a neckline trimmed with lace and a full skirt.

"It was a miracle you got this gown ready in time," she remarked to Conchita.

"It was my pleasure."

As a final touch, Conchita pinned a delicate lace mantilla to Kate's curls. Kate fingered the gorgeous veil and smiled at Conchita in pleasant surprise. "Where did this fancy thing come from?"

"It is my wedding gift to you, *hija.*"

"Oh, Conchita." The two women shared a last, emotional embrace before they left the room and headed downstairs.

Outside on the porch, Kate glanced about. In the yard, Miguel was waiting in the buggy to drive them into town. He grinned as he spotted Kate in her gown and she smiled back at him. Off near the barn, she spotted Pete turning a side of beef over a large fire; the air was redolent with the smell of barbecuing meat.

"You look mighty purty today, Miss Kate," Pete called out.

Kate laughed and waved back as she and Conchita went carefully down the steps. They wrapped a bedsheet around Kate to protect her dress. During the twenty-minute ride to town, the two women held hands and chatted nervously. Conchita fretted over a thousand details regarding the wedding and reception—whether or not she'd made enough cake and potato salad, whether or not Kate had enough warm clothing for the coming winter in Denver. Kate reassured her as best she could, and she realized ruefully that Conchita was more nervous than she was.

They arrived in the churchyard just as the strains of the closing hymn, "Blessed Be the Tie That Binds" spilled out through the open double doors. Conchita helped Kate out of the conveyance and up the steps.

Dora met them in the vestibule. Wearing a lavender organza dress, the widow was glowing with happiness. She hugged Kate and said, "My dear, I've never seen a lovelier bride." To Conchita, she added, ''Mrs. Gonzalez, you're a miracle worker. This gown is divine.''

Both Kate and Conchita were smiling as Dora turned to pick up Kate's bridal bouquet from a nearby table. Kate raved over the stylish ensemble of luscious pink tea roses, baby's breath, and white satin ribbons.

As the closing hymn ended, all three women turned their attention to the front of the church. Reverend Cassidy moved down to the aisle beneath the altar, held up a hand and announced, ''I believe we have present a young couple who wish to plight their troth today.''

At Cassidy's words, a titter of excited laughter passed through the congregation. Kate watched Charlie get up and go stand beside the Reverend, while her father came to join the women at the back of the church.

Jeb reached his daughter's side and offered his arm. ''You ready, Kate?'' he asked.

She nodded, and surprised herself by smiling at her father. Jeb looked quite prosperous today, freshly scrubbed and shaven, in his black suit and red brocade vest. She found to her surprise that she liked the fact that they weren't at war with each other at the moment.

The pianist began a slow processional, and Dora led off the bridal party. Kate glided down the aisle on her father's arm, while Conchita slipped into a seat at the back of the church.

When Kate arrived at the front of the church, and Charlie came to stand by her side, she had eyes only for him. She barely even heard the Reverend say, ''Dearly beloved, we are gathered here . . .'' She hardly even noticed when her pa took his seat at the Reverend's prompting. She was mesmerized by Charlie, drinking in his beauty with her eyes. It was as if she'd never before noticed how tall he was, how broad his shoulders, how dark his eyes, how shiny his black hair. His dark suit fit him superbly, and he smelled so wonderful. As he slipped his hand into hers and winked at her gravely as he repeated a vow, she couldn't believe he was hers . . .

Charlie's heart was overflowing with joy and love. Kate was a vision of femininity in her satin gown and lacy mantilla. A body would never know to look at her that this girl could ride like the wind and shoot as well as any man. How proud he was that she was his! He couldn't wait to get her alone at the hotel in Austin tonight. He'd been without her sweet loving far too long.

Charlie was happy for another reason, too. Just yesterday, he'd received a letter from his partner in the Pikes Peak region, Wayne Burdett. Wayne had hit the Mother Lode at their mine north of Denver. Wouldn't Kate be in for a fine surprise when he took her there and she discovered that they were million-aires? He couldn't wait to see her face. Of course, perhaps he should tell her sooner about their good fortune. No, he decided, let her wait, after giving him hell about living there. Just let her try to belly-ache when he built her the finest mansion in Den-ver!

Charlie jerked himself back to attention as he heard the Reverend request the ring. Taking it from his pocket, he turned to Kate and smiled into her eyes as he slid the heavy gold band onto her finger. She smiled back at him and squeezed his hand as they repeated the rest of their vows. When the Rev-erend at last said, "I now pronounce you man and wife," Charlie drew back Kate's veil and lovingly kissed her. When he felt her sweet lips tremble be-neath his, his control slipped and he pressed his mouth to hers passionately, tasting and savoring her honeyed depths. Then, at the sound of the piano starting up again, both of them turned and swept down the aisle past the smiling congregation.

Outside, in the churchyard, everyone rushed up to congratulate the newlyweds—Conchita, smiling through her tears: Jeb, pumping Charlie's hand; Dora, hugging both of them. The Cassidys offered their fond wishes next, then the rest of the congregation lined up to offer handshakes, hugs, and congratulations.

As the churchgoers were preparing to leave, Kate watched her father move to the edge of the crowd and hold up a hand. With a broad grin, Jeb announced, ''Now everybody, don't forget that you're invited out to the house—''

Jeb wasn't allowed to finish his sentence, for the rest happened too fast. Spuds Gilhooley streaked across the churchyard on a black horse. With horror, Kate watched him raise his six-shooter and she heard the sound of a shot. The next thing she knew, she saw her pa crumple to the ground as Spuds raced off to the west.

Kate's heart lodged somewhere in her throat. Without even glancing at Charlie, she ran to her fallen father. She knelt beside him, uttering a cry of dismay. Her father's white shirt was soaked crimson, he was unconscious, and his face was gray.

As a panic-stricken Dora also rushed over to help, Kate grabbed her father's Colt Dragoon from its holster, lurched to her feet, and waved the pistol at the retreating rider galloping away in a cloud of dust. ''You bastard, Spuds Gilhooley! Now you gone too far! You up and kilt my pa!''

Without additional thought, Kate dashed to the nearest horse, which turned out to be Charlie's palomino. She mounted Corona, yanked on the reins, and dug in the heels of her slippers, mindless of the fact that her wedding dress was now hiked up scandalously, revealing the tops of her white stockings and even her creamy thighs.

As the congregation watched in appalled silence, Kate Maloney galloped off after Spuds, her veil and gown trailing wildly in the wind.

Charlie Durango stepped forward, his expression utterly stunned. He couldn't believe his eyes as he watched his bride ride down the trail in her wedding gown, firing rapid shots at Spuds' retreating figure. He threw down his hat and stamped his boot on the hard earth. The girl had to steal his horse and best him, even on their wedding day. Never in his life had he felt so plumb disgusted.

"Damnation!" he yelled after her, shaking a fist. "If you ain't the most confoundenest female I've ever known!"

Staring after his bride in anger and confusion, Charlie was heedless of the flabbergasted stares of the others. Instead, he was struggling with his most immediate dilemma. Should he go after Kate or tend to her father?

Charlie glanced at his father-in-law, who lay motionless and ashen-faced on the ground. Both Dora and Conchita were kneeling over him. The widow was gripping his hand and weeping, desperately begging him to awaken, while Conchita clutched her rosary and prayed. All the others who stood around seemed frozen by shock.

Shit. His headstrong bride could no doubt fend for herself, Charlie decided, but Jeb Maloney was bound to die without speedy medical attention.

Charlie ran to the fallen man.

Chapter 27

~~~~~~~~ OO ~~~~~~~~

Charlie knelt by the wounded man and laid his fingers against Jeb's throat. He felt a pulse, faint and thready though it was. While the front of Jeb's shirt was drenched with blood, fortunately, the bullet wound was high, well away from his heart and lungs, Charlie judged. With luck, he still might make it.

Flashing a sympathetic glance at the two distraught women bending over Jeb, Charlie sprang to his feet and turned to the crowd. "Someone go fetch the sawbones!" he yelled. "And I need some help carrying this man inside. Now! He's still alive!"

At last, the paralyzed throng sprang into action. Two men rode off to fetch the doctor, while three others rushed forward to help Charlie carry Jeb.

Dora, meanwhile, was clinging to the unconscious man and sobbing heartbrokenly. Charlie laid a gentle hand on her shoulder. "Ma'am, we've got to get him inside."

Dora turned her tear-streaked, terrified face up to Charlie's. "Is Jeb gonna make it?" she asked in a breaking voice. "I don't know what I'd do if I lost him. I think I'd die, too."

Charlie squeezed her shoulder reassuringly. "He's a crusty old fighter, ma'am. And we'll sure give this our best shot. Only, first, we need to get him into the church and tend that wound.''

Dora nodded tremulously and stood, clinging to Jeb's hand as Charlie and the other men carried him inside and laid him down on a pew. Though Dora was still trembling, she quickly went into action to help save Jeb, ripping strips from her petticoat and handing them to Charlie. Opening Jeb's shirt, Charlie used the makeshift bandage to apply pressure to the oozing wound high on Jeb's chest, near his right shoulder. While Charlie tried his best to control the bleeding, Dora wiped Jeb's brow, squeezed his hand, and fretted over him endlessly. Nearby, Reverend Cassidy prayed over the fallen man, while his wife stood wringing his hands.

Conchita was still clutching her rosary and praying. ''Señor Charlie, what about Señorita Kate?'' she asked Charlie half-hysterically.

''First things first, ma'am,'' Charlie replied. ''Soon as we get Mr. Maloney here settled, I'll ride after her.''

''Sí, señor,'' Conchita replied, crossing herself again. ''We must pray that Señor Jeb makes it.''

''Please, Jeb, don't give up,'' Dora added plaintively to the ashen-faced man.

Jeb's bleeding had eased somewhat, and he was beginning to rouse, by the time Dr. Youngblood appeared. While Dora sobbed her joy and kissed Jeb's brow, the patient half-opened one eyelid, coughed, and looked about drunkenly. ''What 'er you doin' here, sawbones?'' he demanded hoarsely.

''You were shot, sir,'' Charlie informed him.

''Hell and high water!'' Jeb tried to sit up, then winced and fell back, his face white as death as he gasped for breath. ''Spuds again?''

''Yes, Jeb,'' Dora told him worriedly as she checked his wound. ''Now, you must lie still, my dear. You've been very badly hurt.''

In the meantime, the thin, elderly physician quickly assessed the situation and opened his black bag. "I'll need a couple of you men to hold him down while we put him out," he directed tersely, taking out a bottle of ether, "and someone else to help me put him to sleep. I need to probe for that bullet—now, before this man bleeds to death."

While Dora uttered a cry of horror, Jeb acted as cantankerous as ever. "Forget it," he protested in a raspy, if vehement tone. "I ain't letting you saw into me, Youngblood. I'd just as soon pass."

At that, a tearful yet equally determined Dora Fuermann shook Jeb's good arm. "Jeb Maloney, don't you dare die and leave me to rear this baby alone!"

There was a mortified gasp, and Mrs. Cassidy slid to the floor in a faint. The Reverend rushed to his fallen wife, while the other men present exchanged embarrassed glances. As Dora Fuermann smiled through her tears at the man she loved, Jeb Maloney grinned back at her idiotically, dropping his guard just long enough for the doctor and Charlie to administer the ether . . .

Out on the prairie, Kate was riding hell-bent-for-leather and rapidly firing her father's Colt at the figure hunched over his saddle ahead of her. Maddeningly, Spuds had managed to stay just out of range, although this did not keep Kate from trying. She'd found extra ammunition in Charlie's saddlebags, and had somehow managed to reload her father's pistol without falling off the horse. Corona must be used to the sound of bullets flying, she mused, since the horse charged on, seemingly oblivious to the gunfire.

"Spuds Gilhooley, you stop and take your medicine like a man!" Kate screamed out at him. "You know you got this coming for killing my pa. I'm gonna shoot you dead if it takes me all day!"

"Sorry, Miss Kate, I ain't aiming to meet my maker just yet!" Spuds called back in a shrill voice as his mount flew over another rise.

"Damnation!" Kate cursed. She rode on, firing her gun and screaming out every vile epithet she could think of.

Dr. Youngblood's makeshift surgery proved a success. The bullet was removed, Jeb's wound cleaned and dressed before he even began to stir.

If Jeb's bellowing and complaining were any indication, the patient had considerably improved by the time Charlie, the doctor, Pete and Miguel carried him into the Maloney ranchhouse. The four men not only had to endure heaving Jeb's massive body up the stairs, they also bore the brunt of his many complaints and curses. Even Dora and Conchita were soon imploring him to be more reasonable, without success.

At last, the wounded man was settled into bed. The ranchhands departed, and the doctor announced that Jeb would probably live, "if putrefaction don't set in and kill him." He and Jeb hurled insults at each other as the physician left.

Afterward, Charlie stood in the doorway of Jeb's room, watching Dora help Jeb sip hot tea. He noted that Jeb's color had improved somewhat. Conchita was downstairs preparing him some beef broth.

"How you feeling, sir?" Charlie asked.

Jeb shrugged weakly. "Reckon I'll live." He managed a wink at Dora. " 'Pears I'll have to now. Looks like I got me some new obligations."

Charlie chuckled as he watched the two of them smile shyly at each other. "Well, sir, I reckon I'd best go track Kate now."

Jeb frowned up at him. "You say she took out after Spuds?"

"Yes sir—with murder in her eye and your Colt Dragoon blazing."

Jeb emitted a feeble chuckle. "Hell, maybe that gal's got a spark of family loyalty in her, after all."

"Of course she does," Dora put in as she wiped Jeb's mouth with a napkin.

"Still, I guess you'd best fetch her back before she gets her fool self hurt," Jeb continued with a frown.

Charlie laughed dryly. "Don't worry about her—worry about Spuds." He shifted from foot to foot. "I'll be taking Diablo, if you have no objection, sir."

Jeb waved a hand unsteadily. "Pete told me the gal up and stole your horse. What a spitfire! Be my guest, son."

"Thank you, sir."

"What about the sheriff?" Jeb continued.

"I hear tell he's up at Georgetown for the day, going to church with his kin. A couple of the men went to fetch him, and I reckon they'll organize a posse by sundown. In the meantime, though, I'd best hit the trail."

"Right, son," Jeb concurred.

Dora stood. "Mr. Durango, hadn't you better take Kate a change of clothing?" She blushed. "I mean, she wasn't exactly dressed for the trail."

"Now ain't that the truth," Charlie drawled cynically. "I'd be right obliged, ma'am, if you'd go to her room and pack her some duds."

Charlie was watching Dora slip from the room 9when he heard the sound of laughter coming from the bed. He turned to stare at Jeb.

"Don't set too well with you that the girl made a fool of you at your own wedding, do it, son?" Jeb asked.

Charlie set his jaw stubbornly and gazed at Jeb through narrowed eyes. "No, sir, it don't set well with me at a'tall. But I reckon that's somethin' else your daughter and me will get settled up between ourselves."

After Charlie left, Jeb napped for several hours. Late in the afternoon, Dora came in to check on him, sitting down in the chair beside the bed. As he stirred, she felt his forehead and murmured with relief, "No sign of fever yet."

Jeb gripped her hand and pulled it away. "Will you quit frettin', woman?"he asked thickly. "I tell you, I ain't gonna die on you. I'm made of stronger stuff than that."

Dora smiled. "I suppose you are. Still, when I think of how I almost lost you . . ." She shuddered as her voice faded into sobs.

"I know, darlin'." Jeb patted her arm to comfort her. "You gonna marry me now, Dora Mae? It's the only proper thing to do, what with the young 'un coming."

Dora bit her lip. "Are you happy about the baby, Jeb?"

He grinned. "Why, I'm pleased as punch."

Yet Dora still looked unconvinced and uncertain. "Jeb, you don't have to say that just to spare my feelings. You always told me you didn't want another child, not after Kate—"

"Now, honey," Jeb interjected with a placating grin, "let's just assume lightning won't strike a man twice in the same lifetime. This baby'll be a real gentle sort, I'm betting. He'll have to be if he wants to keep his pa above ground till he's reared."

Dora couldn't resist a brief smile. "But do you really want this child, Jeb? It's going to be a big responsibility."

Jeb squeezed her hand and spoke with surprising humility. "Honey, I know I sometimes carry on worse than a braying old jackass. But I got a soft spot in my heart, and you've filled it. I want us to marry and be a real family, Dora Mae. And if that means having a young'un who is part of you and part of me, why I think that's gonna be just fine." He smiled rather whimsically. "You know, even with Kate—look at what that gal done today. It made me realize I'm right proud of her."

"Oh, Jeb. I'm so glad!"

As Dora wept tears of joy and relief, the two kissed and shared their bliss.

Afterward, Jeb noted that Dora's expression was still rather preoccupied as she straightened his covers. "Honey, you can keep your ranch," he added quietly.

She looked at him with delight. "You really mean that?"

He nodded. "I've got Conchita to take care of the house here. You can go run your ranch by day . . ." He winked at her. "Long as you come home to me at night. Then, after the baby comes—"

She kissed his cheek. "Maybe by then we can figure something else out." She regarded him curiously. "What changed your mind, Jeb?"

He sighed, grimacing as he shifted in the bed. "Guess today taught me what really matters."

"You worried about Kate?"

He nodded grimly. "I reckon I am. Though I'm sure Charlie will protect her."

"And what about Spuds?"

Jeb heaved a giant sigh. "Well, if Kate don't kill him, I allow it's time him and me settled things up." Catching her alarmed glance, he held up a hand and added, "Peaceably. You know, a man reaches a point in life when he needs some order and harmony."

"A woman does too," Dora added wisely. She leaned over, and they shared a tender kiss . . .

* * *

Kate continued to track Spuds until it was too dark to see. But, toward sundown, he'd managed to get a small lead on her, and when she could no longer see his tracks, she'd been forced to give up for the day. She figured Spuds would have to stop for the night, too. She'd arise before dawn and somehow get the drop on him, she vowed.

Kate stopped near a stream and let Corona drink while she sat against a mesquite tree, munching on some jerky and hard biscuits she'd found in Charlie's saddle bags. Unfortunately, she'd found no change of clothing there. She was glad it was too dark for her to see her wedding gown, for she already knew the garment was ruined—the skirt streaked with dirt and ripped by the brambles she had passed. Conchita would surely kill her when she made it back—

And, unless her eyes had deceived her, poor Pa was already dead. A wrenching sadness rose in her heart at the thought. She realized she must have cared for her father more than she'd ever admitted. Now, she would forge on until she avenged his death, and then—

Kate groaned as she at last thought about Charlie. She watched the moonlight glitter over the wide gold band on her left hand and felt wretched to her very soul. Perhaps there could be a double funeral when she returned, for Charlie was surely going to murder her for making a fool of him today. They'd come so far in their relationship, and now, she'd no doubt ruined herself forever in his eyes by indulging in the very kind of reckless behavior he'd tried so hard to gentle out of her—taking off without giving him a thought, even stealing his horse again.

Hell. She'd never make him a decent wife. This thought filled her with such unbearable melancholy that she bawled all over her ruined satin wedding dress . . .

* * *

Charlie tracked Kate all night long. Luckily, the girl had left a trail a blind man could follow, and he was all but blind in the cold darkness. Still, he was able to make out scraps of her satin wedding dress stuck on bramble bushes, and he even found her tattered lace mantilla, waving like a flag in the breeze as it clung to a juniper.

He figured that, by now, she had to have stopped for the night. He would catch up with her by morning, he was sure. And then he'd reckon with this headstrong wife of his for once and for all.

Kate was up well before dawn, after spending a miserable, cold night out on the prairie, with only the protection of Corona's smelly saddle blanket to hold the cold at bay. She ate the last of Charlie's biscuits, drank a cup of cool water, then saddled the horse and rode off.

She was able to pick up Spuds' trail right away; the tracks led due west. She trailed him for about three miles, then reigned Corona in at the top of a knoll. As her gaze followed the pale rays of dawn creeping over the valley below, she smiled in grim satisfaction.

Spuds was camped below, at the edge of a stand of scrub oak. He was still in his red longjohns, and Lord, did he look a sight. He was crouched with his back to her, struggling to light a fire, fanning the puny flames with his hat.

Kate dismounted quietly, took Charlie's rifle from its scabbard, and stealthily approached her quarry . . .

When Charlie crested the same rise a moment later, he witnessed an appalling sight. Kate stood in the valley beneath him, still wearing her wedding dress—now, considerably the worse for wear. She held his rifle on the bowlegged Spuds, who cowered across from her in his hat, boots, and longjohns, with trembling hands raised.

"Miss Kate, I never meant to harm your pa," she heard the cornered man say shrilly. "Him and me has been making a show of this feud for twenty years now. It's just my horse up and stumbled and the blame gun went off. Next thing I knew, I kilt him."

Kate appeared unmoved, narrowing her aim squarely on Spuds' chest. "Well, whether it was intentional or not, Spuds Gilhooley, you shot my pa, so now I got to kill you. No hard feelings, though."

Kate was pulling back the hammer when Charlie galloped toward them, yelling, "Kate, no! Wait! Your pa's going to live!"

Her eyes wide with astonishment, Kate paused and turned to watch Charlie ride toward her. Her brief moment of indecision was all the desperate Spuds needed. The whiskered man sprang onto his horse and galloped away . . .

Chapter 28

⌒◝◝◟◞⌒

Charlie dismounted near Kate and strode up to
face her. The two merely stared at each other,
the tension thick between them. Charlie disgustedly
eyed his bride—her ruined wedding gown, her
smudged face, her tumbled hair littered with leaves
and twigs. Less than twenty-four hours ago, he'd
married an angel, and now he had a wild-eyed hoy-
den on his hands.

Kate in turn studied Charlie. Lord, he looked
ferocious, his dark eyes blazing at her, his mouth
brutally tight, his whiskered jaw clenched in fury.
He still wore his clothes from the wedding, though
he'd removed his jacket. His white shirt was stained
with sweat and dirt and spotted with blood—her
father's, she assumed.

"Is Pa really all right?" she asked tentatively.

His nod was curt. "Doc Youngblood says he'll
live."

She heaved a grateful sigh, then glanced about
uneasily. "Shouldn't we chase after Spuds?"

Charlie shook his head. "Looks to me like he was
headin' back for Round Rock. Reckon the posse'll
nab him."

"Oh." She flashed him a lame smile. "I'm relieved to hear Pa's gonna pull through."

"Are you?" he challenged. "You sure couldn't be

bothered with hanging around to find out, could you, Kate?"

She gestured her frustration. "What do you expect, Charlie? I thought Pa was dead, and Spuds was making a clean gettaway!"

His hand sliced through the air. "So you just up and run off without even giving me a thought, let me worry myself sick about you—"

She wrung her hands. "I'm sorry if I worried you."

He stepped closer, towering over her angrily. "It ain't just that. We're supposed to be man and wife now, but you acted like the vows between us was never said. You couldn't even trust me to help you with this."

"But Pa's my kin and this was my duty—"

"*I'm* your kin now!" Charlie exploded. "Woman, when are you going to stop fighting me and your pa and half of Texas and start working *with* me instead?"

She bit her lip in acute misery. "Charlie, I warned you that I'm headstrong. I told you I'd never make you a proper wife!"

He crossed his arms over his chest and glowered at her. "Well, we're hitched now, so I reckon we're just gonna have to make the best of things."

She edged closer and touched his arm. "You really are riled, ain't you?"

"Yeah, I am," he said heatedly. "I've put up with your waywardness, your wild ways, and your smart mouth. I've tried to be patient with you. But you've gone way too far this time. By damn, if I have to wallop you to get you into line—"

"If you beat me, I'll leave you," Kate flung at him.

"If you leave me, I'll beat you," Charlie blazed back.

They glared at each other for a charged moment. Then, surprisingly, Kate smiled and, to his chagrin,

Charlie found himself smiling back. It suddenly occurred to him how comic they must look—both of them standing here in their ruined wedding clothes and bellowing at each other like lunatics.

Kate reached out to touch his rigid jaw in a gesture of reconciliation. Charlie flinched as if from a physical blow and regarded her warily.

"So that's what this is all about," she remarked with a smug smile. "You afraid I'm gonna leave you, bounty hunter?"

Charlie slowly pulled a twig from her disheveled coiffure. "Just try it, sister," he muttered, then caught her close for a hard, punishing kiss.

Charlie's lips were ruthless, his tongue an instrument of hot plunder. His kiss announced in no uncertain terms that she was his, lock, stock, and barrel. By the time he released her, Kate's mouth was throbbing, her heart thundering. Dazedly, she watched him stride off to Diablo and take some articles of clothing from the saddlebags. His expression still grim, he moved back toward her, tossing her the shirt, trousers, and boots. "Here, you'd best put these on, then let's head for home," he said gruffly.

"Will we go see Pa—I mean, before we—er—"

"Of course."

Kate started off with the garments, only to stop when she heard Charlie clear his throat. She turned to him, watched a muscle work in his jaw. "Is there something else?"

He stood with his booted feet spread, regarding her intently. "You all right?"

She grinned. "Yes. Though Conchita's gonna flat murder me when she sees this dress."

A smile pulled at his mouth, but he didn't reply.

Kate went off to undress behind a tree. However, she made only a brief show of modesty; soon, she emerged, wearing just her fancy camisole and pan-

talets, and carrying her wedding clothes. She awkwardly extended the garments toward Charlie. ''Can
you pack these up somehow?''

''Yep,'' he replied in a strangely hoarse tone, his
gaze riveted on her lush figure. ''I reckon I can fold
'um and tie 'um to my saddle straps.''

''Thanks.''

Holding his wife's gown and petticoats, Charlie
groaned as he watched her sashay back off in a flut-
ter of lacy underclothes, her saucy behind tempting
him. His loins ached at the sight of her, and he could
barely contain the urge to grab her and take her right
here on the open prairie. Somehow, reason managed to prevail. They were man and wife now, and
he wasn't going to tumble her in the buffalo grass
and spill his seed inside her like some savage. Besides, he was still too angry to trust himself right
now. They were going to consummate this marriage
good and proper, in that feather bed that still
awaited them in Austin. And they were going to
have a long, serious talk, either beforehand, or afterward—

Watching his wife's impudent bottom swing back
around the tree, he winced. Most likely afterward,
he decided.

To his everlasting shame, Spuds Gilhooley had
ridden straight into the clutches of the posse from
Round Rock. The longjohn-clad man had pulled his
horse to a halt and raised his hands, gulping at the
four grim-faced men who surrounded him with
drawn pistols.

''Spuds Gilhooley drop your gunbelt and get
down off that there horse,'' Sheriff Winston
drawled.

Gulping, Spuds did exactly as he was directed.
The pot-bellied sheriff approached his prisoner, spit-

ting out a wad of tobacco on the ground as he drew
Spuds' hands behind him and handcuffed him.

"I'm hereby arrestin' you for the attempted murder of Jeb Maloney," the sheriff announced. Then
he quickly amended, "That is, if Jeb pulls through.
If he passes, I reckon we'll be having us a necktie
party before long."

"I didn't mean nothin' by it, Sheriff," Spuds interjected in a strident voice. "It's just my horse
stumbled and the gun went off—"

"Tell it to the judge, son," an elderly deputy cut
in laconically.

Sheriff Winston helped Spuds back onto his horse,
and the much-sobered prisoner was led off to jail.

Charlie and Kate rode toward home in tense silence. Toward noon, Charlie shot a rabbit, and they
paused to cook it. Realizing that her husband was
still furious at her, Kate made a great show of domesticity, skinning and cleaning the rabbit and setting it to roast over a fire on a makeshift spit she'd
constructed from sharp branches. She was even able
to gather a few wild dewberries to sweeten their repast.

Once the meal was ready, they sat down across
from each other, each of them leaning against a scrub
oak. They ate the succulent meat and sweet berries
in silence, exchanging occasional, wary glances.

At last, Kate could endure no more of the tension.
Setting down her plate, she crawled over to Charlie,
took his plate out of his hands, and set it aside.

"What's this?" he demanded suspiciously.

Before he could protest further, she grinned and
climbed into his lap.

"Wait a minute," he warned, bracing his hands
on her shoulders and glowering down at her.

But Kate curled her arms around his neck and

winked up at him impishly. "Charlie, are you gonna stay mad at me forever?"

"Well, I don't rightly know," he muttered with ill humor.

"I think it's time for us to kiss and make up."

"Forget it," he snapped, even though she watched his gaze darken with desire as it flicked over her.

She nestled her face against his strong neck, delighting as she heard his breathing quicken and felt his arms move to encircle her.

Still, he felt stiff as a statue against her. "Aw, honey, don't be mean," she cajoled. She boldly reached down to stroke him between his legs. "I missed you, sugar."

Kate heard a low, blistering curse, and the next thing she knew, she was rudely dumped on her behind and Charlie loomed over her, waving a fist. "What in the Sam Hill do you think you're doing, woman?"

Kate stared meaningfully at the large, hard bulge now straining against his trousers. "We're married, ain't we?"

"Oh, no you don't," he scolded.

"And why not?"

"Well, maybe I ain't ready to kiss and make up yet," he said stubbornly. "Besides, we're still going to go to Austin and do this proper. You and me got some things to settle—a lot of things."

"Aw, damn it, Charlie," Kate said in disgust, heaving herself to her feet. "I've never known anyone to hold a grudge like you. You're as bad as some women I've known."

"Women? Hold a grudge?" he repeated incredulously. "You got no call to talk after you plumb made a fool of me at my own wedding!"

Now Kate was getting riled, too, confronting him with hands on hips. "Well, maybe you're just mad because I bested you, bounty hunter—because I was quicker on the draw than you.''

"Bull and horsefeathers!'' he denied heatedly. "The day you try to outdraw me, sister, is the day you'll be pulling lead out of your drawers!''

"Is that a fact? Then why are you so put out?''

"I'm put out because you turned your back on me.''

"Well, it's not every day a girl watches her pa get shot,'' she snapped.

"It's not every day that she gets married, neither,'' he snapped back. "But you sure acted like it was nothin' special.''

Kate's features twisted in distress, and she gestured in entreaty. "Aw, honey, that's not true.''

He began kicking out the fire. "Cut the palaver, Kate, and let's break camp,'' he said curtly, "else we'll never make it home before sundown.''

They glowered at each other as they packed up and rode on.

All afternoon, Charlie watched Kate riding ahead of him, with her proud head held high. He was haunted by images of her in his lap earlier. How he'd managed to resist her, he still didn't know.

As angry as he was, his desire for her still burned brighter than his wounded pride. He winced aloud as he remembered her in his mind's eye. Her eyes had been so wide and beguiling, and she'd smelled of cedar and dewberries. She'd looked so sexy in those trousers, her lush breasts straining against her shirt, her feminine warmth seeping into his chest. Her bottom had teased agonizingly against his throbbing manhood, and then her hand—

Charlie bit back a string of blue curses. Even now, he felt himself stiffening into hard, tortured readiness. He groaned, drowning in fantasies of Kate's sweet kisses.

* * *

It was late afternoon by the time they approached the Bar M ranch. Once they were only a few miles from home, Charlie cleared his throat and said, "Before we arrive back at the house, I guess I'd best prepare you for a shock."

She turned to him curiously. "Oh?"

"Yeah." Charlie grinned. "I think your pa's going to get hitched again. Pretty damn quick, in fact."

Kate grinned back at him. "You mean Dora?"

He nodded.

Kate waved him off. "That's no shock. They've been keeping company for ages now."

Charlie laughed. "Wait till you hear the rest. You see, your pa sort of got Miss Dora in a family way."

Kate's mouth dropped open. "You're funning me!"

"Nope. Back at the church, Jeb was arguing with the sawbones, not wanting the doc to cut into him and probe for the bullet. Said he'd rather pass right then and there. Anyhow, that's when Dora up and said, 'Jeb Maloney, don't you dare die and leave me to rear this baby alone.' "

"Well, I'll be damned," Kate murmured with an amazed giggle.

"Dora's announcement made quite a stir in the church, let me tell you. The preacher's wife plain had a spell and fainted dead away."

Kate chortled in delight. "Pa'll never live this one down."

"Reckon he won't."

"And just think," Kate murmured with an expression of wonder. "I'll have a little brother or sister soon."

"Sure looks that way."

"I'm glad," Kate murmured. "Glad Pa's gonna make it—and that he and Dora are getting hitched."

"Sounds to me like you're softening up on your daddy a mite," Charlie remarked.

Kate's expression grew pensive. "I reckon he and I will never abide each other, but yesterday did teach me somethin' . . ."

"Yes?" Charlie prompted.

Reluctantly, she admitted, "Well, maybe I care about him more than I thought."

"He cares, too, Kate," Charlie pointed out sternly. "He was right worried when he learnt you run off after Spuds—just like I was."

Kate was silent, brooding. It astonished her that her father had been anxious about her, just as it saddened her that Charlie still was not ready to forgive her.

They rode onto Bar M land, passing several ranchhands who were gathering longhorns for the fall round-up. Soon, they crested the last rise, galloped into the valley and pulled up by the house. As they dismounted and tied their mounts to the hitching post, Kate glanced at Charlie awkwardly. "After we check on Pa, are we going to—"

He turned to her with a heavy sigh, pushing his hat back on his head. "Kate, the truth is, I'm plumb wore out. I tracked you and Spuds all night long. The sun will be down in a few hours, so we'd best not head out for Austin just yet. I reckon I'll stay at the cabin tonight and we'll get started on our honeymoon tomorrow."

At his unexpected rejection, Kate felt all the color drain from her face, felt her throat constrict with anguish. Though she could see the deep lines of fatigue on Charlie's face, all her tortured heart knew at this moment was, he was leaving her. He was going off to his cabin—and hadn't asked her to come with him! How angry and disappointed he must feel, if he could turn his back on her this way with their marriage only a day old!

"Please, let me come with you," she said with a catch in her voice.

He shook his head sadly. "Kate, you need to spend some time with your pa, and I'm too damn tired to deal with this right now."

"You ain't comin' back at all, are you, bounty hunter?" she accused bitterly.

"Yes, I am. I'm a man of my word, Kate, and I told you I'll be here come morning. It's just that right now . . ." His voice trailed off, and he shook his head. "I reckon I need some time to cool off."

"You're still mad at me, aren't you?"

His stormy gaze flashed up to hers. "Yeah, I allow that I am."

Even as Kate fought hot tears, Charlie caught her hand and led her firmly up the steps. She struggled to rein in her turbulent emotions as they entered the house. She headed straight for the kitchen, with Charlie following her.

Kate spotted Conchita rolling out pie dough at the dry sink. "We're home, Conchita," she called out softly.

With a cry of joy, the motherly woman dropped her rolling pin, rushed across the room, and embraced Kate. "Oh, *mi hija*, Señor Charlie, you're back! How thrilled I am to see you!" She studied Kate's face closely. "Are you all right, *chica*?"

Kate smiled wanly. "I'm fine. How's Pa?"

"Much better today," the Mexican woman assured her. "You two go on upstairs and see him. He and Señora Fuermann have been worried about you."

Squeezing Conchita's hand, Kate left the kitchen with Charlie, then proceeded in tense silence back through the parlor and up the steps.

They made their way down the second floor corridor and found the door to Jeb's room open. Kate felt better the minute she spotted her pa. He was sitting up in bed, sipping a cup of broth as Dora read to him from the newspaper. His color was good, and he appeared alert and comfortable.

Both Jeb and Dora smiled as they spotted Charlie and Kate in the doorway. "Well, daughter, Durango," Jeb called. "Come on in. It's good to have you both back."

"Indeed," Dora added with a radiant smile as she rose to greet them.

Kate crossed the room and hugged Dora. Then she turned to her pa. "I'm right glad you're better, sir," she said awkwardly, touching his good arm.

"Believe me, I am, too," Jeb concurred with a grin. He nodded to Charlie. "Thanks for bringing my gal back."

Charlie shrugged. "She's my wife now."

"So she is." Jeb coughed. "Well, I want you both to know that Pete come in a while ago. Told me the posse rounded up Spuds early this morning. He's rotting in the hoosegow right this minute."

"I'm glad, sir," Charlie said.

"I almost shot him, Pa," Kate added grimly. "But Charlie here rode up and told me that you was gonna make it, after all."

"I'm glad you didn't kill him, daughter," Jeb remarked soberly. "There's been enough violence already." He smiled up at Dora and squeezed her hand. "It's time for a little peace and happiness around these parts."

"Yeah, I heard you two were getting hitched," Kate put in with a smug smile. "Congratulations."

"Thank you," Dora said serenely.

Jeb cleared his throat noisily and glanced from his daughter to Charlie. "Well, I reckon you two can head out on your honeymoon now."

Charlie stepped forward and said stiffly, "Sir, I thought we'd wait on that till morning. I figured Kate would want to spend some time with you, seein' as how you've been injured and all."

"Charlie has in mind staying at his cabin tonight," Kate added awkwardly. "He'll be fetching me in the morning."

"Aw, don't be silly, you two," Jeb said. "I'm healing nicely, and you can still make it to Austin by sundown."

"Jeb's right—you shouldn't be apart right now," Dora agreed.

Charlie glanced about in uncertainty—at Jeb and Dora's perplexed faces, at his wife's stricken countenance. "The horses are plumb whipped," he argued to Jeb.

"Then you can borry a fresh team and take our buggy," Jeb offered magnanimously.

Yet Charlie's jaw tightened belligerently. "If it's all the same to you, sir, I reckon I'll be fetching Kate tomorrow."

Jeb shrugged in defeat.

Charlie strode over to Kate and pecked her cheek, struggling unsuccessfully to steel his emotions against the tears he saw welling in her eyes, the stark vulnerability on her face. "I'll see you in the morning, honey."

"Sure, Charlie," she said thickly, not daring to look up at his face out of fear she would break out bawling.

Charlie hesitated a moment, then turned on his bootheel and strode out of the room.

"Whew!" Jeb said, glancing askance at his daughter. "It didn't go down too well that you left him standing at the church, did it, daughter?"

For once, Kate was too miserable to argue with her pa. She wiped her tears on her sleeve and said, "No, sir, it didn't. I reckon I shouldn't have gone off half-cocked like that, without clearing things with Charlie first." With a tremulous breath, she finished, "I guess I brought this on myself."

Dora came over and wrapped an arm about Kate's

trembling shoulders. "Don't worry, honey, he'll come around . . ."

Indeed, even as they spoke, Charlie had paused halfway down the staircase, anguish welling in him as he remembered the tears in his wife's eyes as he'd left her. At last, he cursed himself for an idiot and slammed his fist against the wall.

This was wrong, he thought. *Wrong*. Sure, he was bone weary and mad as hell to boot, but the two of them were married now. They were supposed to share both the bitter and the sweet together, to work things out as man and wife. Kate had hurt him, but that didn't give him call to hurt her back. Only a bastard would leave his bride like this, and make her cry on what should rightfully be their wedding night. Dora had spoken the truth—they shouldn't be apart right now. In wanting to punish Kate, he was really only punishing himself.

His decision made, Charlie turned and sprinted back up the stairs and into Jeb's room. His wife, Jeb, and Dora turned to him in astonishment.

"Is that offer of the buggy still good, sir?" he asked Jeb tensely.

"Of course, son."

Charlie turned to his wife and took her hand. "Go pack your duds," he told her gruffly. "You're comin' with me."

Chapter 29

‿‿‿◦◦◦‿‿‿

Ten minutes later, Kate and Charlie were seated in the buggy they'd borrowed from her pa. The dappled gray horse galloped over the rolling hills on the public road to Austin. The evening was cool, scented with cedar and freshly cut hay.

The journey proceeded mostly in silence, the only distractions being when they passed an occasional lone rider, or a farmer in his oxen-drawn wagon, heading in from the fields with a load of fall harvest. Kate kept glancing worriedly at the western horizon wondering if they would complete the twenty mile trip before nightfall.

She also wondered what would transpire between herself and Charlie once they arrived at the hotel. Her heart pounded as she remembered the moment when he'd come back for her at the house, and heard his gruff words, "You're coming with me."

It was so strange, she mused. There was a time not long ago when such a terse command would have infuriated her and prompted an instant rebellion. But this time, she'd been surprisingly docile, merely nodding to her new husband and rushing off to pack a bag. She realized that, over the past weeks, she'd actually come to understand Charlie's feelings, that she'd empathized with the hurt he'd felt when she'd left him behind at the church yesterday.

And, more than anything else, she wanted to close this aching gap between them.

Twilight was falling when at last they moved off Stagecoach Road and turned onto Fifteenth Street, passing blocks of open prairie dotted with a few log cabins and clapboard houses before they arrived at Congress Avenue and headed south.

They proceeded down the dark street lined with storefronts and homes. Glancing ahead, Kate chuckled as she watched a couple of teenage boys in homespun lasso a milk cow and pull her out of the center of the thoroughfare. Even in the scant light, Kate could readily tell that Austin proper was a city bursting at its seams from the influx of settlers. Everywhere were signs of growth, from the new lumberyard to the many homes and businesses in various stages of construction. The city seemed to have doubled in size since her father had last brought her here two years ago, she mused. Indeed, Kate had heard recently that the population of the state capital was now approaching 3,500.

A few blocks later, they approached the brightly lit facade of the Congress Hotel. As Charlie pulled the horse to a halt at the curb of the pillared establishment, a slave in livery came forward to take charge of their buggy. Charlie retrieved their two bags and helped his wife out of the conveyance. They crossed the boardwalk, then he opened the massive oak door and they entered a huge, elegant lobby replete with gleaming marble floors, lacy ferns, and plush settees.

At the front desk, the smartly dressed clerk did not bat an eyelash at the scruffy young couple who approached him in their trail clothes. "May I help you, sir?" he asked Charlie politely.

"Yeah. We'll be needing your best room, a hot bath, and some grub."

The man adjusted his steel-rimmed spectacles and fought a smile. "In that order, sir?"

Charlie grinned. "I reckon so."

Charlie signed them in and paid for their room. As the hastily summoned boy picked up their bags and led them upstairs, Kate felt grateful that she'd at last seen her husband smile. She had a feeling that things would work out between them, after all.

The boy led them into a cool, darkened room, and quickly lit the crystal-globed lamps. Kate glanced around in awe at their opulent surroundings—the plush, flowered rug, the Italian tile fireplace, the huge brass bed set next to windows draped in green velvet.

"Oh, Charlie, it's so beautiful!" she cried.

"Yep, I reckon it'll do," Charlie returned dryly, handing the lad a coin.

Pocketing the tip, the young man beamed from ear to ear. "Thank you, sir. Please let me know if there's anything I can do for you during your stay."

He left, and the newlyweds stared at each other awkwardly. Kate stood near the bed, Charlie across from her next to a handsome ladies' writing table. Though only a few feet separated them, suddenly to Kate the distance seemed like a thousand miles. When Charlie dropped the room key on the desk, she practically jumped out of her skin.

He took a step toward her and smiled. "Why so nervous, sugar? We're finally alone, ain't we?"

Kate gulped and wrung her hands. "That's why I'm nervous."

He moved closer, his expression quizzical. One look at her wide, uncertain eyes and trembling lower lip was enough to break the final barriers of his resistance. "Darlin', you don't have to be afraid of me," he said tenderly, stroking her cheek. "I don't want that."

"I'm not. I'm just—"

She wasn't allowed to finish. With a groan, Charlie hauled her into his arms.

The physical nearness, after so many hours of painful alienation, was just the right spark to make their passion erupt into flames. Even as Kate instinctively stretched on tiptoe, Charlie's mouth descended hard on hers. They kissed each other ravenously, their tongues plunging hungrily.

"Oh, Charlie, Charlie." Kate clung to him, delirious with joy, her eyes welling with tears.

They fell across the mattress together, sinking deeply into the feather tick. Their hearts, their breathing, raced out of control. They tore at each others' clothing, Kate popping buttons on Charlie's shirt, Charlie yanking up her shirt and camisole. She cried out wantonly as he took her bare breast in his mouth. The roughness of his bearded face was exquisite sensual torture against her sensitive flesh; the slight, firm nipping of his teeth drove her mad. She raked her nails across his muscled chest and panted ardent words of encouragement.

His hands moved boldly to her waist, unbuttoning her trousers and pulling them down, along with her pantalets. She felt deliciously vulnerable to him, aroused to fever pitch. Her eyes flashed up to meet his, and when she saw the blazing passion reflected there, a hot tide of desire stormed her most secret recesses. When he parted her and stroked her gently, her fingers clawed at his belt buckle, at the buttons on his trousers.

They fumbled with each other's clothing for a few more seconds, and then Charlie possessed her in a single, shattering stroke that set her reeling.

"Oh, darlin', darlin' " he whispered in a tortured voice. "I feel like I'm home at last."

"You are." She placed her hand in his and kissed him with complete trust.

Something broke in Charlie then. He began to

move so powerfully, so deeply within her that she gasped. With a blinding kiss, he held her to him as he moved hard and fast, melding their bodies with each jarring stroke. The friction was acute, and still Kate hungered for more. She began to move with him, rolling her hips wantonly, heightening the tension until neither of them could bear it. Charlie rammed his tongue deeply inside her mouth, again and again, in a brazen sexual mimicry that had her drowning in him. She kissed him back with insatiable hunger, sucking his tongue deeply into her mouth.

He reacted with violent passion, grinding his mouth, his loins, against her. Her soft whimper of surrender drove him wild. His fingers dug into her bottom almost painfully, lifting her to meet his thrusts. He held her firmly to him as he pounded into her with the riveting strokes of his climax. Her fingernails dug into his smooth shoulders as the same sweet convulsions gripped her.

"Oh, Kate . . ." he murmured, collapsing against her. "I love you, darlin'."

"I love you, Charlie." They clung to each other, and sweet tears filled Kate's eyes. At last the distance had been bridged and they were truly one. Man and wife.

They lay there, still clasped together, half-on, half-off the bed, when a sharp rap sounded at the door. Scowling, Charlie glanced from Kate to the door. "Who is it?" he barked.

A high-pitched feminine voice responded to the surly question. "You ordered a bath, sir?"

Charlie glanced back at his wife, and both of them laughed. "Just a minute!" he yelled.

Kate smirked up at him. "We're faster and hotter after each other than they are with boiling the water," she teased in a whisper.

Pushing himself back on his elbows, Charlie gazed down at his adorable wife—her bare breasts with their nipples tight and red with passion, her smooth belly, the delightful place where they were still joined. He winked at her wickedly. "Shall I ask the lady to come in so we can give her an education?"

She playfully punched him in the shoulder. "Don't you dare, Charlie Durango. And you'd best get off of me, you big ox."

Her flash of mettle only made him stiffen to rock-hardness inside her. He grunted in pleasure. "Now look what you've gone and done."

"What I've . . . Charlie!" Kate tried hard not to chuckle, but it was so difficult when he grinned down at her this way. He looked like such a rogue, his brown eyes dancing with laughter, his face dark and sinfully bearded. It felt glorious and somehow illicit, lying here with his throbbing erection still inside her, while the maid waited outside.

He leaned over and nibbled on her underlip, even as his arousal pressed deeper into her, until he was snugly wedged against her womb. "Sugar," he teased, "I think I'm stuck."

"Charlie!" Her protest was half a moan of pleasure. Then she winced in mingled pain and disappointment as he abruptly withdrew. He stood between her spread thighs at the edge of the bed, affording her an excellent view of his turgid organ as he drew up his trousers.

"Just want you to know what you're missing," he taunted.

"Believe me, I do." Her words were strangled.

Chuckling, Charlie helped his wife right her clothing. Then he strode off to the door. He admitted the red-faced maid and helped her drag in the tin bathtub. Two more maids followed with buckets of steaming water. After a couple of trips, the tub was filled.

Once the woman had left, Kate eyed the bath hungrily. "Which one of us goes first?"

"We could bathe together," Charlie suggested.

Kate was outraged. "If you think we can both squeeze into that little tub, you're loco, mister."

He flashed her a devilish wink. "Guess that depends on how snug we can fit together, huh, sugar?"

She stuck out her tongue at him and he laughed.

Kate began unbuttoning her shirt. "Well, I'm not going to stand here arguing with you while that wonderful hot water grows cold."

He grabbed her hand. "Not so fast. This is our honeymoon, sugar, and I'm going to get everything I want."

"You mean you haven't already?" When he only smirked, her expression tightened with suspicion. "Don't tell me you want to be first?"

He bared his teeth in an expression of lascivious pleasure. "No. I want to undress you and bathe you."

She chortled. "And what about me getting what I want?"

"Oh, honey, you will," he drawled meaningfully.

He reached for her, but Kate was not about to become an easy quarry. She dashed about the room, but Charlie easily chased her down and caught her, heaving her squirming body over his broad shoulder. She was giggling in delight as she landed on the soft mattress. Charlie followed, pinning her to the bed and stripping her with a dispatch that made her head spin. He stood to tug off her trousers and boots, and she squealed in feigned indignation when he nibbled on her toes.

He dropped her shapely foot and bowed. "Your bath awaits you, madame."

Kate flashed him a rebellious look, got up, and pranced over to the tub, swinging her hips provocatively. She screamed when Charlie's hand came down playfully on her behind. She turned and tried to swat him back, but he merely swung her up into his arms, ignoring her struggles as he carried her to the tub and deposited her there none-too-gently. She shrieked her outrage as water sluiced all over her face and hair. He sank to his knees next to the tub and stared at her solemnly.

She flashed Charlie a glower as she reached for the soap.

"Oh, no," he said, again grabbing her hand and staring down at her intently. A husky quality entered his voice. "I told you, I want to scrub you."

Further protests were smothered as Charlie kissed Kate and moved the soap intimately over her body. "My God, you're so lovely," he murmured reverently, feasting his eyes on her glowing face and shapely form. He nuzzled her neck, biting gently. She shivered as he moved the slippery cake slowly over her aroused breasts, down her belly, then between her legs. A shudder seized her entire being. He released the soap and began to stroke her again, taking her lips at the same time. She thought she would die of the combined stimulation.

At last, she came up for air. His face was a hair's breadth away from hers, his breath hot and sweet on her lips. "Charlie, are you still mad at me?"

"No." He whispered the word as he slid a finger inside her.

She gasped.

"It's just that we've got to start pulling together, honey," he went on seductively as he roved his tongue over her lips. "Quit fighting each other so much. Would that be so difficult?"

Kate shook her head and kissed him fiercely.

Her senses were in chaos, her breathing shallow, by the time she at last lurched to her feet. "You'd

better bathe before the water grows cold,'' she said
unsteadily.

Charlie didn't move at first, his dark gaze riveted
on her lush, naked body—her upthrust breasts, slim
waist, shapely bottom, and long legs. He hooked an
arm around her, drew her close, and kissed her wet,
bare thigh.

"Charlie, please, I'm getting cold,'' she said,
though the chill in the room was hardly the cause of
her trembling.

He chuckled and grabbed a towel, briskly rubbing
her wet hair and body. He laid the towel on the floor
so she could step out, then went to her portmanteau
to hunt up her nightgown. "I'll let you wear this for
now,'' he cautioned as he pulled the white handkerchief linen over her head. "But once we're in bed,
I'll keep you warm.''

"I'm counting on it,'' she purred. Wickedly, she
added, "So what's next?''

"Next you're undressing me and scrubbing me.''

"My pleasure, sir.''

Smiling up at him coyly, Kate began slowly unbuttoning Charlie's shirt. She pulled it off him and
tossed it on the floor, letting her fingertips slide
down his muscled, hair-roughened chest and bare
belly. She gloried in his moan of pleasure as she
unbuckled his belt and began working on the buttons of his trousers. She heard his breathing quicken
and looked up to find his eyes intensely focused on
her.

"You'll have to sit down so I can take off those
boots,'' she told him.

"My pleasure, ma'am.''

Charlie plopped himself down on a nearby wing-
back chair, resting one booted foot on a stool. Turning her back to him, Kate straddled his leg and began
tugging on his boot. He pushed his other foot
against her behind to aid her efforts.

She yowled indignantly as the boot came off. "Hey, wait a minute," she scolded. "I don't want a dirty footprint on this fine gown."

"I told you, Kate, you ain't going to be needing that gown," he drawled.

With a grudging smile, she pulled off his sock and then turned to his other foot, yanking off the boot and then his sock and his trousers.

He stood. She couldn't take her eyes off his magnificent bronzed body as he strode confidently to the bath. She took in the thickness of his black hair, the broadness of his back, the leanness of his taut buttocks and long legs, the hard, thick length of his arousal—

All in all, he looked good enough to take a bite out of. She promised herself she would have that pleasure before the night was over.

Charlie lowered himself into the tub and grinned at her. Kate came over and knelt next to him on the towel. She grabbed the soap and began lathering his body. Moving lower, her hand brushed his tumescent manhood. She couldn't help herself—she released the cake and grabbed him, smiling at his sharp sound of pleasure.

"Looks to me like you've sprouted a handle, feller," she teased him. Her fingers slipped lower. "May I use it to pull you out of the tub?"

His hand closed over her wrist and he feigned a growl. "Watch out, or I may use it to pull you in."

She chuckled and resumed her ministrations, gliding the soap over his legs and knees, then back up again, teasing him relentlessly.

Studying her husband's glorious body and remembering their fevered lovemaking only moments before, a shiver coursed through Kate. She recalled how they'd declared their love to each other, and tender tears filled her eyes. He was hers now—truly hers. Possessiveness washed over her.

"You had many women, Charlie?" she asked him casually.

He uttered a tortured sound and glanced up at her suspiciously. "Now that's a fine question to be asking at a time like this. What brought that on, anyhow?"

She shrugged. "Oh, I don't know. Seems like you mentioned some others when we was out on the trail. And you sure know how to pleasure a woman."

He grinned lazily. "That I do." As her eyes flashed, he grabbed her hand. "Katie, you can't hold it against me for what I done before we met."

Her chin came up stubbornly and her lips formed a pout. "Perhaps not." She pulled her hand away from his, and the gentle motions of her fingers belied the violence in her voice. "But if I catch you looking at another woman, bounty hunter, I swear I'm gonna kill you."

His eyebrows shot up. "Are you, now?"

"Yep." She eyed him with stormy resolve. "Make no mistake about it—you belong to me now."

He howled with laughter. "You gonna brand my backside, woman?"

"I might just do it," she said primly.

He reached out and ruffled her hair. "You know, I believe you would, you little vixen."

"Count on it." She squeezed his tumescent organ with her hand and kissed him quickly and possessively. He was making a grab for her when she pulled away and added, "What were they like, those others, anyhow?"

Realization flooded Charlie's face and he shook a finger at her. "Oh, no you don't. I ain't playing those games with you. First thing I know, you'll be locking the bedroom door over things I done when you was still a snot-nosed little tyke."

Kate couldn't resist a giggle. "So you been at it that long, eh?"

Charlie muttered an oath and reached for her again, but she was too quick for him, hopping to her feet and hurrying off for a fresh towel. She approached him, her expression impudent, taunting. "Come to me, sugar," she said coyly.

He did. As he climbed out of the tub, her gaze was drawn to his beautiful, glistening body. She rushed forward and began rubbing him down. He grabbed the towel from her hand, tossed it away, and pulled her into his arms.

"Charlie, you're getting me wet!"

"That ain't the half of it," he drawled. Hiking the gown over her buttocks, he went on sternly, "By the way, Mrs. Durango, you ever look at another man again, and I ain't gonna kill you."

Kate's lips twitched. "You ain't?"

"Naw. You'll only wish I had."

"You gonna brand my backside?"

"Nope. I'm flat gonna wear you out—in bed."

Kate giggled and Charlie pulled the gown off her body. He carried his naked wife to the wing chair and plopped her down. He hooked his arms beneath her knees, boldly pulling her hips to the edge of the chair, and, before she could protest, he pried her thighs apart with his hands and buried his face in the sweetness between.

"Charlie!" Kate was shocked, scandalized, and savoring every second. Her thighs instinctively clenched against the exquisite torture, yet she could succeed in closing not an inch against her husband's determined hands and mouth.

"You're so beautiful," he murmured, studying her as he parted her with his fingers and planted quick, tormenting kisses. "Even here. Especially here." Hearing her whimper, he added resolutely,

"I'm aiming to take my time, darlin', so if you don't like it, that's just too bad."

"I—I love it," Kate somehow managed to say as he nuzzled his face against her again.

Indeed, she could barely endure the rapture streaming through her as his rough face abraded her most intimate parts, as his hot lips kissed her and his tongue flicked, stroked, dipped, tantalized. Kate panted and thrust her fingers into his hair, holding him to her. He found her tender nub and tortured it inexorably. When her hips came up off the chair, he took advantage of the moment to draw her even closer, draping her knees boldly over his shoulders. Kate quivered on the brink of madness, her face hot, her breathing frantically sharp. Charlie continued to tease and arouse her until she found her release against him.

Then he slipped two fingers inside her and lowered his lips once again to her swollen mound. Kate couldn't endure the pleasure—it was simply too intense, too wrenching. Her buttocks clenched and her fingernails clawed the upholstery. She tried to tell him to stop, tried to arch away, but it was useless—he held her too tightly, and her mouth felt too swollen for speech.

The next climax seized her with such violence that she was left sobbing. Charlie kissed her inner thighs and whispered soothing words. Then he pulled her off the chair, and she landed on the rug next to him, on her knees, trembling and breathless.

He leaned over and kissed her roughly. "Straddle me," he whispered. "It's going to be so good, so deep. Before it's over, I'm going to make you scream with passion."

She wanted to scream now. As wonderful as her climax had been, his words had aroused her entire body again. But first—

''First, it's my turn,'' she whispered. Then she leaned over and took his erection in her mouth.

Charlie groaned and thrust his fingers through her slick hair. He tottered between paradise and perdition as Kate made love to him with her lips and tongue, sucking and stroking. Hearing his agonized sounds, feeling his hands clench and tangle in her hair, she wished she could take all of him inside her mouth, but her body would do that, and soon. A shudder gripped her at the thought of him embedded against her womb. She had never felt him so hard and swollen—he was like hot iron in her mouth.

As she continued to move her lips over him, her fingers slipped lower, and that's when he grabbed her and pulled her astride him.

''Now,'' he groaned, and she eagerly sank herself upon him.

They both cried out as Charlie fell back on the rug and pulled Kate down with him. He raised his knees and pressed her back, rocking her even deeper onto his throbbing shaft, until he was so high and tight inside her that she thought she might burst—

''Charlie!'' Desperation seized Kate, and her fingernails clawed into his shoulders. She couldn't bear the intensity, couldn't bear for it to stop—

''I want a baby right away,'' he whispered, flicking his rough thumb against the sensitive bud of her passion. ''Do you?''

Kate could barely answer. ''Oh, yes . . . Oh . . . Oh, God!'' She made an involuntary movement and he grabbed her hips with a grunt of ecstasy.

He began to pump, to pound within her, and she did cry out. He sat up, smothering her lips with his as her entire body shook and rapture convulsed every inch of her.

She felt certain she would have dissolved in a boneless puddle had he not held her so tightly. She

could almost feel her womb hungrily drinking in his
seed. If the force of their shared passion was any
indication, she was pregnant already.

He lowered her to the rug and covered her breasts
with tender kisses. ''Oh, darlin' . . . darlin' . . .''

They were just drifting back to earth when they
heard another knock at the door. ''Your dinner, sir!''
a male voice called out.

Charlie and Kate convulsed in tender laughter.

Chapter 30

The next morning, Charlie awakened Kate with a kiss and a succulent breakfast tray, complete with two yellow roses in a slender vase. They sat on the bed together, laughing as they fed each other *huevos rancheros*, sausages, and coffee. Soon, their tray was cast aside in favor of the fevered lovemaking that had kept them awake throughout much of the night.

Afterward, Kate enjoyed the domesticity of watching her husband shave and dress. Then he helped her into her petticoats and frock, and as they headed for the door, she smiled at the thought of what a handsome couple they made—him in his snappy brown suit, gold brocade vest, and beaver hat; her in a stylish gown of burgandy-colored broadcloth and a black silk bonnet complete with burgandy-colored silk ruching and ribbons.

That day, they had a marvelous time touring Austin and shopping. The weather was deliciously cool, although a few dark clouds loomed in the skies. They walked through the halls of the state capital; they drove past the Greek Revival splendor of the governor's mansion. They strolled up and down Congress Avenue, glancing into the many shop windows. Kate was fascinated by the mishmash of humanity trouping past them—elegant ladies in full-skirted dresses and feathered bonnets, businessmen in fashionable frock coats and top hats, farmers in their overalls, and numerous homesteaders in buckskins or homespun. A cloud of dust swirled in the air from the many conveyances clattering down the street—everything from crude ox-carts and spring wagons to splendid custom coaches. One rancher even drove half a dozen longhorns down the wide boulevard.

After having lunch at a quaint little restaurant, they went hunting up a Catholic church, just as Charlie had earlier promised they would. At Saint Mary's on Tenth Street, Kate was disappointed when the young priest informed them that he wasn't allowed to marry non-Catholics; but when he offered to say a prayer for the soul of her dead mother, she found she was at peace. Kneeling with Charlie as the priest intoned the prayer, Kate felt sure her mother would have approved of their marriage. She felt most touched by the fact that her husband hadn't gone back on his word.

Next, they stopped off at a brand new dry goods store on the corner of Seventh and Congress. Inside the store, Charlie paused next to a stack of woolen underwear and winked at his wife. "We're going to need warm clothing for our winter in Denver."

"So we're really going," she remarked sullenly.

He stepped closer and stroked her cheek with his index finger. "Sugar, I told you that if you don't like it there, I'll bring you back home."

"When?" she demanded.

He scowled. "Well, in the Spring, unless you're expecting. In that case, we'd have to wait till you and the babe can travel."

She crossed her arms over her chest and pouted. "Or never."

He shook a finger at her. "Now, Kate. I gave you my word I'd bring you back to Texas, and I meant it. But your safety always comes first with me."

She was broodingly silent.

"Come on, darlin'," he cajoled with a winsome smile. "Pick yourself out some warm duds and I'll pay for them. We're gonna have to leave Austin in the morning, anyhow."

"We are?" All at once, she was crestfallen at the thought of ending their idyllic honeymoon.

"You know we have to get to Denver before the first snowfall," he continued patiently. "And we need to stop by and check on your pa first—you know, tell him goodbye and all."

She sighed. "I suppose you're right. It's going to be a long, hard journey, ain't it?"

He nodded. "But the railroad should cut through to the region in a few more years. I reckon that'll ease things up a bit."

Her full lower lip protruded again. "You got it all figured out, don't you?"

"Kate, like I told you a week ago, sooner or later there's gonna be a war here over this slavery business. We'll be better off in Denver—"

"And what about my pa, left all alone in Texas?" she challenged.

"He'll make out just fine, honey. He's too old to go off and fight, and like you pointed out, he don't even own any slaves."

"You make it all sound so simple," she said resentfully.

"It is, honey."

"Yeah—as long as you get your way."

Charlie groaned his frustration, but further argument was postponed as a plump saleslady stepped up to help them. Charlie left his wife in the woman's capable hands and strode off to choose a sheepskin coat. With the clerk's assistance, Kate dutifully selected a heavy coat, some woolen underwear and dresses to wear in Denver. Charlie came back and persuaded her to add some thick stockings and sweaters. Then, noting her still-pouty expression, he charmed her by insisting that she try on a sapphire blue velvet dress, along with a matching bonnet with feathers and ribbons. Unable to resist, Kate dashed off to the back room with her treasures and quickly changed.

She was all smiles when she emerged in the full-skirted frock and jaunty bonnet, and twirled about before Charlie. The admiring light in her husband's eyes further brightened her mood.

"It's gorgeous," she cried, fingering a fold of the velvet as she waltzed about. "I've never see anything so fine."

"And it's yours."

"It is?"

"Sure as Sunday."

"Oh, Charlie!"

"You look like an angel in it," he added with a catch in his voice. "A green-eyed angel."

Impulsively, she hugged him, and Charlie privately heaved a sigh of relief. He'd been redeemed—at least for the moment.

By the time he got ready to pay the bill, they had both accumulated an enormous pile of clothing, shoes, and accessories on the counter top. Kate wondered how Charlie would pay for it all, then recalled his bragging to her on several occasions that he was well-fixed. Indeed, even as the saleslady totaled everything up, Charlie sauntered up with an armload of lace and ribbons. As his wife and the scandalized clerk watched, wide-eyed, he tossed down a white lace corset, matching lace garters and fine white silk stockings.

"Mustn't forget underclothes," he said solemnly to both women.

The clerk coughed and glanced away in mortification. Kate, on the other hand, could readily see the comic implications of the situation. She turned to her husband and laughed. *"That's* supposed to keep me warm in Denver?"

Charlie turned to the clerk. "Well, ma'am, what do you think?"

The unfortunate middle-aged woman was crimson-faced. "I—I think your wife will do just fine, sir," she said in a strangled tone, hastily gathering up their goods.

Thunder was clapping as they stepped out of the store with their many bundles. Charlie quickly ushered his wife into the buggy and loaded their packages.

Kate began to needle him the instant they pulled away from the curb. "Charlie, you varmint! You all but gave that poor woman apoplexy back there."

He wiggled his eyebrows and feigned innocence. "Which poor woman?"

"The clerk, of course! You know damn well that by now, I'm quite used to your shenanigans."

"Are you?" he asked meaningfully. "You mean you don't think I have another trick or two up my sleeve?"

She responded with a question of her own. "Why did you buy me them wicked duds, anyhow? Are you trying to dress me up like some two-bit Cyprian?"

He grinned at her as he worked the reins. "Well, if a wife is wise, I'd say she'll give her husband just about anything he could find at a bawdy house."

Now Kate was indignant. "Hey! Wait a minute, you lowdown snake! Just how many bawdy houses have you visited, anyway?"

"None, since I met you, darlin'," came his smooth, enigmatic reply.

"Oh, you scoundrel!" Kate batted him with her just-purchased umbrella as they pulled up to the hotel.

Her outrage was short-lived, however. Though it

rained all afternoon, the fierce rhythm of the storm only enhanced their romantic mood as they made love in their big brass bed. The skies cleared late in the day, and Charlie urged Kate to dress up in her new velvet dress for a night on the town. She did, and Charlie couldn't take his eyes off her all evening long. First, they had a fine beefsteak dinner at the hotel restaurant. Afterward, they visited a *fandango* parlor, sipping wine and dancing to the elegant Spanish music.

It was past midnight when they returned to their hotel. Rain began to pour down again, and they made love all night long . . .

The next morning, Charlie tossed the new lace underthings on Kate's lap. "Why don't you put these on now, sugar?"

Sitting at the edge of the bed, Kate glanced up at him. Standing before her, Charlie wore a grin as wicked as the devil himself. He was already dressed in a white shirt and dark trousers. She, however, was still buck naked. He didn't give her much opportunity to put on clothes, she mused. Indeed, the whole time they'd been here, they'd never even opened the drapes, since they would quickly have scandalized the entire population of Austin.

She fingered the flimsy underthings. "I thought you'd get around to these," she murmured, her lips twitching.

His dark eyes roved over her possessively. "Well, we're going to go see your pa this morning. I like the idea of you all prim and proper on the outside, and hot as sin underneath."

Her gaze flashed up to meet his. "Is that how you think of me?"

His reply was hoarse. "Oh, yeah."

She grinned. "Then I reckon I will put these on."

Kate rose and made a great show of strutting about

and slowly, seductively, donning the garters. Charlie reclined on the bed and watched her greedily. Once the lacy straps were in place around her lovely bare thighs, he had to restrain an urge to pull her down on the bed and bury himself to the hilt in her velvety, tight depths.

She picked up the lace corset. "You'll have to help me tie this," she preened.

"My pleasure, ma'am."

Charlie stood, but instead of helping her, he yanked the top of the corset down and took her breast in his mouth.

She shoved him away playfully. "Charlie, you scamp! We're never going to get to Pa's at this rate."

He chuckled and moved behind her. That was a mistake. Never had she looked so enticing as she did with her lovely back partially bared, and the lacy straps of the garters on her bare legs. "Oh, Christ," he muttered.

"Charlie! You keep up them blasphemies and I'm gonna have to wash out your mouth with lye soap."

"You're one to talk! You've got a mouth that would scald a fishwife."

Their shared laughter ended abruptly when Charlie pulled hard on the strings of her corset, bringing the lush contours of her bare bottom sliding against the front of him. Somehow, he managed to tie the strings.

"Now put on your stockings," he said hoarsely.

She chuckled and went to sit on the bed. Picking up one of the stockings, she swung a bare leg outward, propping her heel on the mattress and giving Charlie a full, delectable view of the cleft between her thighs. When his gaze became riveted there, she brazenly widened his view, smiling as she heard his agonized groan.

Before donning the stocking, she let the silk trail

teasingly between her thighs, and watched Charlie gulp as if he were trying to swallow a melon.

"You gonna put them on?" he asked.

Something in his voice dared her to defy him. But she wrinkled her nose at him instead. "Yes, sir. But only because it's such a novelty for me to have you telling me to put clothes *on*."

He threw back his head and laughed. She put on both stockings and adjusted her garters, but as she started to rise, he pressed a hand down on her shoulder. "Honey, we've got to talk."

She raised an eyebrow and glanced baldly at the bulging front of his trousers. "Really?"

"Yeah. About your pa."

She rolled her eyes. "If we have to talk, I want my drawers first."

He fought a smile. "No."

She lurched to her feet, but his hands caught her shoulders, restraining her. "Damn it, Charlie!"

"Kate, before we leave Texas, you're going to have to settle up with your pa, make your peace," he told her firmly.

"Why?" she demanded belligerently.

"Because your bad feelings toward him are the main reason you don't want to leave Texas with me. You'll never be content to live with me in Denver until you let go of your bitterness."

"Aw, bull," Kate scoffed. "Look, I'm not gonna argue this out with you without my damn drawers."

He grinned, then repeated solemnly, "Kate, you need to make up with him."

Now she was angry, flinging away his hands. "Make up with a man who's never had an ounce of tenderness in his heart for me?"

"Sugar, that's not true," he replied patiently. "During the past few days, I've seen you mellow toward him, just as I've seen him mellow toward you."

Though Kate knew in her heart that Charlie spoke the truth, her pride continued to rebel; her mouth grow tighter and sulkier. "That don't mean that he and I will ever be friends."

"He cares for you, honey. Some men just don't show it too good."

She harrumphed. "Well, forget it."

His hands gripped her shoulders again. "Honey, you're gonna have to do it."

"Says who?" she snapped.

"Says your husband."

She crossed her arms over her bosom and glared at him. "Well, maybe *your wife* says you're gonna have to have a busted lip, if you can't learn to mind your own Goddamned business."

His eyes flared with anger. "You just try it, you little firebrand."

Kate was riled enough to do it, but some fragment of caution prompted her to respond in a less violent manner. So she kicked him in the shin instead. Since she was barefoot, the brief jab was negligible. Still, her show of defiance was enough to make her husband roar belligerently and charge after her like a raging bull.

Kate dashed about the room, shrieking as he chased her. "Charlie, no!"

"Now you're gonna get it," he warned.

She tried to evade him, but he soon had her cornered between the bed and the window. He advanced with a nasty grin on his face that promised instant retribution.

Desperate, Kate made a dive for the bed, hoping to scramble over it to safety—

That was her mistake. As far as her husband was concerned, the sight of her bare bottom bobbing in the air sealed her fate. A split-second later, her ankle was grabbed, and then Charlie's hard body landed squarely on top of hers, pinning her face-down to the mattress.

"Charlie, you villain! Let me up!" She struggled, but it was useless in her present, humiliating position. Not to mention the fact that she could barely breathe now due to the constriction of her corset.

"I've been thinking of what I might do," he murmured lazily. "Blister you, or maybe just take my revenge out in a much more pleasurable manner."

"Get off me, you big bull!"

Charlie chuckled and slowly untied her corset. She heaved a deep, desperate breath. Moving aside the heavy silk of her hair, he looked down at her imprisoned beneath him, and though he would burst at the sight of her, naked from the waist up, and below, wearing just the filmy stockings and garters. He could hear her forced breathing; he could see the goose bumps standing out all over her sexy behind. He knew she was every bit as aroused as he was. He stroked her there, his fingers roving up and down her naked bottom and thighs, delighting to the way she shuddered and sucked in her breath. He reached beneath her, kneading her breasts with just the right amount of roughness. Then his fingers moved audaciously to her mound. She cried out, and his manhood strained painfully against the front of his trousers; never had he felt so eager to invade and plunder her slender body. He freed himself with the trembling fingers of one hand while his warm lips worked their way down her back, nipping and kissing.

As his mouth moved lower, Kate was mortified. "Charlie, don't you dare bite my butt."

He did.

Kate cried out in seething indignation and wiggled wildly, yet it was futile. Indeed, she froze when something big, hard, and hot probed between her thighs.

"Charlie, what in the hell are you doing now?" she demanded, her face burning.

"What do you think?" he teased wickedly. He pulled her to her knees and plunged fully into her womanhood.

"My God!" she cried, both mortified and enraptured. "This ain't a barnyard."

He laughed. "No, but there's more than one way to skin a cat."

"Why that's—that's mixing your metaphors!"

"That's what?"

"Never mind!"

Charlie's forearms clenched against her front, wedging her more securely against his thrusting loins. She winced in mindless pleasure. His teeth nibbled her back as he plunged deeper. She whimpered and begged for more. When he moved his fingers to her front, stroking her provocatively, she reacted with violent passion, and he had to tighten his hold to keep her from writhing away.

"This ain't a barnyard, but I'd sure call this mating, wouldn't you, sugar?" he whispered tenderly.

Kate couldn't answer. The oblivion of ecstasy had wiped out all rational thought . . .

Chapter 31

〜〜◯◯〜〜

While Kate and Charlie were preparing to leave Austin, Jeb Maloney was making a visit to the Round Rock jail, which was little more than a small, square stone building on the southern banks of Brushy Creek.

In the crowded outer office, Jeb told Sheriff Winston that he wished to visit Spuds Gilhooley. The astonished lawman quickly led him to the tiny cell.

"Hello, Spuds." Jeb stood outside the bars and stared at his foe, who sat on his bunk in red long-johns, and trousers with suspenders, morosely smoking a cheroot.

At the friendly greeting, the whiskered Spuds heaved himself to his feet, his expression flabbergasted. Dropping his smoke, he crushed it out under the heel of his boot and stepped forward. "Jeb Maloney. You're the last person I expected to see payin' me a social call."

Jeb pulled up a straight chair and straddled it. "I reckoned it was time for you and me to get some things settled."

Not about to look a gift horse in the mouth, Spuds pulled up a chair as well, sat down, and warily faced his enemy. "You may not believe this, Maloney, but I never aimed t' kill ya at your daughter's hitchin'. I'm as glad as anyone that you've pulled through."

"Yeah—now you won't get your scrawny neck wrung," Jeb drawled dryly.

Spuds coughed. "That's part of it, I allow. But I don't take lightly sending off a fellow human being to the bone orchard."

Jeb waved him off. "Whatever. Anyhow, I come in to offer you a compromise—"

Spuds cut him off with a raised hand. "It don't matter. If I'm ever lucky enough to be let out of the hoosegow, Maloney, I swear, I'll leave 'ya be. You can have your dad-blasted crick."

Jeb grinned. "Don't be so hasty, Spuds. I've come to offer to share the crick with you."

Spuds fell back in his chair. "You're pulling my leg."

"Nope. There's no reason a'tall that all our cattle can't water at the same hole. So I'm offering to bury the hatchet."

"After twenty years?" Spuds asked incredulously.

"I figure it's high time. Don't you?"

Spuds' gaze narrowed suspiciously. "So you're offering to share that there crick . . . In exchange for what, Maloney?"

Jeb shrugged. "An end to the feud. And I'll even drop the charges."

Spuds' mouth fell open, revealing his tobacco-stained teeth.

"Well, Gilhooley, are you gonna sit there catching flies, or shake on it like a man?" Jeb demanded gruffly.

"You really mean it?" Spuds asked in a stunned voice.

Jeb nodded. "Soon as we seal the deal, I'll be having a word with the sheriff about busting you loose."

Instantly, Spud extended his gnarled hand between the bars.

* * *

"Where'd you learn about mixin' metaphors?"

It was almost noon, and Charlie and Kate were in the buggy approaching the Maloney ranch. The weather was crisp and cool. Kate wore a lightweight yellow woolen dress and a gold silk bonnet; Charlie had added a leather vest and a wider-brimmed hat to his white shirt and black pants.

Glancing at Charlie, Kate fought a smirk at his taunting question. "Oh, I think it was at one of the schools Pa sent me to. Miss Turner's Institute for Young Ladies, as I recollect."

He grinned. "Oh, yes. That's the place where you hung your teacher's drawers out on the flagpole, ain't it?"

Kate giggled. "How did you know about that?"

"Your pa told me about it, the first day I met him."

Kate could only shake her head. "And you still agreed to marry me?"

"Sure did," he acknowledged proudly, clucking to the horse. "Then, when I saw him bringing you through town a week later, with your hands tied to the horse like you was some kind of *desperado*, I knew I had to have you."

"Why?"

He winked at her. " 'Cause I knew you'd be a woman with spirit—someone feisty and fun."

"And did I meet with your expectations, bounty hunter?"

He grinned. "Honey, you blew my expectations clean out of the sky."

They were both laughing as Charlie pulled the buggy to a halt before the Maloney ranchhouse. Kate's expression abruptly turned moody.

Charlie laid his hand on hers. "Honey, did you think about what I said earlier this morning? You know, about your pa?"

Her mouth tightened in bitterness. "Oh, yes."

"Did you think about what we done afterward?" he added wickedly.

Her lips softened. "Oh, yes."

Charlie kissed her quickly, then hopped out of the buggy and came around to her side to help her out. "Just give it a chance, will you, honey?"

Looking down at his face, Kate couldn't resist; he looked so solemn, yet so tender. "Sure, Charlie."

They went up the steps and into the house together. Kate spotted her father seated near a crackling fire, smoking his pipe. Jeb was dressed in denim trousers and a flannel shirt. Though he was still a bit pale, he appeared considerably improved.

"Hello, Pa," she murmured.

Jeb glanced up and beamed at both of them. He set down his pipe and stood. "Well, if you two ain't a welcome sight. Come on in here."

Kate frowned as she and Charlie crossed the room. "Should you be up yet?" she asked Jeb.

He waved her off. "The doc says I'm mending just fine." He pumped Charlie's hand and surprised his daughter by leaning over to peck her cheek. He glanced from one to the other. "So, how was the honeymoon?"

Charlie grinned. "We had a grand time."

Jeb nodded. "I'm right pleased to hear it."

"What about Spuds Gilhooley?" Charlie asked. "Will he go on trial soon?"

"Nope," Jeb replied proudly, hooking his thumbs in his suspenders. "I went into town this morning and settled up accounts with Spuds. He's already out of the callaboose."

"What?" Kate and Charlie cried simultaneously.

"We're gonna share the crick," Jeb elucidated. "It's time for a little peace around these parts."

Kate and Charlie could only shake their heads.

Jeb chuckled at their reaction. "Now come on into

the kitchen, you two. Dora and Conchita are finishing up dinner.''

The three stepped into the kitchen to find Dora and Conchita conversing gaily as they puttered about. Both women greeted the newlyweds with joyous hugs, and everyone settled down to a hearty meal of beef stew and sourdough biscuits.

"What are your plans?'' Jeb asked Charlie as he dipped his biscuit in the gravy.

Smiling at his wife seated next to him, Charlie replied, ''We need to head out to Denver as soon as possible.''

"Oh, no!'' Conchita gasped.

"Surely you can't mean today!'' Dora added, her expression crestfallen.

Charlie shook his head. ''No, ladies. You needn't fret about us hightailing it before sundown. We've got a heap of business to take care of before we can leave Round Rock. I've got to buy us a covered wagon, a couple of strong draft horses, plenty of supplies . . . That'll take a day or two, I reckon.'' He glanced at Jeb. ''But frankly, sir, we don't have a lot of time to wait around, with winter a' comin'. And we'll need to veer east somewhat, to avoid Injun country.''

Jeb nodded, while Dora put in, ''Too bad there isn't a train . . .''

"Yes, ma'am,'' Charlie concurred. ''But I reckon we'll get there just fine.''

"Jeb and I were hoping you could stay for our wedding,'' Dora continued with a smile.

"When do you two aim to get hitched?'' Kate asked her father.

He shrugged. ''Truth to tell, we were just waitin' around for you youngsters to return. Preacher Cassidy told us to come on in to the church, any time.'' He leaned toward Charlie and spoke behind his hand. " 'The sooner, the better,' were his exact words, as I recollect."

Everyone laughed.

"We could make it tomorrow morning," Dora told the newlyweds. "If that's all right with you two."

"That would be fine, ma'am," Charlie said.

"Are you two planning to stay here at the house until you leave?" Jeb added.

Charlie glanced at Kate, and she nodded. He replied, "We'd be right obliged, sir, if it ain't no trouble."

"Certainly not. I'll have Conchita change the bed in my room," Jeb offered magnanimously. "The bunk in Kate's room is a mite small for a couple."

Charlie turned to his wife again, and she smiled. "Oh, I reckon Kate and I will make out just fine in her room," he drawled, taking her hand and kissing her soft fingers.

The others present coughed or dabbed their mouths in embarrassment, and Conchita rushed to serve the pie.

That afternoon, Charlie went to town to see to his business, promising Jeb that he would let Reverend Cassidy know that he would have a wedding to perform in the morning. After helping Conchita tidy up the kitchen, Dora went back to her own ranch.

Kate went out to sit on the porch swing. She smiled as she realized that, while Charlie had only been gone a few minutes, she already missed him terribly. He hadn't asked her to go along to town, and she knew it was because he wanted to give her an opportunity to make her peace with Pa.

As if the thought had summoned him, Jeb appeared on the porch, crossing over to her with a slip of paper in his hand.

"Here, daughter," he said, awkwardly extending

the slip. "I want you and your husband to have this as a wedding gift."

With a frown, Kate took the bank draft. Her eyes widened as she glimpsed the generous amount. Then, her features tightening in pride, she thrust the draft back at him. "Charlie said you once tried to buy him as my husband. I don't think we want this. Besides, Charlie's well-fixed."

Jeb sighed his frustration. "Daughter, I allow that it was wrong of me to try to buy you a husband. I might add that Durango refused me utterly."

She crossed her arms over her bosom and gazed at her father through narrowed eyes. "That's what Charlie told me. And you can keep your damned money now, too."

Jeb implored the heavens. "Daughter, must you look with suspicion on everything I do? I just want to give the two of you a grubstake. It's only proper. And why can't you do your husband the courtesy of asking him his feelings before you refuse me?"

Kate struggled a moment, chewing her bottom lip as she thought. At last she mentally acknowledged that her father had a point. "All right, then, fair enough," she said, taking the draft and putting it in her pocket. "I'll let the decision be Charlie's."

He nodded. "That's all I can ask."

He stood there for another uncomfortable moment, and she sighed impatiently. Scooting to the far side of the swing, she said, "Sit down, Pa. You shouldn't be on your feet at all, sick as you've been."

"Thank you, daughter." Jeb heaved himself down next to her.

Father and daughter sat in strained silence. Jeb chewed his whiskers while Kate played with a bit of lace on her cuff. Finally, she said rather defensively, "Charlie said I should make my peace with you, before we go."

Jeb made a hoarse sound as he glanced at her. "And is that what you're wanting now, daughter?"

She fingered a fold of her woolen skirt. "I don't know . . ." Then, catching his disappointed expression, she added, "I reckon so."

Her father expelled a huge breath. "I reckon I'm of a similar mind," he said gruffly.

She stared at him, astonished. "You are?"

He made that pained sound again. "When a man faces death, it gets him to thinkin' . . . You're heading off to Denver now. 'Course, you've got to follow your man. But Lord knows when we'll see each other again."

"That's true." Biting her lip in acute misery, Kate whispered, "I'm sorry for the bother I've caused you."

"I'm sorry, too," Jeb replied, shocking her thoroughly.

"You are? Why?" she asked frankly.

He glanced uneasily at his lap. "I know I ain't always been the best pa. Like what you said just now—my trying to buy Charlie for you. That was wrong. And tellin' you all those awful lies about your intended—that was right bull-headed of me, too." He cleared his throat noisily. "I reckon that's what made you run off like you done."

There, Kate had to laugh. "Pa, I allow I would have run off if you'd told me Charlie was Prince Charming straight from the story book."

Jeb chuckled. "Still, I've got to accept my share of the blame for making you carry on like you done. I been thinking a lot lately about what you told me when I brung you back from Nacogdoches—that I always took it out on you 'cause of your ma's death." He coughed and glanced at her lamely. "I never meant to, daughter, but I reckon I did."

"I wasn't always that easy to deal with," Kate offered. "I wasn't the best daughter, either."

"Could be. But maybe I never gave you enough of a chance."

They lapsed into silence, both knowing that the necessary words had now been spoken. As Kate glanced at Jeb, it struck her anew how pale and tired he looked. This man had nearly died, she thought achingly. Bittersweet emotion filled her heart as she realized that even as she was finally making her peace with her father, she was losing him, going far away to start a new life. But she really did love him—she knew that now. And she was so glad they'd had this talk.

Unbidden, Kate smiled as she again remembered that day long ago when she'd run away from school—how Jeb had found her sobbing at her mother's grave, and how he hadn't spanked her. And she remembered another day, when she'd been a child riding her pony, and she had spotted a gleam of pride in her father's eye—

Jeb loved her, too. The realization filled Kate's eyes with tears. She knew now what was really important, what was really being said here.

Kate heard her father groan, and she automatically reached out to steady his arm as he struggled to his feet. He muttered a thank you and started to leave, then hesitated, turning back to her.

"By the way, Durango told me how that Eberhard woman really gave you girls the dickens out in Nacogdoches." He flashed her a sheepish look. "Guess I should have listened."

Kate rose, feeling genuinely touched. "Thanks for that, Pa."

He nodded and spoke behind his hand. "Truth to tell, I never cottoned to that old bitch myself."

Both of them laughed.

"Well, then . . ." Jeb glanced toward the door.

As Kate gazed up at her father, she thought again of how vulnerable he truly was, and how much she was going to miss him. She surprised herself by giving him a quick hug, being very careful to favor his wounded side. He hugged her back just as awkwardly.

"Take care of yourself, Pa—and Dora and the baby," she said as they moved apart.

Jeb nodded. "Godspeed daughter. Come see us when you can."

"I'll make Charlie bring me."

"See that you do." Jeb coughed. "I'm sure you'll be in good hands with Durango. But if that boy should ever give you any grief—"

Kate's giggle cut him short. "Aw, Pa, don't worry about me. It's Charlie you should be frettin' over. Hell, I've made that poor man jump through hoops of fire, and he's been more patient with me than a preacher trying to baptize six drunks."

Jeb Maloney threw back his head and laughed heartily.

Chapter 32

Later that day, Charlie was thrilled to learn that Kate had at last made her peace with her pa. The next two days passed in a whirlwind of preparation for the newlyweds as they got ready to depart for Denver. Charlie was able to buy a covered wagon and two work horses in town; the couple also packed and accumulated the rest of the needed supplies. At night, they lay locked in the throes of passion on Kate's narrow bed upstairs. Just as Charlie had promised, they made out just fine.

Kate and Charlie made a visit to the town cemetery, placing a huge bouquet of flowers on her mother's grave. Along with Conchita and a few other close friends, they watched Dora and Jeb repeat their vows at the church. Kate and Conchita hosted a spur-of-the-moment reception afterward, serving the two dozen guests cake and punch. Dora and Jeb stayed at the house that night, both refusing to leave on their wedding trip until after Kate and Charlie left for Denver.

Her final morning at home, Kate had a long visit with Conchita, and the two women bid each other a tearful farewell. Afterward, she was putting the last few items in her portmanteau when Charlie came upstairs. "I got everything loaded in the wagon," he told her. "And Diablo and Corona are tethered to the gate. Socks is secure in his basket on the front seat, just bustin' to get loose and play with you. You ready, sugar?''

Kate sighed, taking a last look at the room where she'd spent most of her life. She felt a sadness welling, that she was leaving her pa and Conchita, followed by a quick surge of joy at the thought that she was embarking without bitter feelings toward her father, and that she would get to spend the rest of her life with the man she loved.

She smiled bravely at her husband. ''I reckon I'm ready.''

''Great.''

Watching him grin and reach for her bag, she added, ''Oh, I almost forgot.'' She held out Jeb's bank draft to him. ''Pa gave us this. I told him we don't want it, but he said to check with you first and let you decide.''

Charlie glanced at the draft, then grinned and handed it back to her. ''We don't need this, honey. Give it back to your pa and Dora, for them and the new baby.''

''You're sure?''

He chuckled. ''Oh, yeah.'' His expression grew sheepish and he stroked his jaw. ''As a matter of fact, I wanted to make this a surprise, but . . .''

''Make what a surprise?'' she asked suspiciously.

He hooked his thumbs in his trouser pockets and announced proudly, ''You see, my partner and I own a gold mine just north of Denver. We just hit a major vein, which means you and me are gonna be millionaires.''

If Charlie had expected Kate to be delighted, he was in for a shock. ''Charlie Durango, you're pulling my leg,'' she accused.

''No, honey, I swear, it's the truth.''

She balled her hands on her hips; her eyes sparkled with anger. ''You mean all this time you owned a gold mine, and you didn't even bother to tell me about it? And here, I thought you was after me for my pa's land.''

"You did?''

"Well, sure I did,'' she said with more bluster than conviction. "At least for a time.''

"Kate, I told you I wasn't after your pa's ranch. Besides,'' he teased, "I didn't want you to marry me for my money.''

"Why, of all the lowdown—'' Her fists came raining down on him.

"Hey! Stop that!'' he protested, grabbing her wrists. "Anyhow, I was just kiddin'—you know, about you being a golddigger.''

Kate groaned at the pun. "Oh, you were now?''

He released her wrists. "The truth is, I didn't even get word of the strike until right before our wedding.''

She crossed her arms over her bosom and glared at him. "It don't matter. You went and deceived me—again.''

"Don't you even care that we're millionaires?'' he asked incredulously.

"Deception is deception, is what I say.''

"And the money don't matter at all?''

She straightened her cuffs and tossed her curls with devil-may-care disdain. "Well, it might put a different spin on things.''

"Aw, hell.'' Charlie disgustedly slammed her portmanteau shut, secured the latch, and heaved the bag off the bed. "Let's get going. We'll argue this out once we're on the trail.''

She raised her chin defiantly. "No, we won't. I want to get this settled here and now.''

"Kate,'' he warned, shaking a finger at her. "Don't start up, now.'' He grabbed her hand and pulled her resisting body out of the room.

They were still bickering when he pulled her onto

the front porch seconds later. Jeb, Dora, and Conchita watched from the other end of the gallery, where all three had waited for the couple to emerge.

Charlie released his wife's hand and slanted her a stern glance. "I'm putting your bag in the wagon. If you budge from this porch, you'll live to regret it."

Charlie strode off, while Kate ground her teeth in exasperation. Spotting her father, Dora, and Conchita, she stomped off and summarily shoved the bank draft into Dora's hand. "Here. Buy the baby a candy store." To her father, she added, "Thanks all the same, Pa, but Charlie don't want your money."

"Whatever you say, daughter," Jeb replied. "You two take care now. See you stay well away from Injun country."

"Please write us, Kate," Dora added sincerely.

"I will," Kate promised.

For a moment, the four stood there awkwardly. Kate gazed at the three dear people she was leaving, and, all at once, it didn't matter so much that she was angry. Feeling an unaccustomed aching in her heart, she quickly hugged Jeb and Dora. Then she turned to her dear friend and second mother, Conchita Gonzales. The emotion on Conchita's face more than expressed what both of them were feeling at this moment.

Kate tightly embraced her friend. "Chita, I'll miss you," she whispered in a choked voice.

"I know, *corazón*. Promise me you'll write to me, too," Conchita implored with tears in her eyes.

"You know I will," Kate replied, even as her own eyes stung. "And Charlie says there'll be a train to Denver in a few more years. I'll make him send you a ticket."

"Oh, no, Señorita Kate, you mustn't," Conchita protested. "The expense—"

Kate wiped a tear with her sleeve and glowered

at Conchita. "Charlie says him and me are rich now. So if you don't promise me you'll come, Chita, I'm gonna flat bust out crying."

Conchita quickly hugged the trembling girl. "Very well, *mi hija*, I promise."

When the two women at last moved apart, Kate squeezed Conchita's hand and grinned bravely at her pa and Dora. "Hell, Charlie Durango's so gall-durned well fixed, he can send tickets for the two of you—and the baby, too."

"See that he does, daughter," Jeb teased.

"Why, he can send tickets to the whole dad-blamed town of Round Rock."

The others chuckled, and, before she could lose her nerve, Kate turned to leave. As she descended the steps, it occurred to her that she was still supposed to be mad at Charlie. Come to think of it, she loved being mad at Charlie. It sure beat the hell out of bawling like a baby because she was leaving her home and the three other people she loved.

Thus, feigning her most impudent air, Kate climbed onto the front seat of the wagon and stared moodily ahead. Hearing Socks' strident squeal from the basket next to her, she opened the lid, retrieved her kitten and petted the mewling little critter. Still, her obstinate countenance did not waver one bit.

Observing his daughter's continuing show of temper, Jeb ambled down the steps to join his son-in-law at the back of the wagon. Charlie stood at the gate between the two tethered horses, grimly double-checking his load.

"Trouble in paradise, son?" Jeb asked diplomatically.

Charlie grunted as he secured the gate. "She's riled again."

"If you don't mind my asking, how come this time? And what's this business about you being richer than Midas?"

Charlie grinned. "Seems I forgot to tell Kate that we're millionaires now." At Jeb's astonished expression, he explained, "You see, I'm half owner of a gold mine, and my partner just wrote me that we've hit the Mother Lode."

Jeb beamed from ear to ear and pumped Charlie's hand. "Well, congratulations." Lowering his voice, he added confidentially, "Just build her a fancy mansion, son, and give her a baby each year. She'll settle down directly, I reckon."

Charlie chuckled. "I'll give it my best shot, sir." He glanced toward the front of the wagon. "But somethin' tells me it won't be quite that simple."

Jeb spoke behind his hand. "I'll let you in on a secret, son. That gal purely loves to fight."

"Oh, I think I've figured that out, sir." Proudly, Charlie added, "And I think that's what I love about her the most."

Jeb laughed and patted Charlie on the shoulder, then went off to rejoin the two women on the porch. The three watched Charlie climb onto the front seat and heard him say to Kate, "I thought I warned you to stay on the porch."

"Were you planning to carry the porch all the way to Pikes Peak?" she snapped back.

"Well, no, but—"

"Well, if you can't keep your damned head on straight, Charlie Durango, don't blame me. And, furthermore, I'm going to hate your godforsaken Denver. We're going to be headin' back to Texas before the grass snaps back on the trail."

"Now, honey," Charlie responded patiently, flicking the reins. "You're gonna love it there. Just come see it once. Just once."

On the porch, Jeb, Dora, and Conchita laughed, listening to the newlyweds bickering as they drove off into the hills.

In the wagon, Charlie was laughing, too, as Kate continued to lambast him.

How he loved this feisty, outrageous woman. He'd definitely met his match in this spunky female, and he'd been a fool ever to believe he could gentle her.

Indeed, he could now look forward to spending at least the next fifty years taming Kate.

Avon Romances—
the best in exceptional authors and unforgettable novels!

WARRIOR DREAMS   Kathleen Harrington
76581-0/$4.50 US/$5.50 Can

MY CHERISHED ENEMY   Samantha James
76692-2/$4.50 US/$5.50 Can

CHEROKEE SUNDOWN   Genell Dellin
76716-3/$4.50 US/$5.50 Can

DESERT ROGUE   Suzanne Simmons
76578-0/$4.50 US/$5.50 Can

DEVIL'S DELIGHT   DeLoras Scott
76343-5/$4.50 US/$5.50 Can

RENEGADE LADY   Sonya Birmingham
76765-1/$4.50 US/$5.50 Can

LORD OF MY HEART   Jo Beverley
76784-8/$4.50 US/$5.50 Can

BLUE MOON BAYOU   Katherine Compton
76412-1/$4.50 US/$5.50 Can

Coming Soon

SILVER FLAME   Hannah Howell
76504-7/$4.50 US/$5.50 Can

TAMING KATE   Eugenia Riley
76475-X/$4.50 US/$5.50 Can

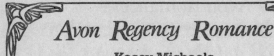
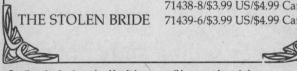

THE LONG-AWAITED
NEW BLOCKBUSTER

KATHLEEN E. WOODIWISS

Forever in Your Embrace

The #1 *New York Times*-

bestselling author of

So Worthy My Love

OCTOBER 1992

AN AVON TRADE PAPERBACK